PRAISE FOR IM

An Unwantec

T0012838

'Imogen Clark deftly peels back the layers of loyalty, family secrets and moral dilemma to examine a family that must make a choice between need, greed and integrity. Pacey, thought provoking and with characters that test the ties of blood, marriage and friendship to the limit, *An Unwanted Inheritance* will have you wondering how far you'd go to uphold your own principles – and how much, or how little, it would take to betray them.'

—Julietta Henderson, author of *The Funny Thing about Norman Forman*

'Lovingly crafted, with flawed and nuanced characters, this riveting story will stay with readers long after the last page is turned.'

—Christine Nolfi, bestselling author of *A Brighter Flame*

'What happens when you drop a bag of cash right in the middle of three siblings and their families? A whole lot of good fun and drama. *An Unwanted Inheritance* delightfully explores the flaws that come with being human as Clark plunges us into a story about what is right and wrong and what it means to be a family. She ratchets up the tension as the story races to its surprising and oh, so satisfying conclusion.'

—Boo Walker, bestselling author of *The Singing Trees*

'Brimful of emotion – a wonderful plot, and characters that you are rooting for, even when you know you shouldn't. *An Unwanted Inheritance* is that gem of a thing: a story to truly lose yourself in – I LOVED IT.'

—Faith Hogan, bestselling author of
The Ladies' Midnight Swimming Club

Reluctantly Home

'Connected by loss, a friendship blooms across the generations in this compassionate and nuanced story of endings and new beginnings.'

—Fiona Valpy, bestselling author of *The Skylark's Secret*

'Imogen Clark is a master at creating flawed, real, loveable characters and exploring their emotions. This novel cleverly weaves together the past and present, and will leave you thinking about the story long after you finish the final page.'

—Soraya M. Lane, bestselling author of *Wives of War* and
The Last Correspondent

The Last Piece

'This is a wonderful novel about the secrets we keep from the ones we love the most. Imogen Clark has a real talent for shining a light on the idiosyncrasies of family life and revealing past traumas, present hurts, and future hopes.'

—Victoria Connelly, author of *The Rose Girls* and
Love in an English Garden

'*The Last Piece* is a beautifully crafted, insightful tale about family and the cracks below the surface of seemingly perfect lives. Clark's characters, with their various secrets and flaws, leap off the page. A most enjoyable and riveting read.'

—S.D. Robertson, author of *My Sister's Lies* and
Time to Say Goodbye

'I couldn't resist going on this journey with the Nightingale family. With emotion on every page and mystery swirling around each character, *The Last Piece* explores how the past can be as unpredictable as the future. I raced through this life-affirming book, which left me buoyed with the promise of second chances.'

—Jo Furniss, author of *The Last to Know*

Where the Story Starts

'Once again . . . Imogen Clark urges readers to turn the pages as the delightfully pleasant façade of her characters' lives begins to crack when the mysteries of the past come to call. Both soothing and riveting, *Where the Story Starts* asks: what if your greatest secret is the one you don't even know exists?'

—Amber Cowie, author of *Rapid Falls* and *Raven Lane*

The Thing About Clare

'Warm and emotionally complex . . . A family drama that's hard to disentangle yourself from.'

—Nick Alexander, bestselling author of *Things We Never Said*

An
Unwanted
Inheritance

ALSO BY IMOGEN CLARK

Postcards from a Stranger
The Thing About Clare
Postcards at Christmas (a novella)
Where the Story Starts
The Last Piece
Reluctantly Home
Impossible to Forget

An Unwanted Inheritance

IMOGEN
CLARK

LAKE UNION
PUBLISHING

Text copyright © 2022 by Blue Lizard Books Ltd
All rights reserved.

Published by Lake Union Publishing, Seattle

www.apub.com

Amazon, the Amazon logo, and Lake Union Publishing are trademarks of Amazon.com, Inc., or its affiliates.

ISBN-13: 9781542032858
ISBN-10: 1542032857

Cover design by The Brewster Project

Printed in the United States of America

An
Unwanted
Inheritance

1

MAY

Caroline found the money in a battered suitcase under the narrow bed in the box room. It had been shoved right to the back wall, a few other boxes pushed in front of it, and she would never have come across it if she hadn't been trying to rescue Monty, her dead father-in-law's cat.

Poor Monty appeared to have been traumatised by the number of strangers who had been traipsing through the previously quiet house of Tony Frost, recently deceased. Caroline didn't blame him. She was spooked by being there too. When she and her husband Max had arrived to retrieve the forgotten cat, the atmosphere inside the house made the hairs on the back of her neck stand up.

There was nothing inherently creepy about the place. It was a perfectly ordinary mock-Tudor detached house, standing in a quiet cul-de-sac of similar boxy houses, built in the eighties and now looking a little self-conscious in a world that no longer valued things made to look like they belonged elsewhere. Which was ironic, Caroline always thought, given how the internet was packed full of fake.

What made Caroline uncomfortable was the feeling that her father-in-law was still there. Tony Frost had filled every corner of his home with the essence of himself, and everything in it shouted his name. Ever since his wife Valerie, Max's mother, had left him over a decade before, he had systematically removed all trace of any taste in furnishings other than his own. The result was rather larger-than-life, reminiscent of a Best Western hotel, with over-sized sofas and lamp-adorned occasional tables in every corner. Valerie's style had been far more modern, all crisp colours and clean lines, but left to his own devices, Tony had filled the space with dust-attracting soft furnishings. The effect was surprisingly feminine, and very dated.

But what made it really impossible to forget whose house you were in were the photographs. They were everywhere. Tony shaking hands with the great and the good, whilst grinning broadly, his head turned at an unnatural angle towards the camera. In some he wore his mayoral chains, in others he was on a golf course, and Caroline wasn't sure whether her eyes should linger on the spectacular tartan trousers or the oversized cap on his head. There were photos of Tony with smiling restaurateurs, with men who looked like Tory politicians (and probably were) and, in one particularly unlikely shot, with the tennis player Andy Murray who must have been in town for some event or other and had rubbed shoulders with Tony just when there happened to be a photographer on hand to capture the moment and preserve it for Tony's gallery.

Tony had considered himself to be a man of some standing in the community, and no one who visited his home would be allowed to forget it. However, now that he was dead, Caroline had the slightly unnerving feeling that he was still in the house, watching them.

What would her father-in-law make of her now? Caroline wondered as she knelt on the carpet of his box room, posterior in the air, trying to coax his cat back out so that she and Max could take him home with them.

'Come on, Monty,' she cajoled, her voice almost a whisper. 'Don't be frightened. I'm not going to hurt you.'

She sounded as if she was talking to a child. Caroline didn't know much about cats, but she imagined that Monty would be scared and she could empathise with that. Nobody liked it when the rug was suddenly pulled out from underneath them, even if they did happen to be a cat.

Gently, she began to slide the boxes out so she could see where Monty was hiding. It was dark under the bed, but it was quite hygienic, with no balls of carpet fluff or dead flies. Tony had kept a clean house, she'd give him that.

The battered suitcase was the last obstacle between her and the cat. Caroline wasn't sure what she should do for the best. If she crawled under the bed, he would either run straight out or stay to defend his corner. She didn't fancy being at eye level with him in his frightened state. She'd seen what those claws could do. Maybe she could pull the bed away from the wall and slip in and pick him up. Probably if she just left him alone he would come out of his own accord when he felt less hunted. But she was on a mission now. She had told Max she would catch the cat and catch the cat she was determined to do.

She grabbed hold of the suitcase by the handle. It was the sort that were all the rage in the eighties: British racing green fabric with faux leather straps and enormous and quite unnecessary buckles. It slid out easily enough, but she could tell from the heft of it that it wasn't empty. She pushed it aside. There was nothing between her and the cat now.

'Out you come, Monty,' she said, exasperation starting to show in her voice. Her back was hurting and she had banged her shoulder on the underside of the bedstead.

3

She reached a little further in. If she could get hold of his collar then maybe she could drag him out, although that probably wouldn't do much to build trust between the pair of them. Then, just as she had predicted, Monty shot out from under the bed, bounded for the door and was no doubt racing down the stairs and straight into Max's arms.

Sighing deeply, Caroline reversed herself back out and sat on her heels as she looked at her under-the-bed bounty. The boxes were mainly packaging for household gadgets – a new DVD player, a Sky box, a matching kettle and toaster, no doubt saved in case the items had to be returned, and then forgotten. The suitcase probably had clothes in, she thought, although since Tony had occupied the house alone there could be no shortage of wardrobe space in its four other bedrooms. And Tony was no hoarder. They hadn't even considered sorting out his things yet; Tony's sudden death was still far too raw for his children to think about that, but from what she had seen, everything in the house had an ordered air to it. It seemed unlikely that a stash of random clothing would be hiding in a case under the bed in the box room.

She unfastened the buckles then felt for the zip's pull. It slid along easily and she dragged the case clear of the bed so she could open it without obstruction. Bracing herself against the possibility of the suitcase containing sex toys or porn magazines or something else that a daughter-in-law shouldn't have to see, she lifted the lid.

Her jaw dropped as she took in the contents. The suitcase was full of cash. There were bundles and bundles of twenty-pound notes, all held together with elastic bands. Caroline had seen moments like this in countless films and TV dramas, where brief-cases are opened to reveal neat piles of crisp currency all tidily held together with bank bands. This was not like that. The money seemed to have been thrown in on a bundle-by-bundle basis, the pile in the centre being higher than around the edges. There was an

4

awful lot of it, though, more than she had ever seen before. There must be thousands of pounds, Caroline thought. In fact, probably tens of thousands, maybe more.

She picked up a bundle, flicked the edges through her fingers and lifted it to her face to smell it. It certainly looked and smelled like real money. She checked a couple of the serial numbers, although she wasn't quite sure why. They were different and non-sequential. There was no reason that she could see to conclude the money wasn't real. But what was it doing hidden under the bed in her father-in-law's back bedroom, and why was there so much of it?

Caroline turned her head towards the door.

'Max!' she called. 'Could you come up here a moment? There's something you need to see.'

2

FIVE MONTHS EARLIER

'If you lot don't get a shift on, we're going to be late,' shouted Caroline from the kitchen. It was a half-hearted reprimand. She was far from ready herself, but getting the four of them out of the house was more of a process than an event and you had to build yourself up to it. There was no sign that any member of her family had taken the slightest notice of her warning. Well, Caroline wasn't going to get herself in a lather about it. It was Christmas Day, and if you couldn't take things easy on Christmas Day then what hope was there?

None of them wanted to go to her father-in-law's house anyway, not even Max, and it was his family. It would be particularly difficult to get the boys to leave home this year as Father Christmas had given them a PlayStation in their stocking and she imagined that the draw of that would be far stronger than any desire to see their cousins. She would have to prise their fingers from the controllers when the time came.

Caroline sympathised with them, though. She would much rather be in her own home on Christmas Day too. Over the years, she had tried to change the Frost family tradition of all congregating at Tony's house, mostly because it made no practical sense; Tony couldn't cook and so, since his wife Valerie had left him, Caroline and Max's sister Ellie had had to make the food, either in their own homes or in Tony's underused and ill-equipped kitchen. Both she and Ellie had perfectly lovely kitchens of their own – in fact, Ellie's was spectacular, in keeping with the rest of her house. But no. They always spent Christmas at Tony's.

One year Caroline had suggested that they alternate between their respective houses, but that idea had hit stony ground.

'You can't expect Nathan to host us all in that tiny flat,' Max had said, ever protective of his baby brother.

'Well, we could do his year,' piped up Caroline, happy to mop up any surplus Christmas Days that were available, but Max had shaken his head.

'It's probably best if we just leave things the way they are,' he said in that way he had of not rocking the boat. 'It's kind of a Frost family tradition.'

Caroline had wanted to point out that Max's father no longer lived in their childhood home and that his mother had upped and left, so there probably wasn't quite as much tradition there as he was claiming. Her own family had disintegrated when she was a child, her father having catapulted them from a perfectly normal existence to what she had once heard her late mother call 'barely living'. As a result, no cosy Christmas traditions emanated from her side, but that didn't mean she wanted to become completely subsumed by what always happened at the Frosts.

'Yes, I understand that, Max, love,' she'd said, delicately judging her tone to strike reasonable and not whinging, 'but it might be nice for Alex and Theo if they got to spend Christmas at home once in a while, make some traditions of our own. It's not fair to drag them out when all they want to do is play with their presents and eat chocolate.'

7

'Oh, they don't mind,' replied Max genially, and Caroline wondered if they were talking about the same children. 'And anyway, they always have a good time when they get there.'

This Caroline couldn't deny. What Tony lacked in catering skills he more than made up for in his other hostly attributes. Her father-in-law was one of those 'life and soul' people who adored having others around him, and he invariably made a huge effort to ensure that everyone else enjoyed themselves as well. He always provided lots of silly Christmassy things to do – it had been blow-up Sumo wrestler costumes the previous year – and the booze flowed generously, which made it all more than tolerable for the adults. She had to admit that despite initial objections, they did generally end up having a lovely Christmas. But that really wasn't the point.

Caroline continued to stir the rum sauce – she was on puddings this year – and hoped that maybe next year they might get a chance to host the day themselves. She might suggest it to Ellie.

3

When they arrived at the house, it looked like a tiny corner of Las Vegas had hit Cedar Crescent. Tony had clearly decided more sparkle was required this year and so had festooned the front of his house with garlands of garishly bright twinkling lights. They flashed in sequence along the gutters and drainpipes in a way that was quite mesmerising. A large cheerful-looking Father Christmas was perched on the garage roof and a white, brightly lit reindeer was grazing nonchalantly on the grass.

'Oh, my God,' said Alex as they rounded the corner into the cul-de-sac. He placed a heavy emphasis on the last word, his eyes sliding sideways to see the effect on his younger brother. He was the eldest of the grandchildren and was just starting to experiment with expletives and blasphemy.

'Please don't swear, Alex,' said Caroline automatically. And then, 'Goodness! What a lot of lights.'

'I bet the neighbours are delighted,' said Max under his breath. A quick glance at the rest of the houses in the cul-de-sac showed that they had adopted a much subtler approach to Christmas decorations.

'That Santa is cool,' said Theo. 'Look, his sack lights up.'

'I think I like the reindeer best,' replied Caroline. The reindeer was quite tasteful, or it might have been in isolation.

As they stood admiring the show, the front door swung open and there stood Tony, dressed in a hat designed to look like a cooked turkey complete with little chef's hats on its legs.

'Merry Christmas!' he called to them. 'Like the light show, boys?'

The boys nodded enthusiastically.

'It's really sick, Grandad,' said Alex, eyes shining.

Tony grinned at them, clearly pleased with the impact his new lights had made.

'And sick is a good thing?' he asked, looking to Max for confirmation.

'Yes, Dad. Sick is good, apparently,' said Max.

'I thought we'd moved on from sick,' said Caroline, but not very loudly in case they were treated to the full range of new adjectives. The language used in their house had definitely taken a turn for the worse since Alex had started secondary school.

'Come in, come in,' said Tony, throwing wide his arms and beckoning them in with an extravagant gesture. 'Ellie and James are here already so we're only waiting for Nathan.'

Caroline relaxed. She hadn't seen Ellie since their book club Christmas drinks the week before and was looking forward to a catch-up.

'We'll just bring the food in,' she said. 'Max?'

Max didn't have to be asked twice and followed her back to the car, the boys making their way inside the house with their grandad. As they huddled under the raised boot, filling each other's arms with the wherewithal for at least part of a perfect Christmas dinner, Max reached across and planted a kiss on the tip of her nose.

'Thanks for this, Caro,' he said. 'I know you'd rather be at home, but it means a lot to Dad to have us all here.'

'Oh, it's okay,' she replied graciously. 'I don't really mind.' And now she was here she really didn't. There were worse ways to spend Christmas. Caroline knew that only too well.

They carried brimming bowls wrapped in clingfilm and endless Tupperware containers into the kitchen where they found Ellie, her cheeks glowing, basting the enormous turkey. Wafts of the tantalising scent of roast meat hit Caroline's nostrils and her mouth watered instantly.

'Mmm. That smells as if it's nearly ready,' she said.

'The joys of pre-cooking,' said Ellie. 'Mrs S would have a fit.'

Caroline gave her a knowing smirk and rolled her eyes good-naturedly.

'You two communicate by code,' said Max. 'It's totally baffling to the rest of us. Who on earth is Mrs S?'

'Mrs Sunderland,' provided Caroline. 'Our Home Ec. teacher. She'd have strung us up for reheating turkey, but if we want to eat before Boxing Day . . .'

'Well, I don't care how you do it,' said Max. 'It always tastes delicious to me. Hi, sis.'

He moved to give Ellie a hug, but she shooed him away with a flick of her tea towel.

'Not now, Max. Crucial moment. James is in the lounge. Grab yourself a beer and go and rescue him from Dad.'

Caroline began opening her boxes to check what each contained and then placing them on the table or in the fridge depending on their contents.

'Where are the girls?' she asked.

'Upstairs, I think,' said Ellie. 'Olivia is sulking because they both got a Barbie but she wants the one that Lucy got. I didn't think it would make any difference who got what, but more fool me, eh? I should have just bought two the same and saved the arguments.'

The thought that the girls should be more grateful peeked its nose into a corner of Caroline's mind but she ignored it.

'And what did Santa bring you?' she asked.

Ellie slid the turkey back into the oven, shut the door and stripped off the oven gloves before shyly proffering her wrist to Caroline. The wrist bore a bangle in what she assumed was eighteen-carat white gold and studded all the way round with brilliant-cut diamonds. It was truly beautiful.

Caroline took Ellie's hand to examine the bracelet more carefully. The diamonds twinkled in the light.

'Wow,' she breathed. 'Somebody's been good this year. That's absolutely gorgeous, Ellie.'

She held Ellie's hand for a little longer, twisting it gently so the diamonds sparkled, and then let it go. Ellie lifted her hand up to the light so she could admire the present for herself.

'Isn't it pretty?' she said. 'I'm such a lucky girl.' Her cheeks flushed pink with pleasure.

'You really are!' agreed Caroline. 'But you deserve to be spoilt.'

Ellie gave a bashful smile then dropped her arm, hiding the bracelet beneath the sleeve of her dress.

'And how about you?' she asked. 'Did you get anything nice?'

Caroline had received lots of lovely gifts from Max, nothing nearly as flashy or expensive as the one James had bought Ellie, but each thoughtfully chosen and carefully wrapped. Suddenly though, the gifts felt too private to share, even with her best friend. She didn't want to spoil them by making them sound silly or trivial.

'Oh, you know. The usual kind of things: perfume, some nice underwear, a couple of books,' she replied vaguely.

'Max always was good at presents,' said Ellie. 'Do you remember that compilation tape he made you when we were in the sixth form where each track was a clue to where he'd hidden your gift?'

Caroline did remember; of course she remembered. It was the kind of romantic gesture that a girl might carry with her for life and use as a benchmark for all future relationships to live up to. She still had the tape, with its insert card made of a photograph of her laughing at some long-forgotten joke, her head thrown back and her pale smooth neck exposed. They no longer had a cassette recorder on which to play it, but she wouldn't have risked playing it anyway in case the machine chewed up the precious tape.

'He is,' she said fondly. 'He gives it lots of thought.'

'And the boys? Were they happy with their stash?' Ellie asked.

Caroline noted the noun, how it implied far more gifts than the boys had actually received.

'It was mainly sports kit,' she replied, 'and the PlayStation that they got to share, but yes, pretty happy.'

'You're so lucky,' sighed Ellie. 'Your boys are so easily pleased. There's no way we could get away with a shared present – there'd be World War Three. I think it must be a girl versus boy thing. Girls are just so much more demanding.'

Caroline had her doubts about this, but it was a well-trodden path between the two of them and she would rather not venture that way today. So she smiled and asked, 'And how about the girls? What did they want?'

'Mainly things that were pink and/or expensive,' laughed Ellie. 'Lucy asked for a Prada mobile phone case! Well, you can imagine what we said to that one.' Ellie raised her eyebrows to suggest what a ludicrous thing such a gift might have been. Privately, Caroline thought what was really ludicrous was that her eight-year-old niece had a mobile phone at all, but again, there was nothing to be gained by saying so.

'Where do they get the ideas?' she asked instead. She meant it as a rhetorical statement but Ellie supplied her with the answer.

'TikTok!'

They laughed and shook their heads at the madness that was the twenty-first century.

'Whatever happened to the Argos catalogue?' asked Caroline. 'It worked perfectly well for us when we were their age. Right, I think I need a drink.' She peered over at Ellie's half-empty glass. 'What are you on? Fizz?'

Ellie nodded.

'Dad was wandering around with the bottle. There might be some left. Or there's some white open in the fridge if you'd prefer that.'

Prosecco gave Caroline a headache and Christmas Day was a marathon, not a sprint.

'I think I'll stick with still,' she said, helping herself to a glass from the cupboard and opening the fridge door. There was next to no food in there other than what she and Ellie had brought with them. Tony was obviously hoping to see out the festive period on leftovers from that day's meal. She grabbed the open bottle, gave a scant glance at the label and unscrewed the lid.

James stuck his nose around the door just as she was pouring.

'Nice wine that, Caroline. Found it in a little chateau down near Bordeaux. It's not cheap, mind you . . .'

He's going to tell me exactly how much it was, thought Caroline, but Ellie interrupted him.

'Are the girls still upstairs?' she asked. 'Could you just go and check on them?'

James helped himself to two more beers from the fridge and then went out into the hallway where he proceeded to bellow up the stairs for his daughters.

Ellie rolled her eyes. 'If I'd wanted it shouting I could have done it myself,' she muttered, and Caroline shook her head in solidarity.

There was the sound of footsteps tripping down the stairs accompanied by Olivia's shrill voice.

'Come on, Lucy. Daddy's calling us.'

Ellie smiled, relieved possibly that just one shout had resulted in the desired result without any more being required. The girls, blonde and really quite cute-looking in matching floaty party dresses, appeared in the kitchen.

'When's food, Mum?' asked Olivia. 'We're starving.'

'I think that's unlikely,' said Ellie, 'and it's not "food". It's the Christmas dinner that your Auntie Caroline and I have slaved over for days. But I'm not sure when we'll be eating. We need Uncle Nathan to arrive first. Why don't you go and see if Grandad's put out any snacks in the snug.'

Olivia wrinkled her nose. 'The boys are in there,' she said with mild disdain.

'But you like the boys,' said Ellie.

'And they'll have eaten all the snacks already.'

'Well, why don't you go and check,' suggested Caroline, 'and if they have come back here and we'll give you some girls-only snacks.'

Olivia's face lit up at this and she swivelled on the spot and left the room. 'Come on, Lucy,' she added as they went, and Lucy trooped out obediently behind her sister.

'Oh, bless them,' said Caroline before Ellie could. 'They're getting so big.'

Ellie smiled indulgently. 'They're tiny really. You wouldn't believe that Liv and Theo are the same age. He's a good head taller than her.'

'Well, Max is taller than James, I suppose,' replied Caroline, feeling prouder of her husband than the comment merited. 'And anyway, there's plenty of time for them to grow. Keep them looking tiny and cute as long as you can, Ellie, that way nobody can mistake them for being older than they are.'

Girls seem to grow up far too quickly these days, Caroline thought, judging by the ones that she saw on the edges of Alex's life. If she had girls, she would keep them well away from make-up and skimpy tops and pouting selfies. There would be plenty of time for all that nonsense, but many of the girls she knew had mothers who were positively shoving their daughters in that direction, as if their child becoming a pseudo-adult couldn't happen quickly enough. Not Ellie, though. On this point at least their parenting values were aligned.

Ellie untied her apron strings and slipped it over her head.

'Well, I don't think we can do much more until Nath gets here. He's shambolic, that man. He needs a good woman to organise him.' Her eyes opened wide and she bit her lip. 'God, was that a terrible thing to say?' she asked. 'Given that the only one he's ever really wanted has upped and left him.'

Caroline pulled a face. 'Probably, but I wouldn't worry about it,' she replied. 'And it's true anyway – he clearly can't organise himself.'

Just at that moment the front door opened and someone shouted, 'Merry Christmas!'

Ellie grinned at Caroline. 'Speak of the devil.'

Nathan, the youngest of the Frost siblings and the tallest, had always been a little bit fuzzy around the edges for Caroline. Nine years younger than Max and seven younger than her and Ellie, he had never really featured in their lives in the same way they had in each other's. Caroline could remember him being born, she and Ellie trying to play with him as if he were their very own living doll. When they were children, Nathan was always the one tagging along and being a nuisance. They used to watch him if Valerie popped to the shops, but they had never actively engaged with him. He was too young to be bothered with.

The last year had been tough for Nathan. His long-term girl-friend, Tasha, who they had all liked, had walked out on him. It wasn't as if they had lived in each other's pockets, and, of course, nobody ever knew for sure what was going on in another house-hold, but her sudden departure had been a surprise. Even though

Tasha was nearly ten years her junior, Caroline had liked her very much and had been sad to see her check out of Nathan's life. Her texts had gone unanswered though. Tash was apparently looking for a clean break from the entire Frost family and not just Nathan. Caroline couldn't help but wonder why it had all gone so wrong, or what Nathan had done to drive her so far away but, despite a huge amount of speculation by her and Ellie, she still had no idea.

There was a thundering of feet as the cousins all ran to meet their favourite uncle. Being the youngest and without the encumbrance of children of his own, Uncle Nathan was always the last adult left on the Twister mat and could generally be found playing 'just one more round' of whatever game was happening long after the other grown-ups had skulked back to their sofas. He also bought great gifts – generally not lavish, but invariably hitting the nail precisely on the head. He was like Max in that. Valerie had trained her sons well.

'Hi, everyone,' he said as he defended himself from the physical onslaught of his nephews and nieces, sweeping Theo up in one arm and grabbing Lucy with the other so that she squealed with delight. 'Sorry I'm late.'

'Again!' laughed Ellie. 'Did Father Christmas bring you an alarm clock because he jolly well should have done.'

'Have I missed something?' he asked, looking slightly crestfallen. He looked at his watch. An expensive gift from Ellie and James the year before, it hung loosely round his thin wrist looking as if it belonged to someone else. 'I thought we said one o'clock.'

'And it's ten past two,' scolded Ellie. 'But it's okay. Caro and I are seasoned professionals, and we anticipated your late arrival and factored it in accordingly.'

'You are at least reliable in your lateness, Nath,' chipped in James, and Caroline saw Nathan's smile slip just a little. Teasing was acceptable from his siblings, but less welcome, it seemed, from his brother-in-law.

'Well, I'm here now,' he said. 'What can I do to help?'

'Grab yourself a beer and stay out of the way,' said Max good-humouredly.

'Ah, Nathan. There you are. Deigned to grace us with your presence, then?'

Tony had appeared in the doorway still wearing the turkey hat and with a glass of wine in his hand. He was grinning broadly, but Caroline sensed that something about his tone was off and immediately, and quite unnecessarily, wanted to leap in to defend her brother-in-law. A look that she couldn't decipher flickered across Nathan's face, but then he returned his father's smile.

'Hi, Dad,' he said. 'Merry Christmas! Sorry I'm late. Can I do anything to help?' he asked again, turning back to Caroline and Ellie.

'Get yourself a drink and get out of the way!' replied Ellie, and Nathan did as he was told.

4

Tony's dining table wasn't large enough to accommodate all ten of them (which was yet another reason to spend the day at Ellie's house, Caroline always thought, as their table was plenty big enough). They had to take a Heath Robinson approach to creating a large enough space by joining two tables of differing heights and widths together and attempting to cover the join with tablecloths that were too big and so trailed on three sides. The effect was very homely, but Caroline regretted that her table dressing never looked quite as she imagined it would because of the various levels and lack of clean lines.

She and Ellie had to take it in turns to dress the table as it was an aspect of Christmas Day that they both enjoyed. Caroline tried to go for a different look whenever it was her turn – something to differentiate one year from another in the photos. She usually favoured traditional reds, golds and silvers, but this year she had opted for a rather left-field purple and was feeling a little anxious about it. Tony had some very definite ideas about what he liked and could make his views known in no uncertain terms if something didn't quite match his expectations. However, as the family made their way into the dining room and saw her choices, their reactions were gratifying, particularly from the female contingent.

'Can I have those pom-poms after?' asked Lucy, fondling the tinsel balls that hung from the backs of the mismatched chairs.

Olivia, sensing that she was about to be outdone, chipped in with her own request and Caroline could feel a row brewing. She had taken a shine to the purple pom-poms herself and had rather hoped she could discreetly pop them back into her bag when they were clearing up and use them to decorate her own kitchen. Ellie, however, was on it.

'For goodness' sake, girls. We haven't even sat down, so let's not start stripping the table just yet. We can worry about who gets what after we've eaten.'

The girls quietened but Caroline could see them sending warning signals to each other with their eyes, already dividing the pom-poms into two neat piles of five in their heads.

Everyone took their places and Caroline and Ellie ferried the various tureens from the kitchen to the table, juggling things around until there was space for everything. The turkey came last, golden brown with the remnants of the heat rising from the breast and filling the room with its delicious aroma. Caroline saw a proud but slightly bashful smile on Ellie's lips as the family applauded the bird and then the cooks in turn. She placed the turkey at the head of the table in front of Tony who was brandishing a glinting carving knife and fork. Max lowered his head as if in deference to his father's position as head of the family. There would come a time, Caroline knew, when those roles would be reversed, but Tony was still a young sixty-five and not yet ready to relinquish his place to his offspring.

'A toast!' Tony said. 'To the cooks!'

There was a general kerfuffle as they all realised the glasses were still standing empty. Ellie tutted, her moment of glory seemingly spoilt through someone else's failing.

'Oh, James! You haven't taken the drinks order,' she said petulantly.

'Mea culpa, mea culpa,' said James, getting quickly to his feet. 'Give me two ticks.'

'Why don't you just carve, Dad,' suggested Max sensibly. 'So the rest of the food doesn't go cold.'

'Actually,' said Tony, lowering the carving knife and passing it, blade first, to Max. 'I think it might be time to hand over this particular duty to my firstborn. We old-timers have to step aside before we get trampled down in the rush to take our place,' he added with a wink at Olivia. 'What do you reckon, Max? You're forty now . . .'

'Forty-one actually, Dad,' said Max quietly.

'Forty-one. Precisely. The perfect age. Do you reckon you're up to the task?'

Caroline wasn't sure if Tony was referring to the task of carving the turkey or something broader, but she hoped it was the latter. Her husband was a good man but he could be over-shadowed by the rest of his family, and James, for that matter. A gesture like this would do wonders for his self-confidence. She looked over at Max and gave him an encouraging smile.

Max looked a little thrown, but he reached for the knife, awkwardly bending his wrist round so he could take hold of the handle. The tiniest flush of colour passed over his cheeks together with a delighted smile, which he quickly turned into a more neutral expression.

'Thanks, Dad,' he said. 'I'm not sure what to say really but, well, thanks.'

'And don't screw it up,' added Tony lightly, taking his seat. It was meant as a joke, but Caroline saw Max's eyes narrow. That was always the way with Tony, she thought. He had a habit of giving with one hand whilst taking away with the other.

'No pressure, Max,' called Nathan from the other end of the table.

But Max was fine. He set to, lifting the crispy skin from the glistening white flesh beneath and was soon carving the meat into even slices as if he had been born to do it.

James appeared moments later with a bottle of red and white wine, one in each hand. Caroline saw him take in the change in status quo but he didn't comment.

'So, this year,' James said, 'we have a mouth-watering, zesty and bone-dry Australian Riesling loaded with zingy lemon and lime notes . . .' He waved the appropriate bottle. 'Or this ripe, black-cherry-scented Pinot Noir, which has particularly silky palate.'

He paused for a moment, as if giving them a moment to pay homage to the wines. Caroline would have been happy with a mid-range Sauvignon from Sainsbury's, but the wine was always James's contribution to the meal and it was obvious that he put a lot of care – and cash – into the choosing of it.

'Tony?' James asked, weighing each bottle in his hands. 'Which is it to be?'

'Red, please, James,' said Tony without looking up.

James, who had been on the verge of reading out the labels, cut himself off abruptly and began to pour.

'I'll sort the kids, shall I?' asked Nathan, giving each child a grin that no doubt made them all feel that they were the favourite.

'Thanks, Nath,' said Ellie. 'There's lemonade, Coke or that fizzy grape juice stuff.'

Each child called out their order and Nath threw his arms up around his head as if defending himself from the onslaught of requests.

Eventually drinks were poured, the turkey and chefs toasted again and the food served. Quiet descended as they all tucked in, occasionally pausing to make appreciative noises. Caroline cast her eyes around the table. Max had been right; it was okay now that she was here. In fact, it was more than okay, it was lovely.

The Frosts were that rare beast: a happy family. Yes, they had their sticky moments from time to time – which family didn't? – but on the whole they were a great bunch and she had always been happy to be a part of it. When she had been invited to their house for Sunday lunch as a girl, such things not being something that happened at home, she had let herself pretend that the Frosts were actually her family, little knowing that that was exactly how things would end up.

All that was missing, really, was Valerie. Caroline didn't like to think of her mother-in-law on days like this. She was single now, never having found someone to replace Tony in her life, but always went on a cruise with a girlfriend at Christmas. Caroline assumed this was to avoid the awkward invitations to join them, or to prevent having to take part in a rota. But she knew that Max would have liked to see his mother on Christmas Day, and her absence always cast a slight shadow over the jolliness of the day, or at least it did for Caroline. Her own mother had been gone for over twenty years and it would have been nice to see her substitute one occasionally. Tony didn't look as if he gave two hoots about his ex-wife as he chatted animatedly to Ellie and Olivia about the worst way to cook sprouts.

'Are we going to play games after dinner?' asked Theo. 'We always do that, don't we, Mum?' he added, looking to Caroline for confirmation.

'We can if you'd like to,' she replied. 'What would you like to play?'

'Sardines!' said Theo, and Caroline's heart sank. Sardines was fine for the children to play on their own but she had no desire to be forced into a confined space, no matter how much she loved her family.

'I'm not sure sardines works that well on Christmas Day,' she said gently. 'How about a board game? Monopoly or Cluedo, maybe?'

Theo looked disgruntled. 'I hate board games. They're boring. And I never win.'

Tony laughed, a warm rich sound. 'Now then Theo, there's a sure-fire way of winning at any game that works every time. Want to know what it is?'

Theo nodded enthusiastically.

'Cheat!' said Tony. 'And make sure you do it better than everybody else.'

Theo's smile fell and his eyebrows knotted together as he looked from his grandfather to Caroline.

'But cheating is wrong, isn't it, Mum?' he asked. He looked so confused that Caroline wanted to sweep him up in her arms and reassure him, but she didn't want to undermine Tony so instead she gave him a huge smile.

'Cheating is very wrong,' she said. 'Grandad is only teasing, aren't you, Grandad?'

She turned her gaze to Tony, signalling with the raise of an eyebrow and the widening of her eyes exactly what she thought of his suggestion, but Tony didn't retract what he'd said.

'Isn't it, Grandad?' she repeated, more forcefully this time.

'Well, it all depends on the rules of the game,' said Tony. 'Sometimes cheating is the only way to play.'

'Like in Cheat!' chipped in Olivia with a note of triumph in her voice. 'That's a game when you're supposed to cheat, isn't it, Grandad?'

Tony turned his attention to her. 'It is, Olivia,' he agreed. 'And there are many others too.'

Caroline could feel her temper rising. She would not have her authority as a parent undermined in this way. She stood up and started to clear the plates, the china clattering as she stacked them into a pile.

'Cheating is always wrong, Theo,' she said firmly without taking her eyes off the plates. 'The way to win in life is to try your very hardest at everything you do. Wouldn't you agree, Max?' She threw her husband a look that she hoped said, 'Back me up here and stop your father from teaching our son that dishonesty is acceptable.'

Luckily Max caught the ball and ran with it. 'It certainly is. Cheating is always wrong. And anyone caught cheating at Cluedo on my watch will be forced to do all the washing-up!'

Everyone laughed and the tension dissipated at once, but as Caroline, laden down with crockery, pushed open the door to the kitchen with her back, she could feel her heart beating hard in her chest. How dare Tony do that? Her boys loved and respected their grandfather and would take anything he told them seriously. And he had just told them that dishonesty was an acceptable way to get what you wanted.

She had just opened the dishwasher with some force and started to slam the plates into it when Ellie came in.

'Are you okay, Caro?' she asked.

Caroline didn't reply, not quite trusting her voice or what she might say.

'Take no notice of Dad,' continued Ellie soothingly. 'You know what he's like. He's just teasing. And the kids know he's only joking. There's no harm done.'

But Caroline knew exactly how much harm could be done by cheating and dishonesty, how the smallest lie could snowball until your whole world came clattering down around you, how lives could be destroyed in the blink of an eye.

'It's no joking matter,' she replied under her breath.

5

After dinner there was generally a lull in proceedings. The men would make a stab at clearing up and then Caroline and Ellie discreetly swooped in and did the bits they forgot. There was a rhythm to it with each knowing what was expected of them.

Caroline, feeling calmer now, headed for the dining room, mainly to check for anything that still needed putting away, but also to make sure that Olivia hadn't swiped all the purple pom-poms.

She was just about to push open the door when she heard voices inside. It was Tony, she thought, and James maybe? She wasn't sure and she couldn't hear what was being said, but something about their hushed tones made her hold back and not go in.

Instead, she went to the snug to check on the children. They were all sprawled over the furniture watching *Elf*. Her boys had pooh-poohed the film earlier in the holidays, claiming to be too grown-up for it, but you could never be too old for *Elf*, could you? Caroline was almost tempted to make them all squish up so she could watch with them, but something about the easy comfort of the four of them together stopped her. She didn't want to disturb the equilibrium. It would no doubt be relatively short-lived.

As she headed back towards the kitchen, James emerged from the dining room looking like the cat that got the cream, with Tony following behind.

'Everything okay?' she asked.

'Absolutely,' replied James, rubbing his hands together. 'Now, shall we open some presents? It's Christmas after all!'

The exchanging of gifts was Caroline's least favourite part of the day. She chose presents carefully and with great thought, but within a strict budget. Ellie's approach was to throw money at the task and, whilst the gifts she gave were never quite as well suited to their recipient as Caroline's, this was often made up for by the sheer wow factor. It didn't matter really. Ellie and James simply had more money than she and Max. It was just how things were and neither Caroline nor Max was in the least resentful, but occasionally it might have been nice if some acknowledgement was given as to how clever her gift-buying had been.

'Kids!' bellowed James down the hall. 'Presents!'

The four children emerged seconds later, and Caroline thought wistfully of how content they had been with the simple pleasure of an old film just seconds before. But James was right. It was Christmas Day and to the children, at least, that meant one thing.

Alex and Theo rushed round her, shoving at one another to get into the sitting room first, with Olivia and Lucy in hot pursuit. Then Tony appeared behind her, the turkey hat now replaced by a full and rather splendid Father Christmas outfit. He had had it, or one like it, for as long as Caroline could remember. She and Ellie had snuck into the loft in the Frosts' old house as children and peeked in wonder into the box where it lived, Ellie keen to show her friend a little part of what happened on pretty much the only day that Caroline didn't spend with the family. There were no costumes at Caroline's house and she relished this glimpse into the kind of Christmases she only saw in films and on television adverts. The outfit pulled a little across Tony's middle these days, but it still made her smile.

Nathan followed behind Tony. Unaware that he was being observed, he looked preoccupied, Caroline thought, as if he was running through something in his head, but when he saw her looking, the corners of his mouth turned upwards and the impression was gone.

'Did someone say presents?' Tony asked as he opened the sitting room door to excited applause.

Caroline and Ellie had already put their gifts into his sack, including the ones that Ellie had bought for Tony himself to give. The overall effect was very festive and Tony played up to the role beautifully, even though the children were a little too old to not recognise him behind the fluffy white beard.

Caroline followed in Tony's wake, slipping quietly to one side and sitting down on the carpet at Max's feet. She watched as Tony made a great show of pulling each gift from his sack, squinting at the label and then delivering it to its grateful recipient. Everyone opened the presents with much oohing and aahing. Ellie and James had been as generous as ever. Her own gift was a beautiful silk scarf and Caroline didn't need to look at the label to appreciate how expensive it must have been, although she did give it a sneaky peek when no one was looking. Max's gift was a butter-soft calfskin wallet, which he was clearly delighted with.

For Tony there was a bottle of whisky in a special presentation box, clearly designed to be a collector's item. As he opened it James chipped in with an explanation.

'That's one to lay down rather than drink, Tony,' he said. 'They go for hundreds, sometimes thousands of pounds after a few years.'

'I'll try to restrain myself,' replied Tony, holding the box up to the light to admire the bottle. 'Did you know there's quite a market for fake whisky?' he added. 'This one is kosher, I assume?'

A look passed between the two men that Caroline didn't like, like a private joke that the rest of them wouldn't get. Ellie would have spent a long time choosing this lovely present for her father, and obviously it would be the real deal. Caroline loved Tony, she really did. He was a kind and generous man who was fun to be around; a room was always jollier when he was in it. But there was an edge to him sometimes that made Caroline uneasy, and a comment like that, coming on the back of what he'd said to Theo at dinner, left a nasty taste.

She would ignore it, though – he was joking, after all. It was just that she didn't find it funny. She turned her attention back to the children who, with sparkling eyes and huge smiles, were comparing their gifts, and the moment was forgotten.

6

The day wore on, becoming more languid as energy levels diminished, and eventually they reached the point in the evening when nothing else of significance was going to happen but no one could be bothered to make the first move to leave. Glasses were sitting empty and had been for some time.

'So, Dad,' Max said. 'Anything new at the council? Or should I say, anything you can tell us about?' He tapped the side of his nose conspiratorially.

Local politics was Tony's thing, more so since he had retired early ten years earlier. He had been an elected councillor for decades, starting at town level and then moving up to the district council on which he still sat. He had even had a year as mayor, elected by his peers, in which he barely seemed to have taken his chains of office off. Caroline had joked to Max that perhaps his father was even sleeping in them, which had gained her a disapproving look. She might be a Frost but she, like James, was only there by marriage and would do well to remember her place.

Tony, the only one amongst them to still have a drink on the go, cupped his brandy glass and swilled the amber liquid around the bowl.

'Not much new,' he replied. 'The wheels just keep on turning. There are a couple of things in the offing' – he glanced over at James and then back to Max – 'but it's a bit early to share the details. Nothing that will be of much interest, though. Housing, that kind of thing. And how about you boys? How are things going for you?' he asked.

He had two sons in the group but it was James who leapt in to answer the question.

'Tremendously, Tony,' he said. 'Life is as sweet as a nut. Did you see the new car?' He gestured towards the curtained window.

They all nodded, although Caroline thought she saw Nathan roll his eyes at Max. It was terribly subtle – she might have got that wrong.

'New last month,' said James. 'It's all about first impressions in my game, making sure that you walk the walk. No one trusts a property developer in a crap car.'

Caroline actually thought cars were for getting from A to B reliably rather than making a statement. Their Seat was six years old but it was perfectly serviceable and had never let them down. But she understood that James had an image to keep up and he did it with gusto. Ellie and James's lifestyle far outstripped hers and Max's, not that these things were of the least interest to them. They had enough for their needs and what they didn't have they saved for. It suited them.

'Next year is looking promising, very promising indeed,' James continued. 'Some big deals in the pipeline and if they come off it's going to make the bottom line look very healthy.'

'And you, Max?' Tony asked. 'How's life in the heady world of paperclips?'

Caroline tried hard not to resent Tony's dismissive attitude to Max's work. It wasn't glamourous being the regional manager of a stationery supplier, but it was a good and steady job, which Max carried out diligently, as he did most things.

'All good,' Max replied. 'We're busy. Customers are buying.'

31

'The paperless office just a pipe dream then?' asked Tony, and Max nodded.

'Seems so. For now, at least.'

Tony never asked about Caroline's work and Ellie didn't have a job, so the attention fell on Nathan. Seemingly aware of it, he shuffled in his seat.

'What's new in website design, Nath?' Tony asked, and Nathan shrugged.

'You know, same old, same old,' he replied, but Caroline noticed that he didn't meet his dad's eye. Nathan had always been private. Even as a little boy he had hidden what he was playing with when they stumbled across him in the house, as if the bigger kids would try to take it from him, although they never had done. Caroline had sometimes felt sorry for him, leading his solitary life when she and Ellie were always together, but if ever she'd tried to join in his games Ellie had pulled her away, telling her to leave him to it, that he preferred it that way.

'But now you've got other irons in your fire, eh, son? That's good,' said Tony with a quick raise of his eyebrows. Nathan gave a single nod but Caroline noticed that Tony's eyes lingered on his son's face for a moment longer. She wondered what he was referring to but there were no more clues to follow.

It was time to go, she decided. She made a show of looking at her watch and then yawned widely. 'Well, Max, I think it's time we took those boys home, don't you?'

Max nodded and got to his feet at once.

'Thank you, Tony,' she said graciously. 'It's been lovely as ever.'

Tony stood up too, pulling down the jacket of his Father Christmas outfit, which he hadn't got round to taking off.

'No, no,' he replied, shaking his head emphatically. 'Thanks go to you and Ellie. You do all the hard work. I just provide the venue.'

It was on the tip of Caroline's tongue to suggest a change might be good, but she swallowed the thought down. This wasn't the time.

'Oh, you're welcome,' she said instead. 'Now, we've left you some turkey and stuffing and some of the leftover cheese in your fridge. There's some of the trifle too. I hope that's okay.'

'Oh, that's most kind,' Tony replied, as if this wasn't the way things went every year. 'Save me venturing out to the shops for a while.'

Caroline and Ellie gathered the children and anything that hadn't been caught in the first sweep for scattered belongings, and then they all stood in the hallway to say their goodbyes.

'Anyone want a lift?' asked Nathan.

Caroline tried to do a quick mental calculation of how much he'd had to drink and when, but gave up. They were close enough to their house to walk so there was no need to trouble herself with the details. The children looked up at their respective parents hopefully, but Max shook his head.

'We're fine, mate. Shank's pony works for us. I'll come back and pick the car up tomorrow, Dad.'

Howls of protest followed from Olivia and Lucy at the prospect that they might have to walk home, which Ellie tried to smother.

'Ellie?' Nathan asked.

Ellie paused for a moment. 'Well, if you don't mind, Nath, a lift for me and the girls would be very welcome. You can walk, can't you, James? I'm not sure there's enough room . . .'

The girls made little fist-pumping gestures, which Alex and Theo studiously ignored.

Finally, they all set off, leaving the glowing reindeer still grazing on the damp grass.

7

FOUR MONTHS EARLIER

Ellie was curled in an armchair in the conservatory, her legs tucked underneath her, perusing cookery books. It was her favourite spot, especially when, as now, the girls were at school and she had some time to herself. The weak January sun was streaming through the glass and even though she could see the frost on the tips of the lawn beyond, she could almost imagine that it was summer. Having the central heating on so high was probably contributing more to the warmth than the sun's feeble rays, but she couldn't be expected to sit in here in the winter without it on. It was freezing.

She flicked over page after page of fussy, complicated-looking recipes, but she didn't fancy any of them. It was too cold to be messing around with dainty little dishes. What they needed was a hearty casserole and some stout jacket potatoes. It was only Max, Caroline and the boys coming for supper and they were always so easy to please. There was no need to go overboard – just something tasty and simple. Her girls wouldn't eat anything that they couldn't immediately identify anyway.

She toyed briefly with the idea of feeding the four children first and getting them out of the way. Max and Caro liked to eat with their boys, she knew, whereas she and James generally had dinner after Olivia and Lucy had gone to bed. She wasn't sure which she would prefer. Exclusively adult conversation had its benefits, of course, but if the girls weren't at the table then she wouldn't have the chance to show them off. She was so proud of them and now that they were growing up a little they were such great company with their funny little turns of phrase and righteous indignation about things that mattered to them.

With a little nod to herself she made the decision. They would all eat together. It was good table manners practice if nothing else, and the kids could always slope off after the main course and have ice cream in the playroom, leaving the adults to their chat.

She shut the recipe book with a satisfying snap. Best to stick to something she knew the girls liked to avoid any drama. She would do her mother's coq au vin recipe. Everyone enjoyed that.

Thinking of her mother made Ellie reach for her phone. They had barely seen each other since she'd got home from her Christmas cruise and Ellie knew that if she didn't make the effort to get in touch then the time would just extend. She dialled her number.

Her mother answered on the fifth ring, sounding a little out of breath and slightly annoyed to have been interrupted.

'Hi, Ellie. It's not a great moment. Can I ring you back?'

Valerie was always busy. Since she had left Tony it was as if she had been granted a whole new lease of life. She had taken up various hobbies – bridge, pottery, Zumba, Nordic walking, creative writing, ballroom dancing, golf. Not all of these had lasted much longer than a couple of weeks, mere flurries of excitement at her newly found freedom, but she was still playing bridge and doing the Nordic walking in the park twice a week. Ironically, it had turned out she was quite good at golf and would have been able to play with Tony had she had a go earlier. She had lost some weight, had a haircut and dyed her grey hair, and now she looked at least ten years younger. Ellie was pleased she had turned her life around so beautifully, but that didn't stop her missing the old version of her mum who could always be found in the kitchen with the kettle poised and the biscuits open.

She sometimes wondered what had caused the transformation. There had been no warning that her mother was unhappy, and Ellie had just assumed that her parents would see out their golden years together. So when Valerie announced that she had left their father just after Nathan went to university it had come as a shock. Whenever Ellie had tried to get to the bottom of what had gone wrong, her mum had always clammed up. Something had happened to force the decision, Ellie was sure of it, but what it was remained a mystery.

'Of course,' said Ellie now, trying to disguise her disappointment but not altogether succeeding.

'It wasn't anything important?' her mother added.

'No, no. Nothing important. It was just . . . but it doesn't matter. I'll catch up with you . . .'

But her mother had gone.

Reluctantly, Ellie uncurled her legs and gathered her book, notepad and pen together. She was expected at the tennis club for the Ladies' Ladder Committee Meeting in half an hour, and then she would just have time to nip to Waitrose before she had to be at the school to pick up the girls. Life was non-stop.

8

Saturday rolled round. The coq au vin was bubbling away on the stove, filling the house with its delicious aroma, and the potatoes were crisping up nicely. All Ellie needed to do was put the veg on to steam at the last minute. Satisfied that all was in hand with the supper, she left the kitchen to go and get herself ready.

'The boys will be here in half an hour,' she called to her daughters as she passed the playroom. 'Please make sure it's tidy in there. Remember, if there's anything that you don't want to get broken then hide it away in your rooms.'

Caro's boys weren't destructive on purpose, Ellie knew, but they were more boisterous than the girls and things did tend to get trodden on or taken apart or lost when they were around.

Hearing the low hum of James's voice on the phone, she paused to put her head round the door into his office. He worked so hard. Rarely did a day go by when he wasn't in there doing something or other. Ellie had tried to tell him that not allowing himself any time off would do him no good in the long run, but James had shaken his head at her.

'You want all this, Ellie,' he said, gesturing at the space, 'then I have to keep at it. I can't afford to take my eye off the ball. I might miss the next big deal and then where would we be?'

She knew he didn't mean to, but James had a way of making her feel a little bit stupid and naive, when she wasn't either. It was true that she had never run a business like he did, but she had had an important job before she gave it all up to have the girls. And nobody was so indispensable that they needed to be available seven days a week, no matter how important they thought they were. But it was true. She did enjoy their lifestyle, so she kept her concerns about James's working hours to herself from then on.

'Caro and Max will be here in twenty minutes,' she whispered.

James was standing with his back to the door, mobile phone pressed firmly to his ear.

'Yes, I know that. Don't worry. It's all under control,' he said testily to whoever was on the other end. The atmosphere suggested that it was a difficult call, so Ellie retreated. She wasn't sure he had even realised that she'd been there, let alone heard what she'd said. Whoever it was clearly had no qualms about working weekends either.

She reached their bedroom and closed the door behind her. This was her sanctuary. When they had moved into the house, a new build that James had had built for them on the edge of one of his upmarket housing developments, he had given her carte blanche to decorate the space as she wished. The en suite and dressing rooms had come with the highest specification fittings, but Ellie had made the bedroom her own with delicate shades of pale pink, pearl grey and silver.

'Do you think it's too girly?' she'd asked when she showed him the mood board that the interior designer had put together.

James had barely looked at it. 'Doesn't worry me,' he said. 'I'll just be sleeping in there. And . . .' He grinned at her lasciviously. 'You know . . .'

Ellie giggled at his insinuation.

'And I doubt I'll be looking at the wallpaper then,' he added with a twitch of his eyebrows.

'And I'm all right choosing this fabric for the curtains?' Ellie had pressed on, running her finger over the burrs in the swatch of pale-grey silk. 'I mean, there are cheaper options.'

'Whatever you want you can have,' he'd said. 'All I want is to make you happy.'

So she had taken him at his word, cut no corners, spared no expense, and now the room made her smile every time she set foot in it.

She nipped into her dressing room to get a clean blouse. Her jeans would be fine, she decided. There was no need to try too hard. Max would be dressed in what he'd been wearing all day and Caro wouldn't mind if Ellie turned up in her pyjamas. Her blouses were all hanging on cedar hangers in colour-coded order at one end of the rail and she selected a boat-necked one in a fifties-inspired print that she thought brought out the blue of her eyes. She would wear her Christmas bracelet as well. She didn't have many opportunities to show it off. It was too beautiful to wear every day and she didn't always think it was appropriate to be quite so ostentatious. But this was dinner with Max and Caro and they had already seen it and wouldn't care about how much it had cost.

She opened her jewellery drawer with the little key that she kept under her make-up bag. It wasn't the safest place to hide the key, but the house had a state-of-the-art security system and a burglar would have to get past a lot more hurdles before he made it up here. The drawer was more to keep the girls from playing with her more expensive pieces than anything else, but having things under lock and key kept the insurance company happy and meant she didn't have to go trailing off to the bank every time she wanted to wear something.

The box for the bracelet was on the top but when she opened it the bracelet wasn't there. She lifted the insert to see if it had slipped underneath but it wasn't there either. That was odd. She was certain she'd put it back the last time she'd worn it. When would that have been? she wondered. There had been the AGM of the tennis club in the middle of the month. She had definitely had it then, but she couldn't be sure about after that. Well, it must be here somewhere.

She picked all the boxes out of the drawer one by one, opening them and peering inside. She really did have some lovely things. James might not have much imagination, but what he lacked in creativity he more than made up for in money spent on her. The bracelet, however, wasn't in any of them. She had hoped that it might have slipped between two boxes but now she was at the bottom of the drawer and she still hadn't found it. Well, where could it be? It wasn't as if it could be stolen. Everything else was still here, and anyway no one came up here except the cleaners, whom she trusted implicitly. Either the girls had found the key or she had put it down somewhere when she got back from the AGM and forgotten to put it away.

Ellie had been a little bit tipsy that night, but she distinctly remembered having the bracelet on when she got home because James had wanted her to wear it, and her underwear, when they made love. She had objected, worried that the bracelet would dig in, but had gone along with it and then . . . That was it. She remembered now. She had slipped the bracelet off when they were in the throes. It must have fallen off the bedside table and rolled under the bed somewhere. There wasn't time to start crawling around now, however. She made a mental note to check later.

She could hear voices floating up the stairs. The Frost contingent must have arrived. Ellie checked her reflection in the mirror and then flew down to greet them. Caro and Max were standing in the hallway chatting animatedly to Oliva and Lucy, Alex and Theo hanging back and shoving into one another so they lost their balance. There was no sign of James. He must still be on his call, Ellie thought. It didn't really matter that he wasn't here to meet their guests when it was only Max and Caro, but she was still irritated that he was working on a Saturday evening in the first place.

'Hi, you lot,' she said as she reached the bottom of the stairs. 'Come in, come in. Is it still freezing outside? Girls, can you take the coats and hang them in the cloakroom, please? Boys, would you like a drink? There's all the usual stuff in the drinks cupboard. Can you sort them out please, Liv?'

They were settled in the lounge with drinks and the log burner blazing before James finally appeared. Ellie thought he looked tired and a little careworn. Maybe she would talk to him about overdoing things again in the morning, but for now she handed him a bottle of lager, which he took with a grateful smile. She watched as he took a sip, appeared to mentally recentre himself and then grin broadly at their guests. The transformation took less than a couple of seconds, but Ellie had clocked it. It was as if he was morphing from James the businessman to James the host. By the time he spoke, all signs of exhaustion had lifted from his face.

'So, what's new in the Frost household?' he asked cheerfully.

Max shook his head. 'Same old, same old. Chasing the corporate dollar as ever.'

'I've told you before, Max mate,' James replied. 'You should work for yourself. No pandering to demanding bosses or grafting to make someone else rich. What I make goes straight into our pockets. No one else takes a slice.'

'Except the tax man, of course,' Caroline said with a smile. There was such an innocence about Caroline sometimes. Whilst James always paid his tax eventually, it was occasionally a little closer to the wire than Ellie would have liked and he was always looking at some avoidance scheme or other. But this would never have occurred to Caroline. In her binary world, tax was due and therefore should be paid. Ellie imagined that this approach to life would be very straightforward.

'The tax man has no complaints,' James said, and winked at Caroline.

'I'm all about the simple life,' said Max. 'I know what's expected of me. I turn up and do the job, and they pay me enough every month for our needs. I don't need any more complications.'

Max had always been the steady one in the family, Ellie thought. He wasn't ambitious, but he wasn't a shirker either. He just got on with whatever needed doing competently and with little complaint. Their father had always tried to get him to strive harder, to better his position, but his words fell on stony ground. Max just wasn't interested. He was no entrepreneur, and no amount of cajoling would change that. Ellie had often thought that the reason she had married James was because he reminded her of her dad. The two of them had hit it off right from the beginning, Tony recognising a kindred spirit in James that he hadn't found amongst his own children.

'You'll never make any serious money, though,' said James knowingly. 'And don't you ever yearn for something more? Let's imagine that money was no object. What would you buy? Go on, Max, name it. There must be something.'

It took Max less than a second to respond. 'I would buy a classic E-Type Jag,' he said. 'Better still, a convertible.'

Ellie thought her brother's eyes seemed to twinkle in the glow of the fire at the thought of the car.

'And what would that set you back, ballpark?' asked James.

'More than I'll ever have,' replied Max. 'But a man can dream.'

'You need to work for yourself, mate,' said James again. 'It's the only way to make any money.'

Max shrugged. 'I'm happy with how things are,' he said, closing James down.

As usual, Ellie was torn between supporting her brother or her husband, and as usual she sided with the latter. How could she not? He had bought her this beautiful house filled with all her beautiful things. They had foreign holidays three times a year and the girls went to the best prep school in the area. And James had made all that happen for her by sheer hard work and dogged determination. A warm glow flooded through her when she thought about it. Her brother's life was pedestrian by comparison.

'So, Els,' began Caroline, apparently to take the spotlight off Max. 'What have you been up to this week?'

And then, as ever, the conversation naturally split into her and Caroline sharing news and gossip whilst Max and James discussed the mid-season position of the Premier League teams until it was time for Ellie to serve the supper.

They all gathered around the huge glass dining table, the children naturally gravitating to the end nearest the door. Ellie would rather they sat a little more interspersed with the adults, but she wasn't about to impose a formal seating plan on a casual supper.

The boys began wolfing down their casserole almost before Ellie had finished serving everyone. She tried not to notice how Olivia and Lucy picked over their plates suspiciously, prodding at unidentified items with their forks, their pretty little noses curled. School had done this to them; she was almost certain they would have happily eaten anything before then.

There were appreciative comments from the adults as they began to tuck in, and Ellie was pleased. She might not have paid jobs like the rest of them, but she could cook.

'Have you seen Mum recently, Max?' she asked. 'I tried to ring earlier in the week, but she was too busy to talk and she didn't ring me back.'

'That woman puts us all to shame,' replied Caroline. 'I don't know how she squeezes everything in. I barely have time to do what I have to and I don't do half the things she does. She makes me feel wholly inadequate, bless her.'

'She is retired though, Caro,' said Max. 'It's hardly the same.'

'I suppose,' said Caroline.

'We've not seen her since . . .' Max puffed his lips out as he counted the weeks in his head. 'Well, it's been a while.'

Ellie shrugged. 'I just wanted to talk to her about Nathan,' she said. 'Did he seem different to you at Christmas? A bit on edge, maybe?'

'I gave up trying to work out what was going on in Nathan's head when we were kids,' replied Max. 'He seemed much the same as always to me.'

Max had many qualities, but reading non-verbal signals wasn't one of them. Caroline, however, had a more finely tuned radar and she seemed to sense something broader now.

'How do you mean, Els?' she asked, tipping her head to one side as she spoke.

'I don't know,' replied Ellie. 'Nothing specific that I can put my finger on. It was more of a feeling, really. I just got the impression that something was a bit off.'

'Maybe it was because Tasha wasn't there,' said Caroline. 'I'm sure them splitting up must have thrown him a bit.'

'Maybe,' Ellie replied thoughtfully.

She threw a glance towards the children, who didn't look as if they were listening but probably were, and changed the subject.

'So, Alex,' she continued in a slightly louder voice. 'How's big school?'

'It's all right,' he said without looking up from his plate.

'Look at your Auntie Ellie when she's talking to you,' remonstrated Caroline, and Ellie saw him look up straight away and make eye contact with her. They were nice boys, she thought, even if they were a little boisterous.

'Which subject do you like best?'

Alex shrugged. 'Dunno. History's okay, I suppose. And I like DT.'

'I like Maths best, don't I, Mummy?' chipped in Olivia, and Theo, who at ten was almost exactly the same age as her, pretended to put his fingers down his throat.

Caroline sighed. 'Theo, don't do that,' she said without much conviction.

'I always think that which subjects you like best has a lot to do with the quality of the teachers,' said Ellie. 'Olivia is lucky that the teachers at Green Mount are exceptional, so it's not that surprising they inspire her.'

'Well, that's true,' replied Caroline. 'What was the name of that idiot who taught us Chemistry, Els? I could never understand a word he said. It put me right off. I blame him for me not being a brain surgeon!'

'And how do you explain not being able to do Physics or Biology either?' laughed Max.

'Well, maybe science just wasn't my thing,' replied Caroline, a slight barb in her voice at the criticism.

'You see, I'm not sure I accept that,' said James. 'With decent quality teachers you can be taught anything. You might not have a latent talent for it, but you can learn.'

'I suspect I was a just a lost cause,' said Caroline. Ellie could see that she was trying to keep the mood light. James could be a bit full-on when he got the bit between his teeth. 'But I did okay in the end,' she added with a little toss of her head as if she was expecting them all to agree. For a moment, Ellie worried that James might actually challenge her on that point. He could push his self-made man agenda a bit hard sometimes. But he kept quiet.

'You did,' said Max supportively, and then, clearly wishing to steer the conversation into less treacherous waters, 'So, I assume you lot will be skiing at half-term as usual.'

Ellie knew how much her brother loved to ski and how the boys would probably love it too if they had a chance to try, but to give him his due, he never seemed to resent the fact that she and James generally went two or even three times a year, whilst he rarely got to go at all.

'Yes, we hope so,' she replied. 'We're going to take the girls to that little chalet we love in Morzine, and then maybe we can squeeze another long weekend in before the snow disappears.'

James cleared his throat, a small sound, but Ellie turned her head to look at him expectantly. It seemed that he had nothing to say, though, so she turned her attention back to her nephew. 'Do they do a ski trip at your new school, Alex?' she asked.

Alex shrugged. 'Dunno.'

'We should look into that, mate,' said Max. 'You'd love skiing.'

'Green Mount runs great trips in the senior school,' said Ellie. 'There's one to Rome next year that looks fab. They visit all the Roman sites and spend a day in Vatican City. Such a great opportunity at their age. We didn't get anything like that, did we? I think Chester Zoo was about the best trip we got.' She looked over to Caroline, smiling at the memory of their outing, but James cut across her.

'Let's not be making any promises just at the moment,' he said, his voice unusually sharp.

Ellie didn't think that any promises had been made, certainly not by her, and she resented being snapped at in front of Caroline and Max, but he was right. Their children were being brought up with a great number of privileges and it was important they didn't develop a sense of entitlement. She had seen that with so many of the children at Green Mount. They spoke as if it was their right to have the best rather than something that had to be worked for, earned. It was easy to lose sight of what was normal. When you were surrounded by the displays of wealth that her children saw every day, they might forget that most people didn't have nearly as much as they had.

'Absolutely not,' agreed Ellie. 'I just said that the trips were great, not that you girls could expect to go on them.' The girls nodded, their eyelashes lowered modestly. The boys nudged each other and smirked. 'We're always telling them how little James and I had when we first met. We were totally stony broke, weren't we? Do you remember that dreadful flat we had over the Turkish bakery, Caro? The one where the kitchen was literally a cupboard and the bed folded into the wall during the day.'

'It smelled amazing though,' laughed Caroline. 'All that delicious bread and baklava baking downstairs just as we were getting in from the clubs.'

'Did you go to nightclubs, Mummy?' asked Olivia, her eyes wide in surprise as if she could no more imagine the two of them in a nightclub than the Queen in a bikini.

She was only ten and Ellie was often surprised by how worldly-wise she appeared to be. Where had she heard about nightclubs, for example? Ellie blamed Francesca, a little girl in Olivia's class whose mother seemed to share far more with her daughter than Ellie thought appropriate. This was harmless enough, though.

'We did, darling,' she said. 'Me and your Auntie Caroline used to go out and dance the night away.'

'Did Daddy go too?' asked Lucy, who struggled with the concept of Ellie doing things on her own.

'Sometimes,' replied Ellie vaguely. 'But you know that Daddy doesn't really like dancing that much.'

Lucy nodded solemnly, as if this was an accepted fact.

'Not even back then?' asked Olivia, clearly seeing this as a rich seam of adult conversation. 'When you were young?'

'Well, we're not exactly old now, Livi,' replied James with a grin, his eyes flicking round the table at the other adults for confirmation, and Olivia raised an eyebrow as if she would dispute that. 'And I was a pretty good dancer in my day, but me and your Uncle Max preferred to go to the pub, didn't we, Max, and wait for the girls to get back to tell us all about it. I reckon they had more fun if we weren't there.' He winked at Ellie and she gave him a grin.

'Not more fun,' Ellie said firmly. 'Just a different kind.'

Olivia stared at them in turn as if trying to spot the young people in the adults she saw before her. She shook her head slowly, defeated.

'As if you've all been friends for all that time,' she said, not quite able to let it drop.

'Actually, your Auntie Caroline and I have been friends since we were your age,' Ellie said.

Ellie could still remember the day that Caroline had arrived at her school, the new girl, pale with neat dark plaits that were impossibly thin at the ends, and which hung down her back like two arrows. Their teacher had sat the solemn little girl at a desk at the front of the classroom and asked Ellie if she wouldn't mind looking after her whilst she settled in. Ellie had been only too pleased to have someone new to befriend and had gathered her bag and her pencil case and changed seats with a proud spring in her step. By the end of that first day, they were firm friends.

'And Uncle Max,' chimed in Lucy, 'because he's your brother. That's right, isn't it, Mummy?'

Ellie smiled warmly at her youngest. 'It is, Lucy. We were all friends together.'

Lucy frowned, her little eyebrows knotted. 'But not Daddy?' she said.

'That's right. Not Daddy. I met Daddy when I was a bit older.'

'And then he made friends with Uncle Max too,' said Lucy. There was a neat order to this that seemed to appeal to her eight-year-old mind.

'He did,' agreed Ellie.

'And then you had us and now here we all are,' added Olivia, her voice suggesting that it was all a job well done. Then something occurred to her and she opened her eyes wide. 'Does that mean I might marry someone that I already know?' she asked, her jaw dropping at the idea.

'You might indeed,' Ellie agreed, not quite able to keep the laugh out of her voice.

'Urgh. Gross,' replied Olivia.

Lucy opened her mouth to ask more questions but the boys, whose plates had long been empty, were starting to kick each other under the table and Ellie decided that the time had come to stop playing happy families.

'Do you four want to get yourself an ice cream from the freezer and go and eat it in the playroom?' she asked.

'Are there white chocolate Magnums?' asked Alex, his eyes shining.

Ellie nodded. 'I bought some especially for you, Alex. I know they're your favourite.'

'Thanks, Auntie Els,' he said without the need to be prompted.

'What a treat,' said Caroline. 'He never gets those at home. Make sure you don't drop little bits of chocolate all over Auntie Ellie's carpets,' she added.

Ellie waved a hand as if such things couldn't matter less, but she had already had a quiet word with Olivia about keeping an eye on where any bits might fall. Olivia looked up at her and gave her an almost imperceptible nod.

The children thundered off leaving the adults alone.

'More wine, Caro?' asked James, waving the bottle at her. Caroline accepted and then James went in search of more beer for himself and Max. Max also stood up and wandered off in the direction of the cloakroom.

Ellie smiled at Caroline.

'They're growing up so fast,' said Caroline just as Ellie was about to say the same thing. The pair of them had always been on the same wavelength, able to guess what was going on in the other's head, sharing likes and dislikes, finishing each other's sentences, sometimes not needing any words at all. The closeness had faded a little after they got married and stopped having the time to share their every thought with one another, but not by much.

Ellie nodded. 'Aren't they just? I'm so proud of them, all of them.'

'Yep. We've made a pretty good job of it so far,' agreed Caroline. 'Go us, eh?'

They clinked glasses.

'Yeah! Go us!' Ellie agreed.

'Go you, what?' asked Max as he wandered back into the dining room and sat down at the table.

'We were just congratulating ourselves on how well our children are turning out,' Caroline said to him.

'And how good you are at choosing husbands,' Max added.

'Yes. That too.'

Ellie felt a warm glow pass through her. Life didn't get much better than this. She loved these people. They were the centre of her world.

'I've made a bread-and-butter pudding for dessert,' she said. 'But I think I might be too stuffed to eat it.'

'Well, I'm definitely not,' replied Max. 'Is there custard?'

'Of course! One bread-and-butter with custard coming right up.'

'Make that two,' said James, coming back in and handing Max a bottle of beer.

'Three!' added Caroline.

Ellie laughed and shook her head. 'Well, maybe I could make a tiny little space for a couple of mouthfuls.'

9

THREE MONTHS EARLIER

Nathan Frost edged his car into the narrow space, positioning himself a little to the left so he could at least open his car door. Who had marked up this car park, he wondered, and had they not considered that people would need to get out of the car they had just parked? At least his Audi was small; no, compact. Wasn't that the term? If he'd still been driving the BMW he would have struggled. Well, every cloud, eh?

He grabbed his portfolio from the back seat and opened the door gingerly, careful not to slam it into the door of the Ford he'd parked next to. He doubted, given the state of the neighbouring car, that anyone would have noticed another dint, but he didn't want to damage his own door. He virtually had to fold himself in half to get in and out as it was. It wasn't really the car for a man as tall as he was, but beggars couldn't be choosers.

Once out of his cage, Nathan arched his back and circled his shoulders until he felt everything realign. Then he looked up at the building in front of him. It was nothing special: a brick and glass multi-purpose office block surrounded by others all exactly the same, each sitting in a sea of tarmac, dotted with little grassy islands and stunted trees, designed to give the illusion of space and the great outdoors. It was a bit of a cliché – there were newly built out-of-town office estates like this all over – but it was nice enough. He wondered briefly whether his brother-in-law had had a hand in building this one, but the thought drifted away as quickly as it had arrived.

This was where We've Got it Covered were based. The unfortunately named umbrella specialists needed a new website and that was where he came in. He suspected it was going to be a cheap and cheerful affair with very little call for imagination, but it was a steady job, quick and easy, and it should keep his boss off his back for a while.

Nathan locked the car and headed across the car park to the building. The name plate on the wall outside told him that his new client was on the second floor. He pushed the buzzer, was let in and made his way up in the lift. It looked as if WGIC, the snappy acronym that they were currently using on their branding, only had a portion of the second floor, but then how much head office space did a company selling umbrellas need? Nathan did a quick mental calculation of turnover based on the square metreage and concluded that the client might be persuaded into an up-sell of rebranding as well. His firm could definitely do a better job.

The current logo had an almost apologetic-looking cartoon umbrella in black with the rainbow-coloured acronym sheltering beneath. Even he could do better than that, and he just did the technical stuff. He would mention the services of their branding department at an appropriate moment in the meeting and see if he couldn't get a result there too. That might get him back in the good books with his boss. He'd had too much time away from work recently. First there'd been Tasha leaving, which had knocked him for six, and then he'd persuaded his GP to sign him off with anxiety. It hadn't taken much acting ability. Even though he had always lived his life on a knife edge, that edge felt sharper and higher with each passing month.

He was okay though, he thought, and holding things together well. He had put all the individual problems in their own little boxes in his head and sealed them up tight so they couldn't escape and cloud his mind. Then he could take them out one at a time and deal with them. Or at least, that was the plan. At the moment, the boxes were all staying resolutely shut but he would get to them in time, he told himself. He really would. He just needed to get into the right mindset.

There was a boy working on the reception desk. Well, not a boy exactly, but a young man who looked barely out of high school, and it was so surprising to see him in what was usually such a female-dominated environment that when he asked if he could help, Nathan temporarily forgot what he was doing there. The boy waited patiently whilst Nathan clattered around in his memory trying to find the name of the person he was due to see.

'Nathan Frost from JM Design Services . . .' He paused, still fishing for the name.

'Oh, you'll be here to see Dad, sorry, Mr Fletcher,' the boy offered.

'Fletcher, yes, that's it.'

'Just take a seat and I'll let him know you're here.' He nodded at a little gaggle of uninspiring chairs in the corner and then rang the message through.

'The bloke from the website designers is here,' he said into the telephone, but in a voice so loud that Nathan could hear the sound coming out of the handset in an office down the corridor. The boy had passed on no name, no company name and the umbrella business belonged to his dad. All suddenly became clear. This was good old-fashioned nepotism at play – not that there was anything wrong with that. Nathan had relied on his own dad often enough. Dads were good like that. They never let you down. Nathan could picture Tony's face when he had stolen a minute away from the others on Christmas Day to talk to him. He had chosen his moment carefully. James and Max were finishing off the washing-up and Tony was putting the last of the dishes back into cupboards. Nathan had cleared his throat and said in as casual a tone as he could manage, 'Could I have a quick word, Dad, please?' He tipped his head towards the door. 'In private.'

Tony had raised an eyebrow but had gestured in the direction of his study and Nathan had followed him down the corridor.

'So?' Tony asked as soon as Nathan had pulled the study door to behind them. 'What's with all the cloak and dagger stuff?'

Nathan concentrated on pulling his face into a grin. 'Nothing to be worried about,' he said as chirpily as he could manage. 'Quite the reverse, in fact. I've been offered an opportunity. Some friends of mine are setting up this business converting camper vans for the yummy mummy brigade. Glamping and all that. But they're a bit short, so they asked if I'd like to go in with them. And I would. It's a great idea and I've seen their business plan. It all looks rock solid. Totally bolted on. But they need to buy the vans so they can get started. And that's where they've come a bit unstuck.'

'And you're wanting to know if you should invest?' asked Tony.

Nathan swallowed. 'Well, yes. It's partly that.'

Tony sat down in his chair so the desk was between them and linked his fingers in front of his face.

'Well, you know me,' he said. 'I'm all for entrepreneurial spirit. I've helped various mates out in my time. But you have to be sure they know what they're doing. If not, it's the fastest way I know to lose your cash. Apart from putting it all on the black jack table, that is.' He winked at Nathan and Nathan's chest tightened. 'So, if you're asking if you should go ahead,' Tony continued, 'then I'd say definitely. As long as you're happy with the business plan, and you trust your mates, of course.'

Nathan nodded enthusiastically. 'The plan's sound,' he said. 'I really think they're on to something. And they are great blokes. Totally trustworthy. The thing is . . .' He paused and ran a tongue over his dry lips. 'I don't actually have the cash at the moment. Not liquid, at least. But I don't want to miss my chance on some great returns. So I was wondering . . .'

'Ah,' said Tony.

There was a pause, and the temptation to keep talking had been almost overwhelming, but Nathan knew that his dad was processing what had just been said and it would be better to let him do that in silence. He waited, his heart pounding in his chest.

'So, you want me to lend you some?' Tony asked.

'To invest,' replied Nathan. 'Yes.'

'How much?'

'Five thousand?' asked Nathan, his voice rising to denote the question mark.

He held his breath.

Tony steepled his fingers and stared straight into Nathan's eyes. Nathan held his gaze although every part of him wanted to look away. Would his dad see through him and figure out what was really going on? It wouldn't be the first time Tony had given him money over the years, but then it had just been the odd hundred here and there to tide him over until payday. This was a far bigger sum. But it wasn't a total lie that it was an investment. It was just that rather than investing in a glamping business, Tony would be investing in his son.

'Okay,' said Tony finally. 'You're my boy, and if you tell me this is a good investment then I'll believe you. Sometimes you just have to go with your gut on these things. Will a cheque do you?'

The feeling of relief had been so intense that Nathan had had to fight hard to stop himself wilting.

'That'd be great, Dad. Thanks. And I'll pay you back with interest when they start making serious money.'

Tony had opened his desk drawer, retrieved his cheque book and written the cheque, signing it with a flourish and then tearing it confidently from the stub. He offered it to Nathan.

'Best keep this to ourselves,' he said conspiratorially, and Nathan had nodded.

'And now,' said Tony, getting to his feet and grabbing a suit carrier from an armchair, 'I need to continue with my other philanthropic duties.' He opened the zipper to reveal the scarlet velvet of his Father Christmas outfit.

Now it was only two months later and Nathan found himself in exactly the same place again, in need of a little help from Father Christmas, or some other form of miracle.

He pulled his mind back to the here and now, smiled at the young receptionist, who also appeared to be benefitting from a benevolent father, and then sat himself down.

Brochures for the umbrella company were displayed on the coffee table in a perfect fan shape, which must have taken the boy a while to construct but was totally unconducive to actually picking one up and having a look. To make the point, Nathan plucked one from the very centre of the design, knocking the others out of position. He flicked through, disappointed to see a range of very drab black umbrellas. Was this what people really wanted? Surely, when the sky was dark and the clouds bursting overhead, a splash of colour would be more cheering.

Still, this wasn't his business. He was just here to sort out the website. Mentally, he started running through ways in which they could make what was fundamentally a very boring product look appealing on a screen. At least, despite everything else that was going on, his creativity seemed to still be breathing, although he wasn't sure how it found the space to spread its wings in his crowded mind. But if he boxed things off into compartments, he could focus on the job in hand and not let the rest of it distract him. This was a blessing. But if he lost his job then he really would be up shit creek.

Mr Fletcher, a stooped balding man with a bent nose and a sharp eye, appeared from the room just down the corridor.

'Nathan?' he asked as he approached, clearly more on the ball than his son. 'Nice to meet you. Come through.'

10

The meeting had gone all right, Nathan concluded as he drove home. Ron Fletcher had been as sharp as a tack but pleasant with it and prepared to listen to suggestions, which was always half the battle. He hadn't managed to convince him on the rebranding, but he had a feeling it wasn't a totally lost cause. He might get someone in the office to mock up a few quick ideas to see if they couldn't lure him in.

For now, however, it was the weekend and he didn't need to think about work until Monday. Unfortunately, that left his mind wide open to the other matters that generally dominated it. Mainly this took the form of a series of questions that he asked himself on a loop. How had he let it happen? What could he have done to avoid it? When had it tipped over from being something that wasn't great but still manageable to total chaos? Where was the path that he'd missed, the one that would have kept Tasha at home with him, the one that would have taken him to a place where what he had was enough for him?

But asking the questions furnished him with no answers. Tasha was gone and with every passing week it became more apparent that she wasn't ever coming back. He was slowly coming to terms with that. There had been no huge row, no door-slamming or insults screamed at one another that could be regretted and taken back later. He couldn't isolate a scene and point to it as being the end of their four-year relationship. He'd wondered if it might have been easier to deal with if they had gone out with the kind of drama that you see on soap operas, the kind the neighbours discuss for weeks afterwards.

'Did you see her go? He was chasing after her, screaming down the street to get her to stay.'

'I swear he was crying, you know, poor bloke.'

'I heard he threw himself in front of her car.'

'You have to feel for him. It's a cold-hearted cow that can leave like that.'

Instead, Tasha had packed a bag and left quietly and without spectacle when he was at work. He had come home and found her side of the wardrobe empty, the coat hangers swinging in the breeze made by the opening door. She had left him a note, propped up against the half-drunk bottle of whisky on the kitchen counter. 'Sorry,' it had said. 'I can't do this any more.'

Nathan had spent that evening in a state of shock, tumbling into a chair and gradually draining the rest of the whisky into a tumbler with shaking hands.

He'd rung her, and that first time she had taken his call.

'Tash,' he'd said, tears making his voice thick. 'Where are you? What are you doing? Come back.'

There had been a silence down the line, but he could hear her breathing, steady, patient.

'I can't, Nath,' she'd said eventually. 'I'm done.'

'No, no, no,' he'd replied. 'You can't be. Whatever it is, we can sort it out. We'll fix it together. Just come back. Please.'

Another pause.

'It's too late,' she'd said. 'You promised you'd change. But you can't. I see that now. Money just trickles through your fingers,

Nath. You're like a child. But that's not the life I want. I need to go before you drag us both down. I'm sorry but that's how it's got to be.'

And then she'd put the phone down and refused to engage again. His calls and texts went unanswered no matter how desperate his messages became.

But Nathan had a plan. He would fix it all, get everything back to the way it was before. He'd do the flat up and buy new furniture and some of those fluffy cushions that Tasha liked so much, and then he'd go and find her. When she saw how together he was she'd come back. She still loved him – he knew that for sure – so if he proved to her that his life was back on an even keel then everything would be okay. This was just a test. A test of his resolve to get things sorted. And he would pass with flying colours.

When he got to his dad's house, he found him on the front lawn practising his putting, the intruder lights floodlighting the grass and casting eerie shadows. His dad had sunk a little metal tube into the lawn and marked it with a flag on a stick. The tiny triangular flag had the initials AF on it, no doubt Ellie's doing. What do you buy a man who has everything? His own monogrammed putting flag appeared to be the answer.

Tony looked up from his shot as the car pulled into the drive and then back down at the ball. He tapped it lightly with the club and it bobbled along the grass and plopped into the hole.

Nathan got out of his car. 'Nice shot,' he said. 'But isn't it a bit cold and dark to be out here?'

'Oh, hello, son,' Tony said, sounding a little surprised. 'I was blinded by your headlights for a minute there.'

'Dad, it's literally freezing.'

'Not when you're focused, Nath. Not when you're focused. But I take your point. Shall we go inside?'

He whipped the flag out of the hole, retrieved his ball and strode purposefully to the front door, Nathan trailing less confidently in his wake. He was suddenly having second thoughts about his plan. If he said it out loud, and to his dad of all people, then there would be no going back. The problem would become real and unavoidable. Of course, it was already both of those things, but somehow when it was just his secret it was easier to twist into a different shape.

But no. He'd been over this a million times. There were no other options available to him. He had reached the point of no return. And if he was going to win Tash back . . .

Inside, the house was bright, warm and welcoming. His dad slipped the putting iron into his golf bag, wiped the ball and dropped it into a pouch on the front.

'Drink?' he asked.

Nathan nodded, not quite trusting his voice.

'Beer?'

He nodded but managed to add, 'That would be great, Dad. Thanks.'

He followed his dad into the kitchen, which was all ship-shape with not a plate or dirty coffee cup out of place. When his mum had first walked out, his dad had been totally lost. Ellie and Caroline had to come to clean and bring food parcels for him as he floundered like a fish out of water in his new domestic situation. Once he got over the shock of having to do everything for himself, however, he had risen to the challenge, and Nathan had to admit that he made a far better job of keeping house than he did himself, and with far more house to keep.

Tony pulled two beers from the fridge and handed one to Nathan, followed quickly by the bottle opener, which was white with an England flag printed on it and played the sound of a cheering crowd when you used it. It had been briefly amusing when it had first appeared around the time of the World Cup but now it felt incongruous in the quiet kitchen.

'So,' said Tony when they were both sitting at the kitchen table. 'To what do I owe this rare honour?'

Nathan shifted a little in his seat. Was he really that transparent? Maybe not to others, but his dad knew him well enough to know that he was unlikely to call in unannounced unless there was something he needed.

Nathan sat back in his chair, snatched a shallow breath and made a determined effort to make eye contact, although it was hard.

'I've got myself into a bit of a mess, Dad,' he said.

His dad eyed him, giving nothing away. 'Okay,' he said levelly. 'What sort of a mess?'

'I owe some money. Quite a lot of money.'

'Ah,' said Tony and took a swig from his beer. 'So, you're after a loan.'

Nathan nodded, feeling relieved that his dad was making this so easy for him so far.

'A loan that you have neither the intention nor the means to ever repay.'

Shit.

'So, more of a gift, in fact,' Tony continued, 'than a loan.'

Nathan could lie, swear that he would pay his dad back, but what would be the point? They both knew they were empty words. His dad was right. He didn't earn enough to repay a loan by more than a few pounds at a time, and there was never anything left at the end of the month anyway.

'Yeah,' he said, his eyes cast low.

'And who do you owe this money to? The bookies?'

Nathan shouldn't be surprised that his dad had nailed the entire problem without his having to utter a word, but he was a little annoyed. He tried so hard to cover his tracks but his dad, it seemed, had had no difficulty following him.

Nathan nodded. 'They've closed my line of credit and if I don't repay what I owe then they'll sue.' Or worse, he thought.

'How much?' asked Tony.

Nathan pursed his lips, squeezing them into a narrow line. Should he tell his dad the full extent of the debt or just what he needed to repay to keep things ticking over for a while? One figure was just about palatable. The other absolutely wasn't.

'Ah, I see. Not sure you can tell me the full amount?' asked his dad.

For God's sake, thought Nathan. How did he do that? He nodded. 'Yeah. That's about it.'

He felt so ashamed. He was thirty-three years old and having to ask his dad to bail him out. Again.

'Come on, Nath. Spit it out. Let's have the whole sorry story and then we know what we're dealing with,' said Tony.

At least he was calm, thought Nathan. Then again, he hadn't heard how much it was yet. He took a deep breath. 'Just shy of twenty-five grand,' he said.

His dad whistled his breath out through his teeth. 'That's a lot of money,' he said. 'What was it? Horses?'

Nathan nodded.

'It's a mug's game, Nath,' he said.

'I was trying to regain my losses, but I made some bad calls, and then, what with the interest payments on top . . .'

But he could see he was on a hiding to nothing. He let his voice trail off and nodded again instead because that was what his dad was expecting, but that wasn't what he thought. It wasn't a mug's game. It was just that he had made a couple of screw-ups recently that had tipped the boat too far and toppled it over. All he needed was this cash to get things afloat again and then he would be okay.

He hated that his dad would be disappointed in him, though. His mind spun him back to when he was eleven years old, being reprimanded for stealing from bags in the cloakroom at school. His parents had been called to see the headmaster to hear of his disgrace. There had been no excuses, he had been caught red-handed, but somehow his dad had managed to persuade the head not to exclude him. It was the summer term and he was leaving the school at the end of the month anyway. His dad had made an argument that his behaviour was a one-off, that Nathan was very sorry and would pay the money back, but there was no point spoiling an otherwise unblemished school record for something that happened so close to the end of his time there.

Of course, it hadn't been a one-off; it had simply been the only time he'd got caught.

On their way home, his mum weeping quietly in the passenger seat, his dad had told him that stealing was a mug's game (that expression again) but that getting caught was just plain stupid. He'd made him clean his car every week, inside and out, until he considered the debt to be repaid and they had never mentioned it again. He was pretty sure Max and Ellie hadn't found out; they had never said anything at any rate. But for a long time after that, whenever he caught his mum looking at him it had been with a cast of disappointment in her eyes. Nathan wasn't sure it had ever entirely gone away.

His dad took a long swig of his beer and then raised his chin and stared at his son down his aquiline nose. 'So the money at Christmas, to invest in your mate's camper van business . . . ?'

Shame dripped off Nathan. He hated lying, especially to his father. He lowered his eyelids and squeezed his lips between his teeth as he prepared himself to confess.

'I lied about that,' he said. 'I'm sorry. I just couldn't tell you what I really needed the money for.'

'But now you can?' asked his dad. 'Because things are suddenly a whole lot worse.'

Nathan nodded.

'I see. And you tried to win it back?'

Nathan nodded again, aware how stupid he looked. 'It would have been perfect but I just picked the wrong bet. I don't have a problem though, Dad. I'm not an addict, not even close. I got myself in too deep but I could stop the gambling whenever I want, except I can't because I've got to pay back what I owe. But once I'm straight then it'll be fine.' Nathan tried to look contrite, but he knew it cut no ice with his dad.

Tony took another drink from his bottle and then set it down on the table. He rubbed his chin and eyed Nathan as if trying to decide what he should do. Nathan knew what he'd do, though. He had always known since that journey back from school.

'Come back tomorrow,' his dad said. 'I'll have it for you then. But this is the last time, do you hear? If you don't sort it out once and for all this time then you're on your own, okay?'

Nathan let out a sigh of relief and nodded. Even though he had been sure his dad would help, it was reassuring to know for certain that he was going to. And he would do things differently from now on. He would pay this debt back and then he would be more careful, calculate risk more effectively, not take stupid chances that might not come off. Gambling was only a mug's game if you either didn't know what you were doing or got too greedy. Nathan had learnt his lesson on both scores.

'Thanks, Dad,' he said, trying to look both sorry and grateful at the same time.

Mission accomplished. The knot that had been tightening in Nathan's stomach suddenly felt less tight.

The intruder lights came on outside, making it suddenly feel as if night had shifted into day and Nathan spotted the outline of Monty, his dad's cat, as he cut a slinky path across the grass, eyes flashing in the harsh glow.

It was only when he was driving home that it occurred to him that it was Friday. Where was his dad going to get twenty-five thousand pounds from at the weekend?

11

When Nathan woke up the following morning, the sense of dread that had recently been accompanying him through his days had lifted. In fact, until he remembered what had happened it felt a bit like waking up on the morning of a holiday. There was that tingle of anticipation that something exciting was in the offing.

This wasn't the same though, he realised quickly. Not the same at all.

His dad hadn't specified a time for him to go back to the house to collect the money, but Nathan was itching to get there. He wanted it in his account before his dad changed his mind, not that he thought he would, but all the same, Nathan would feel much happier when the transaction was complete.

He had a quick look at the day's form on his iPad whilst he drank a cup of coffee. They were running at Lingfield Park and Southwell that afternoon. Nathan had a scan down the runners and riders, deciding where he would put his money. He'd need to clear the debt with at least one of his bookies before then. They had made it clear that his line of credit had stretched as far as it would go. Best if he went back to his dad's this morning, he decided, then there would still be time to repay the debt and place the bet.

There was a car in the drive when he pulled up outside his dad's house. Ellie. Nathan's heart sank. He loved his sister dearly, but she didn't need to know about any of this. It was between him and his dad. And if she knew that Tony had given him the money, who was to say she wouldn't want the same? Actually, he thought, Ellie and James were loaded. Twenty-five grand was probably just change down the sofa for them. Max and Caroline were a different story, though. He was sure that, for all Max made out he was happy with his lot, a nice little lump sum like that would come in handy. If his mum had still been involved in what went on, then she would have made sure that each of her children was treated equally. If they gave to one then they gave to all. Tony was less egalitarian in his approach, driven far more by need than fairness. But whichever way you peeled it, the whole situation would be much easier if Ellie just didn't know.

He knocked on the front door and then walked in, calling out as he did so. Tony and Ellie were in the sitting room. Olivia and Lucy were sprawled on the floor playing draughts, which Olivia seemed to be winning judging by the number of crowned pieces at her end of the board.

'Morning all,' he said. 'How is everyone?'

Ellie's face lit up at the sight of him. She was so sweet.

'Nathan, hi! How lovely to see you. We weren't expecting you,' she said, which was good because that suggested his dad hadn't mentioned he was coming.

'I just popped round to say hello to Dad,' he said, without meeting Tony's eye. 'Great to find you lot here too. How are you, girls?' He dropped down to their level and examined the draughts board. 'I think she's winning, Lucy. You need a new strategy.'

'I always win,' said Olivia smugly.

'She does,' agreed Lucy, as if this was just the way of the universe and there was no getting around it.

'Remind me to teach you some of my killer moves,' he said, winking at her conspiratorially. 'It's no fun being the youngest sometimes, but I could always beat your Uncle Max at draughts.'

'It's not fair if you only show Lucy,' objected Olivia.

'But you clearly don't need any help, Liv,' he replied and then watched as Olivia processed this, not sure whether it was a good thing or not.

'How's it going, Nath?' asked Ellie. She wasn't prying, he knew, but her questions always felt loaded somehow.

'Okay,' he said non-committally. 'You?'

'Same old, same old,' she replied.

This was how these conversations went, with nothing being shared.

'Good,' he said.

He wasn't up for chit-chat. He just wanted to get his money and get out of there, but wasn't sure how to bring the subject up without looking desperate or ungrateful. He threw a glance at Tony, hoping he would take the hint, but his dad seemed to be set on making him wait. Something about his expression suggested he was rather enjoying the power. Well, there was nothing Nathan could do about that. His dad held all the cards.

'Fancy a cup of tea, Nath?' Tony asked, raising his own mug questioningly.

'Actually,' replied Nathan, 'I'm in a bit of a hurry. I was just wondering if you managed to get that stuff?'

Stuff? Nathan cringed internally. For one terrible moment he thought Tony was actually going to make him elaborate on exactly what 'stuff' he was talking about as part of some Machiavellian game of his own.

But then he said, 'Oh yes. It's just upstairs. Hang on whilst I get it for you.'

Tony stood up and left the room.

'You must come for supper one night, Nath,' Ellie said. 'Not tonight, we've got something on. But next Saturday, maybe?'

'That would be great,' he said. 'Just let me check my diary and get back to you.'

She meant well, he knew, but an evening spent with James, filled with little hints at his personal successes, was more than Nathan could stand.

Ellie looked downcast that he hadn't accepted her offer straight away, but she nodded. 'Okay. Well, let me know when you know,' she said.

Tony reappeared clutching a brown envelope that Nathan assumed held the twenty-five grand. Could he make it look any more suspicious? What else could an envelope like that contain? He could feel his heart beating harder in his chest at the thought of so much cash and tried not to make eye contact with either of them, fearful of what he might give away.

Tony handed the envelope over, thick and heavy, and Nathan took it. If they had been alone he would have been more grateful, but with Ellie there the moment felt a little awkward.

'Thanks, Dad,' he said, trying to inject the simple phrase with meaning that Tony would appreciate and Ellie would miss. 'Right,' he continued. 'I'll be off. Lovely to see you, Els. And you too, girls. Remember, Lucy. Killer moves.' He tapped a finger to his nose confidentially. 'I'll see you all soon.'

'I'll see you to the door,' said his dad, following him out.

They stopped on the threshold.

'Just so we're clear,' Tony said. 'I won't be doing this again. If you get yourself in another hole, you'll be digging yourself out. Understand?'

'I know,' Nathan replied. 'And I'm grateful, Dad. I really am.'

'Okay. Just don't tell the others,' Tony added. 'Or your mother. For God's sake, don't tell her.'

12

TWO MONTHS EARLIER

Ellie surveyed the school field and wondered where she should start. The Green Mount School Annual Easter Fair was well and truly underway. Every corner of the hockey pitch was crammed full of money-raising activities, from Sponge the Teacher to Splat the Rat. There were things to guess, things to throw, things to fire at and things to taste, and every stall was manned (or should that be womaned?) by an extra-smiley and super-glamorous mother, each sporting a full face of make-up and a body clad in designer clothes.

Ellie always felt slightly ashamed of the way she sat on her hands when the fair came around, not volunteering for anything at all, but then, she reasoned, they also needed people who just came to spend money, and so she made sure she did that, breaking open new twenty-pound notes as often as the change floats would allow and making sure that plenty of people saw her doing it.

'Where do you want to go first, girls?' she asked Olivia and Lucy.

'Can we have some candyfloss?' asked Lucy.

'We've only just got here!' laughed Ellie, shaking her head and smiling indulgently at her daughter. 'Let's have a go on some of the stalls first and then we can get some later. How about the tombola? Are you feeling lucky, Luce?'

'There's Jade!' said Olivia, deftly slipping her hand free from Ellie's and waving it high in the air. Jade spotted her, waved equally enthusiastically back and then ran across the grass towards them.

'No offence,' said Olivia, 'but it's so not cool to be hanging about with your mum. Can I just have some money and go round with Jade?'

Ellie sighed. The best part about the fair had always been sharing it with the girls, helping them to win things and tempering their disappointment with sweet treats when they didn't, but Olivia was too grown up for that now. Ellie had no option but to smile and let her go, and hope that Lucy didn't want to go as well.

She opened her purse and began to take out a ten-pound note. Olivia dropped a hip, raised an eyebrow and gave her a look that told her it was nowhere near adequate. Well, it all needed spending, Ellie thought, so it might as well be Olivia that did it. It would end up in the same pot, after all. She peeled off two twenty-pound notes and handed them over. Olivia looked as if she might have been expecting more but Ellie silenced any forthcoming complaint with a look.

'Thanks, Mum,' said Olivia and then skipped off arm in arm with Jade.

'I'll meet you at the tea tent,' Ellie called after her, 'in an hour?'

She wasn't sure Olivia had heard her, but it didn't really matter. She wasn't going to get lost on her own school field.

Lucy didn't seem to have any intention of wandering off and hadn't even dropped Ellie's hand. That was the difference between being ten years old and eight. It was also the difference between her two girls. Olivia was by far the more outgoing child, always happy to make friends with strangers or to share her opinion with whoever she could get to listen. Lucy was much shyer, and Ellie worried that she relied too heavily on her sister, was almost living in Olivia's shadow. She tried to encourage Lucy to be more independent, offered to have friends over for tea or to take them on outings, but Lucy always refused. She was happiest when it was just the four of them, it seemed.

Ellie had thought at one point that Lucy might be being bullied at school and had raised it with her class teacher, who had looked surprised and then a little horrified by the question.

'Bullied? No, I don't think so,' Miss Elliot had said. 'We're trained to keep our eyes open for that kind of thing, but there's never been any hint of a problem with Lucy. Has she said something to you?'

Miss Elliot was very young and seemed genuinely upset by the idea that one of her charges was having a hard time and she had failed to spot it.

Ellie was quick to reassure her. 'No, no. Nothing. I just wondered. She doesn't talk about school much and I thought bullying might be the reason. But she doesn't seem unhappy, I don't think.'

Miss Elliot looked relieved. 'Good,' she said, nodding her head reassuringly. 'You really don't need to worry, Mrs Fisher. Lucy is doing so well. She can be a little quiet in class. I think her dyslexia makes her slightly reluctant to contribute sometimes and it can take her a little longer than the others to complete her work, but that's the joy of Green Mount. Because our classes are so nice and small, I can give her plenty of special attention. She's making excellent progress. And the one-to-one time with our literacy specialist is great for her. He hasn't reported any problems to me. Please be assured that she really is in absolutely the right place. Now that you've mentioned your concerns, I'll keep my eyes open for anything untoward, but I'm certain you don't have anything to worry about. Lucy is happy here and working well.'

And so Ellie's fears had been assuaged. Lucy was merely a gentle, sensitive child who struggled with dyslexia and shouldn't be compared unfavourably with her outgoing and sometimes rather brash elder sister.

'Can we go on the helter-skelter?' Lucy asked now. Ellie thought briefly of her brand-new jeans coming into contact with the dirty coir mat and then said, 'Of course! Shall we do that first?'

Lucy nodded and skipped happily towards the stripy wooden tower, pulling Ellie along with her. As they passed other families, she called out greetings and made telephone gestures to suggest they really should get in contact, but she didn't stop to chat. This part of the day was Lucy's. There would be time for chatting later.

13

After it felt like the two of them had tried every stall and been on every ride, and Ellie's purse was feeling considerably lighter than it had done when they'd arrived, it was finally time for Ellie to catch up with her own friends, so they headed to the tea tent. In truth, it was more of a marquee than a tent. It belonged to one of the parents whose contribution to the fair each year was to provide it for the school's use, but they always went much further than just the loan – this was Green Mount, after all. Inside it looked more like the venue for an upmarket wedding than a school fair. All the chairs were covered in pale-pink covers, and garlands of flowers and fairy lights festooned the supporting poles and the canvas ceiling. It was completely over the top but was no less beautiful for that.

At one end was the counter where the drinks and cakes were served and at the other an area with smaller tables and chairs, no doubt taken from the classrooms, for the children.

Ellie, with Lucy stuck to her side, headed to the counter. The chair of the Parents' Association was serving. This was always her job of choice, presumably because it was inside and serving here meant that she would get to talk to just about everyone during the course of the afternoon. She smiled as she saw Ellie approach.

'Your cakes have all sold out first, Ellie,' she said. 'As usual. I even had one man ask me which ones you'd baked so he could make sure he had one of your scones.'

Ellie gave her a little smile, lowering her eyes modestly to take the compliment. She might not volunteer for any of the stalls, but she knew she could bake.

'What would you like, Lucy?' the woman asked, stooping so that she could make eye contact.

Lucy pointed at a chocolate bun covered in M&M's that Ellie hadn't made.

Ellie nudged her. 'What do you say, Lucy?'

'Please,' said Lucy, the one word standing in for the entire sentence, and then, 'Thank you,' before the bun had even made it on to a paper plate.

'And for you, Ellie?'

Ellie didn't actually want anything to eat, and if she did have to choose then she'd rather it was something she had made herself, but that would never do. Quickly she scanned the table for the least complicated item.

'I'll have one of those delicious-looking cookies,' she said, pointing at a plate of misshapen and slightly overdone biscuits. 'And a cup of tea for me and a J2O for Lucy, please.'

Whilst the order was put together Ellie turned to see who was here and spotted a bunch of mums from Olivia's year sitting round a table in the far corner. Then she saw Olivia laughing with Jade in the children's area.

'Look, Luce. There's Olivia over there. Do you want to take your drink and sit with her?'

Lucy nodded and Ellie felt guiltily relieved. It was so much easier to have a decent chat away from little ears. She paid for the items, refusing the change, and then watched Lucy head off to Olivia where she was greeted enthusiastically and a space made for her at the table. With her daughters settled, Ellie made for her own friends.

It was apparent as soon as she arrived that they were in the middle of imparting some choice and rather confidential gossip. The women had all huddled in around the table so their heads were almost touching. Women really were just overgrown teenagers, Ellie thought. This reminded her of her and Caroline as girls, eyes stretched wide and jaws dropped at whatever scandal had just been revealed.

She pulled up a chair from a neighbouring table and the others separated a little to make a gap for her to squeeze into.

'Hi, Ellie,' said Margo with a beaming smile.

Margo was the leader of the gang. Her house was the biggest, her husband's car the fastest and her highlights the blondest; she was the acknowledged alpha female. But she was also lovely, which was how she managed to hold on to her coveted position. Even the young pretenders for her crown were happy to defer to her in all things and the expressions 'What did Margo say/think/do?' were very often to be heard.

'Have you had a good fair?' she asked Ellie, politely breaking away from whatever it was they had been discussing the moment before.

'I have,' said Ellie. 'Although this year was the first time Liv wanted to go round by herself.' She pulled a sorrowful face and the women around her mirrored it, as if they all understood the implication of this coming-of-age moment.

'Oh, I feel your pain,' said Krista, whose youngest was Olivia's age. 'And it only gets worse,' she added with a good-humoured eye roll.

'So,' said Ellie, 'what have I missed?' She wanted them to get back to the conversation that had clearly been in full flow when she had interrupted it.

'Well,' said Fiona, 'I was just saying, you know Emma Powell, who has Daniel in our class and Rosie in year four?'

Ellie nodded. 'The one whose husband left her for his personal trainer,' she clarified.

'The bastard,' said Fiona with a slight pursing of her lips. 'Yes. Her. Well, she's only shown up this afternoon with the most beautiful' – she stretched the word out so the vowels went on forever – 'man on her arm.'

'Well, good for her,' said Ellie, feeling genuinely pleased that something was going well for Emma after the ignominy of having been rejected in such a public and hurtful way.

'But wait, there's more,' added Fiona, holding her finger up to prevent further comment. 'Said gorgeous man can't be older than, what would you say, girls? Twenty-five?'

'I'd say younger,' chipped in Krista.

'Blimey!' replied Ellie. 'Doubly good for her.'

'You can say that again,' said Fiona. 'Honestly, Ellie, you have to see him. I wouldn't be surprised if he was a model. He made me salivate.'

There was a loud groaning and Margo said, 'Oh God, Fiona. Must you?'

'What?!' replied Fiona indignantly. 'Don't tell me you weren't thinking exactly the same.'

There was a general sniggering at the thought of what they might do given half an hour with Emma Powell's new beau.

'I'm pleased for her,' said Ellie. 'Her husband was such a shit. She deserves to have something go well for a change.'

They all agreed.

'I tell you who things aren't going that well for,' said Margo, her voice so low that Ellie struggled to pick it up amidst the rumble of voices in the tent. 'Sarah Coombes.'

Ellie knew Sarah Coombes a little. Her daughter was in Lucy's class and Lucy had been invited round to play from time to time. They lived in a house that made Ellie envious – an old manor house rather than a new build like her place. It was so classy, everything that Ellie aspired to for herself. To the outside world, it appeared that Sarah Coombes had everything going for her. But were appearances deceptive?

'Why? What's happened?' Fiona asked, adopting Margo's conspiratorial tone.

'Well, you didn't hear it from me,' continued Margo, 'but their business has gone bust. They've had to call the receivers in.'

'Oh, that's awful,' said Ellie.

'I know,' agreed Margo. 'They live next door to a friend of mine. Apparently the bailiffs turned up and took the cars, just like that.'

'And your friend saw?' said Fiona. 'God, how mortifying. You'd think they'd do that kind of thing under cover of darkness. Spare everybody's blushes.'

'I don't suppose they care,' said Krista.

'But the worse part,' continued Margo, 'is that they can't afford the fees for here. They've had to pull the kids out.'

'What, now?' said Ellie. 'In the middle of the school year?'

Margo nodded but Fiona shrugged. 'Well, if you can't afford to pay . . .' she said.

'God, that's terrible,' said Ellie. 'Those poor kids. Where will they go?'

'Manor High, I suppose. That'll be one hell of a shock to the system. From here to there.'

'But surely they must have seen it coming?' said Krista. 'I mean, that kind of thing doesn't happen overnight.'

Fiona shook her head. 'I don't know. But even if they had they were hardly going to share the news around, were they? It's not the kind of thing you tell everyone.'

'No, I suppose not,' agreed Krista. 'God, what a mess.'

A stunned silence fell over the table.

'What a mess indeed,' said Margo finally, and they all nodded in sympathy, lost in prayers of gratitude that they were each okay with their cars on their driveways, their houses secure and their school fees paid up until the end of the year.

'I reckon the fair must have done really well this year,' said Krista, deftly changing the subject. 'It seems busier than normal.'

'Someone told me the PTA wants to buy a new 360-degree camera and a drone so the Media department can make some snazzy films. And there was talk of new equipment for the students' gym too.'

'They won't get that at Manor High,' muttered Fiona under her breath.

◆ ◆ ◆

Nobody wanted much supper that evening, so Ellie gave the children beans on toast and put them to bed early. James had had a good day at the golf club and was in an ebullient mood, telling Ellie about how he had played each hole and then who he had been chatting to in the bar afterwards. He knew everyone there, and if he didn't know them, he made it his business to meet them. He reminded Ellie so much of her dad.

'I heard some awful news today,' Ellie said when the golf stories were completed. 'A mum at school has had to pull her children out because their business has gone bust. Apparently there's no latitude on fees. If you can't pay then you're out. That felt a bit harsh to me. I mean, it's the kids that suffer.'

James let out a sigh. 'The school is a business too,' he said. 'They can't afford to carry families who can't afford to be there. Actually, I'm glad to hear there's no leeway. I want our fees to be spent making sure our girls get the best education available, not propping up someone who can't keep their finances in order.'

'But those poor children,' objected Ellie. 'Can you imagine how horrible it will be for them? Maybe I should invite her round for coffee, see if I can do anything to help. What do you think?'

'I'd leave well alone, if I were you,' replied James. 'I'm not sure she'd thank you for interfering. In my experience, people try to keep these things to themselves for a reason. No one wants to be talked about behind their back, nor do they want to be made to feel stupid by some do-gooder.'

Ellie bristled. 'I'm not a do-gooder,' she said. 'I'm genuinely concerned for the poor woman. It's awful what's happened to her and her family.'

'Well, they're not the first and I'm sure they won't be the last,' replied James. 'It's a tough world out there. You need to keep your wits about you to survive. One bad decision or a dodgy throw of the dice and it can all come tumbling down around you.'

Ellie gave a little shudder. 'We're okay though, aren't we?' she said, her voice tiny. She knew they were but she just wanted to hear James say it.

He reached across and gave her a squeeze and she snuggled into him, smelling the familiar peppery tones of his aftershave and feeling the slow beat of his heart through his shirt.

'Of course, we're okay,' he said. 'I've built all this for you and the girls and it's rock solid. You have absolutely nothing to worry about.'

Ellie felt reassured. 'We're so lucky,' she whispered.

'There's nothing lucky about any of it,' said James, trotting out one of his favourite truisms. 'Everything we have is a result of a series of sound decisions. And the best one you ever made was to marry me!' He planted a kiss on the top of her head.

'Oh, was it now?' replied Ellie, rising to his challenge in mock indignation.

'It was,' he said. 'And you know it.'

He was right, of course.

'Now, shall we see if we can find a new box set to watch, or would you prefer an early night?' he asked, running his finger down her spine and letting it come to rest in the waistband of her jeans.

'Oh, I think an early night,' she said, and all thoughts of the day just gone were forgotten.

14

ONE MONTH EARLIER

They had made it a rule that the four of them met up to do something at least once a month. Caroline and Ellie policed it, making sure that the dates were in the diary, but the men were happy to go along with whatever was suggested. Generally, it would be dinner, either in or out, but sometimes they might go to the cinema or a gig. They had even been known to get Max and James to the theatre, as long as it wasn't a musical, which James refused to tolerate despite Max assuring him that it wasn't nearly as bad as it sounded.

This month, a new Italian had opened on the high street and they were all happy to try it out. Caroline was pleased. She liked to think that her tastes were fairly cosmopolitan, but you knew where you were with Italy. To her mind it was hard to beat a simple pasta dish done well and a nice bottle of Pinot Grigio, and it was much easier to relax and enjoy the evening when she didn't have to worry if she'd chosen something she wouldn't like.

Ellie and James were already there when they arrived, perched on stools in the bar area, each with a gin and tonic in front of them. It had been a chilly day for April, but Ellie was wearing a pretty sheer top in a pastel green that radiated positivity and optimism about the season to come. Caroline instantly regretted the black turtleneck jumper she had chosen.

'Oh, you look all ready for spring,' she said to Ellie as she leant in for a kiss. 'I feel a bit like the harbinger of doom.'

Ellie shook her head. 'Rubbish. You look lovely, Caro, and I'm bound to be too cold in this top, but you know what I'm like; a bit of sunshine and I'm convinced I'm in the Med.'

'It'll be summer before we know it,' said Caroline, 'and then it'll be your party. How are the plans coming along?'

Ellie was to be forty on Midsummer's Eve and celebrations for the event had long been in everyone's diary. Ellie winked at her and put her finger to her lips theatrically.

'I'll tell you everything when we're on our own,' she said, throwing a meaningful glance at James. Caroline gave a small nod to show that she understood, and the subject was dropped.

The usual questions concerning the children and their lives in general followed and were answered, and then they were shown through to their table where they discussed the decor, the menu and the ambience of the place, and all concluded it to be to their liking.

'Have you seen that they've started to put up some new houses out on the old road?' asked Max as they waited for the main course to arrive. 'That's not one of yours, is it, James? I didn't see your hoardings.'

Given what Caroline knew was coming next, she was sure her husband would have checked this point before he brought the development up in conversation.

James shook his head. 'No, I don't have anything down that way,' he said. 'Are you talking about the site that backs up on to Marshall's Wood?'

'That's the one,' said Max. 'It's a bloody eyesore. It looks like they're cramming in twice as many houses as it can stand. And the access isn't great either. It'll really slow the traffic down when there are so many cars trying to come out from there to turn on to the main road.'

James shrugged. 'Well, the planners must have thought it was okay,' he said. 'Access and traffic flow are one of the main things they look at. If they hadn't thought it was adequate, they'd have made them put in a roundabout or a set of lights.'

Max seemed unconvinced. 'And it backs straight on to the woods. I thought that was all green belt land.'

'It was,' replied James with another shrug. 'But it got released in the last round of site allocations. The new housing quotas are so high and developers are struggling to get their hands on sites in places where people actually want to live. They keep eating into the green belt.'

'But there must have been objections,' Max pressed.

He was like a dog with a bone. Caroline had already had the benefit of his opinion on the building site more than once and she wished he would just drop it. Conversations like this were always tricky when James was there because he was always going to side with the developer.

'Maybe not as many as you'd think,' James replied. 'The grounds for objections are very specific. You can't just object because you don't like the idea. And if the need for new housing stock is greater . . . well, that's the way the decision will fall.'

Max shook his head, clearly still having difficulty accepting it. 'It would have to be passed by the district council, though, right? They're a proper bunch of reactionary old farts. I can't believe they'd let something like that through.'

'You're just pissed off because they wouldn't let you build that extension on the back of your place,' laughed Ellie.

She was right and Caroline threw her a subtle smirk. Max's view of the planning system had been severely tarnished following his own meagre but unsatisfactory brush with it.

'Well, maybe,' he conceded. 'But still. It feels like it's one rule for the big boys and another for the rest of us.'

'Well, it is,' replied Caroline, one eyebrow raised. 'That's just life. I'm not sure why you find it so surprising.'

The food arrived and Caroline hoped that would break the conversation, but Max just wouldn't let it go.

'I don't know how you put up with it, James,' he said. 'It must drive you absolutely crazy.'

'Don't get me started,' said James, forking pasta into his mouth and then speaking through it. 'Local politics is a bloody nightmare and planning is the worst of the lot.'

'Do we have to talk about planning?' sighed Ellie. 'I get enough of that at home.'

'I bet they're all bent,' said Max bitterly.

'Who?' asked Caroline.

'The planners, of course,' said Max.

James shook his head. 'It's not the planners making the decisions,' he said. 'They just make recommendations.'

Max harrumphed. 'Well, something about it stinks.'

'Anyway . . .' said Caroline, cutting across him and throwing him a warning glance. 'We've just booked our holidays. We're going to this lovely cottage in Abersoch. We've been to a different one just down the road before, but I've always had my eye on this place because the garden backs on to the beach. The boys will be able to spend the entire week in the sea no matter what the weather, and I can sit wrapped up in my thermals and watch them from the patio.'

'I'm sure the weather will be fine,' said Ellie, although she could obviously be sure of no such thing. 'Doesn't it have its own little microclimate there? Someone once told me that it's always warm.'

'I'm not sure about that,' said Caroline. 'But it suits us. Where are you lot going this year? Somewhere amazing, I don't doubt.'

Ellie liked to be warm on holiday, and James liked to be looked after, which generally came together in the shape of some amazingly smart hotel in the tropics. There was the briefest of hesitations and Caroline saw Ellie's eyes flick to James and back. James's focus stayed on his pasta.

'We've not actually booked anywhere yet,' said Ellie.

'That's not like you,' said Caroline, surprised. 'You've usually booked something before the plane has landed from the last one.'

'That's true, but this year there are a few things up in the air around the dates, so we decided to go somewhere last minute instead,' Ellie replied, taking a drink from her glass and avoiding looking at Caroline.

'Excellent plan,' said Max. 'To have no plan, I mean. Plans are definitely overrated. If you don't have a plan then nothing can go wrong.'

'That's what I said,' agreed James. 'And there are so many great deals if you go last minute.'

Caroline thought that the days of great last-minute deals were behind them now that people were happy to go away at the drop of a hat, particularly with the kind of holidays that Ellie and James favoured, but she didn't say so.

'Shall we get another bottle of this white?' asked Ellie as she tipped the previous one over her glass and only a few drops trickled out.

'Let's,' said James. 'And the red too?'

Without giving Max a chance to respond, he stuck his hand up to summon the waitress. Caroline prayed that he didn't click his fingers too – he had an unfortunate tendency to do just that when he was drunk, but luckily his hand was spotted quickly and the order was taken. Caroline didn't really want another bottle of wine. Alex and Theo had football matches early the following morning and it was her turn to take them. Standing on the chilly touchline was bad enough but she didn't relish having to do it with a hangover. Still, Ellie was clearly on a roll and she probably wouldn't notice if one glass was filled a lot faster than the other.

'How's your dad?' Caroline asked. 'We've not seen him for a while, have we, Max?'

'Oh, he's fine,' replied Ellie. 'I saw Nath too, although it was a while back now. He called in on Dad when I was there.'

'And . . . ?' asked Caroline.

'He was good. He didn't stay long, just came to pick something up. He was telling Lucy how he used to beat you at draughts, Max.'

'That's not how I remember it,' said Max with a grin.

'I wish he'd find a new girlfriend,' continued Ellie wistfully.

'One that stays around, you mean,' said James, making eye contact with each of them as if he had just made a highly significant point. Caroline was very fond of James, but sometimes he could be a bit insensitive.

'Don't be mean,' snapped Ellie, giving James an irritated look. 'I'd just like him to have someone so that he isn't on his own. I worry about him, that's all.'

'I don't know why,' said Max. 'He's fine – a perfectly self-contained little unit. Always has been.'

'But is he?' Ellie said, the effects of the quickly consumed wine starting to show in her speech and volume levels. 'Is he really? I mean, what do we actually know about how he's doing? When was the last time any of us went to his house, for example?'

She looked around the group, eyebrows raised. It was true. Caroline couldn't remember when she had been. It was probably when he had first moved in and even then they had shown up without an invitation.

'He's a single bloke. Why would he want us lot traipsing through his house? I certainly wouldn't,' said Max. 'And it's not like we don't see him. He's always popping in on Dad, and I think he sees Mum too. He's just busy. We forget what it's like because we have kids and our worlds all revolve around them, but Nath has only got himself to please.'

Caroline thought Ellie looked less than convinced, but maybe Max was right. And they were so often out anyway. Who was to say that his timing wasn't just a bit off and he called in when they were all somewhere else?

The rest of the evening passed pleasantly, the new restaurant being declared a definite hit by them all, and soon it was time to ask for the bill. When it arrived, James swept it up and began to peruse it, running his eye down the column of figures.

'Result!' he said, and then in a quieter voice, 'They've missed off those second two bottles of wine. Quick! Let's get it paid and get out of here before they notice.'

'They probably haven't got their systems running quite right yet,' said Max.

'Let's see,' said Caroline, taking the bill from James and casting her eye over it. He was right. It only showed the first two bottles. 'We should tell them,' said Caroline. 'That poor waitress will probably have the money taken out of her wages when they work out what happened. That hardly seems fair. And we did drink the wine.' Well, some of us did, she thought. Her glass was still three-quarters full, and Max had barely had anything from the second bottle of red.

She looked at Ellie, who seemed to be weighing up the pros and cons.

'Caro's right,' she said, after a slightly longer time than Caroline thought the decision merited. 'Let's just tell them and pay it.'

James, however, was having none of it. 'Rubbish. It's their stupid mistake. If they can't even keep a track of what they've sold then what do you expect? You can bet your bottom dollar they wouldn't be showing similar scruples if it had been the other way around and they'd overcharged us.'

'Just go and tell them, Max,' said Caroline privately to her husband. 'It won't take them two minutes to redo the bill.'

James shook his head, but when Max stood up and wandered towards the bar area with the incorrect bill in his hand, he didn't object and just looked as if the 'free' wine had been easy come, easy go.

The bill was corrected, less a few pounds as a gesture to their honesty, and then paid. Caroline was pleased. She had enjoyed her evening and now she could eat there another time without her conscience pricking her. Nobody mentioned it again, and when the two couples parted it was with the usual bonhomie. Ellie walked a little unsteadily as they left, laughing loudly at something Max said and then complaining as the chill night air made her shiver. James put his arm tightly around her to warm her up, although Caroline noticed that he didn't give up his coat as Max would have done for her.

She and Max set off towards the taxi rank to get a cab home. The wine thing was still rankling with her.

'You thought I was right, didn't you?' she asked Max. 'About the wine, I mean.'

'Yeah, probably,' he said through a huge yawn. 'I can see James's point about it being their own fault, but we did drink the stuff.'

'Well, they did,' corrected Caroline. 'Ellie was really going for it tonight. I wonder if she'd had a bad day. I might ring her tomorrow.'

Max shook his head at her affectionately. 'Might! Caro, is there ever a day goes by when you don't speak to Ellie?'

'No,' laughed Caroline. 'I suppose not.'

Back at their house they put the babysitter into the taxi they had just vacated and began to shut things down for the night, and soon they were in bed. Max fell asleep quickly as he always did, but Caroline lay awake for a while. The issue with the bill was still bothering her. She wondered whether her refusal to just accept the restaurant's mistake when the others were so happy to let it go in some way separated her from them. They had all been untroubled by the idea of taking something for nothing, but for her it had been unthinkable. It was simply the wrong thing to do.

Caroline prided herself on her honesty. In a confusing world, it was the one pole star that she could always navigate by. Her personal code was clear, her ethos unshakeable. It wasn't that she thought the rest of them were dishonest. She knew that honesty came in many hues between the absolutes of black and white, and she imagined that even honest people generally found a shade of grey that suited them to fit the circumstances.

But that approach wasn't for Caroline. There were no grey areas for her. Something was either right or it wasn't. It was always cut and dried, one way or the other. And, whilst she wouldn't admit it to anyone else, there was another factor that helped her to stick unwaveringly to her convictions. She had refused to steal the wine not just because the waitress might have to cough up for her mistake, or because Caroline wanted to eat in the restaurant again with a clean conscience. She had paid for it because the mere thought of the shame and humiliation of being caught in dishonesty haunted her. Even now, all these years later and as she lay safely in her own bed, just the thought of the mortification of public exposure was making her cheeks burn and her palms sweat.

She had been ten when everything had changed for her. Up until then, life had been very ordinary. She'd lived in a small town with her parents. Her mum was a primary school teacher and her dad worked in an office doing something with insurance. Caroline had taken it for granted, never really appreciating how secure her life was because she had never known anything else.

But it had all fallen apart in a matter of months. Accusations had been made and had stuck to her dad like feathers to tar and then, by association, to her. Caroline had learnt the hard way how fragile a reputation could be and ever since then, she had striven to ensure there could be no opportunity for hers to be tarnished ever again.

15

THE DAY BEFORE

Max sat on the sofa in his dad's house and ran his hands through his hair. He couldn't quite take it in.

His dad was dead.

Max had seen him just last weekend and he had been completely fine, nothing wrong with him at all. And now he was dead. How could that be? It made no sense.

He wished Caroline was here. She would know what to do. Or Ellie, or even Nathan. But it was just him and the paramedics and the police.

They had told him to wait whilst they assessed the situation and so Max, compliant as a child, was waiting. Should he be doing something, asking questions, making sure that everything was being dealt with properly? But he didn't know what to ask, or what ought to be done. He didn't know anything except that his dad was dead.

Overhead he could hear the footsteps as strangers moved about his dad's house, making the floorboards creak. They were talking to one another in low voices and Max couldn't make out any of the words.

He checked his phone again but there were no new messages. They would all be driving here, the gathering of the Frost clan. He wished Caroline would hurry.

Someone was moving slowly down the stairs, heavy-footed and careful not to miss a step. Max sat up a little and looked at the door expectantly. Moments later it opened and the two police officers, a man and a woman, sidled into the room, both looking as if they would rather be anywhere else. It was the woman who spoke.

'Mr Frost,' she said. 'I'm so sorry for your loss, but we need to ask a few questions. It's just routine in a case like this when there's been an unexpected death. May we sit down?'

Max nodded and gestured at the sofa opposite. The policewoman sat lightly on the edge whilst the second one loitered near the door. Max watched as he took in the framed family photographs, all lined up on the sideboard, with a professional eye. He wondered what the other man saw when he looked at them. A normal, happy family.

'So, can you tell me what happened?' the woman asked.

Max brought his attention back to her and tried to concentrate, to get his thoughts in order.

'I came round to pick up a tent,' he said. 'The kids, my kids wanted to camp out, but our tent is too big. Dad has, had . . .' Max stumbled over the change in tense. 'A little two-man job and he said they could use it. I rang the doorbell and let myself in.'

'Is that normal?' the policewoman asked, and Max nodded.

'Yeah. We all have keys, me and my brother and sister. I shouted out for Dad as I came in. I knew he was here because the car was on the drive and the alarm wasn't set. He always sets the alarm when he goes out. But there was no sign of him. So I looked round down here and then, when he wasn't here, I went upstairs. And then . . .' Max heard his voice crack and he took a gulp of air. 'And then I found him on the bed. He was lying there with his eyes closed, like he was just taking a nap. But I knew he was dead. He was grey and . . .'

Max dropped his head into his hands. He needed Caroline.

'I'm sorry,' said the policewoman. 'I know how distressing this must be for you. And did you touch him at all? Did you move anything?'

Max shook his head. 'No, I just rang 999,' he said. 'Do you know what happened?'

'Not yet. The paramedics are with him now and they might have an idea, but there will need to be a post-mortem. It's standard procedure. Now, I appreciate this might be difficult, but I'm afraid I have to ask. Did your father have any particular concerns at all? Anything that he might have been worried about?'

Max picked up on her message straight away. 'You think this was suicide?' he said.

'We're just following procedure,' she replied gently. 'We have to ask.'

Max shook his head. 'No, I don't think so. But Dad wasn't like that anyway. He loved life. He would never . . .' Again he fought to keep control.

'Okay,' said the woman. 'There are no indications that he took his own life, but we just need to make sure. In any event, the post-mortem will probably be able to rule that out.'

'I can tell you now it's definitely not suicide,' Max said adamantly. 'Definitely.'

The front door opened and they all turned to see who had come in. It was Ellie.

'Oh God, Max. I got here as quickly as I could. Are you okay? How horrible for you to find him. You poor thing.' Tears were streaming down her face, but she didn't seem to notice.

Max stood up and threw his arms around her and they stood there for a moment just holding one another.

'And this is . . . ?' asked the policewoman.

'I'm Ellie. His sister. He's . . . was my dad too.'

'We're so sorry for your loss,' said the policewoman again. 'I was just asking Max some questions.'

'They think he might have committed suicide,' said Max.

'No. We're just eliminating the possibility,' began the policewoman, but Ellie spoke over her.

'Dad would never do that,' she said. 'He just wouldn't.'

'That's what I said.'

'Well, there are no signs that that's what happened, but you appreciate we have to ask.'

Max nodded.

'So, do we know what it was yet?' asked Ellie.

Max shook his head. 'A heart attack maybe. I don't know.'

'Did your father have any underlying health issues?'

'Not that I knew. He was as fit as a flea. Ate well, didn't drink too much, played loads of golf.'

Ellie started to sob. 'He was so young,' she said through her tears. 'He had so much life in front of him. Oh, my poor girls. They are going to be devastated. They love their grandad.'

Max put his arms around her again. He felt better when he was comforting Ellie. That was in the natural order of things, him looking after his little sister. It felt right, more right than any of the rest of it.

There was movement from upstairs and the policewoman signalled to her colleague with her eyes. He closed the door to the lounge so they couldn't see what was happening, but Max knew they must be bringing Dad downstairs to put in the ambulance. He was grateful to the policeman. He had enough images in his mind already. He didn't need that one on top.

'What happens now?' he asked.

'Your father will be taken to the hospital. They will do the post-mortem and let you have the results. Then, assuming everything's in order, the coroner will release the body to you for the funeral.'

Assuming everything is in order? Did they think they'd murdered him? Max checked himself. No one was suggesting any such thing. It was just a formality.

There was a light tap on the lounge door and one of the paramedics came in. She was a tiny little thing and Max wondered how she had managed to get his dad down the stairs.

'Hi,' she said with a sympathetic smile. 'We're going now. We'll take him to the mortuary at the infirmary. Here are the details.'

She offered Max a white business card and he stood up and took it from her.

'They will be in touch,' she added.

'Do you have any idea what . . .' Max was going to say killed him, but the words stuck in his throat.

'The coroner will know for sure, but we think it looks like a cerebral aneurysm.'

'A what?' asked Ellie.

'It's a blood clot in the brain,' replied Max. 'That's right, isn't it?' he asked the paramedic.

She nodded. 'Obviously we can't know for sure until we've had the post-mortem result, but that would be our best guess.'

Max saw the policewoman send a warning to the paramedic with her eyes. Speculation was probably not allowed, but Max was grateful. He needed something to latch on to and this would do until they knew for sure.

'Anyway, we'll be going now. I'm so sorry,' she said once again and then slipped out of the room. Moments later they heard the ambulance start up and drive away.

The policewoman stood up. 'We'll be going too. If you have any queries please contact the station.' She too handed him a business card. 'You can expect to hear from the coroner's office over the next day or so, and you might like to get in touch with a funeral director. They can explain the process to you in more detail.'

Max and Ellie both stood and watched as the policewoman and her colleague headed for the door. It felt all wrong to be in his dad's house with these strangers and for there to be no sign of his dad.

'We can see ourselves out,' the policewoman said. 'And once again, we're sorry for your loss.'

Max heard the front door open and then close.

'I didn't offer them any tea,' he said, as if that could possibly matter now.

16

They gathered at Ellie's house. It seemed the obvious place. They had the space, whereas Max and Caroline's house was a little bit cramped for everyone. They might have stayed at his dad's place, but it didn't feel right. Max didn't believe in ghosts, but being in Tony's house without Tony felt like an intrusion.

Ellie was calmer than he would have expected, taking charge of things after the police had left, making sure that the doors of their father's house were all locked and the alarm set. Then she went ahead, anxious to go and break the bad tidings to her girls, whilst he just sat in his car, not yet feeling ready to drive.

He wasn't sure how long he sat there, but by the time he made it to Ellie's house her eyes were redder than they had been and her face had the puffy look it had always taken on when she had been upset as a child. Ellie had never been one to cry discreetly.

She came to the door when he knocked and ushered Olivia and Lucy out of the way to let him in. Olivia was sobbing, the volume increasing the longer she felt ignored. Lucy was quiet and looked more bewildered than upset. Max knew how she felt.

He followed his sister into the kitchen, not really aware of what he was saying to his nieces, and then James appeared. He offered Max his hand and, when Max took it, launched into a brief hug.

'I'm so sorry, Max,' he said when the two men pulled apart. 'Tony was a great bloke, one of the best. It's a real shocker.'

Max nodded. It was true. The death of a parent was something you always knew would happen eventually, but the thought that it might be so soon had never crossed Max's mind.

'I'll put the kettle on,' said Ellie. She was busying about the room, picking things up and putting them away, her hands constantly moving.

'How about something stronger?' suggested James.

'But it's barely lunchtime,' she said, looking at her watch as if time might somehow have got away from her.

'I'm not sure that matters today. What would you like, Max? We've got pretty much everything.'

Max faltered, a decision of any kind being beyond what he could muster just then.

'How about brandy? That's good for shock and I've got a really nice Rémy Martin. Best they had in the shop.'

Max nodded. He didn't know whether he wanted a drink or not, but it seemed important to James that he had one.

'I think I'll join you,' said James, reaching for a pair of cut-glass brandy glasses from a display cupboard. 'Ellie?'

'I'll stick with tea, thanks,' she said.

Max wasn't sure how the drink would help, but when the liquid hit his stomach and then his head, he could see how it might take the edge off whatever it was he was feeling.

Caroline arrived with the boys shortly after. He had forgotten they were at football, even though they had discussed it earlier that morning and then again later when he had rung his wife to tell her what had happened. It was the last match of the season and the boys would normally have been full of it, but Caroline had obviously told them the news and now they were strangely quiet and subdued, understanding what had happened but not being quite sure what they were supposed to do or say. Theo put his arms around Max's waist and squeezed him tight and Max stroked the top of his head.

'I know, mate,' he said, trying to keep his voice even. 'It's really sad.'

He felt Theo nodding his head against his stomach. Alex held back, standing on the kitchen threshold so he could make a run for it if the room became too emotionally charged.

'Are you okay, Dad?' he asked, and Max felt proud that his son was emotionally intelligent enough to understand that this was a difficult moment for his usually steadfast dad. Had he even imagined how he would be feeling if Max had died, putting himself in his own dad's shoes?

'I am, thanks, Alex,' he said. 'But it's a bit of a shock.'

Alex nodded as if he totally understood this. Perhaps he did.

Caroline took the children away to a different part of the house and even though Max wanted to talk to her, he was glad he no longer had to be strong for the boys. It seemed much easier just to stand and stare out at the garden.

Nathan was the last to arrive and Max had to run through the events of the morning again with him. Each time he told the story, it sounded more natural to him, but he still couldn't quite believe it had actually happened and wasn't just the plot of something he'd seen on the television.

'And he was just lying there?' asked Nathan. 'Poor Dad. Do you think he knew anything about it?'

Max was sure he must have. From what he knew, an aneurysm was incredibly painful and not something you were likely to have been unaware of. But then, they didn't know for certain that was the cause of death, and if Tony had been aware of the pain then surely he would have rung for an ambulance. Perhaps he had just slipped away in his sleep, the way everyone hoped to go.

'Maybe not,' he said, to assuage Nathan more than anything. 'His eyes were shut so it could just have happened when he was asleep.'

The idea floated in the air around them. This was what they all wanted to believe and hang on to: that their dad had died peacefully and had known nothing about it.

'So I suppose we'll have to sell the house and everything,' mused Nathan.

Max turned his head sharply towards his brother, sure of what he had just heard but also assuming he must be mistaken. 'What?'

'The house,' Nathan clarified. 'We'll need to sell it.'

'The man's barely cold, Nath,' snapped Max. 'We haven't even got a cause of death, let alone anything else, and you're already talking about selling the house!'

'I'm just trying to be practical,' replied Nathan defensively. 'There's no point sitting on it. It'll only start to deteriorate.'

Max opened his mouth to object but then thought better of it and turned his back on Nathan instead. Getting into a row wouldn't help anything.

Nathan must have realised he had crossed a line and fell quiet, but Ellie, who had just reappeared with a tray of drinks for the children, had half-heard.

'What was that, Nath?'

'Nothing,' replied Nathan, but Max cut across him.

'Nathan thinks we should get the house on the market this afternoon. No time like the present, eh, Nath?'

'Don't be an arse, Max. I was just saying.'

'God, Nathan,' said Ellie. 'How can you even think of that right now?'

Nathan hung his head. At least he had the good grace to look a little ashamed, Max thought. And he supposed they would all approach this differently, would all find their own way of coping with . . . he still couldn't quite take it in . . . with the death of their father.

The day wore on with no one quite knowing what to do or say, but not wanting to be the first to leave. The kids occupied themselves elsewhere, occasionally slinking into the kitchen for something to eat or drink. Every so often the adults would hear the makings of a row building, but then the children would stamp it out for themselves. Olivia appeared more often than the others, wrapped herself around a parent, let out a brief howl and then left again.

Then something occurred to Max and he sat bolt upright. 'Shit! Has anyone told Mum?'

He had long since ceased to connect his parents with one another and in all the upheaval, Valerie had completely slipped his mind.

'I did,' said Ellie. 'I left her a message to ring me urgently and for once she rang back. She's coming over.'

Even though there had been no love lost between Valerie and Tony in recent times, she had still been married to him for thirty years and they had had three children together and four grandchildren. It was only natural that she would be upset – for what they had once shared at least, even if for no other reason. Max's insides clenched at not having thought of her straight away, but there was no harm done. Ellie had everything under control.

Valerie arrived at around five. The boys, unable to stand being cooped up any longer, had migrated into the garden where they had been marauding, but were now on the trampoline with Lucy. Olivia appeared to be directing events from the grass. Valerie went to speak to them first, no doubt hearing their shouts from the road. Max watched as she listened intently to what they had to say and then hugged them all in turn. She always had been good in a crisis.

Then she came and tapped at the huge bifold doors that led from the kitchen on to the patio. James opened them to let her in, pushing the doors wide as if to show just how very big the space was, but at least having the tact not to mention it. Max knew that would have taken a substantial amount of willpower on James's part, and he felt absurdly grateful to his brother-in-law.

If Valerie had been upset by the demise of her former husband then she was hiding it well. Max saw no outward sign of any emotion at all, but as James opened the door and she came into the room, she headed straight for Ellie.

'Oh, my darling girl,' she said as Ellie threw herself at Valerie, sinking her head on to her shoulder and beginning to sob. Max watched as his mum ran a hand gently over Ellie's hair, and something deep inside him wished that it was his head she was stroking. His need to be comforted was so strong that it was all he could do not to go and form a queue behind his sister.

'Oh, Mum,' Ellie spluttered. 'It's so awful. I can't believe he's really gone.'

'No,' said Valerie. 'I thought he'd live forever.'

Something about her tone suggested relief that this was not the case. As if she had read his thoughts, her eyes drifted across and met Max's, held his gaze for a moment. Max felt she was trying to send him a message of some kind, but he was clueless as to what it might be. Probably nothing and anyway, Valerie must have stopped loving Tony or she wouldn't have left, so perhaps it wasn't surprising that she didn't appear to be as devastated by his death as the rest of them.

Around six o'clock, Caroline suggested they should maybe be heading home. She threw a silent look at Max and he nodded his agreement. There was nothing to be gained by hanging around any longer. It wouldn't change anything.

Ellie made a half-hearted attempt to get them to stay.

'We can order in some food,' she said. 'Then no one needs to be bothered cooking.' But it seemed that no one, other than the children, had much of an appetite. Max, having hit the brandy hard and early, had the beginnings of a headache forming behind his eyes and was happy to be led away by Caroline. He needed someone to take control. Caroline could always be relied on to do that.

They were saying their goodbyes at the door when Caroline suddenly slapped a hand to her forehead.

'The cat!' she said. 'Monty. We forgot about Monty. The poor little thing will be terribly confused.' She looked at her watch. 'It's too late to go and find him now, but we'll go over tomorrow and rescue him. Is that okay with you, Ellie?'

Ellie nodded happily. The last thing she would want, Max suspected, would be Monty plucking at her soft furnishings with his razor-sharp claws. He wasn't sure that he wanted to take the cat on either, but now wasn't the time for that discussion.

And so they all left in Caroline's car, Max not being fit to drive, with promises to ring in the morning and hopes that everyone got a good night's sleep. Max always told the boys whenever their lives felt bleak that things would look better in the morning, but this time he wasn't sure that was true.

17

'Max? Could you come up here a minute? There's something you need to see.'

Caroline sat on her haunches and stared at the suitcase full of money she had just found under her father-in-law's spare bed. She didn't think she had ever seen so much cash in real life. She tried to estimate how much there was, but really, she had no idea. A lot was the best she could manage.

The notes weren't crisp and new like you sometimes got from the cashpoint in the high street. These were well used, curling at the edges and with the patina of dozens or maybe hundreds of fingerprints on them. She used cash like this every day, but in such vast quantities the money took on an unwholesome air, as if there was something not quite hygienic about it.

But that was ridiculous, Caroline thought to herself. It was just money. She picked up a bundle, weighed it in her hand as if it were a bag of sugar. She ran a finger down the edge, flicking through the notes like a pack of cards, and then smelled it. When she was in America once, she had been struck by the very particular smell of the dollar bills, but these didn't really smell of anything apart from being slightly musty.

She could hear Max's familiar footsteps on the stairs.

'What's up?' he asked as he got closer to the bedroom. 'You do know that Monty has just pegged it back downstairs. I've locked the cat flap so hopefully he won't have— Oh, my God!'

'Look at this,' said Caroline, although there was clearly no need to point it out. The suitcase stuffed with money had captured Max's full attention.

'Bloody hell!' He ran his hand in front of his mouth and then knelt down next to her. 'Where was that?'

'Under the bed,' replied Caroline. 'I was pulling stuff out to get at Monty and then, as the case was obviously full, I just opened it. I'm sorry. I probably shouldn't have.'

This thought had only just occurred to her. She had only looked in because she'd assumed it would be full of clothes. Cash was the very last thing she had been expecting to find, but now that she had, she wasn't at all sure she should have been nosing about. The money felt private, secret – clandestine, even.

'Well, thank God you did,' said Max, dismissing her fears at once. 'What if we'd just sent the house clearance people in?'

Max seemed to recoil at what he had just said. Tony had only been gone for twenty-four hours and he had mentioned house clearance.

'I'm sure we would have checked things like this before we did that,' Caroline replied kindly. 'And anyway, we're a very long way from that just yet.'

Max nodded.

'How much do you think there is?' she asked.

'Only one way to find out,' said Max, picking up a bundle and beginning to count, peeling the notes off and putting them in piles of five, counting out loud as he went. 'Twenty, forty, sixty, eighty, one hundred.'

When he had ten piles, he scooped them together. 'A thousand,' he said.

He stared at Caroline, eyes wide and lips slightly parted. His little bundle had scarcely made any difference to the piles in the case and yet he was already at a thousand pounds.

'Bloody hell, Caro,' he said.

Caroline began to count as well and soon they had a little production line going, each counting in bundles of one hundred pounds, and then a thousand and then finally making piles of ten thousand pounds, which they secured with elastic bands. After a while, the significance of what she was actually doing left her. She was entirely focused on counting and piling.

By the time they had got to the bottom of the suitcase, there were twenty-seven piles on the bedroom carpet and several notes left over. Caroline was struggling with the basic maths because the outcome for twenty-seven multiplied by ten thousand was so hard to get her head around that she couldn't believe she could possibly be correct.

'So that's . . . two hundred and seventy thousand pounds,' she said. 'Is that right?' She turned to look at Max, who looked as bewildered as she felt.

'Well, yes,' he said. 'Plus . . .' He counted up the remaining notes. 'One hundred and sixty.'

They sat there, stunned, neither quite knowing what to say, just staring at the twenty-seven little stacks of notes.

Finally Caroline broke the spell. 'But why is it here? Why did your dad have two hundred and seventy thousand, one hundred and sixty pounds in cash in a suitcase under his spare bed?'

Max blew out his lips and shook his head.

'I have absolutely no idea,' he said.

18

They sat there for quite some time. Caroline's knees began to ache and she stood up stiffly and sat on the bed instead but they didn't leave the room, as if the money might somehow magically disappear when it was out of sight.

'I feel really vulnerable being here with this much cash on the floor,' she said. 'Does that sound silly? Is the front door locked?'

Max gave her an affectionate grin. 'It does sound a bit silly,' he said. 'But I do understand what you mean. Shall we put it back in the case?'

Caroline nodded but made no effort to leave the bed, and so Max began to scoop up the piles and stack them neatly in the suitcase. When it was all in rows, the money took up less room than it had when it was just thrown in willy-nilly, but how it looked made no difference. It was still exactly the same amount of cash. Over a quarter of a million pounds. It sounded even more when she thought of it like that. A quarter of a million pounds, in cash, in a suitcase.

'What should we do with it?' she asked.

'Well, we shouldn't leave it here for a start,' said Max. 'I'm sure it's perfectly safe. It must have been under there for a while already, but now I know it's here I'll never sleep.'

'Do you think it'll be any safer at our house?' said Caroline.

Max shrugged. 'At least there are people around at ours,' he said. 'This place is a bit isolated with it having the garden all the way round, and it won't be long before the word gets out that Dad isn't here.' His voice cracked a little but he pressed on. 'Someone might break in and it could be days before anyone noticed.'

'There's the alarm,' said Caroline.

'Yes, but they are more of a deterrent than anything. A burglar could be in and out before anyone bothered to come and see what was going on, always assuming that anyone did.'

'They'd do well to find it,' said Caroline.

'Unless they already knew it was here,' replied Max.

Caroline paused, taking in what he had just said. Who might know that? Did Tony owe it to someone? Would someone be waiting for him to return it? The thought was darker than she liked and had sinister overtones that she wasn't used to.

'Why do you think your dad had so much money in the house?' she asked. She could think of a multitude of explanations, none of them good and all making it feel like the plot of a TV drama rather than their lives.

Max shook his head. 'Not a clue.'

'Maybe we should take it to the bank and pay it in whilst we decide what to do,' she suggested. 'It would be safe there.'

Max looked doubtful. 'I'd rather know more about what it is before we do anything like that. And we can't decide on our own. We need to ask Ellie and Nath too, see what they think.'

'Well, of course,' said Caroline quickly. She didn't want Max to think she was contemplating keeping the lot without informing his siblings. 'It's just that it's a lot of money and I'd feel safer if it was nice and securely behind lock and key.'

'I'm sure it'll be fine at ours,' Max said. 'Just until we've spoken to the others. We can stick it in the loft with all the other crap. I defy any burglar to start rooting through all that. And I'll call a family conference. We're going to have to meet up to talk about the funeral anyway. This can just be another agenda item.'

'The others will have a fit when they hear,' laughed Caroline. 'Oh, hi Ellie, Nath. So, we were just trying to rescue Monty from your dad's box room and we found a quarter of a million pounds under the bed.'

'Ellie probably won't even bat an eye. Her share is like loose change to them. I bet Nathan will be interested, though. Money seems to slip through his fingers like water. Did I tell you he was talking about selling this place yesterday? Prat.'

'He was probably just thinking aloud and didn't mean anything by it,' Caroline said. 'We could do with some extra cash,' she added quietly.

Max always said that they had enough money and didn't need any more, but a windfall would be very welcome.

Max nodded. 'We'll be getting some extra when the house is sold,' he said. 'Assuming there's equity in it, which there surely will be. But it will need to go through probate first, and that can take ages.' He screwed his forehead up, deep in thought. 'Okay,' he said, running through the steps out loud. 'We'll take it home with us now for safekeeping. Then we'll tell the others and see if they know why it was there or what it was for. And then we can all decide what to do with it together.'

'That sounds sensible,' replied Caroline. 'Let's find Monty and then we can go home. The boys will be back from school soon.'

And so they headed down the stairs, Max carrying the suitcase whilst Caroline called out for the elusive cat.

19

They drove home via Ellie and James's place to pick up Max's car.

'Are you going in?' Caroline asked as he got out of the car. 'Will you say anything?'

Max wrinkled his nose. 'I don't think I can face them,' he said. 'I'll just take the car and run. They won't mind. They might not even be here.'

'I'll see you back at home then?' she said, and Max disappeared up Ellie and James's long drive.

Monty mewed loudly from the cardboard box on the back seat. He didn't seem at all happy in there.

'I'm sorry, Monty,' she said. 'It's not too long now.'

Caroline had no idea about cats. She hadn't been allowed a pet as a child and so had been nervous of having any since, as if there was some kind of secret key to keeping them that everyone but her knew. Offering to rescue this one from the empty house had been more of an instinct than a thought-through decision. It just felt like the right thing to do and Caroline prided herself on always doing the right thing. And anyway, they could hardly leave him at Tony's to fend for himself.

What did cats need? She stopped at the garage and bought some dried cat food and a bag of cat litter, although she didn't really know what she was supposed to do with it. Maybe someone else would be happy to take Monty when the dust had settled a little bit. That seemed doubtful. The others had looked relieved when she had offered, and clearly had no intention of stepping in to help. How long did cats live? she wondered. How old was Monty?

As if he could read her thoughts, Monty started mewling even louder. Perhaps this was his first ride in a car? He was probably a bit frightened, poor thing. Tony dead, the house filled with strangers, and now dragged from his home to be taken who knew where. No wonder he was crying.

She pulled up outside the house, switched the engine off and considered for a moment. The boys had heard her offer to collect the cat, so she would have to appear with him or they would ask questions. If it hadn't been for that, she might have been tempted to just let him go so he could decide his own fate. Would he be able to make his own way home? Did cats do that, like homing pigeons? But of course, that was out of the question. They would take care of Monty as if Tony had asked them to do it.

Having made the decision, she got out of the car and was about to retrieve the cardboard box when the front door opened and Alex and Theo burst out.

'Did you get him?' Theo asked, his eyes shining brightly. 'Can I see?'

'I did,' she said. 'But he's very frightened so you need to stay calm.'

Monty mewed louder still and the boys looked delighted.

'Is he in that box?' asked Theo, suddenly anxious. 'Can he breathe?'

'Of course he can breathe, you idiot,' replied Alex, punching his brother lightly on the arm. 'There's oxygen in there. We should probably let him out though, right, Mum?'

'Yes, but not here. If he runs away he won't know where to come back to. Let's get him inside and then we can research what to do. I'm sure I read somewhere that you put butter on their paws,' said Caroline, her heart sinking at the thought of little buttery footprints all over her house. 'But maybe we can just feed him and keep him inside for a few days whilst he gets himself acclimatised.'

She slid the box across the back seat and picked it up. She could feel the cat shifting inside, his claws sliding across the cardboard as he scrabbled to get a grip. The movement altered the box's centre of gravity and Caroline gripped it more tightly.

'Can one of you grab the food and the litter from the boot and bring it inside, please? Leave the suitcase. I'll bring that in in a minute,' she said as she headed for the door.

Max was already there standing in the doorway, having beaten her home.

'Someone sounds upset,' he said, standing to one side to let Caroline and her cargo inside.

Caroline pulled a face at him. 'I'm not sure this is the best idea I've ever had. What if he hates us?'

Monty continued to mew plaintively through the box and Max put his hand out and touched her cheek. 'He'll be fine,' he said softly. 'It doesn't have to be a permanent arrangement. Let's just see how we go.'

Caroline nodded at him.

'Thanks for this, Caro,' he added.

She could see tears were not far away and she was reminded that he had lost his father only the day before. That's why she was doing this. For Max. He wanted his dad's cat to be safe, irrational though that might be, and if she could do this small thing for him whilst everything was going on then she would.

'No worries,' she said. 'Can you bring the suitcase in?' She felt her stomach turn at the thought of all that money in the house.

Max nodded. 'I'll put it up in the loft. And I'll make a plan to meet up with the others so we can tell them.'

Caroline nodded, but something about that idea didn't sit right with her. They all got on so well, or she and Ellie and Max and James did – Nathan was a bit of an unknown quantity – but money didn't always bring out the best in people, particularly windfall money. And Caroline was struggling to understand why Tony would keep so much cash under a bed, unless there was something illegitimate about it. If it was all perfectly above board then surely it would have been in the bank.

'Do you think we should try to find out something about what it is and where it came from before we tell the others?' she asked. 'It might be easier to have the conversation if we know what's what.'

Max pulled the corners of his mouth down and wrinkled his nose. 'I'm not sure how we'd do that,' he said. 'Obviously we can't ask Dad. I suppose there might be something about it in his papers, but I doubt it.'

'Might your mum know?' she asked.

'Maybe, I suppose,' said Max thoughtfully. 'But it seems unlikely. And I'm not sure about involving her as well. My gut feel is to keep it between the three of us, and you and James of course, for the time being.'

Caroline wasn't sure. She would definitely ask Valerie if it were up to her. It felt like the obvious thing to do. But it wasn't up to her. This was a Frost family matter and, when the chips were down, she was only a Frost by marriage.

'Okay,' she said. 'Whatever you think's best.'

Monty, who had been quiet for a few moments, began to mew again and Caroline turned her attention to the box as Alex and Theo appeared.

'We can use the washing-up bowl as a litter tray,' said Theo, brandishing it above his head.

'The butter thing is rubbish, Mum,' said Alex. 'I looked it up. We have to keep him inside for two weeks and be nice to him and then he'll work it out for himself.'

'Okay,' replied Caroline. 'Well done, boys. That's very practical of you, although I think there's an old washing-up bowl in the garage that we can use instead of that one.' She grinned at Theo. 'So, shall we let him out?'

The boys started to leap up and down, and then seemed to realise that would frighten the cat so immediately stopped.

'Yes,' whispered Alex.

Caroline peeled away the tape she'd used to seal the box and gently lifted the flaps. Monty sat there looking quite calm. For a moment he eyed them all, and then he hopped out of the box and disappeared through the open door into the kitchen.

'Welcome to your new home, Monty,' said Theo and immediately followed after him with Alex hot on his tail.

20

Ellie didn't quite know what to do with herself. It had been three days since Max had found their dad lying dead on his bed, and since then time seemed to have been playing tricks on her. Sometimes it felt as if she was stuck on that day, and she kept reliving the moment she had taken Max's phone call: the shock, the police, all of it.

And then suddenly time would seem to be marching past too quickly. It had been three whole days and she had done nothing about the funeral or the wake or any of the things you were supposed to dive into after a death. Her heart would race at the thought of all the people she ought to be contacting, but whom she couldn't bring herself to speak to. And that was before you got anywhere near everyone her dad knew in his official capacity. Her mum used to joke that there wasn't a single person in the entire town who hadn't crossed paths with Tony at some point. That could well be true. Was she supposed to contact them all? She didn't even know who half of them were.

So, not knowing which way to turn, she did what she always did in moments of crisis. She rang Caroline.

'If I were you,' said Caroline, her voice calm and unflustered, just as Ellie had known it would be, 'I would put a death announcement in the paper with details of the funeral and then let the news circulate by itself.'

'Of course!' replied Ellie, mentally slapping herself on the forehead. 'Why didn't I think of that? It's so obviously the thing to do.'

'Because your dad just died and it's a really difficult time,' said Caroline.

Her voice was so gentle that Ellie could feel the tears rising up again. She could just about hold herself together as long as no one was kind to her.

'But I don't know when the funeral is yet,' she said, frustrated, aware that she sounded petulant, but not able to help it. 'We're still waiting for the post-mortem results.'

'Then don't do anything for now,' suggested Caroline patiently. 'No one will blame you if you don't make the news common knowledge straight away. People just want a chance to pay their respects, but they can wait.'

'Okay,' Ellie agreed, compliant as an anxious child. 'How's Max coping?'

'Oh, you know Max. Bottling it up. It really shook him, finding Tony like that, but obviously he's dealing with it by pretending it didn't happen. Why do men do that?'

'He's never been that good at showing his emotions,' replied Ellie. 'Something to do with being the eldest and always feeling he had to be the responsible one, I think. He does need to work through it, though. Should I get James to ring him?'

'Yes, that might help. Thanks,' said Caroline. 'It could be that he doesn't want to talk to me but is happy to open up to someone else. It's so hard to tell. Have you heard from Nathan?'

'No. Not a word since Monday. I texted him but he hasn't replied.'

'Men! They're all the same,' replied Caroline with a loud tut. 'And how are you?' She pressed the final word, making Ellie want to cry all over again.

'Up and down,' she said. 'I still can't believe it's true. It's hit us all quite hard. James was very fond of Dad and the girls are devastated.'

'I know. It's so hard to take in,' said Caroline.

Her voice was very steady, and Ellie didn't think it sounded as if she was finding it hard at all, although maybe that was unfair. Tony hadn't been her father, after all, and even though Caroline had known him since she was a little girl, Ellie had always had the impression that she was wary of him, a little on edge in his company, as if she was never sure what he might say next. She might have been right to be wary: Tony could be wildly unpredictable and had a habit of making gentle jokes at the expense of others, but Caroline wasn't a nervous person generally. Quite the reverse. So now it occurred to Ellie for the first time that perhaps Caroline hadn't actually liked Tony very much.

She rejected the thought. It was unworthy and unfair. Caroline was just trying to be strong for her because she was her best friend. The rest of it was all in her imagination.

'Would you like me to pop round later?' Caroline asked. 'I've taken a couple of days off work to support Max, but he's gone into work today. Or if you fancied a change of scene we could meet for coffee in town before school pick-up.'

Ellie leapt at the suggestion. 'Yes! That would be lovely. I think I'm going mad stuck here with all this in my head, and James has just locked himself away in his office. Some big deal or other. I can't remember if he told me about it or not. Everything's a bit blurry to be honest. So yes. The usual place at two?'

'Perfect. And it'll be okay, Ellie. Just take it one step at a time.'

Caroline hung up and Ellie felt ashamed that she had ever had an uncharitable thought about her. She was her best friend and she would be there for her no matter what.

21

Ellie made her way into town a little earlier than she needed to meet Caroline. What she required was a bit of retail therapy to make her feel better. She wasn't quite sure what she wanted to buy, but she was firmly of the view that whatever it was would surely help.

The obvious item would be a new dress for the funeral; something dark, classy and well-cut that she didn't have to worry about when she wore it.

But no. That was for another day. They didn't even have a date yet and buying a black dress was hardly going to cheer her up. Shopping for other clothes seemed somehow frivolous and inappropriate. If she had been a Victorian she would have been in full mourning following the death of her father, and whilst she was glad she didn't have to wear only black for the foreseeable future, it wouldn't feel right, trying on outfits for happier times.

She would buy something for the house. That was a good idea. It could be something they would all enjoy and it was a great way of giving her the boost that spending always provided. Ignoring the window displays in her go-to boutiques, she headed for her favourite interiors shop. It wasn't expensive, but the stuff was always bang on trend and, if carefully chosen, could brighten a room up no end.

As soon as she stepped through the door and her nostrils filled with the scent of whichever diffuser they were showcasing – today it was something with grapefruit that was summery and uplifting – Ellie felt herself calming, the knots in her stomach smoothing themselves out into silky skeins. This was her environment. She knew where she was with a shop. She could move purposefully between displays, always spotting the unusual and being able to picture the perfect place for an item in her mind's eye. It was a skill, she knew. Not everyone had an eye for design like she did. You just had to look at other people's homes to see how easy it was to get things wrong, sometimes quite horribly.

Her attention was caught by a display of tableware, predominantly white but with silver accents. It was classy, to her mind, and spoke quietly of style without being too obvious and showy. She didn't need to buy more white crockery, they had that in abundance, but the silver table runner, candelabra and chargers would be something new. Her existing dinner party table settings were mainly gold, which went well with the dark-red wall in the dining room, but the room had been decorated like that for a while. Maybe a spot of redecoration was in the offing. Perhaps a nice blue? That would work well with silver.

She picked up a sparkly tea-light holder and turned it round in her hands, watching how the light hit the little cuts in the surface and made it twinkle. She saw the shop assistant coming towards her, beaming. They knew her well in here.

'Hi,' said the assistant as she approached. 'Oh, I just adore those. They are so stylish and understated, but they bring sparkle to a table. And they work in both summer and winter, which not many things do.'

'Yes,' agreed Ellie. 'I was just thinking that. The whole setting is lovely.'

'Perfect for a midsummer's dinner party or a New Year's Eve buffet. Can't go wrong really,' said the assistant. 'Have you seen the chargers? That silver rim really sets them off too. Your cutlery's silver, right?'

Ellie nodded.

'Perfect,' she continued. 'Silver chargers, white plates, crystal glassware, and then those lovely little tea-light holders. Totally gorgeous.'

Ellie was aware she was being sold to but she didn't care. It was all true. The setting was breathtaking, particularly if you threw in a few strings of fairy lights and maybe even a couple of the candelabra. She was always worried that something tall on a dining table might block the line of sight, but then again, wasn't that what side tables were for?

'It is. Stunning. I think I'll take eight each of the chargers and tea-light holders, and the runner as well, please,' said Ellie, the familiar buzz that she always got when she bought something new making her nerve endings fizz. 'And two of those candelabra.'

The assistant's eyes shone. Ellie was pretty sure they weren't on commission in here, but who wouldn't get excited at the thought of a purchase like that?

'I'll pay for them now, but could you parcel them up for me? I have a few other things to do. I can bring the car round on my way home.'

When Ellie left the shop, their bank account a few hundred pounds lighter, she felt much better.

The café where she and Caroline liked to meet was down a cobbled alleyway away from the crowds, and whilst it was a popular place, you could usually get a table. Caroline was already there, phone in hand, scrolling, and was so engrossed that she didn't notice her come in until Ellie was hovering right over her.

'Hi, Caro,' she said, bending down to kiss her.

'I ordered you an Americano with milk and a chocolate biscotti. I hope that's okay,' said Caroline.

'Perfect,' said Ellie, settling herself down into the chair opposite, unwinding the long linen scarf from round her neck and stuffing it into the top of her bag. She thought about telling Caroline about her recent purchases but decided against it. It wasn't that Max and Caroline were broke, but she wasn't sure there was spare money for the kinds of things that she routinely bought and she didn't want to appear insensitive. When they came for dinner and saw the new things, she might even pretend that she had had them for a while but just not used them. There was very little chance that Caroline would have noticed them in the shop recently so she was unlikely to catch her out, and it was only a harmless white lie, told with the best of intentions.

'I'm not sure I should have sent the girls back to school today,' blurted Ellie, apropos of nothing but suddenly feeling the need for reassurance that she had done the right thing.

'Were they okay?' asked Caroline. 'Olivia seemed a bit overcome on Sunday.'

'I'm pretty sure that was as much to do with milking the drama as grief for her grandad,' replied Ellie, and Caroline's wry smile told her that she had thought much the same. 'But I think Lucy was genuinely upset and she can be a little' – Ellie picked her word carefully – 'delicate sometimes. I just wanted to make sure she was all right before I sent her back in.'

Caroline's brow was creased, her head tipped to one side as if she understood how delicate Lucy could be, but even Caroline didn't understand how things were with Lucy. Not really.

'Are Alex and Theo okay?' Ellie asked.

'I think so. They didn't want time off school, not that we offered it, and so they just went in as normal on Monday. Theo hasn't really mentioned anything. Alex and Max had a little chat, man to man, but he seems to be coping fine.'

'Will you take them to the funeral?' Ellie asked. This was something that had been on her mind. Her girls were both too young for funerals, she thought, but if Caroline and Max took the boys then it might be difficult for her to do something different.

Caroline stuck out her bottom lip as she considered what to do. 'I assumed we would. Not really given it much thought at all, actually. Why? Do you think that's the wrong thing to do?'

'It's so hard to know,' replied Ellie, who definitely did think that. 'I think I was fourteen before I went to my first funeral, but that was because there weren't any to go to until then. Lucy is only eight. It feels very young to be dealing with a funeral. And I'm sure it'll be quite a big do. I worry that seeing all those adults upset, or at the very least sombre, will spoil all her good memories of her grandad.'

'What does James think?' asked Caroline.

'He thinks I'm making a fuss and that we should just take them, but it doesn't feel right to me. To be honest, Caro, I was hoping that if you didn't want to take the boys either, we could just agree there would be no children.' Ellie watched Caroline's face for any hint of what she might be thinking, but found nothing concrete.

'Yes, I see what you're saying. Let me chat it over with Max. And I'll ask the boys as well. They obviously get a say in it too.'

Ellie wasn't sure that they did. In her view, this was an adult decision and the children would just have to comply with what the adults decided, but Max and Caroline parented differently. It was odd, when she thought about it. She and Max had been brought up with the same rules and values, and yet they had very different ideas about what was best for their children. But then Caroline's upbringing had been very different to theirs. It had been just her and her mum, and on the rare occasions that Ellie had been round to their house she had always been struck by the difference between the two families. Caroline's mother never seemed to want anyone at their house. She hadn't been rude but she was never very welcoming and Ellie always felt like she was intruding. Caroline's mother had always seemed afraid of her own shadow, but Ellie had never really known why.

By contrast, life had been busy and noisy in the Frost household with lots of people coming and going, and decisions often made by committee with lots of good-humoured shouting. At her house there was no peering out from behind curtains or skulking around in darkened rooms; everyone was always out in the sunlight. When you looked at it like that, perhaps it wasn't so surprising that Caroline approached things differently.

There was nothing she could do about it, however. She had made her point, and now she would have to wait until Max and Caroline came back to her. But even if they did choose to take the boys, that didn't mean she would have to take her girls.

'I just wish we'd get the results of the post-mortem,' said Caroline. 'Then we can get on with planning everything. I'm not sure it's good for anyone, it dragging on like this.'

'Well, they need to be sure they know how he died,' Ellie replied. She could feel her eyes starting to brim again and she blinked hard to disperse the tears before they began to escape. 'And I suppose the police will want to be sure that nobody else was involved.'

Caroline stared at her, eyes wide. 'You don't seriously think someone else might have been, do you?' she asked.

'No! Of course not. I'm sure it'll be an aneurysm, like the paramedics thought. But the police have to be sure, don't they? I mean, Dad was pretty young and in good health. It was a bit of a bolt out of the b—' The tears came suddenly. Ellie could do nothing to stem the flow so she just let them fall and soon Caroline joined in, the two of them sitting there, crying into their coffee until they managed to regain control.

'Do you think someone might have wanted to kill him?' asked Caroline when they had stopped crying, and the question was so unexpected that it made Ellie laugh.

'No!' she replied. 'Of course not! The thought never even crossed my mind.' But as she looked at Caroline, she could tell that the thought had crossed hers.

'Anyway, enough of all that,' Caroline continued. 'How are the party preparations coming along?'

Despite her birthday party being almost continuously on her mind until the week before, Ellie hadn't thought about it since they had found her father. Partly this was because it felt disrespectful to be thinking about celebrating so close to a death, but also because pretty much all the arrangements were now in place. All that remained were a few last-minute matters that could only be dealt with nearer the time.

'I think it's nearly there,' she said. 'Almost all the RSVPs are in and there's hardly anyone who can't make it.'

'Of course,' Caroline replied. 'It's going to be the social event of the year. Nobody is going to want to miss it.'

Ellie gave her a wan smile. She had been so excited about it, had rushed round planning and booking things like there was no tomorrow. But now the shine had gone. The whole thing felt overcome by her dad's death.

'I did think about cancelling,' she admitted.

'No! You can't do that. Your dad would have been cross for a start. But also, we've all been looking forward to it. And I think we'll need a good night out by then. We'll have got the funeral out of the way and be ready to let our hair down. Honestly, Ellie, you really shouldn't cancel.'

The idea had been only fleeting and Ellie had come to much the same conclusion as Caroline, but it was nice to have her opinion confirmed.

'Are you sure?' Ellie pressed. 'You don't think people will think badly of me for going ahead?'

'No!' replied Caroline, eyebrows shooting up in emphasis. 'I don't think that at all. And you've put all that effort into it. It would be such a shame to see it go to waste.'

Ellie was glad she'd never mentioned all the cash she'd spent, but that was a factor too. James had said she could have precisely what she wanted and she had taken him at his word. The thought of cancelling now and losing all that money on things that couldn't be refunded or returned made her feel slightly sick.

22

After she had said goodbye to Caroline, Ellie picked up her table-ware purchases and headed to Green Mount to collect the girls. She was early and found a parking spot without any difficulties. Usually she would sit and spend the spare few minutes on Facebook, but that seemed so trivial at the moment, and she still hadn't announced her dad's death so she was avoiding being seen on there in case it looked bad when people did hear the news.

Instead she got out of her car and decided to have a quick restorative walk around the block. It was a lovely day and a breath of fresh air would help to clear her head before the girls came to destroy her peace.

The school was situated in a leafy suburb with not much round it but other houses, but there was a nice little loop that she some-times walked, which took her past a few of the bigger properties. Ellie liked to try to have a nose at them as she passed by, partly looking for garden ideas, but also because it allowed her to indulge in a little fantasy that one day she and James would be able to move up to something as grand as those.

She fished her sunglasses out of her bag – it wouldn't do to be spotted checking out houses – and set off. The biggest places, and the ones that she enjoyed looking at the most, were at the apex of the walk and she covered the early ground quickly so she could slow her pace when she got there. Not that she could see much from the road. Most of the houses had electric gates and long drives, and a couple of them belonged to people James knew through work so she definitely didn't want them to see her, but others were more open and some of them didn't even have electric gates.

When she reached the house that she would dearly love to move to, she slowed her pace right down. There were no cars on the drive so she felt able to have a jolly good peer. It was a Jacobean manor house, gable-fronted with mullioned windows and a box knot garden between the house and the road. Ellie particularly loved the two stone peacocks that sat on the gateposts guarding the house. They must have cost a fortune, she knew, but they were so grand and distinguished. They really made the entrance. Ellie had never been inside the house, but she had done a virtual tour the last time it had been on the market so knew what lay beyond the studded front door. Maybe one day . . .

Time was marching on and she didn't want to be late for the girls, so she picked her pace back up to get to the playground in time. That was when she saw Sarah Coombes. She had completely forgotten that she lived up here. It had been a couple of months since Margo had told her about Sarah having to pull her children out of Green Mount and it had completely slipped Ellie's mind. Before she realised what she was doing, Ellie had called out to her.

'Sarah! Hi.' She took a couple of steps on to the drive.

Sarah looked round, as jumpy as a cat, her hand flying up to smooth down her hair, which revealed a telltale dark stripe down her parting. Her face was free of make-up and her eyes were encircled by shadowy rings, but when she saw Ellie she gave her a crisp smile.

'Oh, Ellie. Hi. Please don't look at me. I'm such a mess.' She gestured to her clothing and Ellie took in the sagging leggings and bleach-stained sweatshirt. 'We're having a bit of a clear-out. I don't know how we've managed to accumulate so much stuff. And I must make an appointment at the salon. I really don't know where the time goes.' Her smile became wider with each sentence until she looked almost manic. 'And how are you?'

'My dad just died,' said Ellie, blurting the information out before she'd had time to think about it. 'So not that great really.'

Sarah tipped her head to one side and pulled a sympathetic face. 'Oh, I'm so sorry to hear that.'

'It's just a bit of a shock,' replied Ellie. 'I'm not sure I've completely taken it in yet.'

'Had he been ill?' asked Sarah.

Ellie shook her head. She could feel her chest tighten, but she was determined not to cry again.

'An aneurysm, they think. It was very quick.'

'Oh, you poor things. Are the girls coping okay?'

Ellie nodded but now she didn't want to talk about it any more and was regretting she had even mentioned it.

'Listen, Sarah,' she said. 'I'm so sorry I didn't ring . . . when everything happened, I mean. I intended to, but then . . .' She let the unfinished sentence hang between them, not sure how to continue.

'Really, don't worry about it,' replied Sarah brightly. 'It's fine. Honestly. There was nothing you could have done.'

'But still,' said Ellie. 'I am sorry.'

Sarah gave her half a smile that didn't extend beyond her lips.

'And now I need to get going,' Ellie added, looking at her Rolex, then wishing that she hadn't. 'If I'm not careful, I'll be late for pick-up.'

Instantly she felt bad for mentioning the school. Was that insensitive of her, even though Sarah must have known that her children were still there?

'We can't have that,' said Sarah with a forced laugh. 'You'll be getting your knuckles rapped.'

'I will,' agreed Ellie, taking a step back towards the road. 'Let's go out for coffee soon, though, have a proper catch-up.'

'Yes, great idea,' replied Sarah enthusiastically. 'I'll ring you.'

But as Ellie walked back towards Green Mount, she knew Sarah wouldn't be getting in touch.

23

It was nearly a week later when Max rang Nathan. Nathan was at work and his boss wasn't keen on them taking personal phone calls, but as long as his body language suggested business and he kept his voice low there was no way of knowing who he was talking to.

'Nath, it's Max,' he had begun, which irritated Nathan immediately as he must have known that Nathan could see the caller display.

'All right,' replied Nathan.

He was having a bad day. He'd had a couple of big losses on the horses the day before, and he was behind on a job for a particularly demanding client who had taken to ringing every two hours to check on his progress. Nathan wanted to scream down the line that he would make much faster progress if the client just left him to get on with it, but that might prompt a complaint and he couldn't risk that. And now here was Max getting in his way as well.

'I'm just ringing because we've had the post-mortem results,' Max said without preamble.

'Okay,' replied Nathan. 'And?'

'Cerebral aneurysm,' said Max. 'Just as the paramedics thought.'

'So nothing that anyone could have done would have made a difference?'

'Apparently not. They said it could have happened at any time, so I suppose it was lucky he was at home.' Max's voice sounded flat and Nathan wondered if his own displayed the appropriate level of grief. He hadn't had time to grieve. He had been too busy keeping all his plates spinning to even think about it.

'Yeah. Suppose so,' he replied.

'Anyway, just thought I'd let you know.'

'Thanks.'

'Ellie is speaking to the funeral directors. To fix a date.'

'Okay.'

'You okay?'

'Yep. You?'

'Yep. Els will let you know.'

'Okay.'

'Right. That was it. See you later.'

'Yeah. Thanks.'

Max rang off, leaving Nathan holding his phone and staring at the back of the head of the designer who sat in front of him. The fact of his dad's death kept taking him by surprise. It snuck up on him and leapt out when he wasn't ready. He'd always assumed his dad would live forever, or at least for another twenty years or so. You didn't think people would be here one day and gone the next. It wasn't in the normal order of things. It took some processing.

Were aneurysms hereditary? he wondered. Would he suddenly wake up one day and discover he was dead?

A thought was pushing itself to the front of his mind. It wasn't the first time it had been there, but the circumstances had been different before, when his dad was alive. He thought about the money Tony had given him back in February. It had made a massive difference, allowing him to pay off the bookies and still have some left to bet with. And he'd done well. For a few weeks he had had some solid wins, big numbers. This was how he was going to make it work, he'd thought, to prove to his dad that it wasn't a 'mug's game' that he could live on his winnings, and this was his profession. It had been the aim, what he wanted to achieve.

But then a couple of races hadn't gone his way, and then a couple more. He found himself betting wildly without real thought or strategy to try to make up lost ground. And now he was back where he had been, only this time it was worse because he had borrowed a larger amount – the twenty-five thousand that he had lost and more on top.

His dad had said in February that it was the last time he would help him out, but Nathan knew that wasn't true. It was just something he'd said to make giving Nathan the money seem less unpalatable. If his dad had been here now, he could have gone to him again and he would have helped. Nathan knew he would.

The only difference now was that Tony was dead.

Nathan thought about the heavy envelope of cash, how his dad had produced it on no notice when the banks were all closed, and reached the only conclusion he could. There must be money in the house. Tony must have kept a supply for emergencies that only he knew about. But now Nathan knew too.

Before he knew what he was doing, Nathan was on his feet, fishing his wallet out of his desk drawer, flicking off his monitor. But then he caught sight of his boss across the office and he sat back down. He couldn't lose this job; he would never get another one. He turned his monitor back on and tried to concentrate. He would go later. He would find that cash, wherever it was hidden in the house. What he would do with it when he did was a question for a different day.

24

Nathan went straight round to his dad's house after work, planning in his head what he would say if he got there and found one of the others already in situ, but as he pulled his car on to the drive the place was deserted. Rummaging around in the glove compartment, he found the front-door key, re-examined his conscience for less than five seconds, and got out of the car.

Even as he crossed the gravel drive he was thinking of likely hiding places. This house wasn't his childhood home. His parents had bought it after he, Ellie and Max had left, so Nathan didn't know how Tony had lived in the house or where he might have stashed cash. He did know his dad, though. Perhaps he could try to think like him and find the money that way, always assuming there was more. It made sense that there was, Nathan supposed. It seemed unlikely that his dad would have the exact amount he had asked for immediately to hand. He must have taken it from a bigger stash.

Nathan opened the door and let himself in, silencing the burglar alarm by punching in the code – the year his parents had married and never changed after they no longer were.

With the persistent beeping silenced, the house fell eerily quiet. Already the air was stale through lack of circulation and human activity, but despite the emptiness Nathan was jumpy, half-expecting his father to appear from another room and ask just what he thought he was doing sneaking around his house. He wouldn't come, though. He would never come again. Nathan didn't want to think about that. He was aware he had been constantly pushing the fact of his dad's death away until he had more bandwidth available to deal with it, but this was most definitely not the moment to start to grieve.

He tried to focus. If his dad had a stash of cash hidden in his house, where would he have put it? A safe would be the obvious answer, although Nathan hoped it wasn't as he wouldn't have a clue what the code might be. He was pretty sure the house didn't have a safe, though. If it had then Tony would surely have shown him. It was the kind of thing he would have been proud of, especially if it was one of those that was secreted behind a painting like you saw in old films.

He made his way to his dad's study, trying not to creep. There was no one here, but he still felt as if he shouldn't be either. Tony had had grand design ambitions for the space, but had never quite got round to it. It was functional, though. It held a desk, an armchair, a couple of filing cabinets and a bookshelf that held a few books as well as lots of manila folders and piles of plans.

He started with the desk drawers – it was as good a place as any – and he had to swallow down his own disgust at going through his dad's stuff. It felt every kind of wrong. He found nothing significant, however. A red fountain pen sat in the pen tray. The three of them had bought it for their dad's sixtieth birthday, the barrel inscribed with his name. It looked as if it had seen some use, at least. As ever, the pen had been Ellie's idea and seemingly she had been spot on. The lower drawers held mainly stationery, but no cash.

He moved on to the filing cabinets but they just contained files, all neatly labelled and hung in alphabetical order as he would have expected. His dad was a stickler for order in business, always had been.

He gave the shelves a cursory look but there was nothing on them that might contain cash. The study was empty. It wasn't surprising, really. If Tony had been hiding cash in the house, he wouldn't have put it somewhere as obvious as his study. Nathan held on to this thought and tried to move it forward logically, as his father might have done. Cash would be kept somewhere out of the way, somewhere unexpected, but also in a room that didn't have a lot of traffic. The family was big and regularly in and out of the house. It would be easy for someone, especially a grandchild, to open a cupboard and inadvertently discover a treasure trove. Following this thread, Nathan headed up the stairs.

Upstairs was even more poignant than downstairs. The familiar scent of his dad's heavy aftershave still hung in the air along with his brand of washing powder and soap. This was where Max had found him, lying dead and alone on his bed. Nathan thanked God it hadn't been him who had found him, so he wouldn't be haunted by that particular mental image for the rest of his days.

Bracing himself, he peered into his dad's room but it looked just as the same as ever. The bed was made and smooth with no suggestion that a body had recently lain on it. There was a large fitted wardrobe, but when Nathan opened the door it was tidy and ordered, clothes hanging neatly, shoes stacked beneath, with no obvious place for the cash. Nathan thought about the contrast with his own wardrobe, which was pretty much empty because its contents rarely made it in there. Nathan's clothes were either on him or on the floor.

Was there a loft? This was something he had never considered before, but houses like this generally had some roof space. He went back out on to the landing and spotted the telltale rectangle in the ceiling, then he found the hooked stick for the ladder balancing on the lintel of the bathroom. The hatch opened easily enough and he pulled the folding ladder down. It screeched in protest, metal grating against metal, the sound shockingly loud in the quiet of the house.

Nathan climbed up, sticking his head through the hatch. It was dark and the light switch not immediately obvious, so he used the torch on his phone to light up the space. There wasn't much there either. A few cardboard boxes neatly piled, the Christmas lights, including the Santa and reindeer that had made their first, and possibly last, appearance last year. Nothing shouted stash of cash to him.

Losing faith in his plan, Nathan didn't investigate the loft any further but stepped down and pushed the ladder back into place. He was running out of options. Maybe he was wrong and his dad hadn't kept money at home. Perhaps it really was just a coincidence that he'd had exactly the right amount on exactly the day Nathan had asked for it.

But of course it wasn't. The cash was definitely here somewhere. Think, Nathan. What would Dad have done with it?

He pushed open all the doors off the landing one by one until he came to the smallest room. It was nothing more than a box room, really: bland, inconsequential, forgettable. And exactly the place Tony would choose.

Quickly Nathan dropped to his knees and peered under the bed. It didn't look like the other spaces he had explored. There were boxes for gadgets that ordinarily his dad would have kept tidily elsewhere. Immediately Nathan knew they were camouflage, left there to hide whatever else was lurking under the bed.

With a racing heart, Nathan pulled all the boxes out, going further and further under until he hit the back wall. But there was nothing there. The boxes were all empty and there wasn't anything else. Nathan sat back, his shoulders hunched. He would have bet on his own life that there was cash in this house, that it was hidden in this room, but he was wrong. If his dad had been keeping money here, then he had made a bloody good job of hiding it or it had already gone.

Nathan hadn't realised how much he had been counting on finding it until it became apparent there wasn't any to find. Now he just felt sick. It would have been his ticket out of the mess he was in. He could have taken the money and no one would have been any the wiser, because no one else knew it was here.

But now he was up shit creek without a paddle. No cash and no way of repaying his debts until this house was sold, and that could take months, years even. Nathan felt his panic sitting heavily in his stomach. He was all out of options.

25

'When are you proposing to tell the others?' Caroline looked over her shoulder and lowered her voice. 'About the cash, I mean?'

Max was buttering his toast, slathering far too much on for Caroline's liking. She worried about his cholesterol levels, and now that Tony had died so young she could feel herself worrying even more. The butter melted and soaked into the toast and Max lifted his knife to load on some more. Caroline's mouth opened to pass comment and then closed again. This was not the moment.

'I hadn't thought,' he said, adding the butter and taking a huge bite.

She knew that wasn't true. Max would have been thinking about how to deal with the money since the moment she had shown it to him. His apparent reluctance to tell his siblings probably meant he hadn't yet reached a conclusion.

'Now we have the post-mortem results, Ellie says she's going to press on with booking the funeral,' Caroline continued, although Max would know this already.

'Uhuh,' agreed Max through his mouthful.

'So, maybe when we meet to talk about the arrangements?'

Max nodded and Caroline felt frustrated at his lack of urgency, but she knew better than to rush him. Even though every night spent under the same roof as the money was making her increasingly anxious, Max moved at his own pace and trying to make things happen more quickly would only end badly. She swallowed down her thoughts and waited for him to speak.

'I'll talk to Ellie,' he said, irritatingly brief.

'Okay,' replied Caroline. Questions brimmed from her brain, but she wouldn't ask them now. Instead she said, 'I saw her yesterday, actually. She's not sure she wants to take the girls to the funeral, thinks they might be too young.'

She could tell Max was listening but he didn't comment, so she pressed on. 'I said that I thought we were going to take our two. Or at least, ask them if they want to go. What do you think?'

'I think Ellie might be right,' he said. 'They are a bit young.'

Caroline stopped filling Alex's lunch box and blinked slowly.

'Oh!' she said after a beat. 'I just thought you'd want them to be there.'

'Well, we can discuss that when we all get together too,' said Max, popping the end of his toast into his mouth and standing up. He put his plate in the dishwasher and moved towards the door.

'But surely what we do with the boys is for us to decide,' Caroline said. 'It doesn't really matter what Ellie and James do.'

'No harm agreeing, though,' said Max as he left the kitchen. 'It'll be easier if we both do the same.'

Caroline stood stock-still, listening to Max's steady tread as he mounted the stairs to go and get ready for work. Since when did they agree their parenting decisions with Ellie and James? Their boys were their business and whether they took them to their grandfather's funeral would be up to just them. Surely?

She was overthinking this. Of course it would be their decision. Max was probably just thinking about the money and conflating it all into the same conversation. Already she could feel how having the money in the house was skewing the natural order of things. The sooner they got it paid into a bank the better as far as she was concerned. And if they didn't want to do that then one of the others could take responsibility for it. She just wanted it out of her loft.

If it was up to her, she thought as she finished off the boys' packed lunches and lined them up next to their polished school shoes and Theo's book bag, she would speak to Valerie. Even if her mother-in-law didn't know exactly where the money had come from, she would probably have a good idea about the possibilities. She toyed with the idea for a moment or two, tossing it backward and forward in her mind, and then decided against it. It wasn't for her to do that, even though it was the obvious solution. It was more likely that Max hadn't decided what to do, or was waiting to see what the others thought, and that was fair enough. But still . . .

When Max left for work, with the usual cursory peck on her cheek, he didn't mention any of it and so neither did she. Even though his inaction was driving her mad, she was not in control here. This was a Frost family issue and she needed to wait for them to move it forward. As she dropped Theo off at school and then headed into work herself, however, she thought that she might message Ellie to ask if she'd made any progress with the funeral arrangements and see if she could help.

26

Caroline was a receptionist at a primary school about five miles from where they lived. It fitted well with the boys as her hours pretty much matched theirs, and now Theo was ten he could walk home on his own, meaning that they all arrived back at much the same time. Sometimes Caroline hung around at work a bit so the boys would have to let themselves into the house and have a little time on their own before she got there. She did it in a very controlled way, but it gave them a little independence. It was important, she believed, to give children space to learn and grow in confidence. She knew other mothers would probably think differently, particularly as Theo was still at primary school, but the walk home was a safe one and the boys got along well. She had no qualms about leaving them to their own devices, at least for a short while – positively encouraged it, in fact.

She would never forget a conversation they had had at Ellie and James's once, when Theo and Olivia had been around seven. They had been talking about independence. After a few glasses of wine, she'd said that she'd often thought about taking the boys to the woods near their house and leaving them alone to find their own way back. The woods were pretty safe and they went there frequently, so Alex and Theo knew their way around and would have seen it as an adventure and not a trauma.

Ellie, however, had been horrified by the idea, so horrified in fact that she had gone quite pale at the prospect.

'How could you even think about doing something like that?' she asked. 'It's so dangerous.'

'Not that dangerous!' Caroline replied. 'I wouldn't leave them at night or anything. I just think it would be good for them to know what to do if there ever was a time they were on their own. And think how grown-up they'd feel afterwards. It would be a real confidence booster.'

'But the woods,' objected Ellie. 'Anyone could be there.'

Caroline smiled fondly at Ellie. 'How many reports have you heard of anything happening to anyone in those woods? They're more likely to be hurt in the playground at school.'

Ellie shook her head vigorously, the movement exaggerated because of the wine she had drunk. 'Well, there's no way I'd abandon my precious girls in those woods. No way.'

Caroline had been cross then. It was as if Ellie was saying she didn't think her boys were precious, that they were dispensable in some way, less valuable to her than the girls were to Ellie, which was obviously rubbish. She had wanted to say that by keeping her children cosseted as she did, Ellie was doing them no favours. Secretly she thought that Olivia, in particular, was developing some rather brattish qualities already, but no amount of wine would have squeezed that truth out of her. She loved Ellie too much and she firmly believed that all mothers were doing their best, no matter how flawed their decisions seemed to be to other people.

The difference in their parenting styles became more apparent the older their children became. Alex and Theo walked home from school alone each afternoon, and seemed to relish the freedom. By contrast, Ellie was always at the playground gate with the car to collect Olivia and Lucy. Granted, Green Mount was a bit more of a walk, but they could have done it by themselves if Ellie had only loosened the apron strings a little.

Then again, Lucy was only eight and Theo hadn't been walking home on his own at that age. Caroline should lighten up a bit. Ellie's opinions could be a bit overbearing, but she wasn't so very different a mother, not really.

When Caroline got to school, she made her way to the office. Children thronged everywhere, like so many little minions in their blue sweatshirts. The youngest ones were so tiny, she thought wistfully. It seemed only two minutes since her boys had been that size. They were growing so fast, the days just racing by.

Her co-worker, Joanne, was already there, working her way through a pile of permission slips and ticking them off on a list.

'Morning,' said Joanne cheerfully, looking up from her list and giving Caroline a broad smile. 'Another day in the mad house!'

She said this most mornings, even though the school almost never resembled anything even close to bedlam.

'Hi,' replied Caroline, slipping off her jacket and hanging it on the hatstand in the corner. 'Anything I need to know this morning?'

'Not yet. Carly has called in sick but she looked so dreadful yesterday that it's not surprising. Mark is going to cover the class with Janine assisting so it's pretty much covered. Nothing else to report.'

The telephone rang and Caroline bent to answer it, sitting down at her desk as she did so.

'Good morning, St Peter's Primary. How can I help you? . . . Oh, I am sorry to hear that. And which class is Ruby in?'

And thus the day began.

Caroline hadn't mentioned Tony's death to her colleagues at school. It wasn't that she had avoided it on purpose, but for the first week she had been quietly processing what had happened, and by the time they'd got to the end of the second week, it felt a little like old news and she worried they would think it odd she hadn't told them earlier. It appeared, however, that the news was out.

'I'm so sorry to hear about your father-in-law's passing,' said the head that lunchtime. He adopted his pseudo-sympathetic face, the one he used for parents concerned about their child's progress. Ears pricked up around the staff room. A death was something new to discuss.

'Thank you,' said Caroline graciously. 'It was very unexpected and a bit of a shock.'

Lesley Hungerford, Year Two teacher and never one to hold back, leant forward in her chair. 'What's this?' she asked.

'My father-in-law died last weekend of a cerebral aneurysm. Max found him,' she said and then listened to the collective gasps.

'Oh, how awful,' said Lesley. 'He was Tony Frost, wasn't he? The council bloke.'

It amused her to hear Tony reduced to such an epitaph – 'the council bloke'.

'Yes, that's right,' she replied.

'He always seemed so full of life when he was mayor,' continued Lesley. 'His picture was never out of the local paper. He was in there most weeks, in fact.'

'Yes,' replied Caroline.

'Seemed to have his fingers in a lot of pies,' Lesley continued. There was something slightly salacious about her tone that Caroline didn't like.

'Yes, he was very busy,' she said, turning her back on Lesley and focusing instead on the kettle.

'Well, please pass on our condolences to your husband and his family,' said the head, and then, as if his pastoral duty was fulfilled, he floated away.

'Wasn't there some rumour about him?' Lesley continued.

Caroline didn't respond, reaching for a mug from the cupboard and a teabag from the caddy.

'I heard that he'd been involved in something . . . now, what was it?' Lesley fell silent for a moment whilst she apparently wracked her brains, and Caroline wished she would just be quiet. Not only did she not want her private family business discussed in the staff room, but it was also so insensitive and disrespectful to be raking over rumours when Tony was barely cold.

'I know!' said Lesley. 'It was that new shopping centre, the out-of-town one. It didn't have planning permission, and then suddenly it did, or something. Wasn't there some suggestion that one of the planners was in league with the developer? Not Tony, of course,' she added quickly with an expression that suggested exactly this suspicion. 'It was just that it happened on his watch.'

Caroline shook her head dismissively. 'I don't know. I don't know anything about it, but I think it sounds unlikely. Tony was a highly respected councillor. He wouldn't have been elected so many times if he hadn't been. And actually, Lesley,' she continued, turning to face her adversary, her expression steely – 'I'm not sure how appropriate it is to be suggesting anything untoward. Not only was he my much-loved father-in-law but it's also been a huge shock for all of us. I'd much rather you kept your rumours to yourself.'

With that, Caroline turned on her heel and left the room, abandoning her cup of tea in the process. She could feel her blood boiling in her veins as she returned to the office, the heat building in her body. She'd never liked Lesley, she was a nasty piece of work – anything for a reaction, that was her motto. But Caroline had probably just played straight into her hands, and in front of other people too. There's no smoke without fire, she'd be saying now, or words to that effect, and the same thought would be tracking through the minds of all the other witnesses to the exchange. People really didn't have any idea of the damage that such careless accusations could do. Caroline, however, knew only too well.

She collapsed into her chair, her heart thundering in her chest as her pulse rose. She closed her eyes and sucked in a breath through her mouth until she felt herself calm a little. She had met people like Lesley before. They were so quick to have a go; all they needed was a tiny little slit in someone's armour and they'd be in there, jabbing and twisting until something was done or said that confirmed their suspicions.

That was how it had been with her dad. It had never been proved that he had stolen money from the fund he was in charge of, but in the end that hadn't mattered. The money was missing, and he was put firmly in the frame for it. Eventually no one cared what had happened; they just wanted someone to blame.

There had been an accident at the football club where her dad had been a coach. A boy a few years older than Caroline and former star of the club had broken his neck diving into the river and the club had been raising money to buy him a state-of-the-art wheelchair. They had raised thousands of pounds and were nearly at the target when the theft was discovered. The money had gone from the account that her father had joint control of.

Caroline had been too young to really understand the vitriol that followed. All she knew was that girls who had been her friends were now turning their backs on her in the playground and calling nasty names after her in the street. She understood later that her mother had endured far worse. The injured boy's family had begun a concentrated hate campaign against them, and it got so bad that Caroline and her mother hadn't dared leave the house. They sheltered indoors, curtains closed, whilst the mob outside chanted threatening slogans. Next came bricks through the windows and worse through the letterbox. Her father had abandoned them, unable to cope with either the taunting or the guilt – Caroline never knew which – and in the end Caroline and her mother had been forced to relocate to a new area where no one knew them. Her mother had never recovered. She had gone from being happy and fun-loving to a woman afraid of her own shadow. Three lives destroyed by gossip and rumour.

Lesley might have thought what she was saying was harmless, but Caroline knew better. And Tony wasn't even here to defend himself, because that's what he'd have done, Caroline knew. He was always telling them the rumours that he'd heard about himself, dismissing them as sour grapes or just laughing them off as ludicrous.

'That's the trouble with public office,' he'd said. 'Everyone will have a pop, even those who have nothing to do with the situation and know even less. All they see is the final decision. That's what they question. What they don't see is the hours of work that go on behind the scenes, the toing and froing between the planners and the developers, the public consultations, the discussions in the chamber. It can take us weeks to reach the right decision and it can get quite heated. But that's because the decisions we're making are important. They affect people's lives. We have to get it right. But of course, Joe Public doesn't know any of that. They just read the final outcome in the paper and automatically assume there's been something dodgy going on. We just have to rise above it all and keep our mouths shut. It's never easy.'

Caroline wished Tony was here right now so he could make that same speech in the staff room. She should probably have tried saying something similar herself instead of just running away. It was too late now, though. If she tried, it would just look like she was protesting too much and that there was definitely something to cover up. God, she hated Lesley Hungerford.

The bell rang and people began to emerge from the staff room to go to their classrooms. Caroline lowered her head and pretended to be concentrating on the papers on her desk, but she could feel their eyes on the back of her neck as they each walked past. Or maybe she was just imagining it. Having been the brunt of gossip and rumour could do that to you. Then she felt someone standing close by her and she looked up. It was Joanne. She put a cup of tea down on the desk next to Caroline.

'Take no notice,' she said quietly. 'The woman's a bitch. She just likes causing trouble.'

Caroline smiled weakly and whispered a thank you.

'He was a good man,' she said, feeling hot tears spring into her eyes and wiping them away with the back of her knuckles.

'Of course he was,' replied Joanne emphatically, and then went back to her own desk. The trouble was, Caroline wasn't entirely sure she believed that any more.

27

Ellie had been so pleased with her new table settings that as soon as she'd returned home after picking the girls up, she had unwrapped them from their tissue paper and admired them all individually. She had even laid a portion of the table just so she could imagine the finished look. She was right about that wall colour, though. The dark red really didn't go with the silver and was actually looking quite dated now. It had been all the rage when she'd had it done, but things had moved on to crisper, cooler colours. She would give her decorator a ring and get him booked in. She might get him to do the hall whilst he was at it, and the downstairs cloakroom. It was important to make a good impression on any visitors and those were the parts of the house they generally saw.

It had been a while since she and James had hosted a dinner party, now she came to think about it, other than Caro and Max coming round, which didn't really count. Ellie ran through a list in her head of the places where she and James had eaten recently and who they owed. Most of the dinners had been return invitations, but there'd been a new couple at Laura and Mark's who they'd got on well with. Maybe she would ask them, with Laura and Mark, of course, and try to build up a bit of a friendship. What had they been called? Sara, that was the woman and . . . Ellie struggled to bring the name of the husband into her mind. She'd always been so good with names. What was happening to her? It began with a C, she was almost certain, something a bit unusual. Charles? Claude? No, Clive, that was it. Sara and Clive. Yes, she'd ring the decorator, and then fix a return date with the four of them after the rooms had been freshened up.

Ellie smiled to herself, pleased with her new plan. She began to dismantle the table setting and then, after a little bit of shuffling around, made room for the new items in the sideboard, except for the candelabra. She left those on the table where she could admire them.

She must also have left the receipt out. She had a little wooden box in which she kept all her receipts in case she needed them again, clearing it out every few months so it didn't become over full, but on this occasion, she'd put the receipt to one side and then forgotten to pick it up. So when James stormed into the kitchen brandishing it above his head, she was thrown for a minute.

'What the hell is this?' he said, thrusting the receipt under her nose and then pulling it away again before her eyes had a chance to register what they'd seen.

'I don't know, James. Let me have a proper look.'

But James was reading from it now, his voice rising as he listed each item. 'Eight chargers. Eight tea-light holders. Table runner. Two candelabra. Two hundred and thirty-eight pounds.'

Ellie was taken aback, not quite sure why James was angry nor what she was supposed to say.

'What about them?' she asked. 'I thought the dining room needed a spruce-up so I bought a few bits and pieces. It's only two hundred and fifty quid, James. I spend almost that much in the supermarket each week. I'll show you what I bought if you like. You'll like them. And I was thinking that we could change the colour of . . .'

'It's all just crap, Ellie,' he snapped. 'Tatty crap. And we don't need any of it. There's nothing wrong with the dining room the way it is.'

'Well, no,' Ellie conceded. 'But it is looking a bit tired and I know how you like the place to look good when we invite your business contacts round.' She could feel her cheeks flare. She wasn't used to being shouted at, especially not for something like this. James loved how beautifully she kept the house; he was always saying so.

'I'm sorry,' she said quietly. 'I thought you'd be pleased.' She thought she might cry, the shock at his anger releasing sudden emotion. Her eyes brimmed with tears and she blinked hard.

'Pleased that you insist on spending above our means?' spat James.

His nostrils were flaring as they did when he lost his temper and Ellie found herself momentarily distracted by that. When had James last lost his temper? She couldn't remember. It had been a while.

'Money doesn't grow on trees, you know,' he continued. 'We can't just print some more when we need it.'

'Yes, I realise that,' she said. She wasn't stupid and she hated it when he talked down to her, as though things were too complicated for her to grasp.

'And don't get me started on how much this party of yours is costing,' he said, folding his arms across his chest and glaring at her. 'I swear several minor royals could get married for less than our credit card bill last month. Honestly, Els, you just don't get the concept of moderation, do you?'

'Now hang on,' replied Ellie indignantly. 'You're hardly one to talk. It's not two minutes ago that you bought that car. There was nothing wrong with the old one.'

'That's work. It's different,' replied James, his tone verging on the petulant.

Ellie didn't see how. It was all money. But she had made her point and she knew she would be on a hiding to nothing pushing it any further. At the end of the day, James could always trump her in this argument, because any money that she had was earned by James, and whilst he said over and over that it was one pot and that she contributed to the household in a non-financial way, they couldn't avoid the truth that she never paid in to their account, only drew out.

'I'm going out,' said James before she'd had time to think where to take the argument next. He was already stalking towards the door. He snatched the car keys from the countertop. 'I'll be late for dinner.'

And then he was gone, door slamming behind him.

Ellie burst into tears. It was the shock of being spoken to like that rather than anything he had said. How dare he have a go? If he didn't like the way she behaved he should talk to her about it reasonably, not fly off the handle at the drop of a hat. What if the girls had seen him shouting at her? How would she explain Mummy and Daddy arguing to a pair of impressionable children? Olivia had already asked her if they were going to get a divorce when she and James had had a tiny spat over something so trivial that she couldn't even bring it to mind now. How would they react to an actual argument? It might damage them forever. Ellie knew this was unlikely, but she was angry with James so she let her fury burn itself out along this unlikely path for a while whilst she calmed down.

Then she rang Caroline. It was an automatic reaction, but as the phone rang out and Caroline's answerphone message played in her ear, she realised that she couldn't talk to Caroline about it. Even though she told her everything and had done for as long as she could remember, this was different. Private. Ellie wasn't sure why, but something was telling her that she should keep this to herself.

◆ ◆ ◆

James came back when she was emptying the dishwasher. The girls were already bathed and in bed. She had concocted a story about a meeting to cover James's absence, but that wasn't so unusual and they had just accepted it without question.

He came straight over to her and put his arms around her, pulling her into a tight squeeze, and Ellie breathed in the familiar smell of him. She loved that their bodies seemed to know exactly how to align with one another. Even when the chips were down, they fitted together, two becoming one. She felt his arms pull her in even closer, as if he were trying to absorb her into him.

'I'm sorry, Els,' he said into her hair. 'I had no right to speak to you like that. It was a total overreaction to something so trivial. I'm sure the things you bought are great. And I love that you keep the house so beautifully for us. It's a big job and you do it really well.'

Ellie nodded her head against his chest, accepting his apology at once. But there was more here, she could feel it.

'Thank you,' she said. 'But I don't understand what the issue was.'

James released her from the hug and pushed her gently away from him so she was at arm's length.

'I'm just a bit stressed, that's all,' he said. 'It's not going that well this month. There's nothing for you to worry about, but a couple of deals I had thought were bolted on have collapsed. I can probably get them back but it'll just take a bit longer than I expected. I guess it's just on my mind, so when I saw the receipt . . . Anyway, I'm sorry.'

He did look sorry, Ellie thought, but mainly he looked tired. The plum-coloured semicircles beneath his eyes were darker than usual and his skin was sallow. He really needed a holiday. They should get a last-minute deal booked like they'd discussed, but this probably wasn't the moment to suggest that.

'I can take the things back,' she said. 'It's no trouble.'

'Don't be silly,' he said. 'It's only a couple of hundred quid. And I bet they'll look lovely.'

Ellie nodded enthusiastically. 'They will. You'll really like them. Did you see the candelabra? They are on the table in the dining room. I thought we could change the colour in there from the red to a nice rich blue. What do you think? It's on my list to ring the decorator.'

James nodded, taking it all in, but he said, 'Let's put that on hold for now, just until I know where we are with these deals. We can do it next month instead.'

'Okay,' replied Ellie. 'And I can keep the table settings?'

'Of course,' he said gently.

28

It was Friday and the Frost family were finally getting together to make decisions about the funeral. Caroline suggested they order food in, and Ellie was happy to go along with that. Their boys were at a sleepover, so Ellie fed Olivia and Lucy before Caro and Max arrived, giving them pizza from the supermarket and trying to pretend it was just as good as a takeaway one. Olivia moaned that they were missing out, but Ellie wasn't in the mood and slapped down her complaints.

When Caroline and Max arrived, Caroline was bearing a plate covered with tinfoil.

'I know we said takeaway, but I thought we might want something sweet afterwards,' she explained, offering the plate to Ellie.

Ellie lifted the foil and took a peek. A delicious warm chocolatey smell flooded her nostrils.

'Your amazing brownies. My favourite. That's so thoughtful. Thanks, Caro.' She leant over and gave her friend a peck on her cheek and Caroline responded with a modest smile.

'I thought we could all do with a little bit of comfort food,' she said. 'Is Nathan here yet?'

'Not coming,' said James, who appeared from his office.

'What?' said Max, passing Ellie a bottle of wine and hugging her in one smooth movement. 'Typical. What's his excuse?'

'Caught up with something he can't get out of, apparently,' replied James, his face suggesting that he didn't believe a word of it.

'It doesn't matter,' said Ellie quickly. 'He's not interested in the details anyway and too many cooks and all that.'

Max squeezed his lips together and let out an audible breath through his nose. 'I've got something else we need to talk about,' he said. 'Something we should all be here for.'

Ellie saw Caroline shoot him a look, eyebrows knotted.

'We have to tell them tonight,' Max said to her and Caroline signalled her agreement with a single tight nod.

'How mysterious you're being, Max,' said James, cocking an eyebrow. 'All very cloak and dagger. Well, maybe we can ring him later. See if we can get him on a video call.'

Ellie thought that sounded like a ridiculous idea. If Nathan was caught up with something else this evening, how likely was it that he would answer his phone? Especially for a video call. However, the others seemed to think it was sensible, so she bit her tongue.

The doorbell rang.

'That'll be dinner,' she said and went to answer it with Caroline following in her wake. They took the food through to the kitchen to dish up.

'I thought we'd eat in here tonight,' said Ellie. 'It's cosier.'

She also didn't want to be reminded of James's outburst over her decor, but it was, in any event, much more relaxed sitting at the round table in the kitchen. It was already set and Caroline filled the water jug and started to dish the starters out. James and Max arrived from the lounge, drawn in by the spicy aromas, and everyone took a seat and started to help themselves.

Once they were all settled, Ellie said, 'So, the coroner's office is happy for us to go ahead with the funeral. I spoke to them this morning but they're a bit busy. The funeral director has suggested a week on Friday after next – two weeks today.'

'But that's . . .' began Caroline, concern written in the lines on her forehead.

'My birthday, yes,' said Ellie.

Her fortieth birthday. The most anticipated event of her year – of the last couple of years, in fact – and to which she had been building up steadily for months. And now it was also the proposed date for her father's funeral.

'Well, we obviously can't have it then,' continued Caroline. 'Have they got any other dates?'

'Not really,' said Ellie. 'Their next free date is the Friday after that, but that's too far away. It will have been nearly a month as it is.' She gave a resigned little shrug. 'Anyway, I've thought about it, and I've decided that the greatest amount of good will be achieved if we go with that date. It's only a birthday . . .'

'Your fortieth birthday,' chipped in Caroline, sounding indignant on her behalf, and Ellie felt immensely grateful.

'And the party's on the Saturday,' Ellie continued. 'It'll be fine.'

'But Els—' objected Caroline.

'I wasn't going to do that much on the actual day anyway,' Ellie said, speaking over her. 'James is working and the girls will be at school. It's fine, Caro. Honestly.'

It wasn't fine. She had planned a long day of shopping and a manicure and pedicure ready for the party, but since James's little outburst the idea wasn't quite as twinkly as it had been, so when she'd spoken to the undertakers and they had suggested her birthday it hadn't taken that long to get her head around it. She would do it for her dad, she thought. He would have appreciated the gesture.

'Well, if you're sure,' said Caroline doubtfully.

Ellie nodded bravely and pressed on. 'So, we need to decide where to have the bun fight afterwards. I was thinking the golf club would be the obvious choice . . .'

◆ ◆ ◆

They had polished off the starters and most of the main course by the time they had a plan agreed, including a clear list of who was going to do what. Ellie had been making notes as they went and now she read through them so that everyone was sure of their responsibilities. The organising fell, in the main, to her and Caroline.

'Good decision of Nath's to be missing,' said James in a tone that might have been interpreted as jokey but which Ellie knew probably wasn't. She was sure Caro and Max would have picked that up too. There had never been much love lost between James and her younger brother. Nathan was too directionless for James's tastes, too much of a drifter.

'It doesn't matter that he's not here,' she said. 'If there are too many people involved it'll get too complicated. It's better that it's just me and Caro really.'

They sat back, relieved that the main task of the evening had been completed without too much difficulty.

James picked at the naan bread and then wiped up the remains of the sauce from his plate. 'So, what is it you want to talk about, Max?'

Max shifted in his seat. 'We need Nathan to be here really.'

'I'll ring him,' said James, picking his phone up from the table and starting to scroll through. 'Better still, let's use Olivia's iPad. Then we can all see him. Hang on.'

He stood up and left the room, appearing moments later with an iPad in his hand. 'Right. Just let me . . . Ah. There we go. And what's the number? Can someone read it to me?'

Max read the number from James's phone and James typed it into the iPad.

'Video call? Yes?' he checked, and then hit the button. They all listened as the iPad tried to connect with Nathan's phone and then Nathan himself appeared, looking slightly confused. He wouldn't have recognised the number, Ellie realised.

'Nath,' James began. 'Good evening to you. We thought that if the mountain wouldn't come to Mohammed and all that.' James swept a glance around the table and gave them all a grin, clearly pleased with himself.

Nathan looked thrown. 'Okay, hi. Is there a problem?'

'No, no. Nothing like that. We've just been arranging your dad's funeral. A week on Friday, by the way. Trust that's okay. But Max has something that he wants to say.'

Nathan's forehead creased and he rolled his eyes. 'It's not a great moment, to be honest, James,' he said. 'I told you I was busy this evening.'

Ellie began to focus on the background of where her brother was. He was outside, and wherever it was was very busy with lots of men all standing facing the same direction.

Nathan snatched a hurried look over his shoulder as if he was expecting someone to appear. 'I can't hear you. It's really loud here. You just go ahead without me. Max can fill me in on whatever it is tomorrow. I'm sorry but have to go now. Bye.'

He cancelled the call but not before the sound of a tannoy announcing the next race filled the kitchen. The screen went black.

'Well,' said James crisply, flicking the cover back over the iPad with a snap. 'And there you have it. The true reason why Nathan is too busy to help with his own father's funeral. He's out enjoying himself.'

'Oh, it doesn't matter,' said Ellie, although she felt like it did. 'It was probably a prearranged thing for work. I'm sure he'd have been here if he could have.'

Nobody spoke.

'Anyway, what is it you wanted to say, Max?'

Max took a moment to consider this proposal, running a hand through his hair and looking at Caroline, who nodded supportively.

'Okay,' he agreed. 'Right. So, here's the thing. We were at Dad's house the day after he died. We went to collect Monty, remember?'

'Oh, how is he?' interrupted Ellie. 'Is he settling in at yours okay? I heard once that if you put butter on their paws—'

Max cut across her. 'He's fine. Anyway, Caro was in the back bedroom trying to coax him out from under the bed and she found a suitcase. And when she opened it, it had cash in it.'

Ellie grinned. 'How like Dad to have a bit hidden in the house in case of an emergency. Was there much there?'

Max paused, smacked his lips for a moment. 'Yes. That's the thing. There was over a quarter of a million pounds. In twenty-pound notes.'

Silence.

The only sound was the distant buzz of the television elsewhere in the house as they absorbed what Max had just told them.

James spoke first. 'Bloody hell.'

Ellie's eyes flicked from Max to Caroline and then back to Max. 'What?' she said, although she had heard what had been said clearly enough. 'I mean, why?'

'I've no idea. Caroline just found it. That's all I know.'

'And where is it now?' asked James.

'At our house. In the loft,' replied Caroline. 'It didn't feel safe to leave it in the empty house.'

'And you found this when?' asked James.

Max cleared his throat, one hand rubbing at the back of his neck. 'The day after Dad died,' he said, without meeting James's eye.

'So, nearly two weeks ago,' said James. 'And you're only telling us this now.'

His tone wasn't exactly accusatory, but Ellie could see which way it might head if he didn't like Max's answer.

'Well, we thought we'd wait until we were all together,' said Max. 'And here we are.'

'Except for Nathan,' Caroline chipped in.

'Yes, except for Nathan—'

'I don't understand,' said Ellie, cutting James off before he could get any further down that track. 'Why was it there? Where did it come from?'

'We haven't got a clue,' replied Max.

'I thought maybe your mum might know,' said Caroline.

'Maybe, but I doubt it,' said Ellie. 'They've been divorced for years. It can't have been sitting there all that time, surely?'

'So what are we going to do with it?' asked James.

'Well, pay it into the bank for a start,' said Caroline. 'I'm sure it's safe, but it's a lot of money to have just sitting in the house.'

James put his hand up. 'Hold your horses,' he said. 'Let's just leave it where it is for now. And maybe we can talk to Valerie. See if she can cast any light on it. She might have an idea, and we don't want to go setting any hares running unnecessarily. Is that okay with you, Max?'

Max nodded. 'That's fine by me. God knows how long it's been under Dad's bed already. A little bit longer isn't going to hurt.'

Ellie noticed Caroline throw him a frustrated look, but he seemed to avoid meeting her eye.

'A quarter of a million big ones,' said James, shaking his head in disbelief. 'Who'd have thought it, eh? Good job you found it too! Can you imagine if it had just sat there until we sold the house?'

Ellie saw Max flinch when James said 'we' but that was unfair. James was her husband. He was just as much a part of this family as she was.

'We need to tell Nathan,' Caroline said. 'You can do that, can't you, Max?'

Ellie eyed Max, wondering how much he was aware of. Max wouldn't know that she and James had lent Nathan money. James was unlikely to have said anything and she certainly hadn't. Nathan was hopeless with money. Max knew that, but he wouldn't have approved of just lending Nathan more rather than encouraging him to be more frugal. And there was no way Nathan would have approached Max and Caroline for a loan. They always said they only had enough for their own needs. There was never anything spare for errant brothers, as far as she could gather.

'Well, we all know how money seems to flow through Nathan's fingers,' said Max.

So maybe he does know, thought Ellie.

'Bearing that in mind,' Max continued, 'I suggest we don't say anything to him just yet. Let's do a bit of discreet digging, see if we can work out why the cash might have been there, and then, when we have a little bit more information, we can tell Nath. It'll keep until then.'

James nodded but Ellie wasn't sure.

And Caroline seemed to have doubts too. 'That doesn't feel right to me,' she said. 'He has just as much right to know as you two. And what do you think he'll do? Break into our place under cover of darkness to try and steal it?'

Nobody spoke. Ellie and Max exchanged a look. That was exactly what they thought. Caroline must have picked up on this because she continued, 'All right. Whatever you think. He's your brother. But I'm not sure it's right to keep him out of the loop like this.'

Max reached a hand out and tapped her gently on her knee. Ellie wasn't sure if the gesture meant 'I hear what you say' or 'stop talking'.

'We'll talk to Mum first,' he said. 'It won't hurt Nath not to know for a few days. And we'll tell him just as soon as we know what we're dealing with. Right. Does everyone agree?'

Ellie nodded straight away. James still looked shell-shocked, his mouth partially open as if this news about the money was all too much to take in. Caroline dropped her eyes to the table and shrugged, but then she nodded reluctantly.

'Good. So you and me will go to Mum's this weekend, Els. We'll need to fill her in on the funeral arrangements anyway.'

'I'll ring her first thing and fix something up,' said Ellie.

The funeral clashing with her birthday suddenly felt of very little importance in light of this new information. There was a moment whilst they thought about the bombshell Max had just dropped, each seemingly caught in their own imaginations, and then Ellie shook her head, as if to expel all dreams about the money.

'Who wants one of Caro's excellent brownies?' she asked. 'I've got some ice cream and there might even be cream in the fridge.'

Later, when everyone had left, she and James were getting ready for bed. James had barely said two words since Max and Caro had left, and he still seemed lost in his own thoughts. She could understand that. It was a lot to take in. She was struggling with it a bit herself. She wished he would say something though. She wanted to chat it through.

'So, what did you make of all that?' she asked eventually, when it became obvious he wasn't going to raise the subject himself.

He sat down on the end of the bed and ran his hands through his hair. 'It's hard to know what to think. A sweet quarter of a million pounds.' He whistled.

'Over a quarter of a million,' corrected Ellie. 'That's what Max said, wasn't it?'

James looked at her, his forehead creased and eyes narrowed. 'That's right. He didn't say exactly how much it was, did he?' His hand went to his temples and he massaged them with the tips of his fingers, seemingly releasing the tension.

'If we don't know exactly how much they found, what is there to stop Max and Caroline from just skimming a little off the top?' he said quietly.

'They wouldn't do that,' said Ellie, horrified by the mere thought. 'Why would they? We're family.'

James shrugged. Ellie wasn't sure what he meant. Was he saying that he wouldn't be surprised if her brother and his wife did exactly that? Or was it rather that that was what he would do if he was in their shoes? Ellie didn't think she liked either suggestion.

29

Caroline's summertime Saturday mornings were so much more pleasant than the winter ones. When the boys were younger, she had encouraged them to go to cricket training once the football season was over, but they had never really taken to it. Now she thanked her stars for that small mercy. It was such a treat to have a leisurely start to the morning after the hustle and bustle of the week.

Alex and Theo had been up for hours, of course. She'd heard from parents of older boys that they'd get to an age when she'd be tipping them out of their beds at midday, but they certainly weren't there yet. The boys were quite self-sufficient though, could get their own breakfasts and find things to do – granted, mainly screen-based – whilst she had a gentle potter about.

Max had gone for a run and she was meandering around the house collecting discarded items and returning them to their correct homes. Today she did the task without mental complaint because her mind was fully occupied with thinking about the evening just gone.

She'd had butterflies before they'd arrived at Ellie's, nervous about telling the others about the suitcase and its contents. She hadn't been sure why she was so apprehensive, but then James zoomed straight in on how long she and Max had known about the money without saying anything to the rest of them, and she'd known at once what had been making her uncomfortable. Even though Max had given a perfectly reasonable explanation for their temporary silence, she could see that it sounded odd.

She tried to imagine what the others would have done if they had found the case, but she wasn't sure she could answer that. Ellie would have been straight on the phone to her, she was almost certain. She was always so transparent about everything, there was no way she would have been able to keep the news to herself. James she was less sure of. He had seemed annoyed by the delay, but Caroline was almost certain that he would have done the same thing in their shoes.

James, Ellie and Max had all been in no doubt that they shouldn't tell Nathan straight away, though. That felt wrong to Caroline. He had just as much right to know, and what did they think he was going to do anyway? The money was in their loft. It wasn't as if he could get his hands on it.

That was why Caroline wanted to pay it into a bank account that all three Frost siblings were signatories to. That way, it would be safe from thieves and they could each be party to whatever happened to it.

Although, wasn't that what trust was for? Caroline had known the Frost siblings for almost her entire life and she would swear they were all basically honest and wouldn't do anything that went against the best interests of one of the others. So if Max and Ellie thought it would be better for Nathan if he didn't know about the money just yet, she should probably just trust their judgement, even though it felt wrong to her.

She picked up five pairs of underpants and two school shirts from Alex's bedroom floor without examining them too closely and dropped them into the washing basket. She would have to remind him to wear a clean shirt every day. At least he seemed to change his boxers regularly, which was a blessing.

The front door banged shut. That must be Max coming in, she thought. She went downstairs and found him in the kitchen standing at the open fridge drinking orange juice straight from the carton. When he saw her, he looked exactly as guilty as Alex or Theo would have done if they had been caught doing the same.

'Sorry!' he said, took one more gulp and then put the carton back in the fridge door.

'Good run?' she asked.

He nodded, smiled. Max ran three or four times a week. He said it helped him clear his head. Caroline wondered if today it had been filled with the same thoughts that hers had been.

She began moving the abandoned breakfast bowls and cereal packets.

'It's such a shame about Ellie's birthday,' she said as she worked. 'I know how much she's been looking forward to it.'

Max shrugged. 'It's just a day like any other. And she didn't seem to mind that much.'

'I thought she was doing a good job of covering it up,' Caroline said. 'I'd have been pretty upset if I had to have my dad's funeral on my fortieth birthday.'

'She's still got the party,' said Max, sitting down to unlace his trainers.

'That's true. I imagine we'll all be ready to let our hair down by then.'

Caroline watched Max. Sweat was dripping from his forehead on to the floor as he bent to fiddle with his shoes. She resisted the urge to swoop in with a cloth and wipe it away.

'I thought there was almost a moment with James last night,' she continued.

'James should learn to wind his neck in sometimes,' replied Max. 'The money is nothing to do with him.'

Caroline wasn't sure she agreed entirely with that. James was married to Ellie, after all, but she could read Max and didn't need to comment. Whilst she wanted to go over the evening yet again, she didn't want to cause a row.

'Have you heard from Ellie about going to your mum's?' she asked.

Max looked up at the big clock above the door. 'It's only quarter past ten, Caro! I'm not sure there's been time.'

'I could come with you,' she said tentatively. Asking Valerie about the money had been her idea in the first place and she wanted to hear what she had to say, even though she could get all the details afterwards from either Ellie or Max, probably both; but Max shook his head.

'I think it should just be the two of us,' he said. 'If you come then we'll have to take James too, and I'm not sure how helpful that will be.'

There had been a tension between James and her mother-in-law from day one, Caroline thought, although Valerie had done her best to disguise it by keeping quiet in his presence and letting Tony do most of the talking. That was quite natural. Ellie was her daughter and what could be more normal than for the men to gravitate together whilst mother and daughter caught up on each other's news? Caroline had noticed, though. She knew both women well enough to pick up the vibe: dislike from Valerie and a kind of regret from Ellie that she couldn't get her mum to see what she saw in the man she had chosen to spend her life with. Looking back, Caroline wondered whether James was just too like Tony for Valerie's liking.

Max was probably right, though. It would be better if it was just the two of them. Valerie was more likely to be open with her children if they were alone.

'Yes,' she said. 'I see your point. Right, why don't you have your shower and then we can pop to the garden centre. I need some more bedding plants for the pots at the front before they sell out.'

She knew Max would rather stay at home with the boys, but Caroline made a point of making them all go out together at least once at the weekend.

'We can take the ball and have a kick about in the park on the way home,' she said. 'And Theo likes looking at the tropical fish. They won't mind.'

'Just as long as he doesn't spend all morning trying to persuade us to buy some like he did last time.'

'I'm not sure we could have fish now we have Monty,' said Caroline. 'Wouldn't he try to eat them?'

As if hearing his name, Monty appeared from the hallway, his ears pricked, and began to rub himself against the table leg. Caroline knelt down stealthily and, making eye contact with the cat, held a hand out to him. Monty inched forward until he was within touching distance and then allowed her to rub him gently on the top of his head and around his ears.

'He seems to be settling in,' said Max, his movement across the room making Monty start and slink quickly away.

'He's still a bit wary,' replied Caroline. 'Like he's not quite sure what's happening.'

'I know how he feels,' said Max with a laugh.

30

Later that day Max and the boys were happily tucked up on the sofa watching a film they had seen hundreds of times but never seemed to tire of. Caroline was surplus to requirements and so she took herself off to the kitchen and fired up the laptop. Ever since Lesley Hungerford's unkind comments about Tony in the staff room, she had been curious to know exactly what she'd meant.

She googled the name of the shopping centre Lesley had mentioned but that only brought up details of opening hours and which shops were there. She tried again, this time framing her search around the news reports. Again, there wasn't much. Various stories tracked the progress of the centre from the initial proposal to its opening, but nothing suggested anything untoward had gone on. A couple of the stories had photographs attached and in one she saw a healthily tanned Tony shaking hands with a man in a hard hat and smiling broadly at the camera. The image of his face there on the laptop, so large and lifelike, pulled her up short and she had to catch her breath a moment before she could carry on. His death was still shocking and seeing him there, looking so very alive, brought tears to her eyes and a lump to her throat.

There was nothing in the stories that suggested the kind of unethical behaviour Lesley had hinted at. Stupid woman, thought

Caroline, cross with herself that she had allowed Lesley's nastiness to get under her skin.

But then she thought about the suitcase full of cash that was currently hiding under the rafters and the doubts began to creep back into her mind. Where would Lesley have got her information from? Caroline wondered. It was probably just gossip around the town. She hadn't heard it repeated because, well, what did she have to do with new shopping centre developments? Also, she supposed, if Tony had been involved then it was likely people would avoid mentioning it when she was there – people other than Lesley, of course. But perhaps they had been talking about it.

Caroline thought about where talking happened online and settled on Facebook. Wasn't there a local group where people posted news and jobs and lost keys and what have you? She didn't really have any time for all of that, but Ellie sometimes filled her in on the more outrageous threads. People got very intense, or so she gathered; everyone had an opinion that they were dying to share. If there had been something suspect about the shopping centre then surely that was the place it would have been raised.

Logging into Facebook, she ignored her ninety-seven notifications and navigated to the local group. Then she tapped in the name of the shopping centre and various threads appeared. It was hard to know which to choose, so she started at the top. The first one was about whether the new centre would steal the trade from the town. Lots of very aerated people had a view. She moved to the next one, which was mainly focused on what an eyesore the centre was. Caroline thought this was rich, bearing in mind the run-down streets that it had replaced. One commenter made mention of how quickly planning permission seemed to have been obtained, but no one else picked up on it. Caroline didn't recognise the name of the person, but then why would she? This was a town of over four hundred thousand people.

After a while she gave up. Just reading through the comments was giving her a headache. Did they not have anything better to do with their time than join in with this pointless tittle-tattle? There was nothing concrete in the posts about the planning process in general or Tony in particular. If there had been anything suspicious then surely someone would have raised it on the page. Unless that kind of post got taken down, of course; she didn't know if that happened. Was it libellous, to make accusations like that? Either way, she had searched and found nothing, probably because there was nothing to find. She snapped the laptop shut and went to see what the others wanted for supper, dispelling all doubts from her mind as she did so.

31

Max still wasn't at all sure about talking to his mum. Part of him didn't want to tell her about the money because the situation was going to be complicated enough without her views on top, but another, and he suspected bigger, worry was that he didn't want to hear what she might have to say about where it might have come from.

Ellie had arranged for them to go early. Valerie had a tee time booked at the golf club that they had to work around, apparently. Max had offered to pick Ellie up on the way, save them going in two cars, and when he arrived he sat outside and tooted his horn. A disgruntled-looking Ellie emerged from the house a minute later, her face screwed into a frown.

'Do you have to do that?' she asked as she opened the door.

'What?' he asked with feigned innocence, although he knew exactly what Ellie was talking about and had only tooted his horn because it pleased him to annoy her stuck-up neighbours. He thought about revving his engine as he pulled away, or even doing the kind of wheel spin that left tyre marks on the tarmac, but decided that maybe that would be a little petty. Tempting though.

'Did you give Mum any idea of what we want to talk to her about?' he asked as they turned out of Ellie's road.

Ellie shook her head. 'No. I just said it was to do with the arrangements for the funeral. I think she thought it was a bit strange that it was going to take both of us to tell her in person, but she'll understand soon enough.'

There was a pause as Max negotiated the roundabout and then she spoke again.

'Where do you think the money came from? Me and James were talking about it but we couldn't come up with a single reason why it would be there.'

'No, me neither,' replied Max neutrally.

He was reluctant to get caught up in speculation. It wouldn't help and it wouldn't give them any answers. Better to wait and see whether Valerie could cast any light on the shadowy stash.

Ellie, seeming to recognise that he wouldn't be drawn, changed the subject and talked about how well the girls were doing pretty much without taking a breath until they had pulled up outside Valerie's apartment.

'How shall we play this?' she asked as they got out of the car. 'Do you want to do the talking?'

'If you like,' he said, not having given the matter any thought. 'It was me and Caro who found the money, I suppose.'

'Okay, let's go then.' Ellie showed no sign of sharing his concerns, stepping lightly towards the building. Maybe he was concerned for no reason.

Valerie lived in an apartment in a purpose-built block. Hers was on the first floor, had joint access via an anonymous staircase and no outside space other than a south-facing balcony like the ones that you got in holiday resort hotels. It was neat, compact and practical, much like Valerie herself.

They rang her bell and seconds later the door buzzed open and they went in and up the stairs. Valerie was standing on the landing as they approached.

'Morning, you two,' she said. She gave them each a hug and then gestured for them to go inside.

The apartment was bright and light and smelled of lilies and fresh coffee. Max saw a fresh pot standing on the kitchen surface along with three cups and a milk jug. There were no biscuits, he noted regretfully.

'Coffee?' Valerie asked, but she was already pouring. Max nodded, pulling out a stool and perching on its edge. He watched as his mother poured confidently, no sign of the slightly tremulous woman he remembered from his childhood. When had that change happened? he wondered. Or maybe she had always been capable and it was his version of her that had been skewed in a different direction. Whatever it was, there was no denying that since leaving Tony she had undergone a major rejuvenation.

'So,' she said when the drinks were all poured, 'what's so important that you two have had to come racing across town to discuss it first thing on a Sunday morning?'

That was another thing that was different about her, Max thought: her directness. It sometimes felt as if she had spent years dancing around subjects and was now making up for lost time.

Even though they had agreed that Max would do the talking, it was Ellie who replied.

'We've booked the funeral for a week on Friday,' she said.

'But that's your—'

'I know. But it really doesn't matter. They didn't have another date that worked, and I still have the party.'

Valerie looked unconvinced, but she let it go. 'So, I'm assuming the crem and then afterwards at the golf club,' she said.

Ellie nodded.

'Okay, I'll put it in my diary. And now, why are you really here?'

Ellie looked at Max, urging him to speak with her eyes.

'The thing is . . .' he began. 'We found some money.'

'At Tony's?' Valerie interrupted.

Max nodded. 'In a suitcase under the spare bed.'

Valerie raised a curious eyebrow as if to say what were you doing there, but there was no point trotting out the cat story again. It was irrelevant.

'And was it a lot of money?' Valerie asked.

Max nodded again. 'About two hundred and seventy grand,' he said. He watched his mum's face carefully for signs of shock but there was nothing there. She gave a single nod, as if he had just confirmed something she had been expecting to hear.

'You knew?' he said.

'No,' she replied, 'but let's just say I'm not surprised.'

'Why not, Mum?' asked Ellie.

Valerie paused for a moment, her eyes passing over her daughter's face. Max got the impression she was trying to decide what she should say, or rather how much, and his anxiety levels began to rise again. He didn't need to know whatever it was. Didn't want to know. But they were here now. The question had been asked and there was no turning back. And anyway, there might be a perfectly innocent explanation, even if it was quite difficult to imagine what it might be. She took a mouthful of coffee before continuing.

'I'm not surprised because there was always cash in the house. Granted not quite that much, although there might have been, I suppose. I used to stumble across it when I was cleaning. And then I got quite good at finding it. He never had much imagination, your father.'

'But where did it come from?' asked Ellie. 'And why did Dad have it at home rather than in a bank?'

Valerie folded her arms across her chest, hugging herself tightly. 'I asked him much the same,' she said.

'And?' asked Max.

'Do you want what he told me, or what I suspect was the truth?'

'Both?'

'Okay. He told me that it was perfectly normal to hang on to cash at home because if he put it in the bank the tax man would take half of it.'

'So he was just dodging tax,' said Ellie. Max thought he caught a hint of relief in her voice, as if she had been expecting something much worse. He thought dodging tax was bad enough. His tax had always been collected by his employer so he had paid what was due from the day he started work without question. He didn't have much time for anyone who tried to cheat the system. If you had a big tax bill to pay, then that simply meant you were fortunate enough to have earned a lot of money.

'But that's not what you thought,' he prompted.

'No,' said Valerie. 'There was an element of that, I'm sure, but mainly I think he kept the money in the house because he didn't want anyone to know about it. If he had total control of it then he could avoid any awkward questions.'

'What kind of questions?' asked Ellie.

'Where it had come from. Where it was going. That kind of thing,' replied Valerie.

This was all a bit vague for Max and he was struggling to grasp hold of whatever it was his mum was telling them.

'But why would he want to do that?' he asked.

Valerie looked at him with something like pity in her eyes and he suddenly felt both ignorant and stupid. What was he missing here?

'Bribes, you mean?' said Ellie.

Max turned to look at her. How did his baby sister understand what was being said here when he was completely in the dark?

'Bribes! What kind of bribes?' he asked. 'I'm not sure I'm following this. Are you saying that there was something dodgy about Dad?'

'Oh, my lovely innocent boy,' said Valerie. She reached out and put her hand on his forearm, gently applying pressure in an affectionate squeeze. 'I'm sorry to be the one to tell you this, Max, but your father didn't always play things exactly by the book. There were parts of his dealings that were a touch on the shady side. I always found that it was better not to ask too many questions.'

Max couldn't process what she had said. He ran his hands through his hair, blinking stupidly at Valerie. He wasn't sure he believed her. If his dad had been up to no good all those years then surely he would have noticed something, but he had seen nothing out of the ordinary. Tony was a perfectly ordinary bloke, a bit loud sometimes, but not dishonest. Surely.

And yet, two hundred and seventy thousand pounds in a suitcase under his spare bed did seem to tell a different tale, and one that would fit in with what his mum was saying.

'So, who does the money belong to?' he asked.

Valerie shook her head, her palms raised. 'Now that I couldn't tell you,' she said. 'It could have been his, although I wouldn't want to look too closely at where he got it from. It could have been in transit to someone else, in which case they are going to be pretty annoyed that he's up and died on them.'

'But what should we do with it?' Max asked, suddenly feeling like a child taking advice from a trusted teacher and not a man in his forties who could decide such matters for himself.

'That's up to the three of you, I suppose,' she said. 'I don't want to sound uncaring and I'll be here for you all, of course I will, but what Tony was or wasn't up to is none of my concern any more.' She gave them a wan smile, as if she was exhausted by just the thought of dealing with the aftermath of his dad's death. 'And where's Nathan in all this? I assume, given that he's not here now, that you haven't told him about the money.'

Max saw Ellie's head drop to avoid any eye contact with their mum. What was that all about? he wondered. There were too many signals that he couldn't read flying around here.

'No,' he said. 'We thought we should try to find out a few more details before we . . .' His sentence drifted to a halt.

'Probably for the best,' replied Valerie. 'Money does seem to fall out of Nathan's pockets as fast as it goes in. And I know your dad dug him out of a few holes over the years. Nothing major, just a few hundred here and there, but he does seem to be the one who can't manage his money. Tony used to say it was the last time he'd put his hand in his pocket, but then he always coughed up when Nathan asked. He could be a bit of a softy, really, especially where Nath was concerned. Youngest child and all that.'

She gave them an apologetic smile, but Max had always known that the three of them were treated differently and it had never bothered him. And he wasn't really that surprised that Nathan had been sponging off his dad, although it was annoying. He and Caroline could have done with the odd windfall over the years. A few hundred pounds here and there would have come in handy. But he could be the bigger man here and not make a fuss.

This was all going round in his head when his mum spoke again.

'Has he had money from you as well, Ellie, sweetheart?'

Max turned to see what Valerie had seen. Ellie's cheeks were burning and her expression fluctuated between confusion and anger.

'Well, yes, but we thought it was a one-off . . .' she said.

Valerie's shoulders drooped and her head tipped to one side as she took in her daughter. 'Oh, my darling, trusting girl,' she sighed. 'I was always telling your father that he was doing Nathan no favours by bailing him out. Maybe he finally shut up shop and refused to pay and so he came to you instead. How much did you give him?'

'Ten thousand,' said Ellie quietly.

'What?!' said Max, turning to face his sister. How had she paid their brother ten thousand pounds and not told him?

Valerie shook her head knowingly. 'That's quite a leap up from where he was. What did he say he needed it for? An investment in some sure-fire scheme?'

Ellie nodded. 'We thought we were helping him make some money,' she said. 'That's why we gave it to him. If we'd thought we were just servicing a debt . . .' She bit her lip in thought. 'Well, actually, I might still have given it to him. He is my baby brother after all, and James and I have the cash. But I'm not sure James would have been so amenable.'

Max was really struggling to get his head round what he was learning. 'Hang on!' he said, putting his hands firmly down on the countertop. 'Let me get this straight. You're telling me not only that my father, rather than being the pillar of the community that I thought he was, was actually up to his neck in corruption, but also that my brother has been taking handouts of thousands of pounds from my sister. And I knew nothing about any of it.'

Valerie turned the corners of her mouth down and gave him a sympathetic look, which made Max feel like an idiot. There really wasn't any need to answer his question, it seemed.

'Shit,' he said, holding his head up with his hands.

There was a pause whilst they all absorbed the new information they had each learnt. The fridge hummed and the clock on the wall ticked loudly.

Ellie was the first to break the silence. 'Should we be worried about Nathan?' she asked. 'I mean, do you think he's got himself into a real mess, money-wise?'

Valerie shook her head. 'He's still got his flat and his job so things can't be too bad.'

Then Ellie's eyes opened wide and her mouth dropped opened slowly. 'You don't think it's drugs, do you?' she asked. 'You hear such terrible stories. But he looks healthy enough. I mean, he doesn't look like a drug addict.'

Max had to agree. Nathan was the image of a man at his peak.

'I'm sure it's not drugs,' said Valerie, touching Ellie gently on the arm. 'If there'd been any suggestion of that I'd have been all over it. He is my son, you know. I wouldn't have let him struggle through something like that on his own.'

Ellie nodded, reassured. 'So just debt then,' she said. 'That's more manageable. But that gets us back to where we started. What are we going to do with the money?'

'That, my lovelies, is up to you,' replied Valerie. 'I wish I could be more help, I really do, but it isn't anything to do with me any more. You're going to have to decide that for yourselves. And now, I hate to rush you, but I really do need to get off for my golf match.'

She stood up and began to tip the half-drunk mugs of coffee down the sink, removing the dregs with a swoosh of water from the tap in much the same way as Max's understanding of his family had just been washed away.

Slowly he got to his feet, confused and dazed by what he had heard. At the door, Ellie kissed their mum on the cheek and Max squeezed her shoulder. They were just leaving when Ellie stopped and turned back.

'Is that why you left Dad?' she asked Valerie. 'The shady dealings?'

Valerie looked her straight in the eye. 'Let's just say it was a contributory factor,' she replied.

Max and Ellie didn't speak in the car on the way back, each still reverberating with the shockwaves of what they had learnt. When Max pulled up outside Ellie's house, this time without any of the high jinks of earlier, he switched off the engine and they sat there for a moment.

'What now?' he asked, when it became apparent Ellie wasn't going to speak.

'God, Max,' she said with a deep sigh. 'I don't know. I suppose we should all get together and run through the options.'

'With Nathan?'

Ellie shrugged. 'I don't see that we have much choice. He's got as much right to be there as we have.'

Max paused, considering this. 'Did you really give him ten grand?'

Ellie nodded. 'Although it seems it might have barely touched the sides. I thought we were doing him a massive favour. It's a lot of money . . .'

Max agreed. More than he could imagine having spare to give to someone else.

'. . . but not in the grand scale of things, it appears.' She pressed her lips together so tightly that their rosy hue disappeared, leaving harsh white lines across her face, like scars. It was clear Nathan had more than blotted his copybook with her and would have some making up to do.

'And what did he say he needed it for?' asked Max.

Ellie shrugged. 'He told us it was to invest in a business, just like Mum said. James was all for it. Nath said he'd cut us into any profits.'

'And now? When you know that Dad gave him money too?'

'I have no idea,' she said. 'What takes lots of money? He doesn't exactly live a flash lifestyle.'

Max thought back to the video call the other night. 'You don't think he's got a problem with gambling, do you?' he said. 'I mean, he was at a racecourse when we rang him and it's a pretty good way of losing money fast.'

Ellie thought for a moment. 'Maybe, I suppose. Although I wouldn't say he was the type.'

'Is there a type?' asked Max. 'I mean, I wouldn't have said that my dad was shady an hour ago, but it seems I'd have been wrong.'

'We don't know that for sure,' replied Ellie sharply. 'We only have Mum's word for it and she has a bit of an axe to grind.'

'But if not, then where did the money come from?' said Max.

They were going round in circles. Too many revelations and too much still unknown. Max's head was spinning with it all. But they were going to have to get to the bottom of it somehow or other.

'We need another family conference,' he said. 'Definitely with Nathan there as well. Could you fix something up? I'd do it, but you usually . . .' His sentence faded away. It seemed important not to make any assumptions just then. He needed to hold tightly to what he knew for sure, which currently wasn't much.

But Ellie nodded. 'Sure,' she said. 'I'll do it. James isn't going to believe all this,' she said as she reached for the handle and opened the door.

Max wasn't sure whether she meant the fact that Tony had been bent or that Nathan had tricked them out of ten grand, but he suspected it was the latter and that made him sad. Was he so naive that the fact his family weren't who he thought they were had never touched his consciousness? Maybe he was but, he decided as he watched Ellie disappear up her drive and started the engine, he'd rather be naive than corrupt.

32

Ellie stood and stared at their house before going in. It felt like a perfectly normal Sunday morning. James was on the drive, hosepipe in hand, cleaning his car. The girls were on the trampoline; she could hear their shrieks even though she couldn't see them from where she was.

But nothing was normal. It felt as if someone had turned her upside down and shaken her.

James, somehow sensing she was there, looked up and gave her a wave. 'You're back soon,' he said. 'How did it go?'

Ellie had the strange, other-worldly feeling that she needed to decompress from one situation into the other before she could share what she'd learnt.

'Fine,' she said. 'I'm just going to make a cup of tea and then I'll tell you all about it.'

'Okay,' said James cheerfully, turning the hose head on to a more vigorous jet, which he aimed at a white teardrop of bird poo on the windscreen. 'I won't be long.'

Ellie slipped into the house and immediately felt calmed by the familiar things that surrounded her. She breathed in the smell of their family, not really able to identify particular elements but recognising it as a whole. Her home. Her world. Safe, secure, slightly rocked by what she had just learnt about her father and brother, but still fundamentally unassailable.

As she moved about the kitchen making tea, she pondered what James was going to say about the money they had given Nathan. He'd be annoyed, she suspected. It was only ten thousand pounds but James didn't like to be hoodwinked. It was going to leave a sour taste between her husband and her brother for a while. Ellie didn't want that. The Frosts (she still counted herself in their number even though technically she was a Fisher) were tightly bound together, always had been. It was unthinkable that something like this would get between them. Yes, Nathan had been underhand, or actually downright dishonest, but what if he had other issues he was battling with that she knew nothing about? She and James should rise above it all and accept what he had done graciously.

The more she thought about this approach, the more she liked it. She could persuade James to go for it too, she thought. He liked to be magnanimous. And when she explained that Max hadn't even been aware that Nathan had been sharking around for money, then James would be persuaded that they were at least less innocent than him.

Ten minutes later James appeared, slipping his feet out of his wellingtons at the back door and coming stocking-footed into the kitchen. His hands were red and mottled from long exposure to hot soapy water and he dried them on a towel before sitting down next to her.

'That for me?' he asked as he picked up one of the mugs of tea and took a drink. 'Thanks. Just what I needed. So, what did your mum say? Could she cast any light on the money?' His voice sounded eager, enthusiastic for news.

Ellie really wasn't sure where to begin, so decided to impart the information in the order that it had been given to her.

'Mum said that Dad always kept money in the house. He said it was so the tax man didn't find out about it . . .'

James nodded approvingly. 'Wise bloke.'

'And partly so that he always had cash available if he needed it.'

It took James less than a blink of an eye to work out what she meant.

'The wily old bugger,' he said, a grin spreading across his face. 'Well, I never knew for sure, but I'd heard the rumours.'

'What rumours?' Ellie asked.

'You know, that your dad was the fixer for the council. If you wanted something sorted then he was your man.'

'Oh!' she said. He made it sound like a good thing, a worthy job that could only be fulfilled by a very special kind of person.

James tapped at his lip with his forefinger. 'So that means the cash is now going begging, I suppose,' he said.

'I suppose so,' said Ellie.

'So, neatly spilt three ways that makes' – his eyes shot to the ceiling as he did the arithmetic in his head – 'about eighty thousand each. Nice.'

'It's a bit more,' said Ellie. 'Max said that there's actually two hundred and seventy thousand in the case.'

'Ah, the missing thousands,' said James. 'It's good to know exactly how much we're talking about. Not that I don't trust Max and Caroline, but transparency is important so we don't have any misunderstandings. In fact, I'd feel better if we saw the case for ourselves, just to be sure—'

Ellie pulled a warning face at him.

'—but I can see that's not really practical,' he continued, switching direction neatly. 'Anyway, twenty-seven divided by three is ninety grand apiece. Very nice.'

It sounded as if he was saying most of this to himself, clarifying ideas in his own head rather than talking to her. Maybe he was already working out how they could spend the extra money. There was the holiday, of course, still unbooked. And the decorator. And her party coming up. A nice little windfall was just what they needed.

'There was one other thing,' she said. 'Apparently Dad had been bailing Nathan out recently too. So when he came to us and we gave him the ten thousand, it wasn't as life-changing as he made out.'

Ellie held her breath, ready to face the tempest from James, but he barely seemed to be bothered. She wondered if he had even heard her.

'James, did you get that? About Nathan? I said that . . .'

James waved a hand as if dismissing the information. 'Well, we won't fall for that again,' he said. 'Nathan has burnt his boats on that score. It just shows, Els, how trusting we are and how conniving he is. You don't set out to con your own family like that.'

'I'm not sure he was trying to con us,' interrupted Ellie, inexplicably needing to defend her little brother despite his actions. 'I think he just got into a bit of a mess.'

'Face it, Ellie,' said James. 'Everything about him is a mess.'

'Not everything,' she said, because she felt she ought to, but she was struggling to think of a part of Nathan's life that ran smoothly. 'He has a job.'

James pulled a face that suggested that was a pretty poor effort. 'We can make allowances because he's your brother, but he won't be getting any more money from us. So,' he said, standing up and putting his mug in the dishwasher, 'ninety grand.' His face settled into a look of satisfaction as if it had been him who had earned the money. Then he left the kitchen to go, Ellie assumed, into his office, which was where he spent most of his time these days.

She put her mug into the dishwasher too and set it going to wash the breakfast dishes. That had gone very smoothly. Next, she would fix the meeting up so they could all agree how to move forward. She wondered whether she should get Max to bring the suitcase with him so they could dish the cash out there and then, but she decided that maybe that looked a little bit greedy. Better to agree in principle first and then deal with the practicalities after that. Then again, she thought, there wasn't really anything to agree. There were three of them so they would split the money three ways. It was a no-brainer.

33

There was a lot to do when you were organising your own birthday party. For a while, Ellie had hinted to James that it might be nice if he were to make the arrangements for her, but it soon became apparent that her comments were falling on stony ground, and so she had given up. In any event, she wanted the evening to be perfect, so there was to be no leaving things to chance. She also wanted the look of the evening to be a surprise, so she had even held off from discussing some of the details with Caroline. The party was very much her baby.

She had toyed with various themes – everyone did the seventies or eighties, so she had rejected those early on. For a while she had thought about an *Ocean's 11* theme, set in a mock casino, which would give everyone the chance to dress up to the nines, but in light of what she thought they had just discovered about Nathan it was probably for the best that idea had fallen by the wayside. A Gatsby theme was a nice idea too, but James really wasn't the fancy dress sort.

In the end, there was only one theme she could go with, given that her birthday was the twenty-first of June – A Midsummer Night's Dream. Using a pallet of the palest of pinks and pearlescent whites she hoped to create a magical, almost ethereal, effect. She had found a place that would create a flower tunnel for her guests to enter through, and which would also be perfect for Instagram shots. The room itself would be transformed from the function room at a boutique hotel in town into a fairy grotto with a canopy of tiny lights overhead and strings of pearls trailing down twisted with garlands of white and pink flowers. It was going to be breathtaking, the most talked-about party for years to come, or so Ellie hoped.

Of course, all that stylish beauty didn't come cheap. James had given her a budget to work with, but she suspected his thinking didn't expand much beyond a helium balloon archway and maybe some flowers for the tables. He didn't really have any idea what she had booked, or how much it was going to cost.

Ellie had had a little wobble when he had told her about the deal that had gone off, but now they had this cushion of money from her dad she was sure it would be fine. James loved her, would want her to have the best fortieth birthday she could. And he also loved to show everyone just how well they were doing. A really classy affair would enable him to make the kind of social statement he liked.

It was just a shame that the funeral was going to be the day before. There would be so much to do. She would just have to trust the party planners and make sure she had got as much as possible sorted the day before. Then she could concentrate on saying a proper goodbye to her dad.

Tears sprang into her eyes and suddenly she was weeping, deep juddering sobs that wracked her entire body. For a while, Ellie gave way to her grief and let it do its worst. By the time it had passed, she was left physically worn out by the effort, and mentally bereft.

When she had gathered herself again she picked up her phone and sent a message to the Frost family WhatsApp group.

We need to talk about Dad's money. Here. Wednesday 8 p.m. RSVP (@Nathan that means you!)

She hoped that the reference to money and mentioning him by name would be enough to get Nathan to show up. They all had to be there this time; they couldn't move forward until they had agreement and they couldn't do that until they sat down together and discussed it.

The replies started to ping in and within ten minutes they were quorate.

34

Max had been very quiet since he'd got back from his mum's. Caroline was desperate to find out what she had said, but she knew better than to push him. He would open up when he was ready and until then she would have to be patient. And there was the rest of life to get on with. The money might be sitting under their roof waiting to be dealt with, but the boys and work and the house still needed attention and Caroline was beginning to resent the amount of brain space that the whole issue was taking up. She made a conscious effort to try not to think about it. It didn't go that well.

By the time they had had supper and were settling down to watch whatever Sunday night drama was on, she thought she might burst if she didn't find out what had happened.

'Well?' she began, disappointed that she sounded so impatient when she hadn't intended to. She softened her tone. 'What did Valerie say?'

They generally sat apart in the lounge, each sprawling on a sofa facing the television, but now Max got up and came across to where she was sitting. Caroline sat up a little, pulling her legs in to make room for him. Then he wrapped his arms around her and squeezed himself into her. The angles of their respective bodies weren't ideal for this and the clinch felt awkward and a little uncomfortable, but

Caroline tried to sink into it for Max's sake. Whatever was going on in his head, it was clearly causing him some challenges.

She waited until he pulled away, then looked at him expectantly. He hadn't been crying but his eyes were red-rimmed and glassy, as if tears were only a moment away. It was hardly surprising. It had only been two weeks since he'd lost his father, and without a funeral yet, it must be hard for him to start to move beyond the shock.

'It's okay to cry, you know,' she said gently.

Max swallowed, nodded, took a deep breath to steady himself. He clearly had no intention of letting the tears go, not if he could help it at least.

'So, today was weird,' he began.

'Weird, how?' Caroline asked.

'Well, I learnt that my dad was bent and my brother is basically a thief.'

Caroline heard what he said but she couldn't take it in.

'What?' she said, incredulous. 'How do you mean?'

Max pulled himself away from her and went back to the sanctuary of his own sofa.

'Put it this way. Mum wasn't even vaguely surprised there was so much cash at Dad's. He always had money in the house, apparently. He told her it was a tax dodge but she basically said that he used it to pay backhanders.'

Caroline was horrified. Backhanders? Wasn't that something that happened in films? 'What kind of backhanders?'

Max shook his head, looking almost as bewildered as she felt. 'I've no idea. Stuff to do with the council, I think. Ellie seemed to know all about it. Not what Dad was up to but the idea of bribes in general.'

Caroline's jaw fell. 'But how? How did she know about that kind of thing?'

Max shrugged. 'James, I suppose. Maybe everyone in the property world is up to no good. I don't know. I don't really care, to be honest. I've got enough to worry about with this.'

Caroline wanted to probe a little deeper but she knew that if she did Max might shut up like a clam.

She switched tack. 'And Nathan?'

'He's been getting bits of money out of Dad for years, apparently. And then recently he got Ellie to give him ten grand. Ten grand! Made out to her that it was for some deal that he had going on and that he'd be eternally grateful, but actually he's been dipping into Dad's pocket too, so this was on top of all that.'

Caroline tried not to think about all the things they could have done if they'd had access to a magic money tree like that. They were fine as they were, but still it rankled a little to know Max's siblings had been playing the game with a different set of rules.

'And your mum knew?' she said instead.

'It seems so. God, what a mess.' Max ran his hands through his hair. 'I don't know which is worse, Dad dying or finding out about all this other stuff.'

'Try not to overthink it,' said Caroline. 'It doesn't make a difference to anything, not really.'

Even as the words left her mouth, she knew they weren't true. This fundamentally altered who Max understood his father and brother to be. It didn't matter how she tried to smooth it over. It was still a huge thing to take in.

And also, she could feel the old panics beginning to rise in herself. If Tony had been up to no good and it all came out then it would be their family who would be in the firing line. The nudging as they walked past, the unspoken words that echoed loudly behind them, the spoken accusations.

And by the time that happened, it wouldn't matter whether the rumours were true or not. There was no smoke without fire, that's what people always said. It hadn't mattered that no one had proved anything against her dad. The suspicion alone had been enough for the witch hunt to start. It was the same here. Tony was dead so there would be no action taken against him, but she knew that gossip was all it took. Caroline's face went cold and clammy, and she felt sick as she thought about it. She couldn't go through all that again. She absolutely couldn't. It had ruined her life once and it couldn't be allowed to do that again.

But at this moment the important thing was Max. He had to find a way of dealing with all this and Caroline would be there to help. She swallowed down her own fears and dug deep to find a smile.

'And Ellie's fixed a meeting for Wednesday,' she said. 'So we can talk it all through then.' She tried to sound reassuring. 'I'm sure it won't be as bad as it seems now, when we really get to the bottom of what's been going on. Maybe that's how things work and we've just been really naive not realising.'

Caroline wasn't sure saying this was going to help Max come to terms with any of it. Just because everyone was being dishonest didn't make the dishonesty any easier to deal with. And was Valerie any better? By turning a blind eye to what was going on and then leaving Tony without saying anything, was she condoning his behaviour? Caroline thought that she probably was. Being party to someone else's dishonesty was tantamount to being dishonest yourself in her book; in everyone's book, surely? It was certainly as black and white as that for Max, she knew. Although wasn't there some rule about not having to speak out against your spouse? Caroline wasn't sure. Not that it mattered. This was hardly a court of law, just a family trying to work out what to do for the best.

35

Caroline felt nervous. It was ridiculous. She had been best friends with Ellie for almost as long as she could remember and had been married into the Frost family for well over a quarter of her life. She thought she knew them all almost as well as she knew herself and she couldn't remember a single occasion when she had felt anything other than entirely comfortable in their company. But as the clock ticked round to the hour appointed for the meeting about the money, Caroline became aware of an unfamiliar twisting in her stomach.

It was groundless, this anxiety, she knew. The meeting would be fine. It was obvious what they should be doing with the money and so it wasn't going to take them long to agree on that. It was more that for the first time since they were children, she had discovered something about them all that she hadn't known – that not even Max had known. This was what was making her uncomfortable, the feeling that she had thought she knew her way around them all, and now someone had opened a previously hidden door and she'd discovered a whole new corridor she hadn't realised existed.

Still, what did she know about the world of local politics, or property development for that matter? What had she ever wanted or needed to know? It wasn't all that surprising that there was a murky underbelly she hadn't come across before. Probably if you lifted the stone on any side of life you would find something unsavoury lurking beneath. Tony had moved in circles she neither knew nor understood so she might have guessed that there would be aspects to him that she hadn't known about.

But it wasn't just Tony who had secrets, it seemed. Nathan did too. Caroline had never known that much about Nathan's life. She and Ellie were constantly in and out of each other's houses and she was married to Max, so he was an open book to her, but what Nathan got up to had always been a bit of a mystery. When they were younger, he was just the little brother and she hadn't taken much notice of him. As an adult he had kept himself to himself, joining the family for birthdays and Christmas but then slinking back to his own life. Caroline had never thought it odd. The Frosts weren't all joined at the hip, after all. But now, discovering that he had been 'borrowing' money, she was beginning to wonder what else she had missed about him.

Did it matter? He was still just Nathan, Max's little brother, good with the kids and generally a fun person to have around. These new discoveries didn't change that and Caroline was working hard at convincing herself of this. It had been a surprise about Tony and Nathan but not a disaster, and she and Max could just pretend that they had half-suspected it all, and then keep their mouths shut.

As she gave final instructions to the babysitter, assuring him that they wouldn't be late and there were snacks out in the kitchen, Caroline thought again about the suitcase in the loft. There had been no mention of taking it with them and so she hadn't raised it. It would be so much easier to discuss the money in the abstract than if there were bundles of twenty-pound notes winking up at them. Caroline wanted to clarify whether Max had agreed this with Ellie, but she didn't want to ask in case he hadn't thought about it. Instinct was telling her to leave the case exactly where it was.

As they turned the car on to James and Ellie's drive, Nathan's scruffy little Audi was already there. Max pulled up to one side, careful not to block Nathan in. Caroline wondered whether this was tactical, but then remembered that her thought processes and Max's were nothing alike. It wouldn't have occurred to him that anyone might want to leave in a hurry and with a minimum of fuss.

'Now we know why he sold that flashy BMW,' said Max as he climbed out. 'Basically, he couldn't afford it. What an idiot.' It sounded as if he was speaking more to himself than her, so Caroline didn't reply.

They knocked on the door then let themselves in as they always had done. Max was about to call out, but Caroline put a restraining hand on his arm.

'The girls,' she whispered. 'Don't shout. They'll be in bed.'

Max nodded, understanding at once, and led the way through to the sitting room where James and Nathan were sitting, each holding a bottle of beer. They weren't talking to one another, each lost in their own thoughts, but that wasn't unusual and was certainly no indication of anything being amiss.

James stood up as they walked in, smiling and opening his arms to welcome Max into a hug. He was looking tired, Caroline thought, fine lines showing around his eyes and his skin grey, despite the sunny few weeks they had enjoyed recently.

'Hello, you two. Ellie is just saying goodnight to the girls, but she'll be down in a minute. Beer, Max? Glass of wine, Caro?'

Max nodded but Caroline declined, midweek drinking being something that she tried to avoid. Whether that was for better or worse was something she had yet to decide.

Ellie appeared moments later. She gave them both a hug and then, when she was sure everyone had what they needed, sat down.

'Right,' she said. 'Who starts?'

They all looked at one another, not quite sure what the etiquette was. Then Max spoke. As the eldest sibling it seemed natural he would lead the discussion. He was already stepping up to his dad's position in the family, trying to fill his shoes. This wouldn't come naturally to him, Caroline knew, and so she threw him a supportive little smile.

'I assume you've filled Nath in on our discovery, Els,' he began, 'so I don't have to retell the tale.'

Ellie nodded.

'Good job it was you that found the money, Caroline,' Nathan said. 'If it had been me, I'd have swiped the lot and not told any of you.' He grinned, looking round at them all for a response, but the comment fell flat. Only James laughed.

'It was a joke,' said Nathan. 'God, you lot. Lighten up a bit, would you. Of course I wouldn't have nicked it.'

Caroline smiled at him and tried to look as if she knew that, but she could tell no one believed him entirely. She knew how it felt to be the kind of person no one quite trusted. It wasn't a good place to be.

Then a mobile phone began to ring. They all glanced at one another, each looking irritated that whoever it belonged to hadn't switched it to silent when they had this important business to discuss. It was James's phone and he pulled it out of his pocket and stared at the screen.

'Shit,' he said. 'Sorry. I have to take this.' He stood up and strode towards the door, his attention immediately focused on the call.

Ellie's lips pursed together. 'I'm so sorry,' she said. 'I have no idea what could be more important than this right now.'

'Shall we wait for him?' Max asked, but Ellie shook her head.

'These calls can go on forever. You just carry on and I'll fill him in with whatever he misses later.'

Max pressed on. 'So, we've found the money and now we need to decide what we should do with it. Before we do anything, I think we should pay it into the bank so we know it's safe. Nathan's cat burglary talents aside, Caro and I feel a bit vulnerable with that much cash sitting in the house.'

Caroline nodded.

'I can see that,' said Ellie. 'Anyone could take it. You haven't mentioned it to anyone, have you?'

Max looked at her as if she were stupid. 'No! Of course not. We haven't told a soul and it's well hidden, but I'll still be happier when it's safely sitting under lock and key. We were thinking we should open an account with the three of us as signatories.'

Ellie nodded enthusiastically. 'That sounds good to me. Then what?'

'Then we have a bit of a problem,' said Max. 'We don't know why Dad had the money. It might not be his. He might have been holding on to it for someone else. That's another good reason for paying it into the bank. Then it can sit there for a while and if any-one comes forward to claim it, we can pass it to them.'

'And there's probate too,' said Ellie. 'We won't be able to do anything until the executors have released the estate. Do we know who the executors are?'

'Is there a will?' asked Caroline. In all the talk of the money, no one had mentioned one.

'There will be,' said Max. 'It'll be in his study at the house or with the solicitors. I'll find out.'

'Do we need the will to decide what to do with this cash?' asked Ellie. 'I assume it just divides everything between us. Or does Mum get something?'

Max shrugged. 'I doubt it. They've been apart for over ten years.'

Nathan sat forward in his chair and put his hands up to stop the discussion. 'Hang on, hang on. Am I missing something here? We have the cash now. I think it's fair to assume that it was Dad's, so surely we just split it three ways and then you can all do what you like with your share. Bank it or spend it or whatever. But there's no need to pay the whole lot in.'

Max lifted his gaze and met his brother's eyes. 'Listen, Nath,' he began, 'I don't know what your current situation is and there may well be plenty of reasons why you want to get your hands on the money as quickly as possible, but that doesn't make it the right thing to do.'

Nathan set his jaw, clearly irritated by the implication. 'What I want to do with my share of the money is neither here nor there,' he said. 'I just don't see any point in getting caught up with bureaucracy and red tape when we can just distribute the cash between the three of us and keep schtum.'

'Well,' said Ellie, 'I suppose he's got a point.'

'No, Ellie, he hasn't,' said Max firmly. 'He just wants to get his hands on his share fast. But that isn't going to help us think all this through and make the best decision.'

'What is there to think through?' asked Nathan, the volume creeping up in frustration.

'Could you keep your voice down, Nath?' asked Ellie. 'You'll frighten the girls.'

'Sorry,' said Nathan a little more quietly. 'But my question remains. What is there to think about?'

'Well, as I said before, we don't know whose money it is. It might not even have been Dad's.'

'Of course it was Dad's,' scoffed Nathan. 'He always had cash in the house.'

Max raised an eyebrow and Caroline thought she saw Nathan look a little sheepish. How did Nathan know that? Just how many times had Tony dipped into this treasure trove to help Nathan out? she wondered.

'Still, I'd feel more comfortable if we paid it in first and then decided from there,' said Max, standing firm.

Nathan was becoming more agitated. He folded his arms, unfolded them again, ran his hands through his hair. Caroline could see what an effort it was for him to keep control.

'Okay. Let's vote on it,' said Max. 'But we'll go with the majority vote because it doesn't look like we'll ever get unanimity. Agreed?'

Ellie and Nathan both nodded solemnly.

'Right,' Max continued, 'those in favour of paying the money into the bank now raise your hand.'

Caroline assumed that she didn't get a vote so she didn't move. Max's hand went up. Caroline watched as Ellie moved her eyes between her brothers and then slowly raised her hand.

'Oh, for God's sake!' snapped Nathan, getting to his feet. 'This is bloody ridiculous. Let's just take the money and be done with it.'

'You're outvoted, Nath, two to one.'

'So it would appear. Well, I've got places to be so if you'll excuse me.'

He stalked out of the room and a few seconds later they heard the front door slam. Ellie jumped as the sound reverberated around the house.

Max slumped in his chair, the corners of his mouth dragging downwards. 'That was exactly what I didn't want to happen,' he said. 'Damn.'

Ellie gave him a sympathetic smile. 'Don't worry. He'll come round. He'll see that it makes more sense. We've done him a favour, really, slowing things down. And then we can distribute the money between the three of us when we know who the executors are.'

Max nodded.

'It doesn't look like James is coming back either, so I think we'll get off, Els,' he said. 'It's work tomorrow. I'll look into interest-paying bank accounts, and I'll swing by the house to see if I can find the will.'

Ellie nodded as they both stood up. Caroline stayed where she was. She was trying to process what she'd heard but was struggling a little because none of it was what she had been expecting.

'Are you coming, Caro?' Max asked.

Should she say what she thought now, in front of Ellie, or would it be better to chat it through with Max first? What was the best thing to do? The meeting had been called to discuss these very issues and she had assumed that one of them would have voiced what she had been thinking so that she wouldn't have to. As they hadn't, she had no option but to say it herself, and there was no time like the present.

'The thing is . . .' she began, looking from Max to Ellie and then back to Max again. 'The thing is, I don't think we should take the money at all.'

36

'So, what does she want to do with it?' asked James when Ellie was filling him in on what he had missed. He had been on the phone for most of the evening and it was only now, at bedtime, that they were together.

'I don't really know,' replied Ellie, lifting the duvet and slipping underneath. 'They left pretty much after that. Max seemed just as surprised as I was, and as Nathan had already stormed off anyway, he decided that we should all go away and reconsider whilst he looks into things. I'll ring her tomorrow to see what she meant. And before that we had a vote about paying it into a bank account whilst we decide what to do next. Nath didn't want to do that, but it's okay because me and Max outvoted him.'

James had been getting undressed as she spoke, but now he stopped, one sock on and one off and stared at her.

'You voted in favour of putting it in the bank?' he said. From his tone, Ellie got the feeling she had done the wrong thing, but surely that couldn't be right. What else were they to do with such an enormous amount of cash? Keep it in a suitcase like her dad had done?

'Well, yes,' she said, feeling flustered and a little thrown. 'Of course.'

James sat down heavily on the bed, the air rushing out of his lungs as he did so. He shook his head. 'We need to get that changed,' he said. 'We can't let them pay it in anywhere.'

Ellie was confused. 'But why not?'

James took a deep breath, as if he was having to explain something to a particularly stupid child, and Ellie started to feel defensive. She might be a lot of things, but stupid wasn't one of them.

'At the moment, that money isn't registered anywhere. It's untraceable. As soon as we pay it in then there will be record of it.'

He nodded at her, urging her to follow his train of thought without having to spell it out, but Ellie was lost.

'So?' she said.

'No record means that it's as good as not existing at all. As soon as it goes into a bank then people will start to ask questions about it. The bank. The Inland Revenue. Do you know how much will be left after the tax man gets his hands on it? Barely half. And for what? Just so Max and Caroline don't feel nervous about having it under their roof? We can have it here if they're that worried. I don't mind taking the risk if it saves us one hundred and twenty grand.'

Ellie's jaw dropped. 'That much?'

'Well, yes. For the whole amount. So that would be forty thousand lost for us.'

'God,' said Ellie. 'I see.'

'I'm with Nathan,' said James. 'We should just split it three ways now and then if Max and Caroline want to pay theirs into a bank that's their decision.'

Ellie could feel her cheeks blush. How had she not realised that something so seemingly simple would have such enormous ramifications? But then, she wasn't the business person here. How was she supposed to know? Perhaps if James hadn't been so distracted by his phone and had been there then . . . but there was no point thinking like that.

'I'm sorry,' she said quietly.

'Don't worry,' said James softly. 'Just ring Max tomorrow and tell him you've changed your mind. You can explain why if you like. It obviously hasn't occurred to him either; he's such an innocent sometimes. I'm sure it'll be fine when he understands just what's at stake. But it's pointless to shoot a flare up into the sky for the world to see. No one knew the money was there so no one will know if we just divvy it up between us.'

James got into the bed next to her and gave her a peck on her nose.

'The sooner we can get it all sorted out, the better. Then you can stop worrying your pretty little head about it. Lights out or do you want to read for a bit?'

As Ellie lay there in the dark listening to the sounds of the house, she thought about what James had said. It would be strange having so much cash. Usually she paid for everything by credit card, although she had seen people at tills who kept wads in their wallets. Seeing the money just there for anyone to steal had always made her nervous. She imagined thieves following them out of shops and jumping them in a dark alley. But you never heard of that kind of thing happening. This was England, a perfectly civilised and safe country. There was no reason why you couldn't carry cash, just as long as you took sensible precautions.

Still, she couldn't imagine making any large purchases in cash. It was more likely to be smaller things, twenty pounds here, twenty pounds there. It was going to take a very long time to work their way through ninety thousand pounds like that. The thought made her smile and she drifted off to sleep with images of twenty-pound notes floating through her head instead of sheep jumping fences.

37

The next morning, having the conversation with Max about the bank account was almost the first thing that James mentioned.

'I have an early meeting,' he said as he ate a piece of toast standing up, 'but make sure you ring Max and tell him that you've changed your mind about paying the money in. I'm sure he won't do anything hasty, but better to be safe than sorry.'

Ellie looked at the clock as the front door slammed behind him. It was just after eight. Was that too early to ring? The banks didn't open until nine so Max couldn't do anything before then, but she needed to make sure she caught him before he left the house in case he didn't pick up his mobile messages. They wouldn't thank her for a call so early when the household was chasing its tail to get out on time, but that couldn't be helped.

She dialled their landline, assuming there would be more chance of someone answering that, even if it was one of the boys. Within a couple of rings, a very anxious-sounding Caroline answered and Ellie realised that receiving a call on the landline so early would generally mean bad news.

'Caro, don't panic. It's only me,' she said quickly, to ease her nerves. 'I just wanted a quick word with Max before he left. Is he there?'

'Oh, Ellie. Hi,' Caroline replied, breathy with relief. 'Yes. Hang on.'

Ellie heard her call for Max and moments later he came on the line.

'Hi, Ellie. Is everything okay?' he asked.

'Yes. It's just that I was telling James about what we decided last night, and he says that if we pay the money in there's a good chance that we'll get stung for tax on it. So I'd like to change my vote. I'm not saying that we should split it now, just that we shouldn't pay it in, at least until we've checked whether James is right.'

There was a pause that went on for so long Ellie wasn't sure Max was still there.

'Max? Did you get that?' she said.

'Sorry. Yes. Just thinking it through,' Max replied. 'I suppose he might be right. I hadn't thought of that. And inheritance tax is how much?'

'Forty per cent.'

Max whistled and Ellie pulled the receiver away from her ear.

'Okay. Well, thank James for me, would you. I was going to the bank this morning so it's a good job you caught me. I'll hold fire. But I'll go to the house and see if I can find the will. We should get that started at least.'

Ellie felt relief run through her. 'That's great, Max. Thanks. Sorry to be so flaky.'

'No. You're right. Thank you.'

'Is Caro there? Can I have a brief word?'

'She is but she's racing to get out of the house with the boys. Can it wait until tonight?'

'Yes, of course,' Ellie replied brightly, trying not to show her resentment that her best friend had better things to do than to talk to her, even though she knew she was being ridiculous. 'Tell her I'll ring her later, would you?'

'Will do,' said Max. 'Got to go now. See you.'

And then he was gone. Ellie stood with the receiver in her hand for a few moments. Well, that was good about the bank at least. She would text James to tell him. He'd be pleased. But really what she wanted was to quiz Caroline on what she had meant about not wanting to take the money at all. However, that, it seemed, would have to wait.

She put the phone back in its cradle and went to chivvy the girls along for school. She found Olivia in the hall, checking through her bag to make sure she had everything she needed and ticking everything off on her fingers.

'Good girl, Livvy,' she said. 'Where's Lucy?'

Olivia rolled her eyes. 'She's in her bedroom. Crying. Again.'

Ellie's heartstrings tugged a little.

'What's the matter?' she asked as she headed up the stairs.

'The usual,' sang Olivia in a matter-of-fact way.

Ellie got to Lucy's door and knocked lightly before opening it and putting her head around.

'Are you okay, Luce?' she asked.

Lucy was sitting on the floor. Her reading book was lying upside down against the skirting board. It looked as if it had been thrown there. Her unbrushed hair was sticking to her face, which was blotchy and damp with tears.

'Oh, Lucy,' Ellie said, going in and dropping to her knees so that she could hug her daughter. 'What on earth is the matter?'

She wrapped her arms around her. Lucy felt tiny and fragile, as if one squeeze too hard could break her little bones. Lucy leant into the hug but then Ellie felt her stiffen and she pulled away.

'It's not fair!' she spat.

'What isn't, poppet?' asked Ellie, although she had a fair idea.

'Why can't I do it when everyone else can? I try just as hard as them. Harder. Chloe Davenport gets a new reading book every day. She says I'm stupid. I'm not stupid, am I, Mummy?'

'No, of course not,' reassured Ellie. 'And it's very wrong of Chloe to say something like that. Everyone reads at different speeds. It's fine. And if Chloe reads so quickly then she probably isn't understanding the meaning of the words properly.'

Ellie knew she shouldn't criticise another child, but she was cross. It was so unjust that Lucy was being made to feel bad for something that just wasn't her fault.

'And,' continued Lucy, gulping back the sobs, 'she told everyone else that I'm too stupid to read.'

'But that's not true, Lucy. You're not stupid, far from it. Your brain just works a little bit differently to everyone else's.'

'Well, I wish it didn't,' shouted Lucy and flopped back into Ellie's embrace.

Ellie hugged her tightly. She would do anything she could to make Lucy feel better. It must be so hard for her to understand, particularly when Olivia read with such ease. Miss Elliot, Lucy's class teacher, was fantastic with her. Ellie would try to have a quiet word when she dropped the girls off, ask her to keep an eye on this Chloe. She sounded like a nasty little girl, although Ellie knew that she was probably perfectly lovely. No different to Olivia, in fact.

'Come on now,' she said gently. 'We need to get ready for school. Shall I do your hair? Would you like plaits or ponytails today?'

'One high ponytail,' said Lucy. 'So it swings when I move my head. Like an actual pony.' She shook her head to illustrate.

'Great idea!' said Ellie. 'Pass me your brush and a bobble.'

Twenty minutes later they were all in the car, Olivia and Lucy enthusiastically discussing what the plot of the forthcoming Disney release might include, all thoughts of reading speeds forgotten.

38

Caroline couldn't concentrate. No matter how hard she tried to focus on the pupil absence numbers she was trying to collate, her mind was firmly on the money. Max had spoken to her briefly before he left for work about the reason for Ellie's early-morning call. Apparently, James thought that paying the money into the bank might make it attract tax. Well, what was wrong with that? If tax was due on the money then they should pay it. That was what it meant to live in a civilised society where everyone played their part. The law stated that forty per cent of any inherited money above a certain amount should be paid in death duties and so that's what should be done. If everyone tried to avoid paying tax, where would they be? The country would grind to a halt.

What she didn't understand was how James could baulk at paying the tax when the whole amount was a windfall anyway. It wasn't as if he had earned the money himself. It had literally just dropped into their laps. It was pure greed to want to take it all, as well as being against the law. He was showing his true colours by wanting to keep it secret, that was for sure.

Caroline felt pleased that the possible implications of paying the money into a bank hadn't occurred to her and Max. Their thought processes hadn't been tarnished by such considerations.

You could call them naive if you liked, but she'd rather be naive than have a mind that worked like James's appeared to.

However, paying the money into the bank or not was not the main problem as far as she was concerned. It was true that it had taken her a while to get her thoughts in order, that she had had her head turned by the sheer quantity of cash, but now she was over the initial shock of the discovery, she was clear about what she thought.

The money was dirty, tainted, unclean. It had either been given to Tony as backhanders for services rendered, which was illegal, or it was there waiting to be used to pay someone else off, also illegal. Either way, Caroline was certain that it would be wrong to take it. It wasn't theirs to take, and it probably wasn't Tony's either. It would be tantamount to theft.

What they should do with the cash was crystal clear to her as well. They must take the whole lot to the police and get them to investigate where it had come from. Then, if the police could find nothing untoward, they would get it all back. It could then form part of the estate and would be distributed in accordance with whatever the will said, less any tax owing. It was as plain to her as the nose on her face.

Yet this manifestly correct course of action hadn't been suggested by any of them the night before, not even Max. To be fair, they hadn't got very far into the discussions before Nathan had taken his bat home over the bank account issue, so maybe the ethics of taking the money for themselves would have come up later. Somehow, Caroline doubted it.

However, she wasn't going to let it go. She would be the voice of reason, or morality. The money wasn't theirs to take and so they shouldn't take it, particularly when they suspected there was something dubious about it, and she would argue the point until she was blue in the face if she had to.

It would help if she could get Ellie on her side, she thought. At the moment she was distinctly outvoted. She could persuade Max, she was sure, but it was clear that neither Nathan nor James, who would no doubt seek to control Ellie's vote, would agree with her. But if she talked to Ellie so that she understood her thinking then they could outvote Nathan and would be able to do what was right. She would ring Ellie tonight, she thought, talk it through with her and get her to see things from her point of view.

Satisfied with her proposed course of action, Caroline forced herself to concentrate on the job in hand and pushed the money to the back of her mind.

39

Max rang Caroline in his lunch hour to tell her that he had tracked down the will. It was, as he had suspected, with Tony's solicitor, who had told him that it contained nothing unexpected. The estate, including the proceeds from the sale of the house, was to be split three ways between him, Ellie and Nathan with some small cash gifts for each grandchild. Valerie wasn't mentioned. The executors were the solicitor and Max.

'Just you?' asked Caroline. 'Not the other two?'

'No. Just me and him,' said Max matter-of-factly.

'I wonder why Tony did that,' she continued.

'I assume because I'm the eldest, and he thought it would all run more smoothly if there were only two of us dipping our oar in. The solicitor knows what he's doing and there's no reason why I can't act in the best interests of us all. It's a pain in the backside, though. There's quite a lot to organise, and if I leave it to the solicitor then he'll obviously charge us for his time.'

Caroline sat quietly for a moment.

'Do you think your dad made you executor because you're the most trustworthy?' This wasn't something that had ever occurred to her before, but in light of recent developments, Caroline couldn't help but wonder.

'No!' replied Max, his tone indignant, and Caroline worried that she had overstepped the Frost family boundary line.

'But think about it,' she continued, not quite willing to let her train of thought go. 'Remember what we've learnt about Nath over the last few days. I'm not convinced that he'd always act in the best interests of the beneficiaries.'

There was a pause in which Caroline assumed that Max was reluctantly conceding that she might have a point.

'And Ellie. Well, I love her dearly but she does have a tendency to chase after butterflies.'

'That doesn't make her untrustworthy,' said Max.

'No,' agreed Caroline. 'Maybe I chose the wrong word. I just wonder whether there was a reason why your dad picked just you to be executor.'

'If I know Dad, it'll have been driven by practicalities – not wanting too many cooks spoiling the broth, and all that,' he said. 'Anyway, I have to go. We can talk about it later.' And then he hung up.

Caroline wasn't convinced. Tony didn't do things on a whim. If he'd chosen just Max and run the risk of upsetting the other two then there would be a reason. Then again, from what they were learning about Tony, perhaps being trustworthy wasn't as important to him as it was to her and so hadn't been a consideration at all. Or maybe, given what Tony knew would need to be distributed when he died, he had thought that neither Nathan nor James should be involved. Because it was James that she had her doubts about in the Fisher family, she realised. It wasn't Ellie at all. Ellie had never done anything dishonest, as far as she knew. And Ellie had never been afraid to stand up for the right thing.

An uncomfortable twist in her stomach pulled Caroline back. Of course Ellie wasn't untrustworthy. How could she have given that idea even a second's credence? No wonder Max had been so short with her. She would need to apologise when he came back down. She sent a short apology up into the ether for Ellie as well, just in case.

Still feeling guilty, she picked up her mobile to ring her.

Ellie answered after two rings. 'Hi, lovely. Good day so far?' came the cheerful voice, clearly glad to be hearing from her. Caroline dispelled the last of her doubts about her lifelong friend.

'Oh, not bad,' she replied. 'Same old, same old. You?'

'I'm in full-on social gathering organisational mode. My party and the funeral.'

'That sounds a bit grim.'

'It's quite hard doing them together – excited about the party, sad about the funeral, you know.'

'Well, if I can do anything else to help then you will say, won't you?' Caroline offered.

'Thanks, but it's fine. I think I'm sorted. There was something that I wanted to talk to you about though, Caro. You know last night . . .'

Caroline sat up a little and listened harder.

'I just wondered what you meant when you said you didn't think we should be taking the money at all.'

Caroline took a deep breath as she ordered her thoughts. She hadn't been sure that anyone had even heard her say that, let alone thought they wanted to hear her opinion. But of course, if anyone did it would be Ellie.

'Well, just that really,' she said. 'It feels wrong to me. We don't know what the money was doing at your dad's or what it was for. There's a suggestion that it might not be entirely above board. I just think we should hand it over to the police to investigate and then, if it turns out that it is completely legit, they'll give it back to us and we can divvy it up at that stage, knowing we've done the right thing.'

Ellie went quiet on the other end and Caroline could picture her thinking about what she had just said.

'Do you really think the money is dodgy?' she asked after a few moments.

Caroline paused, weighing up her answer. If she told the truth there was a clear implication that she must think the same about Tony. She didn't want to upset Ellie, but the thought must have crossed her mind too. In fact, from what Max had told her about their conversation with Valerie, Ellie had already learnt that Tony wasn't whiter than white. In that moment, she decided it was more important to be completely honest about how she felt. That was going to be the key to getting this sorted out effectively – honesty.

'I can't see any other reason why it would have been hidden like it was,' she said, hopefully leaving it open for there to be a perfectly reasonable solution.

'Yes,' Ellie said. 'I thought that too.'

Encouraged, Caroline continued, feeling her way for unexploded bombs as she went. 'So, if that's right, then it strikes me that the money was got unlawfully, or it actually belongs to someone else. And either way, just because I found it doesn't mean that I, or we, have any entitlement to it.'

Caroline carefully sidestepped mentioning Tony by name or suggesting that he had any part in the money being in his house. She could sense Ellie nodding down the phone.

'I take your point,' she said. 'I'd not really looked at it like that.'

'I was going to bring it up last night, but then Nathan stormed off and it didn't feel like the appropriate time. I don't want to cause any bother, but I really feel we have a duty to do the right thing. I actually feel that quite strongly,' she added, feeling that she might be pushing at an open door.

'What does Max think?' Ellie asked.

'Oh, you know Max. He sees my point of view but if Nathan was to say we should take it all and put it on the three thirty at Chepstow, he might be persuaded to do that too.'

'I'm not sure that's fair,' chipped in Ellie.

'No, of course not,' laughed Caroline. 'He's not *that* easily swayed. But he's so laid-back that he's happy to take on board what everyone says. Take the tax thing that James said. Yesterday he was all set to pay the money in to the bank. Today he's not going to.'

'But that's because the situation's changed,' said Ellie. 'He hadn't thought about the inheritance tax angle before . . .'

'Yes, you're right,' Caroline said quickly, not wanting the conversation to get sidelined into a discussion about Max's failings. 'So, you think I've got a point?' she added. 'About handing the money over to the police.'

It would be perfect if she and Ellie were thinking along the same lines over this. They usually did, but if they agreed now, then between them they could probably get Max and James to do the right thing.

'Yes,' said Ellie. 'And if it turns out there's nothing wrong with the money – which is probably going to happen – then we've lost nothing and we'll all feel better for being sure the money is perfectly fine to spend.'

'Precisely,' said Caroline.

When she put the phone down twenty minutes later, Caroline was pleased that progress was being made. Maybe they could avoid another gathering. If Ellie spoke to James and Max got Nathan on board then they could just move forward without any more arguments. Caroline couldn't help but think that would be for the best.

40

Nathan was going to have to get himself a new mobile phone. He had turned his current one off to avoid the daily texts and phone calls that came in from all quarters, demanding repayment of debts. Every time it rang, his blood ran cold in his veins. And on top of that, he had set his ringtone as one of his all-time favourite songs, which was now ruined forever – he would never be able to enjoy listening to it again without a rising sense of panic.

But he couldn't carry on like this, with his phone resolutely switched off. He did actually need to use it – for checking the form and odds if nothing else. It was just this bombardment of messages from his creditors that he wanted to avoid. Briefly, he indulged the idea that if he didn't reply to the increasingly threatening messages they would just give up and leave him alone, but that was rubbish, of course. They would find him whether he turned his phone on or not, although ignoring them might buy him a little more time.

Time was all he needed. Getting hold of the money was finally no problem. God bless his dad and his stash of cash. Nathan allowed himself a moment of congratulation for his own instincts. He had known there was cash hidden in that house. It was just incredibly bad luck that by the time he'd gone looking for it, Caroline and Max had already found it. He assumed they had known about it too and possibly needed it just as badly as he did. It was all very well, this whiter-than-white act the pair of them put on, but at the end of the day why else would they have been hunting round the house? He'd heard their ridiculous cat story, but it really didn't ring true. If all Caroline was looking for was the cat, how come she'd opened the suitcase? It made no sense. No. They had definitely been searching for the money too.

Nathan cursed out loud at the thought of his bad timing, a single explosive expletive that made the old lady in the sandwich shop queue next to him jump and turn her head to see who had been so uncouth. He half-smiled an apology at her. He really wasn't in the business of upsetting old ladies.

There had been a spanner thrown into the works the previous evening, though. Paying the money into the bank? What was that all about? Cash was king. Everyone knew that. They should just split it three ways, and then the others could do what the hell they liked with their share, and he could use his to get the loan sharks off his back. Ninety grand would be more than enough to get a fresh start, but he had to act quickly. The interest on his debts was building up at a terrifying rate and the longer it went on, the less chance he had of coming out of it with both his legs in full working order.

When he reached the front of the queue, he ordered a sandwich and a doughnut and then had to copper up from the coins in his pockets to pay for it. The bank had put a stop on his cards. All he had left was a single credit card, not yet maxed out, which he was saving for a true emergency. The man in the queue behind him tutted as he palmed the coins, counting them one at a time. Nathan threw him an aggressive glare, but he knew he would have been just as irritated if the situation were reversed.

Lunch in hand, he set off to the patch of green space at the back of his office to eat it and ring Max. His brother might not take the call. He was funny about what he did in work time – so twentieth century of him, but then that was his brother all over. But even Max had to stop for lunch, and Nathan might be fortunate with his timing. It was about time Lady Luck put in an appearance.

He sat down on the grass as far away from the other workers as he could and took his phone out of his pocket. The dead screen was reassuringly black. Tentatively he switched it on and watched as colour spread across it. Then there was the usual cacophony of notification noises as all the messages he had received that day and thus far ignored landed.

Nathan felt sick. How the hell had he got himself in this deep? He was an idiot. But he would sort it out. He would get his share of the money, pay off the debts and then he'd make some changes, get his life back on track. He could do it; he knew he could. He just needed the little leg-up that this cash would give him. He dialled Max's number.

Max answered quickly, but his voice was lowered as if he was worried about being overheard.

'Nathan. I can't really talk now,' he began.

'Max, wait!' said Nathan. 'It won't take more than a couple of minutes. We can't pay that money into the bank. It's total madness. It makes no sense. You should just split it up and then we can each do what we want with our shares.'

He paused, waiting for the objection, ready to counter it, but Max said, 'Actually, Nath, I was wanting to speak to you about that. Ellie rang this morning. She's been talking to James and he said that if we pay it in it's likely to trigger a tax point so we'd lose forty per cent in inheritance tax.'

Shit. Nathan hadn't even thought of that. A forty per cent deduction wouldn't leave him with enough to clear his debts. In fact, that would be worse than not having anything. To make a partial payment but to still have the interest accumulating on the balance with no way of repaying it would be even more of a nightmare.

'Well, we definitely can't do that, then,' he said, desperate to get his view across. 'It would be stupid.'

'Yeah, I agree,' said Max, and Nathan felt first surprised and then relieved.

'So, we're going to go back to the first idea and just divide it now?' he said.

'I suppose so. We'll need to decide, of course, but if we can't pay it into the bank then I'm not sure what else we can do.'

Nathan's breath came rushing out in relief. 'No,' he said. 'Me neither. It's the obvious thing.'

'Right, I have to go,' said Max. 'But I'll be in touch soon. Okay?'

'Yep,' replied Nathan. 'That's great. Speak soon. Have a great day.'

As Nathan turned his phone back off, steadfastly ignoring all the flashing messages, he felt lighter. It was going to be all right. He would have the cash soon and then everything would be okay. He ate his lunch and then whistled his way back to the office.

41

Lucy seemed brighter when she got home from school. No one had been mean to her about her reading, and Miss Elliot had singled her out for praise on her art project. God bless Miss Elliot, Ellie thought as she listened to a bright-eyed Lucy recount the tale. That was what they were paying for at Green Mount. Each child really was seen as an individual with individual needs. She couldn't believe that her girls would get that level of attention in a state school where the classes were twice the size.

James was home early as well, but in a far worse mood than Lucy. He barely said hello as he stalked across the hall heading for his office.

'You're back early,' Ellie called cheerfully after him. 'Good day?'

His office door slammed in reply.

'Nice to see you too, darling,' she muttered under her breath. He'd calm down, she thought. He got like this sometimes, difficult and withdrawn. It was generally something to do with his work. He was such a perfectionist and when things didn't go entirely the way he wanted he took it very much to heart. Ellie loved that about her husband, the drive he had to succeed no matter what the obstacles. So she forgave him the occasional lapses of humour. And manners.

Ellie got on with the after-school routine, listening to Olivia read, cajoling Lucy into doing the same. Then a quick tea before they headed out to the girls' ballet classes. Olivia had the makings of a lovely little ballerina. Lucy preferred her horse riding, but ballet was important for posture and balance, so Ellie made her stick at it.

Ellie settled down in the waiting room with the other mothers. She didn't really know any of them, not being Green Mount mums, so she gave them all a pleasant but unengaged smile, and pulled her phone out and started to scroll. However, she couldn't help but listen in to the conversation of the women sitting next to her, despite their lowered voices.

'They found him hiding in the boys' changing rooms,' one mother was saying. 'He was black and blue and covered in scratches from where they'd made him stand in the holly bush. Fran said he was still shaking when she got him home. She's thinking about suing the school for emotional trauma.'

'It's shocking,' said the other. 'And where were the dinner ladies when all this was going on?'

'Didn't see a thing, apparently. Or didn't look, more like.'

'Has Fran been to see the head?'

'Oh yes. Got some crap about boys being boys and it just being harmless fun, but of course, they'd keep their eyes open from now on.'

'They always say that. Just paying lip service, really. Nothing ever changes. And what about Aiden? How's he?'

'Fran says he's having nightmares. I'm not surprised, poor lamb.'

Ellie resisted the urge to look up and take a better look at the two women but from what she remembered they both looked perfectly nice and not at all rough. Their children were in a ballet class, for goodness' sake. Hearing stories like that just went to confirm what she already knew: state school was a bear pit where only the strongest could survive.

After the class, they headed home, Ellie hoping that James's mood would have improved, but when they opened the front door she thought she could sense a chilly atmosphere still hanging over the house. She had been going to talk to him about her conversation with Caroline, but she judged that this wasn't the moment. However, after she had put the children to bed and was sitting at the kitchen table, working her way through the lists for the funeral, he wandered in and raised the subject himself.

'Did you speak to Max?' he asked as he poured himself a glass of wine. 'About the cash?'

Ellie nodded, pleased to have some good news to impart. 'Yes. It was like you thought. He just hadn't thought about the tax implications. He's totally happy to hold off.'

James swallowed and gave her a brief smile.

'That's good. Saved ourselves a fortune there, then,' he said.

Ellie paused before she replied. She wanted to tell him what Caroline had said, was judging whether this was the moment, but he seemed to have forgotten his earlier mood and she didn't want him to have the impression that everything was sorted with the money now when it wasn't quite.

'I spoke to Caro too,' she began. 'We had a bit of a chat about it all. You know what she said last night, about not wanting to take the money at all . . . ?'

James rolled his eyes and made a tutting sound. 'Yes. What does she want to do with it? Donate it to the donkey sanctuary?'

'No! Of course not,' laughed Ellie. 'But she is worried that the money isn't entirely legal. She thinks we should hand it over to the police so that they can look into where it came from. Then, when we get it back, we can split it up.'

There was a pause of about five seconds whilst James processed what she had just said. And then he exploded.

'What the fuck is she talking about, the stupid woman? Hand it over to the police? Is she completely mad? Just split it three ways and give us our share. It's not fucking rocket science. Jesus Christ!'

They had a strict 'no swearing in the house' policy in case the girls overheard, and Ellie was more concerned about making him stop shouting than what had actually made him start. On top of that, she really didn't appreciate him bad-mouthing her friend and the wife of her brother.

'James, for goodness' sake, stop that,' she hissed at him, lowering her own voice to not much more than a whisper. 'The girls. They'll hear you. You'll upset them.'

'They need to hear!' he shouted. 'This is going to affect them too.'

Ellie was completely lost. 'What on earth are you talking about? What is?'

James looked so anguished that Ellie thought he might actually burst into tears. He ran his fingers through his hair and rubbed at his eyes with the heel of his hands. Then he seemed to come back to himself and he forced a smile of sorts.

'I just mean that if we can get our hands on ninety grand now then it would be handy.'

Alarm bells started to go off in Ellie's head. What was he talking about?

'But it's only ninety grand,' she said. 'I mean, obviously that's a lot of money, but in the grand scheme of things . . .' Her sentence tailed off as she saw James's expression. Ellie felt suddenly sick. It was obvious that there was something not right here, not right at all.

'James?' she continued. 'What's going on?'

James took a deep breath, then blew it out in one sharp release as if he were about to dive from a very high board. He chewed at his bottom lip for what felt like forever as Ellie, her heart beating hard in her chest, waited for him to speak.

'James, you're scaring me,' she said. 'Just tell me. What is it?'

James wouldn't look at her, his eyes darting left and right. He pulled up a chair next to her and sat down heavily. He took a large swig of his wine.

'You know I told you that I had a deal that hadn't gone the way I hoped,' he began.

Ellie nodded.

'Well, it's left us with a bit of a cash flow problem.'

Ellie wasn't quite sure what the implications of this were. Business was James's domain and she never really took much notice of the ins and outs.

'How do you mean?' she asked.

'Well, we don't have any liquid assets just at the moment.'

Relief flooded through Ellie. That didn't sound too bad. They had assets, just nothing they could put their hands on immediately.

'Okay,' she said. 'So, ninety grand would be handy. I get that.'

'It would,' he began. 'There are bills that need paying and others that are just over the horizon. The mortgage for one, and the bill for the school fees will land next month.'

Ellie nodded. She had never had anything to do with this kind of thing before. James sorted the family finances. Her duties lay elsewhere. Then something occurred to her.

'The mortgage?' she said. 'But we don't have a mortgage. Didn't we pay it off years ago?'

'Yes,' James replied. He ran his hands up and down his forearms as he spoke, as if he were cold. 'But don't you remember, we borrowed against the house again so that I could secure that big development out on the other side of the bypass.'

Ellie remembered that vaguely. 'Is that the one that keeps stalling?' she asked.

'That's the one,' he said. 'The whole site got caught up in red tape which messed up all the cash flow. I should have been shifting the houses by now, but we've barely got started.'

Something still wasn't adding up in Ellie's head.

'But we hardly borrowed anything,' she said. 'The mortgage payments can't be that steep. And if we're a bit short at the moment, couldn't we just cash in a bit more of the equity on this place, just to tide us over? Then we can pay it back off when those houses are up and start to sell.'

The look that crossed James's face was one she had never seen before. Panic, fear, she wasn't sure which it was but she definitely didn't like it.

'What is it that you're not telling me?' she asked him.

'The thing is, Ellie . . .' He put his hand over his mouth, rubbing at his stubbled chin. 'The thing is, we're pretty much borrowing up to the hilt on this place already.'

Ellie didn't understand. That was definitely not what she had agreed to. She might not know much about the workings of James's business, but she wasn't stupid. She would never have agreed to mortgage the entire house. It was far too risky.

'No, we're not,' she said. 'You've got that wrong. We only borrowed a hundred grand. I remember quite clearly.'

And then a bell sounded in her head, loud and long, bringing her to a new understanding. He had done it without her. He had borrowed against their house without telling her.

For a second, the kitchen seemed to be spinning before her eyes and she grasped the lip of the table to hold herself steady. This couldn't be happening. She and James were a team. They told each other everything. Other women's husbands had secrets, but not hers. She had always felt sorry for the wives who'd had the wool pulled over their eyes; sorry for them, but also slightly superior.

What kind of marriage could it be if they didn't share those simple, basic truths with one another?

And now, exactly the same seemed to be happening to her. A glance at James told her she was right. He looked as if his world had just collapsed around him, shoulders hunched and expression mournful.

'You did it without telling me,' she said simply, her voice calm and quiet for fear of waking her daughters. 'You borrowed money against our home, the most important thing we have, and you lied about it.'

'I didn't lie,' objected James, but they both knew he was splitting hairs. Lying. Hiding the truth. It all amounted to much the same thing.

'You knew that I would never have agreed, but you went ahead and did it anyway. Behind my back,' she continued.

'Only in the short term,' he said. 'I only needed the money for a couple of months, just while the planning permission on that site was sorted out. And then . . .'

And then again. Another horrible light bulb moment. A spotlight was suddenly shining on the darker parts of her world, and Ellie was able to see them clearly for the first time.

'And then Dad died,' she said, finishing his sentence for him. 'Is that it? Dad was going to fix the planning for you, so you borrowed against the house. And now he's not here so you have to go through the proper channels just like everyone else.'

James didn't speak and Ellie knew she was right. Her mind flicked back to the conversation they'd had after she and Max had spoken to their mum. Hadn't James suggested that all he had heard were the rumours about Tony being the council 'fixer'? But now he seemed to be saying that he had known that Tony was up to no good all along. However, Ellie was still reeling from the mortgage issue. She couldn't deal with his smaller consequential lies, not now. And then something else dawned on her.

'Oh my God,' she said slowly. 'Is that what the money in the suitcase was for? Is it what he needed to make things run smoothly for you?'

'And you,' interrupted James. 'And his granddaughters. It's for all of us, Ellie. And I don't know what that money was actually for,' he added. 'It could have been something else entirely.'

'Caro's right, though,' said Ellie. 'It is dirty money. Whether it was for your deal or someone else's, it's money that didn't really belong to Dad.'

'We don't know that,' said James. 'And to be honest, Ellie, it's a bit late for us to be seeking out the moral high ground now.'

'Us! Us!! I have done nothing. Absolutely nothing.' Ellie was outraged that he should tar her with the same brush as himself and her dad.

But James was having none of it. 'Nothing!' he shouted at her. 'Who is it wants the best holidays, the most expensive soap in the bathroom, the latest shoes? That's you, Ellie. I'm not bothered about all that crap. And the school. Have you any idea how expensive it is to send two children to that money pit? Fees, uniforms, trips, the right car to turn up to collect them in. Most families could live quite happily on what that all costs us. How much do you think Max earns? Less than you spend on fresh flowers, I bet.'

Ellie didn't know what to deal with first. This was all too much and it was coming at her too quickly. She started by defending herself.

'But you never told me I was spending too much,' she said, tears pooling in her eyes. 'I didn't know. You just let me do it. If you'd said something, I'd have stopped. I am capable, you know. But you never did. You just let me go on, willy-nilly. How can that be my fault?'

She stopped. There was no point shouting at each other. Nothing was going to be gained by that. What they needed was a solution. She pulled herself back and took a deep breath.

'So, what are we going to do?' she asked more calmly.

James slumped forward and rested his head on his forearms on the table. 'I don't know. I'm doing my best to keep it all going. There's that other site out near the waterworks. I have reasonable lines of credit with the local tradesmen, so if I can just keep them going on-site then we should get those houses finished within a month. A couple of them are sold already, so a marketing push should help me clear the rest. Then, if we rush them through to completion that should be enough for now. After that, I can work on getting the planning permission through for the other site. It's not a disaster, Els, not at all. Like I said before, it's just cash flow.'

'So we just need enough to cover the mortgage for a few months,' she said. 'Well, that can't be too hard.' Her heart seemed to have dropped back down from the base of her throat into her chest.

James nodded. 'And the school fees,' he said.

Ellie's heart leapt back up. They *had* to find the money for the school fees. That was imperative. She had seen what happened when they weren't paid. The image of Sarah Coombes shifting bin bags into her garage filled her mind. She pictured the faces of the other mothers at the school fair when they told her about Sarah's downfall, the delight in their eyes at the misfortune of another. And Ellie had joined in, blissfully unaware that she was only a few short steps from the edge of the precipice herself.

'We must find the school fees,' she said. 'That's a priority. We can't put the girls through having to change schools. It's far too damaging. And they shouldn't be punished for our mistakes.'

She chose her pronoun carefully, understanding that this was not the time for blame and recrimination. They were firefighting here, and they had to do it together.

'We'll find the fees,' James said. 'But can you see why that money from your dad would be fantastic right now. It would tide us over perfectly.'

Ellie did see that. She could see that perfectly plainly. 'Okay. So, what do we do?' she asked again.

James thought for a moment, and then a smile spread across his face. 'We don't have to do anything,' he said.

Ellie was thrown back into confusion, her brain struggling to keep up with all the new information.

James, reading her expression, continued. 'You and Nathan are in favour of taking the money now. So it doesn't really matter what Max and Caroline think. You two outvote them. You simply have another vote and let the decision follow the majority.'

He was right. In one way, the answer to their problem was incredibly simple. They all knew that Nathan wanted the money straight away, so together the pair of them could make that happen.

'But if we do that,' she began, 'we risk falling out with Max and Caro. I don't want that. Caro is my best friend and Max is my brother.'

'And we find ourselves up a particular creek without a paddle,' said James. 'Right now, it's either us or them, Ellie. You are going to have to decide where your priorities lie.'

42

Ellie was reeling. She lay in the dark trying to think through all the ramifications of the evening's revelations, but it made her too anxious, so instead she was trying to make a practical to-do list in her head. Beside her James was asleep. For a while after they turned out the light she could tell from the depth of his breathing that he too was struggling to drop off, but then his body's rhythms evened out and now she was certain she was the only one awake. How many nights had he lain awake whilst she had slept innocently on? Now the roles were reversed. He had had time to get used to the situation, and seemed to have found a way to sleep through it. For her, it was all horribly, shockingly new.

In the maelstrom of emotions that she was drowning in, two things were crystal clear: they needed to get hold of their share of the money, and they needed to do it without falling out with Max and Caroline.

Ellie could feel her cheeks burning at the thought. That was something else. They would have to secure the money without having to confess to Max and Caro just how close to the wire she and James were. She couldn't bear it if that came out. It was so embarrassing, so shaming. It was bad enough that James had taken all the equity out of the house without her being aware. That made her look like such an idiot as well as putting a huge crack down the image she liked to portray of them as a strong team. On top of that was the truth about her dad and just what the money might have been lined up for. Backhanders received by Tony and then recycled to be paid back out to others. Was that really how it all worked? Ellie truly didn't think it was, but then, as had been proved quite categorically that evening, there was a lot Ellie didn't know.

The thought of having to explain exactly why James had run up against a problem made her feel sick. Worse still was the idea that if her dad hadn't had his inconveniently timed aneurysm, she would never have known that her home was at risk. James would have borrowed against it and then paid it all back before she was any the wiser. That had been the plan. Was it better to know or to have been in blissful ignorance? Ellie really wasn't sure.

There was one element of luck that was on their side, though. Neither the mortgage nor the school fees needed to be paid until the end of the month. That gave them two weeks to sort it all out. Granted, there was a lot happening in those two weeks – Ellie's stomach turned over at the thought of exactly how much money she had already committed to for her fortieth birthday party – but it still gave her time to speak to Caroline and Max clearly and calmly and get them to change their minds. She had done it once, after all. Max had been determined to pay the money into the bank at the beginning, but when she'd explained about the tax implications he'd been quick enough to do a U-turn.

And Ellie didn't know what Max thought. He might not agree with Caroline about not touching the money. In fact, it hadn't sounded as if Caroline had really discussed her thoughts with him at all. The way she had explained it to Ellie, she had just assumed they would all want to make sure the money was theirs to take before they split it up. Caroline had always been scrupulously honest. It was one of the things Ellie loved best about her, the way her moral compass always pointed out a clear path for her to follow. But it was more of a hindrance than a help now. They didn't have time to waste debating the finer points of what was right and wrong. Caroline just needed to agree with them and let them get on with distributing the money before she and James ran out of time.

It wasn't that easy, though. Although she and Nathan could easily outvote Max, if they did that she would be riding rough-shod all over what she knew Caroline wanted and that would mean putting their friendship in jeopardy. Who would she choose, Ellie wondered, if it was between James and Caro? Well, that was obvious, even though it was difficult to acknowledge the thought that she might ever have to make such a decision.

Maybe it would be better to try to talk Caroline round to their way of thinking so that no one needed to fall out. Ellie was sure that if she explained exactly why she and James needed the money, told her about the school fees . . . But then Ellie had never told Caroline about Lucy's dyslexia and how she struggled so hard to keep up, so Caro wouldn't automatically understand why a switch to a state school would be so devastating for her. Ellie would just end up looking like a snob and that would be sure to make the situation worse.

Ellie had never really unpicked why she had kept Lucy's difficulties to herself when she told Caroline everything else, but she knew it was something to do with feeling embarrassed that her second daughter was somehow less than outstanding. It was an ugly thought and one she didn't like to examine too closely. Of course, Ellie didn't truly believe it. She loved Lucy just as much as she loved Olivia, but having to explain away Lucy's far from glittering academic record in terms of a learning difficulty that had never before been mentioned might make her seem like one of those pushy mothers they both hated, who made feeble excuses to explain why their child was not at the top of the class.

So Ellie had just never mentioned it. And now it would look peculiar if she suddenly pulled it out of the bag at precisely the moment she needed a reason to take the money from the suitcase.

It was all so very complicated, or so it seemed in the small hours of the morning. Her dad used to say that the night was always darkest just before the dawn. Well, that was certainly the case now.

James spluttered in his sleep and rolled over. That was something else Ellie didn't dare unpick: just how very angry she was with him for getting them to this point in the first place. But it wouldn't help anything for her to vent her fury now. The time for recriminations was when the mess was sorted out. Then, and only then, would she let rip at James.

In the meantime, she had given Caroline the impression that she agreed with her about handing the money over to the police. Hell, she *had* agreed with her when they had spoken, little knowing how quickly the situation would change, and with it her mind. She would need to see if she could gently push Caroline along the same path as the rest of them.

Of course, they could just press on and leave Caroline out in the cold, but that was the last thing Ellie wanted to do.

43

Nathan rang Ellie the very next morning. This was a rare event. Usually her brother only replied to her messages rather than initiating contact himself, but as soon as Ellie saw his name flash up on the screen of her mobile phone she knew exactly what he wanted.

'Hi, Nath,' she said. 'I can guess what you're ringing about.'

'Are we any further forward?' he asked without bothering with any niceties. Ellie thought about commenting on his lack of social grace, but what would be the point?

'No,' she said.

'Why the hell not?' His voice was spiky but also guarded, and Ellie wondered if he was worried about being overheard. 'I spoke to Max and he said we weren't going to pay it into the bank any more. So, what's the delay?'

Ellie took a breath to give herself time to get her thoughts straight. 'I don't know,' she replied simply. 'There's no reason, as far as I know. Maybe Max has just been too busy to get it sorted.'

She wasn't about to tell Nathan what Caroline had told her. That really wouldn't help and anyway, if Caroline wanted to delay things with this integrity issue of hers then she should be the one who took the flak for it.

'Why don't you ring Max and ask him?'

'I did that already,' snapped Nathan, 'but he's not picking up.'

'You know what he's like about taking calls at work,' she said.

'So, I'm ringing you instead. The thing is, Els . . .' His tone became lighter and more friendly and Ellie got the impression that he was trying to soften her up. What was it about the men in her life? Did they all think she was a pushover? Nathan didn't know that she knew he had lied to her and James about the money they'd given him. He had no idea exactly how steep the hill he was climbing really was.

'. . . the thing is,' he continued, 'I could really do with that money. Like now.'

Well, couldn't we all, she thought but didn't say.

'Then you need to speak to Max,' she said dismissively. 'He's the one with all the power, or at least all the money.'

The irony wasn't lost on her. The most plodding, least dynamic of the siblings was suddenly the one in control of both their destinies. Or perhaps his wife was. Ellie still hadn't got a handle on the situation between Max and Caroline.

'I just thought—' Nathan began, but Ellie cut him off.

'You're the one that needs the cash right now, so you can do your own chasing,' she said firmly. She was thinking that if they both pushed at once there was more chance Max would cave in, but she would let Nathan ford that stream first, then it wouldn't look as if she was as desperate. In fact, if Nathan did the groundwork, she could possibly emerge from this without any of them having to know just how desperate the situation was for her and James.

Nathan sighed loudly down the phone. 'Okay,' he said. 'But will you ring him too. Just so he knows that you're on my side. Please.'

He drew the word out like he had done when he was little and, despite everything, Ellie caught herself smiling down the line at her baby brother.

'Oh, go on then,' she said. 'Seeing as you asked so nicely. You ring him this evening and I'll try tomorrow.'

'Okay,' he replied, and then he was gone without even saying goodbye.

Ellie considered her next move. Caroline would be at work as well so she would have to wait until she got back home, but Ellie thought she would like to speak to her before Max got there. That way she could test the waters a little on just how strong this conviction of hers really was.

With this in mind, she drafted a quick text.

Hi Caro. Fancy a cuppa after work? Shall we pop over to you around 4?

A couple of minutes later a simple thumbs-up emoji arrived from Caroline.

44

Alex and Theo were already home when Caroline unlocked the front door. The hallway was strewn with school detritus, dropped and left where it had fallen like a snake sheds its skin. She picked her way through, scooping up a sweatshirt, a tie and two schoolbags as she went.

'Hi, boys,' she called out. 'I'm home. Did you have good days?'

A muffled sound that could have been anything but which she chose to interpret positively came from the lounge where the boys would be ensconced in front of the games console whilst they decompressed from their day.

Caroline put the dropped items at the bottom of the stairs for the boys to ignore the next time they went to their rooms, and then went to make sure the kitchen was fit to receive Ellie. It wasn't too bad. There were crumbs and a dirty butter knife on the work surface where someone had made themselves a sandwich without using a board, and a bottle of squash stood, lidless, by the sink, but that was all.

She had just begun the task of emptying the dishwasher when there was a tap on the back door and Ellie appeared, Olivia and Lucy slinking in behind her and then immediately disappearing to find their cousins.

'Only me,' she said, coming in and giving Caroline a hug. 'Good day?'

'Not so bad,' replied Caroline. 'Much the same as always. You?'

Ellie shrugged. 'Oh, you know,' she said sadly.

Caroline hadn't thought about Tony's death all day. Quickly, she recentred herself. Living with Max, who kept his emotions somewhere close to his bones, it was easy to forget that he and Ellie had lost their dad in shocking circumstances three weeks before. Caroline knew what it was like to lose a parent, and in difficult circumstances too, so she berated herself for forgetting Ellie's pain in and amongst everything else that was going on.

She pulled Ellie back into her and gave her another hug, harder this time and, she hoped, loaded with more significance.

'Oh, your poor lamb,' she said soothingly. 'It must be so hard, especially with the funeral still being so far away.'

She could feel Ellie nod against her chest and she squeezed a little tighter. After a moment or two, Ellie pulled herself away. Her eyes were dry but Caroline noticed how deep-set they looked, hollowed out by dark shadows.

'Are you okay, Ellie?' she asked. 'Is it all too much, the funeral and the party? I'm here for you, you know. You only have to ask.'

'I know,' said Ellie. 'Thank you, but it's all in hand. It's just a lot to take on board, that's all.'

'Of course it is. How are the girls coping?'

'They're sad, when they remember,' smirked Ellie.

Caroline smiled and rolled her eyes. 'Yes, the boys are the same. It's quite hard for them to take it in. They know they're supposed to be upset, and I think they are really, but they can't quite manage sad twenty-four/seven.'

Caroline was curious as to what Ellie had decided about taking the girls to the funeral, but she felt instinctively that this wasn't the time to ask. She and Max had finally agreed that Alex and Theo should go. It was up to Ellie and James what they did with their kids. Wanting to move the conversation on, she asked about the party preparations. Usually this would have lifted Ellie's mood, but today even that seemed to leave her flat.

'It's pretty much done,' she said, barely even smiling. 'Just a couple of last-minute things on numbers and catering that I can't do until nearer the time.'

'Oh, Ellie,' said Caroline. 'I'm so sorry this is happening. It's all such crap.'

Ellie looked at her, eyebrows raised. 'Well, it's not like you can do anything about it,' she replied a little sharply, which pushed Caroline slightly off-kilter.

'Well, no,' agreed Caroline, 'but still. I wish it was a bit easier for you.'

'Thanks,' said Ellie. She flicked her fingernails and Caroline wondered if she had done something to upset her, but then Ellie pulled out a chair and sat down. 'Any chance of a cup of tea?' she asked.

Caroline, momentarily having forgotten her hostess duties, jumped to it. 'Yes, sorry. I should have asked. Earl Grey, mint or builders'?'

'Mint, please,' said Ellie and slumped back in the chair.

Something really wasn't right here, Caroline thought. Something more than the party and the funeral.

Two minutes later they sat opposite one another, each cupping steaming mugs in their hands, but the conversation was still faltering. Thirty years of friendship meant they could sit in silence without it being an issue, but Caroline sensed Ellie had something to say that she just wasn't vocalising.

'What's up, Ellie?' she asked when it became clear that Ellie wasn't going to begin herself. 'Apart from the obvious, I mean.'

Ellie paused before she spoke, taking a deep breath and letting it out again slowly. Caroline got the impression that Ellie was deciding what she should tell her, and the thought sent tiny sparks of alarm tingling down her spine. Since when did Ellie pick and choose what to say? They told each other everything. That was how it was, how it had always been. Their friendship was the 'warts and all' kind. She tried again.

'Has something happened? Something more than just the funeral and everything?'

Caroline watched her friend's face carefully as it fleetingly registered a raft of emotions suggesting some kind of turmoil going on inside, but then Ellie said, 'No. Not really. It's just all getting a bit on top of me.'

That wasn't it, Caroline was pretty certain, but she was happy to run with that until something closer to the truth came out.

'I'm not surprised,' she replied. 'You're grieving, and on top of that you have all this other stuff to deal with and that's not to mention the day-to-day difficulties of being a wife and mother. It's enough to bring anyone down.'

Ellie nodded and bit her lip, but she still didn't open up. Caroline took another sip of her tea and tried a different tack.

'Oh, I meant to tell you. You'll never guess who popped up on my Facebook page,' she said, pivoting the conversation in a more light-hearted direction. It was a something and nothing of a story, an unrequited childhood crush of hers, who had disappeared and been forgotten, only to reappear on social media looking far less attractive than Caroline remembered. Ellie rallied a little as they gossiped about him and other people from their childhood and for a while it was almost as if nothing was wrong, but Caroline could still feel the sting of whatever it was Ellie wasn't sharing.

Eventually, Ellie finished her drink and put her mug down decisively, signalling her intention to leave, the thing she had come to say remaining unsaid. Caroline felt it was now or never.

'Did you have something you wanted to talk about, Ellie?' she asked, looking directly into her friend's eyes. Ellie immediately dropped her gaze to the floor, telling Caroline everything she needed to know. 'Come on. Spit it out. What's worrying you?'

Ellie put her hand to her mouth, found her thumbnail with her teeth. 'You know what you said about the money,' she began. 'About wanting to hand it over to the police.'

So that was it, Caroline thought. She must have been talking to James. He'd have decided it was a terrible idea, and told her to come round and talk some sense into her. Caroline felt herself bristle. What did it have to do with James? She was perfectly entitled to have her own views, and to pass them on to Ellie. But then, she thought, in reality the money had as little to do with her as it did with James. It was a Frost sibling issue and both of them were excluded from that particular gang.

'Yes,' she said simply. If James had sent her here to change her mind then she wasn't going to make it easy for him.

'Well, me and James were talking, and we're not sure it's the right thing to do.'

'That's not what you thought yesterday,' said Caroline, aware that her tone was snippier than usual.

'No,' agreed Ellie, 'but I've had a chance to think about it since then. If we hand the money over then everyone will find out about it. There's bound to be a leak of some sort. And it's not going to cast Dad in the best light.'

'Possibly not,' conceded Caroline.

'And I'm not sure that's something we should put his memory through, not on purpose at any rate,' Ellie continued.

It crossed Caroline's mind that perhaps Tony should have thought about his reputation before he started hiding enormous stashes of cash in his house.

'I'm not sure that's the point,' she replied. 'If the money is illegal then we shouldn't touch it. If it's clean then we can just go ahead.'

Ellie's brow furrowed. 'But can't you see that just by asking the question it makes it look like we think Dad was up to no good.'

Caroline raised a sceptical eyebrow as if to say of course he was up to no good. No one who is up to any good has that quantity of money hidden in a suitcase under a bed.

'Well, anyway, we think it would be better not to open that particular can of worms and just distribute the cash now,' Ellie continued. She almost sounded as if she were bruising for a fight, and Caroline felt herself straighten up mentally, preparing herself to return her punches.

'And I don't,' she said.

'To be honest, Caro,' said Ellie, her lips narrowed, 'it doesn't really matter what you think. Or Max, for that matter. Nathan and I can outvote you.'

This hadn't occurred to Caroline, but of course Ellie was right. They had gone with the majority vote from the start, outvoting Nathan about putting the money into the bank before they had realised the potential tax implications of doing so. But surely this was different? Something as fundamental as this would need them all to agree, wouldn't it? She hadn't even had a chance to discuss her thoughts with Max yet – she had been planning to do so when he got home from work – but she felt confident he would see things her way. But that didn't matter if Ellie and Nathan pushed through what they wanted to do by sheer force of numbers.

'But it's wrong!' she said, her voice shrill. 'You know that, Ellie. We discussed it and you agreed with me. It's theft, plain and simple.

249

Until we know the money was Tony's and obtained entirely legally then it's not ours to take. I don't care what you think. Nathan has his own agenda so he's not looking at things logically. And you and James hardly need it. Much better to wait until we know for sure.'

Ellie stood up. 'Who needs what is beside the point,' she said. 'It's the principle. If we take it to the police, then questions will be asked. People will start casting aspersions on Dad's integrity and he's not even in the ground yet.'

Caroline saw that Ellie was fighting to hold back the tears so decided to back off, even though her comment about Tony's integrity really needed addressing.

'Let me talk to Max,' she said more gently. 'And then we can decide what to do for the best.'

Ellie wiped at her eyes and gave her a weak smile, clearly also anxious to dispel the tension of a moment before.

'Okay,' she said. 'See what he thinks. We just need to get it sorted out, Caro. The whole situation is making me so stressed and I've got enough on my plate as it is. It would be better if we could just agree and move on.'

Caroline nodded sympathetically, but as far as she was concerned nothing had changed. They still needed to make sure the money was legal before they started throwing it around. Max would see that, she was sure.

'I'm glad we've had this talk, Caro,' said Ellie, sounding as if it had been concluded to her satisfaction. She moved towards the back door. 'Let's get the whole thing done before the funeral, shall we? Then we can bury Dad and forget about it.'

Caroline gave her a smile but she wasn't about to agree with her. There was no way this would be sorted by then.

45

Max had barely got through the door before Caroline was on him.

'We have to talk about the money,' she said before he'd taken his jacket off. 'Ellie popped round this afternoon and I think there's something going on there. She's putting quite a lot of pressure on us to just hand the cash out to everyone.'

Max rubbed at his shoulder to relieve post-work stiffness. His skin looked pasty, she thought, and there were fine lines around his eyes that hadn't been there before all this had happened.

'Well, why shouldn't we do just that?' he asked. 'We're both jumpy about having it in the house. So splitting it would be the perfect solution.'

Caroline started. She hadn't expected this reaction and she needed to make him see that it would be entirely the wrong thing to do before he just caved in and took the easiest path out of the problem.

'But it wouldn't—' she began urgently.

'Hang on,' Max said, putting a finger up to silence her midflow. 'I thought we'd agreed that paying it into the bank was a bad idea.'

'That's not what I'm talking about,' Caroline said. Then she swallowed. She was about to accuse Tony of being bent. However she spun it, Max wasn't going to take kindly to it. 'It's more a question of integrity.'

Max threw her a quizzical glance.

'We don't know where that money came from. We might be taking something that doesn't belong to us. We have to know why it was there or if it's owed to someone else. Without knowing that then taking it for ourselves is theft. And I can't do that, Max. I can't steal it.'

Max stuck out his lower lip as he considered her words. 'Okay,' he began. 'So how do you propose to find that out?'

'I think we should hand it over to the police, let them investigate. And then if it's clean we'll get it back, and if it's not the police will do what they should with it, and that will show it wasn't ours to take in the first place.' Caroline scanned his face carefully, looking for any clue that he was with her. For a couple of seconds there was nothing and her heart fluttered in panic.

'I get where you're coming from,' he said slowly. 'But I can't see Nath agreeing to that. What did Ellie say?'

Caroline noted that he had just assumed she had already spoken to Ellie, and of course, he was right.

'It's a bit strange,' she said. 'Yesterday she totally agreed with me. Today she's totally against.'

'No mystery there,' said Max, pouring himself a glass of water from the tap and taking a drink before he continued. 'That's James speaking.'

'She said she was worried about it leaking and damaging your dad's reputation.'

Max's eyebrows shot up and Caroline was tempted to comment, but she bit her tongue. She was treading a fine line here, and it was the concept of them stealing the money that she wanted Max to focus on, not Tony himself.

'What do you think, Max?' she asked instead.

He cocked his head on one side as he went over both arguments in his head. Caroline's eyes never left his face.

'On balance, I'm with you. But I can see Ellie's point of view as well.'

Caroline knew that she needed to make her point more clearly. She needed him firmly on her side and at the moment she could see that he could still go either way.

'It's wrong to take it, Max. It's as clear as the nose on my face,' she said. 'What if whoever the money does belong to found out that we had it? It wouldn't be that difficult to find us. We're easy enough to track down. What if they demanded it back, threatened me and the boys? We have no idea who we're dealing with here, what kind of people. And what if other people found that we'd taken all that money? It wouldn't just be your dad's reputation on the line then.'

She let the thought hang in the air so Max could catch up with where she was.

'I'd just feel much happier if we let the police deal with it,' she continued after a moment. 'And then, if it's all totally legitimate, we'll get it back and everything will be fine.'

'Okay,' said Max, nodding slowly.

'The trouble is, Ellie and Nathan could outvote you. But I feel so strongly that handing it over would be the wrong thing to do. This isn't as simple as a little bit of tax. This is about the rights and wrongs of it. This is fundamental to the kind of people we are.'

Max sniffed, taking in what she had said before he spoke again. 'I agree that it's not ours to take,' he began. 'And you're right, Ellie and Nathan can outvote me, just like we outvoted Nath before.'

Caroline needed to lead him slowly through her thought processes. She was used to doing that. She adored Max, but sometimes his thinking was downright pedestrian.

'You should say that for something as serious as this there has to be unanimity,' she said.

'Well, that would never work,' replied Max quickly. 'Even if we could talk Ellie back round, Nath will never agree.'

'Perhaps he would if the alternative is no money at all,' Caroline said sharply.

Max's face went dark and Caroline realised she was treading a thinner line than she had realised.

'I really don't want us all to fall out,' she said in a softer tone. 'But I feel so strongly about it. It's just wrong to take the money. You can see that, can't you?'

There was a pause, then Max nodded. 'Yes. I see that,' he agreed. 'God, I wish we'd never found the bloody stuff. Who knew a quarter of a million pounds could cause so much trouble? Let me speak to the others myself. We're going round in circles here, but if I talk to them, I'll have a better idea of where we stand.'

Caroline could feel her throat thickening. She hadn't realised she was so close to tears. She wasn't quite sure where it was coming from, this strength of emotion. But she couldn't have anyone accuse her and Max of theft or cheating the system or, in fact, anything dishonest at all. She knew people always assumed guilt if there was any hint of wrongdoing. There were already some who were suspicious about Tony and his business dealings. Valerie, for one, and she was better placed to know than most people, but also Lesley at work and she hadn't just conjured that rumour out of thin air. She must have heard something unsavoury about him to think as she did.

And it was a very small hop from people accusing Tony to people accusing her and Max. Caroline had been there. She knew how it stung to have all eyes on you, accusing you of something. She had seen people's expressions as they reframed their opinions of her based on what they believed her father had done. She might have only been a child, but it had left its scar on her. It hadn't just been her father who had been accused of taking the money for the wheelchair. It was the whole family, tainted by association, because they looked at her and her mother and wondered, if her father could steal money from a disabled boy, then who knew what the rest of the family was capable of? Her little family, blown apart by the accusations, had never recovered, and there was no way she was going to let anyone do that to Max and the boys.

She just couldn't let it happen a second time.

46

Max could feel things spiralling away from his grasp and he didn't like it. He definitely understood where Caroline was coming from with her argument. She was right that they knew nothing about the provenance of the money, and it was obvious there was something dodgy about it. Anyone could see that. Why else would it have been hidden as it was? So he could see the sense in getting it checked out before they spent it. He didn't want anything to come back and bite them at a later date.

There was also the issue of reputation to consider. Nobody wanted to be accused of being dishonest, he assumed, and least of all Caroline.

Caroline had always been scrupulously honest. It was one of the things he loved most about her. If she got given the wrong change in a shop she would own up. If a delivery contained items she hadn't ordered, she sent them back, even though he was sure it was legal to keep unsolicited goods. Whichever way he cut it, the money was clearly dubious, and the honest thing to do would be to hand it over to the police and let them decide what happened next.

But his siblings apparently didn't see things like that. It had been obvious from day one that Nathan just wanted to get his hands on his share, but now it seemed Ellie felt the same way – or at least James did. It actually made no difference which of them was leading the other. If that was the position Ellie had decided to take and she sided with Nathan, then they were two to one against him. Even if they included spouses in the vote, he and Caroline would be on the losing side.

Max had left the house to go for a walk and clear his head. If they had a dog then that would have given him the perfect excuse. He had always thought that just walking without a purpose was a strange thing to do. Maybe he could buy a lead for Monty. Did cats wear leads? He thought probably not, and he didn't really want a dog, so walking on his own it would have to be.

He pulled his mind back to the matter in hand and began running through the points. There was also the tax issue to think about. If they handed the money over to the police, then it would surely alert the authorities to its existence. They all spoke to one another, he assumed, in some convoluted way, especially when such big sums were involved. The police may well conclude that the money was clean, but merely by asking them the question would they be forfeiting forty per cent of it? Did that make sense? Max wasn't sure.

As he stomped along the street, hands in pockets and head down to avoid eye contact with anyone else, he tried to decide what to do. Should he be siding with his siblings or his wife? That was basically the question, and the answer was obvious. His wife. It was a no-brainer.

But was she right? There was no point causing the enormous row he knew was coming over something that was a mere whim. Who should he be trying to talk round here? Caroline or Ellie and Nathan?

He wished he could chat it through with someone else, but who was there? His friends were no good. It would be a huge ask to keep such a juicy story to themselves, and even if they tried to anonymise it as they recounted the tale to open-mouthed acquaintances in the pub, it wouldn't be that hard to fit the pieces together and bring it back to his family. There was Valerie, but she had made her views pretty clear. She had divorced Tony and whilst she was still his mum, she had left her ex and his dodgy dealings in her past.

'For God's sake, Dad,' he said out loud. 'What a mess.'

What would his dad have advised him to do? Keep the money! But that wasn't the point. That wasn't what he was searching for here. At a more fundamental level, and going back to first principles, what would his dad have said? Well, Max knew the answer to that, unhelpful though it might have been. Tony would have told him to follow his instincts.

'Always go with your gut, Max,' Tony had said. 'Learn how to separate your head from your heart and be sceptical about them both. Either one can take you up the wrong path. Instead, follow what your gut tells you. That won't ever lead you far astray, even if it feels like it might sometimes.'

So, what was his gut telling him? Max was surprised to discover that he knew what that was immediately.

47

Max called Nathan first. His brother picked up on the first ring, as if he had been hovering over the phone just waiting for it to leap into action.

'What's going on?' Nathan asked at once. 'What's the hold-up?'

Max's heart sank. Why had he done this? He had nothing new to tell Nath, nothing that he would want to hear anyway, and there was no way he would be able to discuss Caroline's proposal with him rationally. All he had achieved by calling was to put himself in the firing line for more flak.

'Just a few logistics to iron out,' Max said cagily. 'I wanted to keep you in the loop so you know where we are. Speak soon.'

He ended the call.

His walk was taking him past some huge houses, he noticed. Some of these, tucked away behind electric gates and hidden up long drives, were even bigger than Ellie and James's place. What did people need with all that space? he wondered. Maybe the families that lived there hated one another and had to have plenty of room to avoid unnecessary contact. Max couldn't really understand that. When the three Frost siblings had been growing up, there had been friendly fire between them but no real hostility. And his household now was calm and ordered. It must be horrible to live in a family that fought.

An unwelcome thought shouldered its way into his head. Wasn't a fighting family precisely the uncharted territory that he was about to march into himself? If he and Caroline stuck to their guns, or Caroline's guns at least, it was going to cause one almighty row from which there may never be any return. He couldn't imagine having a family at war. But surely, he thought as he passed yet another huge house, this one with ridiculous stone peacocks on the gateposts, it would never come to that. The three of them were too close. They were never going to let something like a bit of cash cause fissures to open up between them. Everyone would get a bit aerated whilst they tossed the options backward and forward, but they wouldn't fall out, not seriously anyway. They were all right-thinking adults who could see both sides of any argument. After all, he had no difficulty understanding everyone else's point of view, so it wouldn't be a problem for the rest of them.

He rang Ellie, holding the phone tightly to his ear as if that would somehow cement the connection between them.

'Hi, Max,' she said. She sounded less cheerful than usual, he thought, but then it was Friday evening, the end of a long and challenging week for all of them.

'Hi. Listen, Ellie,' he said, 'I just wanted to sound you out on this money business.'

'Oh, yes?'

'I gather Caroline's told you that she thinks we should hand the money over to the police,' he continued, listening hard for any subliminal signals that Ellie might be giving off.

'She has,' Ellie replied cautiously.

'And what are your thoughts?' he asked neutrally.

There was a pause. Max realised he was holding his breath so as not to interrupt the silence and alter what Ellie might be about to say.

'It's difficult, Max,' began Ellie. 'On the one hand, I can see where Caro is coming from. I think we can all agree that the money is probably suspect. It doesn't take a genius to work that out. But if we take it to the police, well, I just think awkward questions will be asked. And it won't only be about Dad. We'll all come into the firing line. Nathan has clearly got himself into some kind of financial pickle, which I wouldn't want investigating, and James's business really doesn't need that kind of scrutiny right now either. I mean, Caro is right that the honest thing to do would be to report it, but sometimes life just isn't that black and white.'

Max listened. Ellie sounded so calm and reasonable and he could totally understand her point of view.

'So, if we had to vote on it . . .' he said.

'I'd vote against handing it in,' she finished. 'I'd opt for just taking the cash and splitting it between us now. It's the rational thing to do. I know it's not ideal for very many reasons, but it's the best option in a field of bad ones.'

A pause.

'And,' she continued, 'Nathan would vote with me, so that would mean it didn't really matter what you thought.'

Her tone had changed. Her voice was sharp, brittle as broken glass. She was warning him. It was polite and reasonable, with no suggestion of an argument, but underlying her words was the clear understanding that she would get her way and there was nothing he could do to stop it. He heard her loud and clear. But he wasn't going to be browbeaten by the pair of them.

'I'll have a think,' he said. 'Speak soon.' He ended the call.

He set off back home again, his pace faster now as his mind became clearer. Ellie had used words like 'difficult' and 'awkward' to show that she understood that this wasn't at all clear-cut, but when push came to shove, her position was crystal. There had definitely been a threat in her words, veiled and civilly delivered, but there nonetheless. If he didn't vote with them they would gang up together and he would be out in the cold.

That was the trouble with having three children. It was the main reason he and Caro only had two, despite her pushing for another. With three you were either all together or someone was being left out. Over the years, it had generally been Nathan on the outside, but that was mainly because he was so much younger. They didn't really notice the nine years now they were adults, or he didn't at least, but it had been an almost insurmountable gap when they were kids. It was inevitable that he and Ellie, being a more conventional two years apart, would grow up together whilst Nathan had tagged along on his own, for all intents and purposes an only child.

Max had never really considered how that might have felt for Nathan, watching as his siblings shared private jokes that he could never understand. Max knew he had never excluded Nathan maliciously – it had always been as a result of his age and nothing else – but now he wondered. Had Nathan felt less supported than he and Ellie had, less loved, even? Could how they had treated him when he was a child have led to his difficulties as an adult?

No, Max told himself, that was ridiculous. If anything, Nathan had been showered in love and attention because he was so little and often quite cute. There was no correlation between Nathan now and some kind of childhood deprivation of affection. If he had got himself into a mess then it was of his own making and not the fault of his family.

But feeling like the outsider . . . Maybe that was something Max was beginning to understand. The thought that it might be he who was pushed out of the tight little band left him with a strange and unfamiliar sensation. And he didn't like it.

As he rounded the corner into their road and saw the generally comforting outline of their house, he felt a tension starting to build across his shoulders and up his neck. Whatever happened next, someone he loved was going to get hurt. Max was in for a fight that he really didn't want to have.

48

Ellie opened her eyes on her fortieth birthday and immediately concluded that she didn't feel any different. For nearly ten years, she had been anticipating this day – first worrying about it, slowly getting her head around the idea and then, ultimately, almost looking forward to it. A new decade was something to be celebrated; after all, many people never had the luxury of getting there. And everyone she knew who had reached the milestone before her seemed to be enjoying it. Apparently, going into your forties brought with it a kind of inner self-confidence and calm that women in their thirties just couldn't match. After all, didn't life begin at forty, and all that?

Ellie wasn't feeling that calm about hers, however. There was far too much happening over the next two days for that. At least the funeral wasn't until two, so there was no need to start racing around straight away. She could enjoy the pre-school time with the girls and James. They would have treats lined up, she was sure, so she could focus on enjoying that and move into funeral mode later.

The real celebration would be the party the next day. That was okay. She was forty, not fourteen; she could wait another twenty-four hours to step into the spotlight.

She pushed a foot over to James's side of the bed but found an empty space. It was clear from the temperature of the sheets that he had been gone for some time. A cold shiver of dread ran through her as she thought what he might be doing, but she told herself that he was just as likely to be up early arranging surprises with Olivia and Lucy as trying to rescue his failing business. In fact, she knew it was probably a bit of both.

Now that she was aware of what was going on, she had noticed that his sleeping patterns were more erratic than they had been before. It was all so very hard to process. James had always been the steady one in their marriage, the rock that she clung to when things got bumpy. To see him losing his footing now was discombobulating and Ellie didn't like it at all.

But it was okay, she thought. Everything was in hand. They just had to get through the next two days and then it would all be sorted out, for the time being at least. Ellie had deliberately avoided the question of the money over the last week. Each time she'd spoken to Caroline, they had steadfastly ignored the subject. She had avoided it on purpose to give Caroline time to come round to their way of thinking so they didn't have to argue. Caroline must have known the writing was on the wall, especially now she knew that she and Max could be outvoted.

There was no need to crow, though, or rush to a conclusion. She and James still had over a week before the bills needed paying. That was plenty of time to get the funeral and party out of the way and distribute the cash so they would have it ready when the direct debits were drawn. Caroline had made her point, just as she was entitled to do, and now, knowing it would be overruled, there was time to conveniently overlook it and move on.

It had felt strange, though, having conversations with her best friend, all the time knowing there was an underlying subtext, an elephant in the room. It was the first time it had ever happened between them and Ellie didn't like it, but at least it would be the last. And it wasn't as if they were short of other things to say to one another with so much going on. It would be nice to get back to normal, though. She was looking forward to it all being dealt with and in the past.

Ellie shuffled up in bed a little and rearranged the pillows behind her until she was comfortable. She regretted not having had a quick word with James the day before about what her 'birthday surprises' were likely to be, because now she didn't know whether she was supposed to be getting up or whether breakfast in bed was on the list. She imagined it would be. The girls still thought that to be served a meal in bed was the height of luxury. She had better stay where she was.

She reached for her phone and texted James.

Morning. It's my birthday!!! What's happening? Shall I stay put?

She heard the text land, and then some shushing and whispered giggles. It seemed her birthday celebrants were just outside her bedroom. Then the door burst open and the three of them appeared, Olivia balancing a packed breakfast tray and James hovering just behind in case of disaster. Lucy followed, solemnly carrying a pile of presents in front of her rather like a pillow with a crown on top.

'Happy birthday, Mummy!' they all called out, James included.

'Oh look!' said Ellie, shuffling back in the bed so she was sitting up against the headboard. 'What's all this?'

'It's breakfast in bed,' said Olivia proudly. 'Which we know is your favourite thing.'

James winked at Ellie over Olivia's head and blew her a kiss.

'And what do we have?' asked Ellie. 'Crunchy nut cornflakes and a croissant and juice and coffee! Wow!'

'And a flower,' said Lucy. 'I did that part. I got it from the garden, didn't I, Daddy?'

'And I put the milk in a jug so the cornflakes didn't go soggy,' said Olivia, pleased with her planning.

'Well, it all looks perfect,' said Ellie. 'Shall we ask Daddy to clear a space on the bedside table for it all?'

Lucy looked disappointed that the tray wasn't going to sit on the duvet like it did in the films, so Ellie added, 'So we don't spill the coffee and the juice.'

'I've got your presents,' said Lucy unnecessarily, as this much was obvious. 'Do you want to open them?'

'She has to eat her breakfast first,' said Olivia.

'Of course,' said Ellie. 'And it all looks so delicious.'

She would have to tell James to talk them out of this in future. Eating with an expectant audience was no fun. She reached for the cup of coffee, which was disappointingly tepid when she took a mouthful. She worked hard to control her expression so the girls wouldn't see and moved on to the croissant. The cereal was more than she could be bothered with.

'You have to eat the cereal first,' said Olivia, not missing a thing.

Ellie sighed internally.

'Oh yes, silly me,' she said, and swapped the plate for the bowl. 'We don't have much time before school, though,' she added. 'So I might have to finish my breakfast when you have gone. Now, what have you got there, Lucy?' she asked, giving Lucy a wink.

Lucy beamed. 'I told you. Presents,' she replied. 'And they're all for you!'

Ellie hadn't asked for anything in particular, and was glad, given the recent revelations about their financial position, but she couldn't help feeling a tiny bit disappointed when she opened the gifts to find a selection of her favourite things, tried and tested items from safe shops. Lovely, but just a little bit dull, she thought, then scolded herself for being ungrateful.

By the time all the beautifully wrapped boxes were opened, they were getting precariously close to being late for school.

'I'll take the girls, if you like,' offered James as Ellie raced to get herself ready.

He was being thoughtful, but Ellie wanted to be in the playground herself, today of all days. Still, it was rare for James to make an appearance at school, and it would do no harm for him to be seen.

'Why don't we all go together?' she suggested. 'A family outing.'

She could tell from his expression that James thought this to be a colossal waste of time, but today was her birthday and the funeral of her father, and so he smiled his agreement.

'Nice idea,' he said.

'And don't forget, girls, that there's an extra-special treat today. You'll be staying for after-school club and then Sophie's mum is going to pick you up and take you back to her house for tea and a sleepover. Have you got all your things ready?'

Ellie had checked the bags herself the previous evening. Olivia would pack the kitchen sink if left unsupervised.

'I don't want to go to Sophie's house,' moaned Lucy.

Sophie was more Olivia's friend than hers and they had a tendency to leave her out of their games, but needs must. Ellie had decided that the girls shouldn't be at their grandad's funeral and this was the best solution she could come up with in the absence of all their usual family babysitters, who would all be at the funeral too.

'Come on now, Lucy. It's just for this evening. You'll be fine. Right. Let's clean teeth and then we can all jump in the car.'

Somehow, her birthday morning in the playground didn't go quite as Ellie had imagined it in the many months leading up to the big day. Only a couple of women rushed over to give her hugs, and there were no gifts or cards. She wasn't sure whether it was James's presence that put people off, or in the morning rush they had forgotten about her, or simply that no one thought Ellie Fisher's fortieth birthday was that big a deal. Maybe they were all waiting until the party, Ellie told herself. That made sense, she knew, but as she and James climbed back into the car to drive home, she couldn't help but feel a little defeated by her disappointment.

'What's the plan for later?' asked James as they drove home, as if they were meeting friends for brunch and not attending her father's funeral.

'Everyone is coming to ours first, and then the cars are picking us up around one thirty,' she said. 'Not Mum, though. She's making her own way there.'

James nodded, taking in the information.

'And please can we not mention the money,' Ellie added. 'I don't want things to get awkward. Today is going to be hard enough as it is without starting a row.'

James opened his mouth as if to say something, but then seemed to think better of it and nodded. 'Okay. I have a few bits and pieces to do in the office first,' he said. 'If that's okay.'

Ellie's disappointment grew. Was she really going to have to be on her own on her birthday morning? She could feel a seed of resentment that her dad was stealing her thunder growing inside her, but she squashed it. She had chosen to sacrifice her birthday. She could hardly complain when it actually came to pass.

So she spent the time arranging her presents and then began the task of getting ready. She had chosen to go with a black suit that she already had rather than buying something new, teaming it with a midnight blue silk shirt. It was classy and understated and nothing about it shouted that it was her birthday. She would brighten it up with some jewellery though.

She flicked through her favourite pieces in her mind and settled on the diamond bracelet that James had bought her for Christmas. That would be perfect. It wouldn't be on display all the time as it would be hidden by the cuff of the shirt, unless she lifted her arm and then it would sparkle and Ellie would feel secretly better that even on this very sad occasion, a part of her still twinkled.

She went to her jewellery drawer and it was only when she looked into the bracelet's box and found it empty that she remembered she had mislaid it. Her heart beat a little faster. It was an expensive piece, not a trinket, and she ought to have taken care of it. She recalled that the bracelet was under the bed somewhere and she got down on her hands and knees to search for it.

Forty-five minutes later her back was aching – surely nothing to do with turning forty, not so soon – but the bracelet was still missing. Ellie sat down at her dressing table and let out an enormous, shuddering sigh just as James came into the room to begin getting ready.

'Oh, what's up, babe?' he asked when he saw her. 'It'll be all right, you know. We just need to get today out of the way and then we can start to move on.'

Ellie's bottom lip quivered. 'It's not that,' she said. 'I can't find my bracelet, the one you bought me for Christmas. I'm so sorry. I think I might have lost it. I've looked everywhere. I know I had it here last, I remember taking it off, but now I can't find it.'

She looked up, ready to take a tongue-lashing for having mislaid her very expensive gift, but rather than preparing to chastise her, James put his hand across his brow and his cheeks reddened.

Ellie saw in an instant what had happened. 'Did you sell my bracelet?' she asked, not wanting him to tell her that he had, but suddenly certain that was where it had gone.

'Pawned it,' he said quietly.

'Pawned it!' Ellie was horrified. People like them didn't pawn things. She didn't even know where there was a pawn shop or how you would go about getting money from one.

'But I'll be able to get it back when we get the money,' he added quickly. 'I'm so sorry. I was desperate. I just didn't know what else to do.'

'But my bracelet. That was mine. You can't give me a present and then take it back,' Ellie said indignantly.

And then something else occurred to her. 'Hang on. I first realised it was missing not long after Christmas. That's months ago. You told me the cash flow problems only started when Dad died. But that can't be true. Not if you took the bracelet in January.'

James sucked in a huge breath and let it out slowly before speaking. 'The reason why it's so bad now is because we didn't have much in the war chest to start with. Our life is expensive, Ellie. And my money doesn't come in every month like a salary. Some months are better than others. So I had to borrow a bit from our savings to tide us over and then . . .'

This was a surprise to Ellie. She knew that their savings were temporarily gone. If they hadn't been then they could have paid the mortgage and the school fees with those. But for it to have started going wrong so long ago? That was something new.

'Why didn't you talk to me?' she asked, shaking her head as if that could change the situation. 'You should have told me what was going on. We could have figured it all out together.'

She stood up and went to put her arms around James. She should perhaps be angry with him but he looked so very forlorn that she just felt sorry for him. His head hung low, his shoulders rounded.

'I didn't want to worry you,' he said. 'I thought I could sort it all out without you ever finding out. It was a blip, that was all. And then . . .'

Ellie squeezed him tightly and they stood in silence for a minute or so.

'God, what a mess,' said Ellie. 'Thank God for Dad's money, eh? At least we can get ourselves out soon. But you have to promise me that you will never let things build up like this again. We're a team, James Fisher. I'm here to help.'

She felt James nodding.

'I'm sorry about your bracelet,' he said. 'I'll get it back, I promise.'

'Let's not worry about that now,' Ellie replied, suddenly feeling like the grown-up. 'It would have been too much for the funeral anyway. I'll wear my pearls instead. Far more suitable than diamonds.'

They broke apart. She was going to be brave, Ellie decided. Then, when this was all over, she could look back and feel proud that when their backs were up against the wall, albeit temporarily, she hadn't fallen apart.

'Listen, why don't we go out for coffee?' James suggested. 'I know it's not much, but we can have cake to celebrate . . .' His face fell again. 'Oh shit. I forgot to get you a cake.'

Ellie grinned at him. 'It's all in hand,' she said. 'Do you think I'd let that happen? No cake?! There will be one at the party tomorrow, don't you worry. And as for today, a cake in a café would be perfect. But only if it's chocolate.'

49

Ellie sat at one end of the front row of the crematorium, with spaces left for James and Nathan. Her mum, sitting at the other end, was perching right on the edge of the bench, as if she was ready to leap up and walk out at any moment. Caroline and her boys were tucked into the row behind. The boys looked smart in matching chinos with shirts and ties, although Theo kept tugging at his collar, trying to give his neck a little more space.

Ellie felt a pang of regret that she hadn't brought Olivia and Lucy. It was strange that there was a family gathering and they weren't there. She dismissed the thought. It was the right decision to protect the children from this sadness, whatever Caroline thought, and Lucy was still a lot younger than the others in any event. Behind her, she could hear some fidgeting, Caroline issuing warnings in a low voice, and she felt smug. If her girls had been here they would have known how to behave.

She risked a look at the room behind her. The crematorium was full, every seat taken and with standing room only for latecomers. There were people at the back and against the side walls. It was astounding, really. Had Dad had so many friends? It seemed hard to believe. He barely talked about anyone other than his golf buddies. She had seen them sitting a couple of rows behind her, sombre in dark suits and black ties. The rest must be people he'd known in an official capacity through his positions as councillor and then mayor. Then there would be a few hangers-on as there always were at these things. Ellie noticed a couple of her mum's friends, there to give her moral support, no doubt.

Overall, though, the room was packed with people who had all taken the time to come and pay their last respects to Tony Frost. It was touching and Ellie couldn't help wondering whether there would be so many people at her own funeral. She doubted it.

The woman playing the keyboard at the front had been working her way through a series of generic hymn tunes, which all sounded vaguely familiar without actually being recognisable, but then the music changed to the Elgar they had chosen for the arrival of the coffin. There was a general shuffling and pushing back of chairs as the congregation stood up.

Ellie didn't want to look but she couldn't help it. There he was, her dad being carried up the aisle. Max and Nathan were at the front, the coffin resting awkwardly on their shoulders. Nathan was taller than Max and she worried about the box sliding to one side. There was a look of grim determination on Max's face as he gripped it firmly, his fingers white. Nathan seemed to have taken himself to a different place and looked untroubled by his task. James was behind Max, evening things up a little, and the remaining three places were filled by the undertakers.

They made slow progress up the aisle as 'Nimrod' built to its crescendo. Ellie blinked hard, swallowing back her tears. She couldn't cry yet. She needed to hold on for as long as she could because she knew that once she let her emotions have full rein that would be it. There would be no stopping them.

The men balanced the coffin on the stand at the front of the room, the professionals running a final check that it was stable and secure before making a discreet exit. James and Nathan slipped in beside her, Valerie making herself even smaller so they could squeeze past, and Max into the row behind.

The coffin looked huge, although Tony hadn't been a particularly big man. A simple bouquet of white lilies was resting casually across the lid as if someone had left it there and would be back to pick it up at any moment. The coffin seemed to be sucking all the energy out of the room as it sat there, all eyes drawn to it.

Ellie made a conscious decision not to look. If she did it would make her think of what was inside, and that would bring the tears that she was trying so hard to stem. She was grateful they no longer sent the coffin trundling off down a little conveyor belt and into the furnace. Apparently it would stay precisely where it was for the duration of the service and then the undertakers would deal with it when all the mourners had left. That, at least, was a comfort.

Ellie could hear Caroline reassuring Max in a low voice. As eldest sibling, he had been volunteered to give the eulogy. He wouldn't be relishing that prospect, she knew – who would? Ellie had almost suggested that James do it, to save the three of them the additional pressure, but given the nature of the connections that had appeared between her husband and her dad since his death, it was probably just as well that she hadn't.

As the final chords of 'Nimrod' faded away, a tall, angular man in a shabby suit appeared and stood at the front. Ellie recognised him as the man who had come to the house to talk to them about the service and to whom she had given a potted history of her dad's life. He smiled at the congregation but the smile seemed obsequious and didn't spread further than the corners of his mouth. Tony hadn't been religious, so a total stranger doling out platitudes at his funeral was how it was to be. Ellie didn't let herself dwell on that either, her brain skipping quickly between thoughts before it had the chance to get too deeply embroiled in any of them.

The man announced the first hymn and the keyboard sprang into life again. There were a couple of readings, commonplace but appropriate, and then it was Max's turn. Ellie heard Caroline whisper 'Good luck' as he got to his feet. He walked to the front, a few sheets of paper in his hand, and stood behind the lectern. Then he took a deep breath, composed his face into a smile and began to speak.

'Anthony Gerald Frost was born in 1953, the second of three siblings,' he began.

Ellie took a shuddering gulp, preparing herself for what was to come, but as Max worked his way through their dad's life, she found she was more interested than anything else, losing herself in the reassuring facts. When Max reached her parents' wedding she looked across and gave her mum a little smile, which her mother acknowledged with a nod so tiny that she barely moved at all.

Max trotted over their births and early childhood, telling gentle anecdotes about family holidays, and Ellie's stomach knotted again. Her family had always been something she was sure of. In an uncertain world it had always been there to keep her safe. Even when Valerie deserted them and the planes of her world had wobbled a little, Ellie had known where she was. But now, with these new revelations . . .

Max had moved on to Tony's public service, listing his achievements and accolades. Was it Ellie's imagination or had the atmosphere in the room shifted from benignly supportive to something more edgy? There was certainly some shuffling amongst the mourners, but perhaps that had been there before. It was quite a long time to sit still, particularly for the more elderly of their number. She focused her attention on Max. He had been going great guns, but now that he was beginning to sum up with glowing praise for their father, Ellie could see he was finding it harder to maintain his composure. As he approached what must surely be the end of his speech, he began to speed up, as if he was racing his emotions to the finish line, unsure of who would get there first.

And then it was over. He lifted his notes from the lectern and made his way back to his seat, carefully not looking out over the sea of faces. Ellie threw him a reassuring smile as he passed her and mouthed 'Well done,' but she wasn't sure he noticed.

She still wasn't crying. She couldn't decide if that was a good thing. She was allowed to cry, wasn't she? There was nothing preventing her. Then her eyes strayed towards the coffin and the thought of her dad lying cold and alone inside was enough. The tears came. She riffled in her clutch bag for a tissue and then remembered that she had one ready, her fingers having been wrapped tightly round it all through the service. Quietly she dabbed at her eyes, although the tears were flowing down her cheeks so quickly that her eyes were wet again as soon as she wiped them.

James reached for her hand and squeezed it and she gave him a grateful look. She could hear Caroline sniffing behind her, a discreet blowing of her nose. But they were nearly through this part. Just one more hymn and then they would be released into the summer sunshine. Ellie could hang on until then.

She didn't even look at the service sheet as the pianist played 'Lord of all Hopefulness'. The words were so achingly sad that she just couldn't bear to read them. Instead, she focused her gaze on a spot on the ceiling just above the coffin. There was a cobweb, she noticed. It must have been there for some time because a little snowflake of dust had got caught and was now gently swaying from side to side.

Then there were the closing words, a brief prayer and they were free to leave. Except they weren't, were they? They had duties to perform. More than anything, Ellie wanted to bolt for the car and get the driver to whisk her off to the golf club bar where she could down a swift drink without even tasting it. Instead, the family had to form a receiving line to thank everyone who had taken time out of their busy days to come, in case they didn't want to go on to the golf club. She wanted to nip to the Ladies first, check her make-up and put on a quick slick of lipstick so she could at least pretend to herself that she looked presentable. But she couldn't leave her brothers to deal with the mourners alone and she could hardly touch up her face there, in full view of the coffin. Actually, her dad would probably have found that funny, but she couldn't take the risk of offending anyone else. The mourners would just have to take her as they found her, smudged mascara, dry lips and all.

As they made their way back up the aisle she felt a gentle tap on her elbow. She turned to see Caroline smiling at her. Her make-up had more or less gone too; just a little bit of grey shadow blended into her lids remained. Her expression was a picture of resigned sympathy.

'Happy birthday, Ellie,' she mouthed sadly.

50

Caroline ushered Alex and Theo to one side as Ellie, Nathan and Max formed a line to greet the guests. Normally Caroline would have stood at Max's side to support him, but she could hardly ask the boys to do that, and so she had the perfect excuse to bow out. A month ago she wouldn't have even questioned that as a member of the family, it was right to stand in the receiving line. Now, though, with what she had learnt about the Frosts since Tony's death, she wasn't at all sure she wanted to be part of it. She didn't have the sense of belonging that she'd had before. Even though they hadn't exactly closed ranks, Caroline felt excluded in a way that was new. And hurtful.

She became aware of someone at her side and looked up to see Valerie. She was soberly dressed in neat black trousers and a cream blouse, the light colour striking against the sea of dark. From the state of her make-up, it didn't look as if many tears had been lost over Tony during the service.

'Well, that went okay,' she said. 'Good to get it out of the way at long last. And I thought Max did very well. I'll ring him later and tell him so.'

Caroline looked at her in surprise. 'You can tell him yourself at the golf club. I think there's room in one of the cars if you'd like a lift.'

'Oh, I don't think I'll be going to that,' Valerie said briskly. 'I've come to show my respects, as is right, but that's enough. We'd been divorced a long time and, as I think you're discovering, Tony wasn't always an easy man. Anyway, I'm sure those three'– she cocked her head in the direction of the receiving line – 'are perfectly capable of coping without me hovering around in the background. So, if you could say well done to Max for me that would be very kind. I'll see you all tomorrow at Ellie's party anyway.'

And then she disappeared into the milling throng of people, leaving Caroline feeling a little stunned. Valerie seemed to have a residual bitterness towards Tony that she hadn't realised was there. In fact, Caroline had had no idea that there had been any issues between them at all, other than falling out of love with one another. As far as she had known, the couple had just drifted apart and then split up as so many people did after their children left home.

But maybe there was more to it. Caroline thought about the jibes that Lesley had made in the staff room at work. It made her wonder exactly what Valerie had been putting up with for all those years. It was turning out that there was plenty about the Frost family she hadn't been aware of.

Still, there was no point worrying about it now. She ushered the boys outside to wait for Max, keeping her head held low to avoid meeting the eyes of well-wishers.

Half an hour later, Max and Nathan appeared at the car. Max looked pale and weary. Nathan looked much the same as he ever did, apparently unfazed by the ordeal.

'Thank God that's done,' he said. 'I had no idea who most of those people were, did you, Max?'

Max shook his head.

'I think we got away with it, though,' Nathan added. 'And I'm sure no one really expected us to know everyone.'

Max nodded. He really did look drained. Caroline was going to have to show him some real TLC when all this was over. She slipped an arm around him and squeezed him to her gently. He submitted for a moment and then took a deep breath, pulling back his shoulders and standing tall.

'Right,' he said decisively. 'And on we go.'

51

The golf club had done them proud. There were fresh flowers on the reception desk and the tables and chairs in the bar had been moved to the edges of the room to make a bigger space where people could stand and chat about the deceased. In fact, it looked as if it had been arranged for a party rather than a funeral, but maybe that was appropriate, given Tony's love of life.

The club's steward, a balding, portly man with kind eyes, was hovering around the door and pounced on Max as soon as they arrived.

'Can I just say,' he began, his hands clasped in front of his chest like a supplicant, 'how very sorry we all are for your loss, Mr Frost. Tony, Mr Frost senior, was a true gentleman. Never a harsh word for anyone, always a joke and a ready smile, even when his game was off. And so generous with his tips.' The steward blushed slightly, as if he had crossed a professional line by mentioning money. 'Not just to me,' he added quickly. 'But to all the staff right down to the most junior pot-washer. He will be sorely missed here, I can tell you.'

Max gave him a sad smile and reached out a hand to tap the man on his shoulder. 'Thanks, Martin,' he said. 'That means a lot. And the place looks great.'

The steward pulled himself up and stood a little taller, although he was still barely bigger than Caroline.

'We've done our best to give him a good send-off,' he said proudly. 'If there are any problems just come and find me and I'll sort them out.' Then with a little nod of his bald head he bustled away.

'That's nice,' said Max thoughtfully. 'Dad was popular here, I think.'

'And generous,' said Caroline, raising an eyebrow.

'Let's not start that,' said Max sharply. 'Let's just focus on getting through this afternoon. Come on. I don't know about you, but I need a drink.'

It took them an age to get to the bar, shuffling through all the well-wishers. Now they were here, there seemed to be even more people and Caroline wondered if a number of them hadn't bothered with the crematorium and had just been waiting for the party to come to them at the club.

Max was buttonholed almost at once by someone she didn't recognise, and so Caroline slipped away to find Ellie. She had a card and present for her in her bag and she wanted to find a quiet moment to give them to her. She caught sight of Theo and Alex heading out to the putting green, clubs in hand, followed by the club's professional. When he saw Caroline he gave her a questioning thumbs-up and she nodded and smiled. Everyone was being so kind, which made it worse that she was harbouring such mean-spirited thoughts about Tony. She resolved to put the recent revelations out of her head, at least for today, and to focus on remembering the man she thought she had known for most of her life.

Scanning the room, she eventually spotted Ellie talking to her aunt, with James loitering loyally at her side but clearly not engaged in the conversation. She decided to bide her time. There was no rush. Instead, she looked for a friendly face she could say hello to.

Most of Max's relations and family friends, people who had known them both since they were children, were here somewhere.

She was just setting off in the direction of a couple of Max's cousins when someone pulled her roughly by the crook of her elbow, stopping her in her tracks. She turned round, assuming it would be one of her sons and readied herself to complain, but it was Nathan.

'Sorry, Caroline, could we have a word?'

He was smiling and his tone belied the force of his gesture.

'Yes,' she replied, shaking herself free from his grip.

He seemed to realise then that he might have been a little heavy-handed and muttered an apology, his arm dropping back to his side.

'Shall we go outside?' he suggested. 'It's so noisy in here.'

He gestured to the doors that led out on to the terrace beyond, and Caroline made her way through the people until they found a quiet place, away from prying ears.

'The thing is . . .' he began.

Caroline's heart sank. Could they not just have a day without thinking about the bloody money? She was honestly beginning to wish she had never found it.

'I could really do with getting my share of that money you found,' he said. His voice was gentle but Caroline could see the strain in his face as he spoke. 'There are things I need to do, and it's getting quite urgent now. And I'm not sure why we have to have all this delay. You can do what you please with the rest of it, but I really need my third, like now.'

Why was he having this conversation with her? And when Max wasn't here? Surely this was a matter for him to deal with. But then maybe Max had enough on his plate already, and, she had to admit, it was her convictions that were causing the delay.

She took a deep breath. 'Well, I think, actually we both think, that the money is probably dodgy in some way.'

Nathan rolled his eyes. 'Of course it's dodgy,' he hissed. 'All the more reason to get it out of the way before anyone realises we've got it.'

'But that's the thing, Nath,' she said. 'I don't think we should be doing that at all. We ought to hand it over to the police, let them deal with it.'

Nathan looked as if he might explode. 'What?! Are you mad?' he said, trying to keep his voice low, the effort it was taking showing in the lines on his face. 'Why in God's name would we want to do that?'

'Well,' said Caroline, thrown slightly by the vehemence of his reaction, 'because it's the right thing to do. It's not our money to take. We don't know whose it is. So until we're sure . . .'

'Of all the fucking stupid ideas,' Nathan spat. 'What exactly has this got to do with you, anyway? You're not family. It's up to us what we do with our dad's money.'

That stung. Caroline could feel her cheeks start to blaze. Not family? She had almost been a part of the family for longer than Nathan had. Who was he to say that she didn't belong?

'I don't think this is the time or the place,' she said, turning away from him so he wouldn't see her struggling to keep her composure. 'You should remember where you are and show a little respect.'

Then she walked smartly away from her brother-in-law, her throat constricting as she struggled to swallow down her tears. Who did he think he was, talking to her like that? And here, of all places? She headed for the ladies' cloakroom to compose herself. Her urge was to go and direct her outrage at Max, tell him how appallingly his brother's behaviour had just been, but this was not the time. Max didn't need to hear it right now. No, she would protect him

285

from it today and they could deal with it tomorrow. Or the next day. There really was no rush.

The ladies' cloakroom was mercifully quiet and Caroline made her way to the wash basins and looked at herself in the mirror. Her cheeks were a little flushed, but apart from that there was very little outward sign of the turmoil going on inside her. She thought about splashing water on her face but her make-up was barely holding on as it was, so instead she put her wrists under the taps and let the cold water trickle over her veins. It was a trick they'd used at school discos to cool down and she had no idea if it made any difference to her temperature, but the sensation of the cool water flowing across her skin was calming if nothing else.

There was the noise of a bolt sliding behind her and she looked up and saw the reflection of Ellie emerging from the cubicle.

'Oh, Caro,' Ellie said, then immediately came and threw her arms around her. Caroline turned round and hugged her hard.

'Happy birthday, Els,' she said, planting a kiss in her hair. 'How's it going?'

Ellie pulled away and gave a doleful little smile. 'Oh, it's okay, I suppose,' she replied bravely. 'Everyone is being so kind. I just wish Dad was here to see. He would have loved all this fuss being made about him.'

'Yes,' Caroline agreed. 'He would. I can just picture him now, standing in the middle holding court.' Tears pricked in her eyes and she blinked fast. 'Listen, I've got your birthday present. I know it's not ideal, giving it to you here, but I wanted you to have it today, on your actual birthday.'

She opened her bag and retrieved the card and a little box wrapped in gold paper with ivory curling ribbon cascading from a bow on the top. The corners of the card had bent a little in the bag and the ribbon was a touch squashed. The overall effect was less impressive than Caroline had hoped for.

'Happy birthday, Ellie,' she repeated, and handed the gift over.

Ellie beamed at her. 'Thanks, Caro,' she said and Caroline thought that she looked truly grateful. 'Can I open it now?'

'Well, it's your present and your birthday, so I'd say the answer to that is yes!'

Ellie went for the card first, carefully pulling back the envelope. Caroline had spent a long time choosing what she hoped would be the perfect balance between humour and sentiment and she watched Ellie's face carefully as she read it. It seemed that she had got it just right and Ellie grinned at her and wrinkled her nose.

'That's lovely. Thanks. God, we've been friends for a long time, haven't we? Just thinking about it makes me feel old!'

'Well, don't think about it then,' laughed Caroline. 'Open your present.'

Ellie turned her attention to the little box and Caroline held her breath, watching as she released the ribbon from its bow and slid the paper away. Ellie lifted the lid and gave a little gasp. Inside were a pair of exquisite butterfly earrings, white gold and studded with diamonds. They had cost more than Caroline had intended to spend, but when she saw them she knew they would be the perfect gift.

'Oh, Caro,' said Ellie looking up, her eyes glistening. 'They're so beautiful. Thank you.'

This time Caroline's cheeks flushed with pleasure. She could still do something right, it seemed. 'You are very welcome, Ellie,' she said. 'I know today isn't quite as you'd planned it, but at least we're all together.'

As soon as she said it, Caroline realised that of course they weren't. Olivia and Lucy were missing. She watched Ellie's face for any sign that she might have upset her, but Ellie was looking again at her butterflies, lifting them up so they caught the light. Then she swept up the wrapping paper and dropped it in the bin.

'Come on,' she said. 'We'd better get back out into the fray. I need to speak to Dad's best mate from school. Peter Hopkins? You remember him, don't you? He's a bit creepy I always think, but his heart's in the right place.'

Caroline did know him. 'Uncle Peter' had been one of those men she hadn't wanted to be alone with when they were younger. He had never done anything untoward, but there was always the suspicion that he might.

'Is he here? I haven't seen him,' she said.

'He wasn't at the crem,' replied Ellie. 'We knew he'd be late. He left a voicemail saying he had something on that he couldn't get out of, but he'd do his best to get here to raise a glass to Dad later on. Hopefully he's here by now.'

As she opened the door to leave, she gave Caroline a lovely smile. 'Thanks for the earrings, Caro,' she said. 'They're perfect.'

And then she was gone, lost in the sea of people.

Caroline had had enough. She would have quite cheerfully gone home, using the boys as an excuse and leaving Max to it, but the boys were perfectly content so that was that. Perhaps she could slope off to a quiet corner and loiter until she could decently leave. No one would miss her. She was very far from being the star turn here.

She skirted round the edges of the room hoping not to make eye contact with anyone. There were plenty of people that she recognised, but she wasn't feeling up to talking to them. The little run-in with Nathan had completely taken the wind out of her sails, and even though she was unlikely to have such a confrontational conversation with anyone else, it had put her off trying. She needed to avoid James too. He would no doubt be gunning for her as well.

Quickly and quietly she made her way out through a side door and went to find the boys. Maybe if she gave them a nudge she could persuade them that they were ready to leave.

52

When Max woke up the day after his father's funeral his head was pounding as if he had spent the previous day just slamming it against a wall. He groaned a little and put his hand to his forehead, massaging the space above his eyebrows, although it didn't seem to ease his discomfort. It was the brandy that had done it. If he'd only had the sense to stick to lager he would have been fine, but someone had bought him a brandy quite late on in the evening and before he had realised, one had turned into several.

The funeral was now split into two distinct parts in his mind – the early part that he could remember and the latter part, which was decidedly hazy. It had gone off well though, he thought. His dad would have enjoyed it, all those people there swapping anecdotes about him, being the centre of attention, even in his absence. Max had managed to talk to most of the people that he should have, he thought, even if the latter conversations were a little foggy.

There had been one towards the end of the night with his dad's best friend Peter. Max couldn't remember exactly what they had said but he had an idea that there was something significant about it. He tried to reach deep into his memory bank, but whatever it was had gone.

And today he had to do it all over again.

Whose idea had it been to have the funeral and Ellie's birthday party on successive evenings? Well, that was Ellie, of course, who was no doubt skipping round her huge house bright-eyed and bushy-tailed. It was probably just him who was the worse for wear. No one else would have been that stupid.

He opened his eyes and was immediately confused about where he was until he recognised the curtains of the spare bedroom. God, he must have been bad if Caroline had made him sleep in here. He turned his head gingerly to the right and saw a glass of water and two paracetamol, no doubt left there for him the previous night. She was so good to him. Sometimes he didn't know what he would do without her. He hoped he would never have to find out.

He leant over and scooped up the pills, throwing them into his mouth one at a time and then swallowing the water down greedily. He'd be fine once he got moving. He'd had worse hangovers than this and still managed to function.

He found Caroline in the kitchen, batch cooking for the coming week. She gave him a knowing grin as he appeared.

'Morning,' she said. 'How are you today? Bit fragile?'

Max screwed his face up into a grimace. 'A bit,' he admitted.

'Fancy a bacon sandwich?' she asked with a sympathetic smile.

He nodded gratefully and sat down at the table. 'And a cup of tea would be brilliant,' he added.

He watched as Caroline bustled around the kitchen. She had clearly exercised far more self-restraint the day before than he had, judging by her general perkiness this morning.

'I thought it went well yesterday,' he said, hoping he was right.

'Yes, I did too,' Caroline replied as she dropped three rashers of bacon into the pan she had just been frying onions in. They sizzled immediately. 'Your dad would have been very proud of you all. And your mum said to tell you that the eulogy was lovely. Now, you just need to shake off that hangover in time for round two this evening.' She smirked at him, then fished the bacon out of the pan and flipped it over.

Something triggered in his head, a memory of an uncomfortable moment that he couldn't quite pin down. 'Did you speak to James?' he asked, feeling his way between emotional responses and genuine recollection to try to create something he could grasp hold of. 'Yesterday, I mean. I think he was an absolute arse to me. It's a bit foggy but I'm pretty sure he really lost it about Dad's money. He had a right go at me, said that we had no business holding the cash to ransom and that Ellie and Nath outvoted you and me anyway, so we should just get it shared out and stop messing about. He was bloody rude, actually.'

'That's not like James,' said Caroline. 'Maybe he'd had one too many as well and that, with the pressure of the day . . . Actually, Nath had a bit of a pop at me too.'

'Oh?' Max asked. 'About the money?'

Caroline nodded. He knew she was trying to shrug it off as unimportant, but he also knew his wife.

'Are you okay?' he asked. 'What did he say?'

Caroline shook her head as if it wasn't important, but Max could tell from the way she wouldn't meet his eye that she had been upset and was trying hard not to show it.

'It was pretty awful, to be honest,' she said when he pressed her. 'He got quite heated, but I don't think anyone else noticed, so that's good at least.'

'I'm so sorry you had to deal with that,' he said, suddenly feeling responsible for his brother's actions. 'For God's sake! It was Dad's funeral. Could they not have left it alone for one day? I'm beginning to look at those two in a very different light. They're like vultures.'

'Don't apologise,' Caroline replied, her brow furrowed. 'It's hardly your fault. You're not your brother's keeper. Or your brother-in-law's for that matter.'

'No, but Nath has no business being rude to you. I'll speak to him about it.'

'Please don't,' she said. 'It really doesn't matter. Tensions were running a bit high yesterday, that's all. It's understandable that he got a bit overwrought.'

She passed him a steaming mug of tea and he took a sip of the scalding liquid, hoping the heat would take his mind off the throbbing in his head. He opened his mouth to speak, closed it again. They were going to have to concede defeat over the money. Caroline must surely realise that. It didn't matter how adamant she was that she was in the right; at the end of the day Ellie and Nathan didn't agree, and even the strongest of moral convictions wasn't as strong as a two-to-one vote.

But now wasn't the time. It was Ellie's party later so they could just focus on that and forget all about the money in the loft. Or at least try to.

53

Ellie thought her party venue looked perfect. In fact, as she had come into the room she had actually gasped at how magical it all was, which was precisely the effect she'd been shooting for. Tiny lights twinkled in branches suspended from the ceiling and ivy cascaded down walls and over tables as if they were actually in some moonlit glade deep in a forest.

She had purposefully kept away all afternoon – that was what you paid party planners for – so she would get the same impression as her guests on arrival, and now she was certain that she had done the right thing. All the impact and none of the stress. Perfect.

Behind her, Olivia and Lucy were squealing in delight as they saw the room. They pushed past her and began to twirl on the spot in the middle of the space, their pink velvet dresses spreading out around them like petals on a tulip. They looked beautiful with their hair curled and their sparkly ballerina pumps catching the light as they moved. They would be here until ten, at which point Valerie had volunteered to take them, along with their cousins, back to her house for a sleepover.

She heard and managed to ignore the very different kind of sharp intake of breath that had come from James when he saw how the room was decorated and no doubt worked out exactly how far over budget her spending had gone.

But it wasn't something to worry about just now – all that was for another day. Today she was a princess, albeit a slightly old one, and nothing was going to spoil her moment. She hadn't been the centre of attention like this since her wedding day and she had forgotten how much she liked it. She was a chip off the old block in that regard. Thinking about her dad brought a lump to her throat but she swallowed it down. Today was not about him.

In the far corner of the room, the string quartet she had hired for the early part of the evening was setting up, the musicians, discreetly dressed in black, taking instruments out of cases and moving music stands around. Ellie headed over to introduce herself with James and the girls in tow. Then she had a quick last word with the party planners after which, finally, Ellie had her first glass of champagne in hand and was ready to greet her guests.

Shortly after seven thirty they began to arrive, no one wanting to be late or to miss out on anything. Ellie had been billing the evening as 'the party of the summer', and it seemed that her hype had been accepted as gospel truth. Everyone had made an effort with their outfits too and Ellie felt touched. She greeted her guests with grace and made sure they all had a drink, smiling bountifully all the while. She loved to be the hostess.

Caro and Max arrived with Alex and Theo just before eight. Ellie went over to welcome them and just caught a raised eyebrow from Max and a look from Caroline that she couldn't quite identify. Ellie bristled a little. She was used to sour grapes and people being catty about displays of wealth, even though she and James were quite frugal by comparison to many of their friends, but she didn't expect to see it from her own family, and certainly not Caroline. In the past, Caroline would have been bubbling over with excitement, just as she herself was, but since this issue with the hidden money something seemed to have shifted a little, their attitude to spending changed. Ellie wasn't ashamed of how much the party had cost them, far from it, but knowing that the foundations of it were built on sand and not rock made her feel uneasy. The last thing she needed this evening was any suggestion from Caroline that she thought the party was extravagant rather than magical.

Ellie's thoughts were interrupted by Alex and Theo who raced into the room, Theo dropping to his knees and skidding across the expanse of polished dance floor, nearly sending a couple flying. Ellie couldn't help herself and the reprimand was out of her mouth before she had the chance to think about it.

'Theo!' she shouted. 'For goodness' sake. Don't do that!'

Theo dropped his head and immediately stood up. 'Sorry, Auntie Ellie,' he said at once and Ellie nodded at him, apology accepted.

Then she looked up and saw Caroline. Her expression was tight, lips pressed together as if she was trying to stop what she wanted to say from escaping. For a moment, Ellie felt bad for telling off another woman's child in public, and her nephew at that, but she dismissed the thought. Theo was old enough to know how to behave. There was no excuse for stupidity and if Caroline couldn't control her own children then it was left up to Ellie to do it for her.

She didn't want any unpleasantness, though, not tonight. So she altered her expression into a beaming smile and went across to hug Caroline.

'You look gorgeous,' she said, which was true. She turned her eyes to her brother. 'You too, Max.'

'He looks better than he did this morning at any rate,' replied Caroline with a laugh, which dispersed the tension of the moment before. 'You were a little worse for wear, weren't you?'

'Nothing that a couple of cups of strong tea couldn't fix,' he said with a grin. 'This looks amazing, Els.' He cast his eyes around the room. 'Happy birthday, by the way. I'm sure we must have bought you something lovely. I'm just not quite sure what.'

Ellie rolled her eyes at him. 'I don't know how you put up with him, Caro. Yes, Max. You bought me the most beautiful pair of earrings.' She pulled her hair to one side to reveal the butterflies. 'And your thoughtful wife gave them to me yesterday.'

'Oh, they look lovely,' said Caroline. 'Perfect with that dress. I'm so pleased you like them.'

'Yes,' agreed Max. 'Well done, Caro.'

James appeared at the same moment as a waiter bearing a tray of glasses brimming with pale, bubbling champagne.

'Hi, you two. Welcome to A Midsummer's Night Dream – or nightmare, depending on your point of view.'

It was meant as a joke but Ellie didn't find it funny.

'Only teasing, Ellie,' James added quickly. 'Do you want one of those or shall we get ourselves a real drink, Max?'

James and Max disappeared in the direction of the bar while Ellie put her empty glass down and picked up two full ones, offering one to Caroline.

'To birthdays,' she said. 'May there be many, many more.'

They chinked glasses.

Caroline put the glass to her lips and drank half its contents in one go.

'Blimey. You look like you needed that!' said Ellie, tipping her head towards the half-empty glass.

Caroline raised her eyebrows. 'It's been one of those days. Well, weeks really,' she said, finishing off the rest of the glass. 'But this place looks amazing, Ellie. Really spectacular. And you look gorgeous too. Happy birthday!'

Caroline lunged at her, throwing her arms around her and squeezing tight. She held on just a little bit longer than Ellie thought was necessary in a public space, but just as she was starting to feel a little uncomfortable Caroline loosened her grip. There was something here that required further investigation, Ellie felt, but now was not the moment. Guests were arriving all the time and she needed to be available for everyone, not just Caroline.

'I'd better go and circulate,' she said, 'but we'll catch up later, okay?'

Caroline nodded enthusiastically. 'Yes. Go, go! Greet your public.'

She shooed her away playfully but Ellie thought she could see something behind her smile. Maybe she had had a row with Max on the way there? Well, whatever it was, it wasn't Ellie's problem. This evening was all about her and she wasn't going to let anything get in the way of that.

54

The evening ticked on and Ellie was delighted with how everything was going. Her party appeared to be a roaring success. The guests had arrived nice and early and ready to celebrate. They had all appeared to be suitably amazed by the beauty of the midsummer night's glade she had arranged, with phone cameras being employed left and right as they captured images of themselves to share with less fortunate friends who didn't get invited to such elaborate events. The DJ had correctly read the room as well, and was nudging more people towards the dance floor with each track he played.

She could finally relax, Ellie told herself, and allow the tension of the last few weeks to lift, if only for an hour or so. Waving across the room to Margo and some of the other school mums who were standing in a group on the far side of the room, she put her glass down and danced her way on to the dance floor, urging her friends to join her. They did and soon they were all dancing in a circle to a Take That classic. There were no handbags in the centre but there might as well have been.

It didn't take long for Olivia and Lucy to notice, and soon they were in the circle too. Ellie felt such pride in her girls. They were beautiful and becoming so self-assured too, holding their own in this room of adults. There weren't many children who could do that with confidence. As she looked at them, jigging from side to side, their faces alive with the joy of the moment, her heart swelled. They were her single greatest achievement and she knew she would do whatever it took to keep them safe.

Caroline was standing with Max, and Ellie beckoned her over to dance with them. Caroline beamed back, then turned to try and drag Max along with her, but Max was having none of it. He shook his head amiably and tried to release his hand from hers, but Ellie could see from the angle of Caroline's body just how hard she was tugging him and how much he was resisting.

Then somehow she seemed to lose her footing at exactly the moment that she let Max go and the sudden release made her fall to the floor. Ellie started, almost feeling the thud in her own body and was about to race over to help, but Caroline seemed to be all right. She struggled to her feet, all embarrassed smiles, waving the attention away from herself. Then she kicked off her shoes and made her way to where they were dancing. Ellie thought she was swaying a little as she walked. Just how much champagne had she consumed? she wondered. But then, it was approaching ten o'clock and everyone was a little merry by this point, herself included.

They had always danced together, Ellie and Caroline. They had started as little girls, when they'd made up routines to show Valerie and Tony, strutting their stuff in front of mirrors side by side. School discos had followed, at first awkward and not quite sure of themselves, and then later with their shaky confidence boosted by elicit alcohol. Nothing had changed with the passing decades. There were certain tracks that would always pull them to the dance floor like some Pavlovian response. This time it was S Club 7.

Caroline, apparently recovered from her tumble, joined Ellie, standing between Lucy and Olivia and taking their hands so they could dance together in a long line. The girls joined in enthusiastically, aware, no doubt, that their time at the party was coming to an end and wanting to eke out every last moment of pleasure.

'This is a great night,' Caroline shouted across to her, even though the music wasn't so loud as to prevent conversation. 'I haven't had such a good time in ages.'

Ellie felt gratified, even though she wasn't sure exactly why Caroline thought this when all she had done so far was talk to Max and consume free champagne. But maybe that was all it took to have a good time; an opportunity to let her hair down and an excuse to drink more than was wise.

'Thanks,' Ellie mouthed back as she bounced up and down to the music.

Something in the corner of the room caught her attention. Max and James appeared to be involved in a heated conversation. Ellie could guess the subject matter. Irritation rose in her like a fast-moving tide. How dare they do this? She had specifically told James not to bring the subject of the money up, not tonight, but it looked as if he just hadn't been able to help himself.

The two men were squaring up to one another now, standing less than a foot apart. Ellie cast her eyes around the room to see if anyone else had noticed, but the situation appeared to be contained to just the two of them. Still, that was two people too many. She needed to get them to knock it off.

'I'll be back in a mo,' she mouthed at Caroline and her daughters, then headed off to get the men under better control. When she got closer, it was clear they must have been building up to this point for some time.

'It's not up to you,' James was saying as she approached. 'It's a majority vote and we don't need Caroline to agree with us. I'm not sure what it's got to do with her anyway. She's the one causing all this bother. She should just keep her do-gooding nose out.'

'She's my wife!' Max replied. 'Of course it's got something to do with her. It's as much to do with her as it is with you, in fact.'

'Yes, but I'm acting in Ellie's best interests,' James began.

300

'I fail to see how this is in my best interests,' hissed Ellie when she was close enough to speak without being overheard. 'Will you two knock it off? This is not the time.' She threw a particularly vicious look at James, who she assumed had been the perpetrator.

'I'm sorry, but it has to be said, Ellie,' replied James. 'This has been going on long enough. It's ridiculous that we are all being held over a barrel by Caroline's over-inflated sense of right and wrong when, quite frankly, she doesn't get a say in it anyway.'

'For one,' said Max, crossing his arms and straightening his spine as he spoke, 'Caroline appears to be the only one with any integrity at all. The rest of you are happy to just take what might not be ours, finders keepers. In fact, if it weren't for Caroline's conscience, we could have just kept it all for ourselves and you lot wouldn't have been any the wiser. Maybe that's what we should have done. It would have saved us a hell of a lot of hassle, that's for sure. But that never even occurred to us. We did the right thing. We told you about it. But I'm starting to wonder whether you'd have done the same if the boot had been on the other foot.'

Ellie, horrified though she was, didn't want them to examine that idea too closely. She wasn't sure what she would uncover. She definitely wouldn't have just kept the money for themselves. But James?

Nathan appeared, and latched on to what was being discussed straight away.

'What I've never quite understood about the story was what your whiter-than-white wife was doing nosing around in Dad's stuff in the first place,' he said viciously.

Caroline stepped forward then. Ellie hadn't realised she had left the dance floor and automatically looked back to see where her girls were, but they had taken the opportunity to sneak to the bar to order one last juice before they had to leave. Ellie wasn't sure how much Caroline had heard, but she hoped that it hadn't included

James's little diatribe as well as Nathan's. There were tears trickling down Caroline's face, her mascara making them run black. She had heard some of it then, Ellie thought.

'I was just looking for Monty,' she said, her voice almost more sob than words.

'And you thought he might have unfastened the suitcase himself and just snuggled in, did you?' asked Nathan. The sneer in his voice was unmistakable.

'No!' wailed Caroline. 'I opened the case because I was curious, okay? I really wish I hadn't, but I did. I can't take it back. And now look at all this bad feeling it's caused.'

'Well, it's not going to cause any more. Not today at any rate,' said Ellie, putting her palms up to silence her brothers on one hand and her husband on the other. 'This is my party and I'm not going to have you spoiling it with your stupid, petty fighting. You'll have to agree to disagree for now, and then you can leave it alone for tonight. Okay?'

Max nodded. 'Fine by me. I didn't bring it up in the first place.'

'James?' she said, focusing on her husband with as much menace as she could muster.

James nodded, slouching and hanging his head without meeting Ellie's eye. Nathan nodded too, although he looked like he had done when they were little and always had to have the last word in any argument.

'Good,' she snapped. 'You two are behaving like children. It's pathetic. Speaking of which, it's time the kids went home. I'll go and find Mum, see if she's ready to take them.' She looked up once more, eyeing James and Nathan, and raised a pointing finger. 'And I mean it. No more, okay?'

Caroline was still looking bewildered by the argument. Ellie wrapped an arm around her shoulders. She could feel her body trembling.

'Come and help me get the kids rounded up,' she said gently. She lifted her hand to Caroline's face and wiped away some of the tears with the pad of her thumb. Caroline looked broken but she allowed herself to be led away by Ellie without any objections.

'I'm sorry, Els,' she mumbled. 'I didn't mean for this to happen.' She was definitely slurring her words a little now. 'I don't want to cause all these arguments. But I just know it's the wrong thing to do, just taking the money. It's like stealing. In fact, it is stealing.'

Ellie could feel her anger building again. 'Let's just drop it, Caro,' she snapped. 'Not tonight.'

Caroline looked wounded by her words and more tears ran down her cheeks, but she nodded her agreement meekly. 'Okay,' she mouthed. 'Sorry.'

Ellie didn't have the bandwidth for this now. This was her long-awaited fortieth birthday party. Nothing and no one was going to spoil it, least of all members of her own family.

She scanned the room for the children and found them sitting round a table at the far end of the room. Alex seemed to be trying to flick peanuts into an empty glass and the others were egging him on. The behaviour of her own children declined substantially when they were with their cousins. Did Caroline and Max not parent them at all? There always seemed to be very little by way of discipline. Those boys did pretty much whatever they wanted, it seemed to Ellie. They were as good as feral, or they would be in a few years if they weren't reined in now.

'Right, you lot,' she said as she approached them. 'Time to go. Get your stuff together and I'll find Grandma.' She silenced a potential objection from Olivia with a look.

Valerie was by the bar talking to a former schoolfriend of Ellie's who had often been at the Frost house for tea when they were children, and was now a consultant radiographer.

'Can you keep the kids here,' she said to Caroline, who still looked as if she might break down at any moment, 'and I'll go and get Mum.'

Without waiting for an answer Ellie headed towards the bar. Her equilibrium was returning to normal. She would get the children off to her mum's and then she could concentrate on enjoying the rest of the evening. Caroline would have to fend for herself. If she couldn't snap herself out of whatever she had going on, then Ellie would just have to leave her behind, because she definitely wasn't going to let Caroline's issues spoil her night, not when everything else was so perfect.

55

The evening wasn't panning out at all the way Caroline had intended. She and Ellie had been looking forward to it for so long, chatting over what they would wear, who Ellie would invite, the food. They had spent hours making lists of the songs they loved, without which any playlist would be incomplete. Every angle had been covered in their quest for the perfect party.

And now it was precariously close to ruin, or it was for Caroline at least. Nathan's vicious attack had cut straight through her. He hadn't accused her of stealing but he might as well have. After everything she had done to try to steer them all to the right decision.

But they had no integrity, none of them. They were all cut from the same cloth as Tony. Except Max, of course. He understood. He could see how strongly she felt about the money.

The more she thought about how wrong they all were, the more her upset was beginning to build into something closer to anger. How dare Nathan talk to her like that? Who did he think he was? Just because it was becoming crystal clear that he would have stolen the money for himself if he had found it, that didn't mean it was right or fair of him to tar her with the same dishonest brush. Had he been suggesting that she was nosing around Tony's house looking for something to pinch? The idea was preposterous. She had never stolen anything in her life and, unlike him, she was not about to take what wasn't hers right from under the noses of the people she loved the most.

Caroline's lips pulled into a tight knot as she thought about it. And James was no better. Hadn't he basically said that what happened to the money was none of her business? Like it was any of his! He was only part of the family by marriage. She had been like one of the family for as long as she could remember so had just as much say as he did in the matter, and probably more.

She really wanted another drink, but that would mean going to the bar and she wasn't entirely sure where her bag was. That said, it was probably a free bar. That would be James all over. Making a fuss about the money she had found whilst at the same time doling out free drinks all night to over a hundred people. James was all about how things looked. He always had been. He was basically flash. Just like Tony.

Feeling really angry now, she was about to go and get herself another glass of wine when Ellie reappeared. Caroline thought she had gone to get Valerie to take the children home, but there was no sign of her mother-in-law. The children appeared to have scarpered too.

Ellie was frowning at her. 'Mum is just saying her goodbyes,' she said. 'Where are the kids? I thought I told you to keep them here.' It sounded like she was talking to a servant, not her best friend. Caroline's already spiked hackles rose further still.

Ellie cast her gaze around the room and located her daughters on the dance floor.

'The girls are there,' she said with a fond smile. 'Where are your two?'

Caroline looked around for them, although if she moved her head too quickly her sense of balance was sent dangerously off-kilter. There was no sign of the boys.

'Oh, for God's sake,' hissed Ellie. 'Can you not keep control of your own children, Caroline?' Then she added under her breath, 'Those boys are basically feral.'

It took Caroline a moment to process what Ellie had said, and the clear implications behind it. When she had, she got to her feet, pulling her shoulders back and pushing her chin up defiantly.

'I beg your pardon,' she said.

'I'm sorry, Caroline, but they are,' replied Ellie, not looking in the slightest bit sorry. 'They were supposed to stay put, but where are they? No sign.'

'Well, my boys might be a little wayward at times, but at least they're not spoilt, ungrateful brats like your two,' spat Caroline. Instantly she regretted it. She didn't mean it. Olivia did have a tendency to be a little bit entitled, but she wasn't a brat. Not really. But before she had a chance to take the words back Ellie was on the defensive.

'My girls are not spoilt,' she said, carefully enunciating every syllable so there could be no mistake. 'We're just very fortunate that James earns enough to let us give them the best in life.'

'Oh, I see,' said Caroline, her eyebrows high. 'And we can't do that for our kids? Is that what you're saying? That your girls are somehow better than my boys because you have money to throw at them? But where's that money coming from? That's what I'd be interested in finding out.'

Ellie shook her head in disgust and turned away from Caroline to bring the conversation to an end. But Caroline couldn't let it go. The gap between them was opening up rapidly as Ellie went to join her girls on the dance floor. Caroline would have to raise her voice to be heard over the noise of the music and the party. And raise her voice she did.

'Is that where all your money comes from?' she shouted. 'Is your husband as bent as your dad was?'

Ellie's back was towards her, but she could tell from the way she stopped moving that she had heard her. Another flush of regret washed through Caroline. She whipped her head from side to side to see who else might have heard her. The people standing nearby had gone perfectly still. They shot glances at one another and then back at Caroline to see what she was going to say next. Ellie still didn't turn around. Anger seemed to be radiating out of her.

In the spotlight of unwanted attention, Caroline thought she might cry. She hadn't meant it. She was drunk and she was upset after what James and Nathan had said, but this was Ellie, her best friend. She didn't want to fall out with her as well. She could feel eyes burning into her as the number of people who were aware that something was afoot grew. She wanted to run to Ellie, to throw her arms around her and tell her that she didn't mean it.

But Ellie still didn't turn to face her, and the longer she showed Caroline her back, the more Caroline's anger was refuelled. What she'd said was true, after all. If Tony wasn't bent then why did he have all that money in the house? Hiding huge amounts of money in a suitcase under a bed wasn't the action of an honest man. And James and Nathan were as bad. They just wanted to hush it all up, avoid death duties, steal the money. It was all dishonest – tantamount to theft, in fact. They were all as bad as each other. Only Max had shown any doubts about claiming the money for themselves. If the rest of them weren't actually bent, they had morals that wouldn't stand scrutiny.

And she wanted no part of it.

Caroline stalked across the room towards the toilets, trying hard to hold on to what dignity she had left. She could feel heads turning as she went.

Opening the door into the Ladies, she ran straight into Valerie.

'Ah, Caroline. I'm just going to take the kids home with me now. Is that okay?'

Caroline, not trusting herself to not make matters worse, just nodded. Valerie's eyes narrowed.

'Are you okay?' she asked.

Caroline nodded again. 'Thanks for taking them,' she managed and then disappeared into the shelter of the toilets.

56

Caroline sat on the loo in a locked stall, not wanting to come out. She could hear the beat of the music from the party, but wasn't able to make out the tune. She had had enough, she decided. The party was totally spoilt for her. The things Nathan had said about her were still ringing in her ears but now, with a little distance, she questioned them. Did he really think that she had done something wrong by even looking in the case in the first place? And there it was again – the shame of having her integrity questioned. It felt just as it had when she had been a girl: that leaden feeling in her stomach, the fear that they were all whispering about her behind her back, that no one could trust her. That was exactly what she had been trying to avoid by being honest about the money, and yet she appeared to have found herself in exactly the same place.

But worse, far worse than all of that, was what she had just said to Ellie. Yes, she had been provoked, but still. That was no excuse.

She felt sick. She wasn't sure if it was what had been said or the champagne. She had definitely drunk too much of it too quickly, but she had been trying to shake off the low-level disquietude that had been hanging over her ever since Tony died. She had wanted a break from it, just for one night, just for Ellie. But it had backfired. She was too drunk to have a good time now. She had accidentally crossed the line.

Carefully, she stood up and went to wash her hands. When she looked at her face in the mirror she could see that her eyes were glazed and her colour high. She looked terrible. She should go and apologise to Ellie, make it up. That was the right thing to do. It wasn't too late. She could fix this.

But when she got back to the party, it was very clear that Ellie didn't want her. She was on the dance floor now, arms raised and head thrown back, letting the music pulse through her body, seemingly without a care in the world. She was with a bunch of women Caroline didn't recognise; Green Mount mums, no doubt, and Caroline felt a stab of jealousy. That was *her* place, at Ellie's side where she had always been since they'd been girls.

But not tonight. Caroline had forfeited her spot next to Ellie because of her behaviour. And this party would forever be tainted for her, spoilt by the unfortunately timed explosion of pent-up and pressured resentments. It was no wonder Ellie had sidelined her. She didn't want her own memories spoilt too.

She should go home, she decided. She didn't have the boys to worry about and Max was now happily talking to a group of men, laughing at someone else's tale, pint glass in hand. No one needed her. She would slip away quietly and with no fuss. She could send Max a text, rather than interrupting his night. That was the best thing to do. Then he would know where she was, but wouldn't feel obliged to leave just because she had wanted to go. And Ellie would understand. Caroline would ring her in the morning, explain that she hadn't felt well and so had left without any fuss. Ellie probably didn't care whether she was there or not, to be honest. Not after what she'd said.

She edged her way along the wall towards the exit, back under the entrance arch thing, which was truly beautiful, to where the cloakrooms were. The girl on duty looked surprised that she was asking for her coat so early and Caroline muttered something about the babysitter having called. A lie. Where was her precious integrity now?

The taxi rank wasn't far from the venue and soon she was whizzing her way home, composing a text to Max as she went.

The house was silent, but she had left a number of lights on to deter burglars so the place felt welcoming when she opened the door and let herself in. She stood in the hallway, not quite knowing what she wanted to do. It wasn't even eleven o'clock. Regrets flooded through her. What had she been thinking, leaving the party so early like that? Was it too late to call another cab and go back?

But that was a ridiculous idea, she knew it was. She would have one more glass of wine and wait for Max to come home. There was a bottle of rosé open in the fridge. That was just what she needed. Something crisp and cold. Unsteadily, she made her way into the kitchen, poured herself a large glass and took it through to the sitting room to drink.

This was all the money's fault, she thought as she sat there, glass in hand. If she hadn't found it, then none of them would have argued and she would still be at her best friend's party in her rightful place at her side instead of sitting at home on her sofa alone.

Maybe the others were right. Maybe it was her point of view that was suspect, and they should just share the money out between them and move on. Caroline's fuzzy brain tried to concentrate on that idea for a moment. But even through the fog of alcohol she knew she wasn't wrong. Tony had been up to his neck in God knew what. That much was obvious. Why else would you stick that much cash in a suitcase under a bed? There was something off-colour about the whole thing. And therefore, it was as plain as the nose on your face that they shouldn't take it. It was theft by association, or whatever the term was. She wasn't sure of the exact legalities, but really that didn't matter. The important thing was that it *felt* wrong and that was surely deterrent enough.

She should just get rid of the money. That was the sensible thing to do. Getting rid of it would stop all this aggravation, and then they could just get back to how things were before, how things were meant to be with their two families being best friends and without all this sniping at each other.

The solution was so clear to her now, and it was up to her to fix things. She was the one who had spoilt everything by finding the money in the first place so she should be the one to sort it out.

And she would.

Feeling more decisive than she had in a long time, Caroline drained her glass and made her wobbling way upstairs. On the landing, she opened the trap door, pulled the attic ladder down and then, swaying slightly, grabbed hold of the steps with both hands and hauled herself up. She giggled quietly as she nearly missed her footing, even though the house was empty and there was no one to hear her.

'Oops-a-daisy,' she muttered. 'Don't want to come a cropper, Caroline. That would never do.'

She pulled herself up into the space and flicked on the light. There was the case, hidden in plain sight with all their others. It would be a bit tricky getting it back down through the trap door on her own, she thought, but not impossible.

Once she had retrieved it, she got down on her knees and lowered the case through the hole, making sure that she didn't lose her rather precarious balance. Then she let go of the handle and the case fell on to the landing with a bump. Caroline giggled again. She felt like a particularly noisy cat burglar.

She edged her way back down the ladder and soon she was on the landing next to the suitcase, which seemed to have survived its adventure intact.

Caroline carried the case down to the kitchen, poured herself the dregs of the rosé and got what she needed for her mission. This was the obvious answer to the problem and she wasn't sure why she hadn't thought of it before.

When she opened the back door, it wasn't quite dark, being the longest day of the year, so she didn't need a torch or the outside lights to see. That was good. She didn't want to draw attention to herself.

With a strong sense of purpose, she took the suitcase out on to the back lawn. The night was so quiet and still, without a breath of wind. She knelt down on the cool grass with the case next to her and opened the lid. The cash had shifted as the case had been moved about and had all settled at one end. Caroline took a long look at it. A quarter of a million pounds. A quarter of a million little digs and needling comments and uncomfortable looks. A quarter of a million lies.

She took the box from her pocket and lit a match, shielding it with her cupped hand. Then she nestled the tiny flame beneath a curling twenty-pound note at the bottom of the case and sat back to watch.

57

VALERIE

I always knew Tony Frost was a bad lad. He was the kind of man your mother warned you about, all big, wide smiles and twinkly eyes. In the end, he even managed to charm my mother, which was more than I ever did, although that's another story.

We met in the queue for the cinema. Jaws – *Christmas 1975. I was with my then best friend Jill. Tony and his best friend Peter were behind us and, of course, we got chatting. I later learnt that Tony would chat to anyone, anywhere, but at the time I felt special, as if he was bestowing all his attention on me and me alone.*

He was completely relentless in his pursuit of me, never once giving us the chance to drift back into two pairs. By the time we got to the kiosk to buy our tickets, it had been decided that we would all sit together. Tony made a beeline for me. I remember that Jill was a bit put out because, whilst Peter was great company, he was no looker. Fortunately, he was quite shy with it, so the most he managed during the film was resting a nail-chewed hand on her knee.

Tony was a completely different matter. Chief Brody had barely found the first shark-mangled body and Tony had already managed to get his hand into my bra. I'm still not sure how he did it from that position. He must have had double-jointed wrists. Or, more likely, it was just years of practice.

Anyway, it was the perfect film for what turned out to be a first date. Every time there was a jumpy moment I screamed and he wrapped his arm closer around me. When the final credits rolled, he had saved me from danger so many times that I was perfectly happy to let him kiss me. It only seemed fair.

Seven months later, Max was conceived and three months after that we were married in a small registry office service that my parents refused to attend because of the improprieties, although, as I said, my mum came round to the idea eventually.

So I should have known from the start that I was getting myself into deep water. Just how deep remained shrouded in darkness at that stage as I didn't have a crystal ball handy. There would have been nothing that I could have done, though, even if I had known where we were heading. I got sucked into his orbit like a meteor into a black hole.

Now, don't get me wrong. Tony Frost was a great bloke to be married to. He was the life and soul of any room that he chose to wander into. People were drawn to him like moths to a flame. If there was ever a table that seemed to be having more fun than all the others, you could bet your bottom dollar that Tony was sitting at it. It was a talent, I suppose, making people feel at their ease.

And to start with I was more than happy to be a part of it. I mean, why wouldn't I be? I was one half of the most popular couple on the circuit, and because Tony knew everybody, it was a pretty big circuit. After we were married, it was a never-ending round of cheese and wine parties and safari suppers. We were rarely at home, even after the children arrived. We must have spent a fortune on babysitters and they loved to come to us because Tony was so generous with his tips. I didn't know anyone else who tipped their babysitter, but Tony did.

But I'm getting ahead of myself. When Max was born, a bit of a surprise as I said, we just absorbed him into our life with no difficulty.

316

He was an easy child, passive, happy to go with the flow, and we dragged him along to parties with us. He'd sleep where we left him and was always content to be settled by anyone who gave him a kind smile.

Ellie was born about two years later. She was very different. It was all about her right from the moment she arrived. She demanded attention and screamed the house down if she didn't get it. She used to run me ragged and our social life took a nosedive for a while whilst I got her into a routine that suited her.

I'd given up work by this point. Tony had insisted and I could see that it made sense for me to stay at home with the kids. Money seemed to be no problem and it was the seventies so there were plenty of other women at home to spend time with. I joined clubs, we went to toddler groups and that kind of thing.

It was okay, but my friends from before I was married seemed to drift away. I lost touch with Jill somehow, something I could never have imagined happening before. I suppose it's quite common really, people floating away in different directions, and at the time I didn't really think much of it. I was busy with the children and my new life. Looking back though, I can see that Tony just didn't encourage any part of my life that didn't include him. He was too wrapped up in where he wanted to go and it was my job to go along with him.

Nathan was another accident. Well, maybe it's fairer to call him a surprise. We had worked out what caused babies by then, but what with Tony's spur-of-the moment attitude to life it was easy to get caught out. Ellie was six and a half and already at school and we thought our little family was complete with two children, one of each. What could be more perfect? I was even thinking of going back to work and regaining a bit of my independence, but finding out I was pregnant again put the kibosh on that idea.

I sometimes wonder if that was my last chance to get out from under Tony's smothering. If I could have gone back to work, I'd have had the chance to stretch my wings, cut out a little bit of life for myself, away from Tony and the kids.

Now, please don't misunderstand me, I wasn't unhappy then. Far from it. Life was exciting; there were always people at the house, parties, laughter, Tony holding court. But I was very much Tony's wife. Some of the more obnoxious of Tony's acquaintances even called me Mrs Tony, like I had no identity of my own. Either that or I was of so little significance to them that it wasn't worth the effort to remember my name. So I would have relished the chance to break free, just for a bit. Then it would have been less irritating to be referred to as 'Mrs Tony' at home.

But Nathan coming along was the end of that plan. The freedoms that came with both Max and Ellie being at school were snatched away from me and I was sent straight back to the beginning – an elaborate and rather cruel game of snakes and ladders.

And then Tony got his first seat on the council.

◆　◆　◆

I can remember when it started as if it were yesterday, although I had no idea at the time what it all meant or where we would end up. Tony had moved up from the local council to the district one by then. It was an obvious move for him. He was a big fish and he needed a bigger pond to swim in. He didn't work for the council as such, he had an uninspiring job in an office, but he liked to feel that he was in the middle of things, influencing how they worked. That was why he concentrated on the town planning and development side of things. He used to say it would be his legacy, shaping the town the way he thought it should be.

Anyway, Max was thirteen and his life revolved around football. He was a huge Liverpool fan, I think mainly because of the romance of the team more than anything else. His bedroom walls were plastered with posters of players. He seemed to know everything there was to know about them and talked about little else.

One day Tony came home from work grinning like a Cheshire cat. After a fair bit of winding Max up, Tony finally told him that he had managed to get his hands on a pair of tickets for the Sunday match against Manchester United, and not only that but that they were in the directors' box at Anfield. I had no idea about football, but even I knew that was a pretty big deal.

I thought Max was going to burst, he was so excited, and Tony was delighted to have done something that brought his son so much pleasure. He was buzzing with it for days and I remember thinking that it was lovely to see them both so happy.

The tickets came with a sit-down lunch before the match, and so we had to buy Max some smart trousers to wear because he couldn't go in his Liverpool tracksuit. Apart from that expense, we apparently didn't have to pay a penny for the tickets. I queried that with Tony, asking him how much they had cost. I wanted to make sure that Ellie and Nathan didn't miss out; it was important, I thought, to keep everything nice and even between the three of them.

But Tony said he had mentioned what a big Liverpool fan Max was to some bloke he knew, and that he had been able to call in a favour and get the tickets for free. I had no idea just how big a favour that was at the time. It just never occurred to me that there was anything amiss.

Anyway, Liverpool won four–nil and they were both as high as kites when they got back. Max talked about nothing else but his day out for months.

And that was how it started. There was nothing big, nothing that would cause questions to be asked. The odd ticket here, the odd night away there. I honestly didn't think anything of it. It all seemed perfectly legitimate. Tony told me that the treats were a perk of the job and I just took what he said at face value. I had no reason to do otherwise.

It was the conservatory that first made me suspicious. I really wanted one. The woman next door had had one built on the back of their house, and I have to admit that I was envious of it. I must have mentioned it to Tony because the next thing I knew he brought a bunch of brochures home. These were for something altogether more flash than she had next door, all ornate metalwork and a fancy roof. When I questioned it, Tony gave me some guff about only wanting the best for his Val and I fell for it. I mean, I was getting the fanciest conservatory on the street; why would I object to that?

But I think in my heart I knew there was something off about the whole thing. Tony was earning a good salary, but this wasn't really in keeping with what the conservatory must have cost.

After that, we seemed to have more disposable income than we'd had before. Instead of a self-catering holiday on the Costa Brava, we were doing posh hotels in the smart bits of Majorca, and then going more than once a year. Our friends started to joke about Tony's perma-tan and he used to laugh it off, saying that he just had the kind of skin that held on to colour. But I knew it was all the free trips to Praia da Luz.

Then someone said something at one of those interminable dinners we had to go to. It was when Tony was mayor, and I was in a cubicle in the ladies' loo when I overheard a conversation going on by the washbasins. I didn't know who it was, I didn't recognise the voices, but I knew they were talking about Tony before they mentioned his name. Something just clicked, all the levers falling into place.

But of course, I'd known there was something wrong before then. There was no way Tony could be earning the money we seemed to have from just his job. Men used to come to the house, often late at night. Tony would usher them into the dining room and close the door. I'd hear the hushed voices, but not what was said. You couldn't tell me that it was all above board. I knew it wasn't; how could it be?

But I just didn't want to know. What Tony got up to was his business, I decided, and the less I knew about it the better. The kids never gave it a second's thought. They had grown up with a busy house, so late-night visitors didn't even tickle their radars. If they heard the whispered, sometimes desperate, tones of the conversations that took place in our dining room then they never asked me about it, but I suspect they were all totally oblivious. Just like I pretended to be.

There were always rumours of untoward goings-on at the council – I bet there are about most public bodies – but they stayed as just rumours. I lived life on a knife-edge, always assuming that any knock at the door would be the police and that Tony would be caught and publicly shamed. I became a nervous wreck, not daring to go out in case someone accused me of something.

But the knock never came. As far as I know, no one ever suggested anything directly to Tony's face, and there was never any suggestion of police involvement. I could feel people staring at us sometimes on the rare occasions we went out together, conversations that hushed as we walked into a room. I think that either there were suspicions that couldn't be proved or the whole scandal was too big and cut too deeply for anyone to try.

It was a bit like living with a man who is having an affair. You might spot the telltale signs, but unless you actually catch them in flagrante, you can just pretend you're mistaken.

That's what I did. The trips and the favours and the extra money and the stream of anxious-looking men at my door late at night. I ignored the lot and steadfastly refused to see what was staring me in the face.

My way of dealing with what was going on around me was to try to make myself invisible. If Tony was larger than life then I would be smaller, so small, in fact, that no one would notice I was there. I ran a perfect house. I made sure everyone had everything they needed and

I stayed firmly in the background where I hoped no one would catch sight of me.

That strategy worked, but at a price. I had no life of my own. I didn't really want to get close to anyone in case they started to ask questions, so I kept myself distant. Most of my friends had floated away by then as our children had all grown up, so no one really noticed that I had disappeared into my kitchen. The kids just assumed that was what I preferred. They already had one parent who lit up the sky like a firework. They didn't need two. It hurt a bit that they didn't know I had been bubbly and vivacious too once, but sometimes I even doubted that version of myself had ever existed. It all seemed such a very long time ago.

And then finally, when Nathan turned nineteen, I left. I felt bad about that, of course I did. Nathan had only just gone to uni to do his web design course and I knew it would be unsettling for him, for all of them, but I suddenly felt I had done enough. It was like a switch flicking in my head. One day I could put up with it and the next I had absolutely had enough. It was my time. I had supported them all just like I was supposed to, but now they had lives of their own and it was the right moment for me to reclaim mine.

I had just had my fiftieth birthday, which Tony and I celebrated with a first-class trip to Venice. I don't even like Venice that much – it smells and it's too busy – but it was one of Tony's favourite places. I made the decision to leave on the plane on the way home, and then it took me a month or so of dithering before I finally took the bull by the horns and packed my bags.

Tony was devastated. He hadn't seen it coming at all – why would he have done? – and he couldn't understand why I seemed to have suddenly made such a huge decision without any build-up of arguments. I didn't really give him much to go on, to be honest, because I didn't want to give him the opportunity to lie and deny what I knew was the truth. So I told him I didn't love him any more, which wasn't strictly true. I did love him, or at least I loved what I knew was at the core of him; that cheeky young man who had accosted me in the cinema queue and made me laugh.

What I didn't love was the person I became when I was in the shade that he cast around him. Sometimes you just have to make a selfish choice, don't you? This was mine.

58

Max was enjoying the party. Apart from the brief skirmish with James and Nathan earlier, it was going well and his hangover from the day before had all but gone.

He was standing at the bar when he felt his phone buzz in his pocket. He pulled it out and peered at the screen. It was a text from Caroline. Confused, he scanned the room for his wife, wondering why she would be texting him when they were in the same place. Then he turned his attention back to his phone.

I've gone. Didn't feel great. Am ok. See you at home x

It wasn't like Caroline to just disappear like that, and certainly not without telling him in person what she was doing. She had been a little bit drunker than usual, he supposed, but this was Ellie's fortieth birthday. They were always going to be drunk.

So there must be something else going on, and the obvious thing was the row with James and Nathan. Max urged his memory to play ball. Had Caroline been there when James was shooting his mouth off? Ellie certainly was, he remembered, but how much had Caroline heard? Enough to make her want to go home?

But she had gone off with Ellie after the row. Ellie would have looked after her, he was sure, so it all would have been smoothed out. He hadn't checked though, had just left them both to it. Max reprimanded himself. He should have made sure Caroline was all right when the row had blown over. He knew how wobbly she was about the money. Why hadn't he done that? And now poor Caroline had gone, left her best friend's birthday party and returned to an empty house on her own.

Guilt washed over him. He dialled Caroline's mobile and then the landline, but they both rang resolutely out. She was probably asleep.

But what if she wasn't? He was going to have to leave too to make sure that she was okay.

He abandoned his pint and went off to find Ellie to tell her what was going on. He couldn't sneak away from his sister's party like a thief in the night as well.

Ellie was with a group of women, glass in hand, head tipped back as she laughed at whatever had just been said. Max took her by the arm and gently pulled her away from the group.

'I have to go, Els,' he said quietly. 'Caroline has gone home by herself. I think she must have been upset by . . . well . . . I don't want to leave her on her own. So I'll go too. It's been a great party though. Thank you.'

Ellie looked a little glassy-eyed but she nodded her understanding, her head moving slowly and deliberately as if the action was taking huge concentration.

'Okay,' she said. 'Tell Caro . . .' she began but didn't finish. 'It's a great party, isn't it?'

Max gave her a quick smile and then left her to it.

There was a snake of taxis waiting at the nearby rank and he hopped into the front seat of the first one and gave his address. It was a shame they had both left Ellie's do early, but then again it had been a difficult couple of days, what with the funeral as well. And Ellie seemed to be having a great time, which was the main thing.

The taxi pulled up outside their house and Max paid the driver and got out. There were lights on inside. Maybe Caroline was still awake. Letting himself in, he called her name but got no reply. He moved through each room in turn looking for her. The sitting room was empty, as was the kitchen, although there was a drained wine bottle on the countertop.

Max tried upstairs, but when he went into their bedroom the curtains were still open and there was no sign that Caroline had been in there since they'd left for the party hours before. Max's confusion was starting to turn to panic. Where on earth could she be? What if she had never actually made it home? Visions of her being attacked or snatched flooded through his head.

He moved towards the window and peered out into the gloom of the garden. There was something on the lawn, a lump that wasn't usually there. His eyes struggled to make it out in the dark. Was it something the boys had left there, or a full laundry basket? As he peered harder its shape emerged from the darkness. It was a body, not sitting upright but slumped over a box of some sort but he couldn't make out any more details. Was it Caroline?

With his heart banging in his chest, he rapped on the glass with his knuckles and called out to her, but the double glazing didn't let the sound penetrate. Really anxious now, he turned on his heel and raced down the stairs, taking them two at a time, a hundred questions flying through his head as he moved. What was she doing outside slumped over like that? Had she hurt herself? He prayed it was nothing serious.

The back door was unlocked and he flung it wide in his desperation to get out.

'Caroline! Caroline!' he shouted, sprinting across the grass towards her. 'Are you all right?'

Caroline's form was completely inert. Max came to a skidding halt next to her, immediately dropping to his knees. He put out a hand and touched her forehead. It was warm and he immediately calmed a little. He hadn't really thought she was dead, not really, but the memory of finding his dad was still so hauntingly fresh.

Caroline stirred, moaned a little, then opened her eyes. It took her a moment to focus on his face and then her expression collapsed into one of pure misery.

'Oh, Max,' she moaned. 'I'm so glad you're back. It's not good. It's making such a mess of everything. So I've got rid of it.'

She was more drunk than he'd seen her for years, her words all slurred together, their meaning mangled by wine.

'I don't understand,' he said gently. 'What are you talking about, Caro? What have you got rid of?'

Caroline looked at him as if he were entirely stupid. 'The money, of course. I've got rid of the money.'

She was making no sense. It was the middle of the night and there was nowhere she could have paid it into even if she'd wanted to. He started to worry that she might have handed the lot over to a passing tramp in an altruistic but misguided gesture.

'How do you mean?' he asked, keeping his voice calm and patient. 'Got rid of it?'

Caroline tipped her head back and looked up at the dark sky, now dotted with stars. Then she waved her arms about extravagantly.

'Poof!' she said. 'Just like that. Poof!! Like magic.' Then she hiccupped and let out a little giggle.

Max was doing his best to hold on to his temper now. He would take her inside and give her some coffee and then maybe she might start making a little bit more sense.

'Come on,' he said, putting his hands under her armpits to haul her to her feet. 'Let's get you into the warm.'

Caroline's feet scrabbled a little in the damp grass, but then she found purchase and staggered to her feet, and Max got his first chance to see what she had been slumped over.

It was the suitcase.

Even though the garden was dark, he could see at once the charred remains of twenty-pound notes. As Caroline stood up, ash was released and blew away into the darkness. Max saw the corner of a note flutter upwards like a black-edged butterfly.

'Oh, my God, Caro,' he said as he watched. 'What the hell have you done?'

Caroline swayed slightly on the spot and pulled a petulant face. 'I got rid of it,' she said, her bottom lip sticking out like a child's. 'It's caused nothing but trouble from the moment I found it, so I decided that it would be better for everyone if I just made it disappear.'

Max felt sick. A quarter of a million pounds gone up in smoke in his back garden. The others would kill him. This would be the end of the family. There would be no coming back from here. Their relationships with James and Nathan were already stretched to breaking point. How would he explain that Caroline had just torched the lot?

Adrenaline coursed through Max's body, making him feel very cold all of a sudden. This was a disaster, worse than any of the scenarios they had come up with when they'd been trying to decide what to do with the money. Simply destroying it wasn't something any of them had even contemplated, for obvious reasons.

Caroline had started to cry now, but Max was struggling to find sympathy for her.

'But the thing is, Max,' she began. She wiped at her eyes with dirty hands and left sooty tracks across her cheeks. 'The thing is, I failed. I couldn't do it. I can't even do a simple thing like setting a fire. It just wouldn't catch light and it kept going out. And then I used up all the matches.' She kicked despondently at the empty matchbox on the grass.

Max looked again at the suitcase, dropping to his knees so he could see it close up. She was right. Now that the wind had taken the ashes from the top, he could see that most of the notes were still intact, although a few were a little singed on the edges. He let out a huge breath.

'For Christ's sake, Caroline,' he snapped. 'Do you know what you nearly did?'

'I did it for us,' Caroline replied peevishly. 'I'm tired of us all falling out. We never fall out, me and Ellie. We're friends. Best friends. But all this' – she kicked the suitcase and the bundles of notes shifted – 'this has made us argue. And I don't like it, Max. I don't like anything about it. I want it gone. I want it to all be finished with.' She aimed another wobbly kick at the suitcase but barely made contact. 'I want it out of our lives so I don't have to think about it any more.'

Then she launched herself at him, throwing her arms around his neck and sobbing into his chest.

'I know,' he said, feeling tender towards her again now he knew she hadn't managed to destroy all their futures. 'Let's go inside and tomorrow we can have a proper talk about what we need to do. I think the time has come, Caro, when we need to reconsider our position on all this, for the good of the family if nothing else.'

As he said this, his wife's head pressing hard into his chest, Max knew he was right. This couldn't go on any longer. He had been prepared to stand at Caroline's shoulder and back her up – that was his duty and the right thing to do, but not indefinitely.

He still believed she was probably right about the money being dirty. But that in itself wasn't enough. He had his brother and sister to think about as well. This was not just about Caroline's integrity and sorting right from wrong. That much was clear from the increasingly desperate reactions of James and Nathan. It was obvious that they both had agendas he knew nothing about. Why else would they be so aggressive?

But their motivations were none of his business. He didn't need to know what they wanted their share of the money for. What he couldn't let happen was for the family to fall apart. His dad was gone and he was the head of the family now. The huge responsibility of that position weighed heavily on him. They had always been so close, the three of them, and he wasn't going to let anything change that. The Frost family was not about to disintegrate. Not on his watch.

He would talk to Caroline when she was sober. There must be something they could do, some compromise she would be happy with, even if it meant giving their share to the Cat's Protection League. All he had to do was work out what that compromise looked like and then make the proposal to her in a way that meant she would see he was right.

He loosened Caroline's grip on him a little and bent down to close the case before a gust of wind came and swept more of the money away.

'Let's go to bed,' he said quietly. 'And then we can see how this all looks in the morning. It won't be as bad by then, Caro. I promise.'

As they stumbled back into the house, Max really hoped that was true.

59

Caroline felt terrible. A team of little dwarves seemed to be chipping away at the inside of her skull and the contents of her stomach roiled when she moved. It felt safest to keep her eyes closed, but then the room span so violently that it made her feel worse. It was morning, though. She could tell by the colour of the curtains that it was light outside. Was she still drunk?

Her body went cold and clammy before the wave of nausea overtook her and she just managed to stumble out of bed and into the en-suite bathroom in time.

'Morning!' came Max's mocking voice from the bedroom. 'Can I get you anything? Water? Paracetamol?'

'How about a new head?' she said weakly as she curled herself around the toilet pan. 'And a new body whilst you're at it. I think I may actually be dead.'

She heard Max getting out of bed and then he appeared in the en suite, smiling sympathetically.

'You were certainly going for it last night,' he said. 'I haven't seen you in that kind of state since we were students.'

'God, I'm so sorry. I didn't spoil the party, did I?' Caroline suddenly felt panicked. She had no memory of leaving the party or how she got home. She assumed Max must have seen she was too drunk and brought her back, but what if she had disgraced herself at Ellie's beautiful do first? She threw a worried look at Max, the sudden movement making her head spin, but he was grinning at her.

'No,' he said. 'You didn't spoil anything. Well, apart from about a grand. You pretty much trashed that.'

Caroline's brow wrinkled as she tried to work out what on earth he was talking about. 'Shit. Did I break a window or something? Tell me, Max. What was it? I have this horrible feeling that I embarrassed myself somehow, but I honestly can't remember any of it.'

Feeling a little less fragile now, she stood up gingerly, threw some cold water over her face and stumbled back on to the bed, pulling the duvet over herself.

'Well . . .' began Max.

Caroline screwed her face up whilst she waited to hear the worst.

'You left the party on your own,' he began.

Caroline was immediately confused. That was so unlike her. She wracked her brain to think why she would have done something so out of character. And then it came to her. The row with James and Nathan. Fragments of what she had overheard floated round her head, not quite solid enough to grasp hold of but still painful. 'Do-gooding', 'over-inflated sense of right and wrong' 'majority vote'. She really didn't need to have the full sentences to get the gist of what they had said. And hadn't there been something with Ellie too? That felt unlikely, but there was something gnawing at her gut that she couldn't identify.

'I think I must have been upset by the row with James and Nath.' She paused, looking at Max for confirmation. 'There was a row with James and Nath, right?'

Max nodded.

'So, then I came home on my own. Without saying goodbye. Shit! What will Ellie think of me?'

'Ellie was fine when I spoke to her,' said Max. 'I'm sure she understood.'

Caroline relaxed back into the pillows. That was okay then. The last thing she would ever want to do was upset Ellie, and especially not on her big night. But it seemed she had just got a bit upset and decided the party would be better off without her. That was okay. It could have been worse.

'It was what you did when you got home that's the interesting part,' added Max. He raised an eyebrow and Caroline suddenly felt like a child being told off by a parent.

But there was nothing in her memory bank for that part of the evening. It had been completely wiped. The last thing she thought she remembered was sending Max a text, although she couldn't quite piece together where she had been when she did that.

'What did I do?' she asked in a small voice.

Max came and sat down on the bed next to her. The movement made her stomach turn over, but she kept control. He was half-smiling at her, so whatever she had done couldn't have been that bad, surely.

'If I said the words "garden", "suitcase", "matchbox" to you, would that help?' he asked.

She tried to think of any possible situation in which those words could be put together but came up with zero.

'No?' asked Max. 'Let me put it another way. So I came home and found you sitting on the lawn surrounded by ash and dead matches having tried to set fire to Dad's money.'

Caroline's hand shot to her mouth. 'Shit!'

Was that it? Had she solved the problem of what to do with the money by letting the whole lot go up in smoke? Nausea of a different kind engulfed her.

333

'It's okay,' Max said quickly. 'You're a terrible arsonist. I reckon you probably destroyed about a thousand pounds, maybe a little bit more, and there are a few notes with crispy edges, but basically it's still intact.'

Caroline dropped back once more. Thank God. The money was a nightmare but it wasn't up to her to destroy it. That was something they would never have come back from.

'But I do think,' Max continued, 'that we have reached the point where we need to compromise. I know how strongly you feel about the money and what we should do with it, Caro. But at the end of the day, it's up to me, Ellie and Nath. I can't sit back and let us tear ourselves apart over it, not when they can outvote me anyway. If you really can't take any of it then that's something I can live with, but I can't let this bickering go on any longer.'

Caroline felt as if the world was collapsing around her. Max had always taken her side. Ever since they had been married, even before that, when there had been things that she and the siblings had disagreed about, Max had stuck with her. Partly it was because they generally shared a point of view, but also she had always believed that he had made a conscious decision to put his wife and his own family ahead of his siblings.

But had she been wrong? Now, when they were facing the biggest test to their relationship ever, Max was showing his true colours and bending towards his siblings and away from her.

60

Ellie's party had been a hit and, for the most part, she had had a wonderful time. The compliments had flowed – about the venue, the food, the cake, her outfit, all of it. Everyone seemed to have agreed that it was a party to beat all parties. Mission accomplished.

If it hadn't been for the row with Caroline. Ellie replayed their conversation in her head, ashamed. She knew she had started it. She had called Alex and Theo feral. They were, but that wasn't the point. And her saying that had prompted Caroline to say what she really thought of Olivia and Lucy. Ellie's lip curled at the thought of it, but she couldn't find it in herself to be angry. Olivia was a bit of a princess. Caroline had only said what she already knew.

But it was the fact that she had said it. That was what hurt. And the things about James and her dad too. And in front of everybody! That would take longer to forgive.

But she wasn't thinking about Caroline now. She wasn't going to let her spoil this morning as well as last night.

It was quiet in the house without Olivia and Lucy. Part of Ellie longed to go and pick them up from her mum's so they could all relive the details of the party together, but on the other hand, it was nice to have a little bit of space to bask in her good memories of the evening alone, to cement them so she could draw on them again in the future.

She rolled over and reached for James's warm, familiar body, but his side of the bed was empty and cold yet again. Ellie sighed. He would be in the office already, juggling figures, trying to balance the books.

She resented that she couldn't even have this morning free of the stress he had caused them. He hadn't said anything about the cost of the party yet, but she knew that was coming her way. She had seen how he'd been mentally totting up the bill through his slightly forced smile.

But she wasn't going to let any of that spoil her moment. The party had been everything she could have hoped for, except for the small skirmish between her brothers, which she was happy to pretend hadn't happened.

She reached for her phone and began scrolling through her photos. There were endless selfies snapped with all her friends, and she looked wonderfully happy in all of them.

But there were none with Caroline, not even from the beginning of the night. Of course, Caroline had drunk too much champagne and had had to bow out early, but that didn't explain why there weren't any photos of the two of them at the start of the evening.

Ellie knew why they were missing, though. She just hadn't wanted any photos with Caro. It had been as simple as that. She didn't want her memories of her party to be spoilt by anything. They hadn't fallen out by then but she had known it was coming. Something in her had foretold the inevitable. Even without what had been said at the party, there was no way the two of them were going to be able to go on as they had done in the past, not with the issue of the money hanging over them.

With the funeral and the party finished, she was going to exercise her vote and make Max hand over the money, and knowing how Caroline felt about that, the result would be a fracture, a fissure, a rift. No matter how close they had been in the past, this was going to push them apart. Caroline would never forgive her for taking the money and she would never forgive Caroline for standing in the way of maintaining the life she loved. It wasn't Caroline's fault that James had miscalculated so badly, but it was her fault that she was withholding the wherewithal to fix things. What had been said at the party about the children was inconsequential really. They had both been drunk and on edge. Sometimes words were spoken ill-advisedly in the heat of the moment. But what Caroline had said about her husband and her father . . . those things were harder to forgive, not least because Ellie suspected they were true.

Ellie threw back the duvet and slid out of bed, the euphoria of the successful night before suddenly sucked out of her. They were back to the cold reality of their situation. James had remortgaged their house without her consent and the fees for the school that was keeping her younger daughter afloat were in jeopardy. Her friendship with Caroline, in its current form at least, would be collateral damage. It was a bleak truth, Ellie knew, but there was no way around it.

61

'Nice weekend?' Joanne asked Caroline as she sat at her desk on Monday morning.

What was Caroline supposed to say to that? She had been to her father-in-law's funeral, ruined her best friend's party, fallen out with her entire family and tried to set fire to a quarter of a million pounds. Just your standard weekend.

'Oh,' added Joanne, 'it was the funeral, wasn't it? How did it go?'

Caroline smiled wanly. 'It was okay. Actually, it was lovely. I'm sure Tony would have been delighted by it.' She turned her attention to her monitor, not wanting to engage in any further discussion of her weekend.

All day, her mind kept returning to the Frost family right and wrong, what to do and what to let go. Reputation and what other people thought. Mistaken beliefs. She and Max had had a serious talk after her hangover had lifted the day before. He had explained to her that whilst he understood her worries around the provenance of the money, they had no grounds other than suspicion for thinking it was illegal. And there was too much at stake to proceed on 'maybes'. They had to assume that all was just as it appeared, that the money belonged to Tony and it had been his choice to stuff it under a bed rather than bank it, and then share the cash out. It was the only sensible solution, certainly the only one that would keep the family intact.

Caroline could tell that he didn't want to let her down or be seen to be taking his siblings' side over hers. But really he had no choice.

He would tell Ellie and Nathan that she had changed her mind. He had no other option. She would have to find a way to live with it, for the greater good.

But in her heart she couldn't help but think the damage had already been done to the family. Too much had been said that couldn't be unsaid. And sometimes, there was no going back from that.

She sat back and pushed herself away from her desk. Joanne was working through a spreadsheet on her screen but looked up at Caroline's sudden movement.

'Can I ask you something?' Caroline asked her, not really sure what she was going to say but desperate to talk to someone else about what was troubling her.

'Of course,' Joanne replied. 'What's on your mind?'

Caroline paused for a moment, trying to get her thoughts straight. 'Imagine there was something you felt really strongly about,' she began. 'Something that was going to affect all the people that you love most in the world, but none of them agreed with your take on it.'

Joanne's brow creased as she tried to follow what Caroline was saying. 'Okay . . .' she said slowly.

'What would you do? Stick to what you believed because you were certain that was right, or compromise for the good of the group?'

Joanne put her hand to her face and tapped her lips with the tips of her finger whilst she thought.

'Well,' she said. 'My dad always said to thine own self be true – Hamlet and all that. But my mum thinks you should always think of others before yourself. She was a Girl Guide. I think they instil that in you from an early age.' Joanne laughed and Caroline smiled back.

'Well, that's a vote for each, then,' said Caroline. 'Which doesn't really take me any further forward.'

Joanna screwed her nose up as she contemplated. 'I think I'd be tempted to go for the greater good,' she said.

'Even if you think that's the wrong thing to do?' asked Caroline. Joanne nodded.

'And what about what other people think? What if you do the thing for the greater good and people think the worst of you for it?'

'Ah well, that's easy,' said Joanne. 'Then I'm with Aristotle.'

Caroline stared at her, mouth slightly open. 'What?'

'Another of my dad's favourites,' replied Joanne with a raise of an eyebrow. 'Aristotle said there's only one way to avoid criticism and that's to do nothing, say nothing and be nothing. Something like that anyway.'

Caroline let that sink in for a moment.

'You can't live your life worrying about what people will think of you,' Joanne continued. 'I mean, I'm all for having principles and sticking with them unless there's a good reason to swerve away. But who cares what anyone else thinks? Honestly, Caroline, that way disaster lies.'

Caroline's head was spinning.

Joanne threw her a questioning look. 'Have I helped or made it worse?' she asked.

'Helped. I think . . .' replied Caroline. 'You're quite wise, aren't you? For a school receptionist.'

Joanna winked at her and turned back to her screen.

62

The new week had begun and Max was pleased to have both the party and the funeral behind him, although it did mean he was going to have to tell Ellie and Nathan that he would agree to handing over the money. He had thought all day that he would ring them as soon as he got home from work, but now the time had come he still couldn't quite bring himself to do it. Even though he and Caroline had agreed they had no choice, he hated seeing the sadness in Caroline's eyes. If he could have done anything to make things different then he would. But they had been over and over it. There was no alternative.

So when there was a knock at the front door, Max was half-expecting it to be Ellie or Nathan, come round to wrench the money from them by force. He wanted to tell them about how Caroline had tried to burn their inheritance, but he doubted they would see the funny side, not just at the moment, anyway. Maybe in the future they would all be able to laugh about Caroline's solution to the conundrum they found themselves tangled up in, but right now they would probably just be angry that she had managed to reduce the balance of the cash by a thousand pounds. Max wasn't even sure that was the amount – it was just a guesstimate and could have been less, or more. He would have to count the blessed stuff again and he wasn't sure he could find it in himself to do that.

But when he opened the door, ready to defend his wife from his siblings, he was surprised to find his dad's friend Pete on the doorstep. Tony and Pete had been inseparable since school and his dad had always been full of stories of their antics – childhood money-making schemes that had gone wrong, near misses with the local bobby for knocking on doors and running away, the odd tyre let down. It was all just high jinks of which his dad had always seemed inordinately proud, as if being in mild trouble was a badge of honour to the pair of them.

Pete was looking well. He was dressed in expensive-looking casual wear, as if he was on his way to a smart dinner engagement. A pink cotton sweater was hanging from his shoulders and there was a sharp crease down his shirt sleeves and up his trouser legs. He struck quite a contrast to Max's evening attire of jersey shorts and scruffy t-shirt.

'Good evening to you, Max,' Pete said as Max opened the door. 'Sorry I'm a little bit early.'

Early for what? Max wondered. Pete made it sound as if he was expected, but Max was at a loss. He had no idea what he could possibly want.

'No, not at all,' he said. 'Come on in.' Max stood aside to let Pete step inside.

'I won't stay for long,' said Pete. 'I just wanted to bring you the surprise I mentioned.'

Pete looked extremely pleased with himself. Max had only the vaguest memory of a conversation with Pete at the funeral. Had he said something about a surprise, but in the trauma of the day, Max had totally forgotten? It appeared they had arranged that Pete would drop whatever it was round this evening. Max wondered if he would be able to get away with pretending he knew what he was talking about.

He led Pete through to the sitting room. Pete was clutching a plastic carrier bag, which apparently contained the surprise. It looked to be the same size and shape as a brick. Max hoped it wasn't. He wasn't sure he could muster the enthusiasm that Pete was clearly expecting for a brick.

In the sitting room, Max gestured for Pete to sit down, but he seemed too excited to relax. He bounced up and down on the balls of his feet like a high diver preparing to go off the top board. Then he handed over the plastic bag, almost thrusting it at him in his eagerness.

'I hope you don't think it's a waste,' he said, suddenly bashful. 'But I was so grateful to your dad that I had this made for him. I'm gutted he never got to see it. He would have loved it.'

Max had no idea what to expect. His fingers grasped the neck of the bag and he paused, not really sure that he wanted to see whatever it contained.

'Go on, then,' urged Pete. 'Open it. Sorry it's not wrapped or anything.'

Max opened the bag and slid his hand inside. His fingers touched something flat, hard and smooth and he closed them round it and drew it out. It was a brick, or at least it was brick-shaped, but it was made of transparent Perspex and set in the centre was a purple rectangle. Max had no idea what he was looking at.

'It's the stake,' said Pete, nodding enthusiastically as if this would mean something to Max. 'Your dad's stake. His investment in my business.'

Max was completely lost. Now he looked at the brick a bit closer, he could see that the purple thing in the centre was a pile of twenty-pound notes, stuck there like a fly in amber.

Finally, Pete seemed to realise his confusion.

'You have no idea what that is, do you?' he said with a grin.

Max shook his head. 'No idea whatsoever,' he agreed. 'Sorry, Pete.'

Just then Caroline appeared in the doorway. She still looked a little pale, Max thought; part prolonged hangover and part having to deal with all this heartache.

'Peter,' she said. Caroline had never been able to use the shortened version of his name. 'How lovely to see you.'

'Max didn't tell you I was coming, I assume,' Pete said. 'I suppose I didn't pick the best moment to make arrangements – at the funeral, I mean. Sorry about that.'

'No, it's my fault,' said Max. 'I just forgot. So, you were about to tell me what this is.' Max held the block up so that Caroline could see it. 'Pete's brought us this. It was a gift for Dad, but he never got to see it. He was just about to tell me the story behind it.'

Caroline settled herself in a chair, ready to listen.

'It goes back decades,' said Pete, finally sitting down. 'Me and your dad were just kids really. But I had this offer made to me. A friend of a friend was retiring and he had a job lot of second-hand Rolexes to sell. None of your dodgy fakes, these were the real McCoy. He was a trader but he was retiring to live in Spain with his missus. So he'd been winding down his business and these were the last few that hadn't sold. He offered them to me for ten grand. That was a lot of money back then. Far more than I could afford. But I knew that this bloke had made a good living from the business and I really wanted a piece. I tried to knock him down, but he was having none of it. He knew the value of what he was selling.'

Max concentrated hard, but had no idea where this was going or what it had to do with his dad.

'Well,' Pete continued, 'I could get my hands on five grand from other sources, but I was struggling to find the rest. So I asked your dad if he'd come in with me, a sleeping partner, if you like. And because we were mates and he trusted me not to screw it up, he lent me the other five. So, that' – Pete nodded at the block – 'is the return of his investment.'

Max held the block up to the light and then he could see that rather than just having a twenty-pound note stuck on the front and back of a cardboard box and fashioned to look like a pile of twenty-pound notes, it could actually be real. He felt for a seam or opening of some sort so the money could be released from its prison, but the block was completely smooth.

'So there's . . .' he began.

Pete nodded. 'Yep. There's five grand in there. Your dad's investment returned. I'm retiring myself now. I've sold the business on to my nephew.'

Caroline spoke. 'It's very nice, Peter,' she said. 'A lovely gesture, I mean. But wouldn't it be better if you could actually get at the money?'

Pete looked irritated at her suggestion, his grin fading. 'I think Tony would have liked it,' he said with a little shake of his shoulders. 'I mean, I'd given him the return on his money before. This was more a little commemorative gift for him, to say thank you for having faith in me all that time ago. It was a bloody good investment as it turned out. Rolex watches not only hold their value year on year, but have become more in demand, especially some of the classic designs. I've made a pretty good living off it, what with the Rolexes and other second-hand jewellery. Your dad's investment brought him a return of sixty times what he gave me. You'd not get that kind of interest in a bank.'

Max looked at the Perspex block, weighing it in his hand as he did the maths. 'So that means that you gave him back, what? Two hundred and ninety-five grand?'

Pete grinned at him proudly. 'Yep. Pretty good, eh?'

'And was this money in cash?' asked Max.

'Oh, my God,' said Caroline under her breath, which seemed to throw Pete off his stride a little. He looked at her uncertainly.

'Yes. He asked me for cash, not a bank transfer,' he replied. 'Wanted to avoid the tax man, I imagine.' Pete winked but when he saw Caroline's face, his confidence seemed to slip and he started to play with a heavy gold chain that hung around his wrist.

'And how long ago was this, Pete?' Max asked.

Pete blew his cheeks out as he tried to remember. 'Well, a few months back, certainly. It's taken me a while to get round to having that made.' He nodded at the block a little sheepishly. 'But I guess it would have been around February time.'

Was this it? The answer they had been searching for? Max threw a look at Caroline, who had gone pale.

'I think we found the money,' Max said. 'At the house. It was in a suitcase under the spare bed.'

Pete grinned. 'That sounds like Tony. Always was a cash man.'

'It was a little bit less than you said, though,' said Max. 'About twenty-five grand less, in fact, but maybe he'd dipped into it since you gave it to him.'

'Had he bought a new car, been on any holidays?' Pete asked.

Max shook his head. He was starting to have an idea where the extra money might have gone, but he wasn't going to tell Pete of his suspicions.

'Yes, it'll have been something like that,' he said. 'God, Pete, you have no idea what a relief it is to find out where that money came from. We've been tying ourselves in knots over it.'

'Well, there you go,' said Pete. 'Mystery solved.' He got to his feet with not a little effort. 'I'm just sorry I didn't get the present sorted before . . . well, before he died. I know I told you already, but I'm going to miss old Tony more than you could believe. Friends for sixty years. It's not something you get over in a flash. He was a great bloke.'

Pete's bottom lip quivered and his hand shot up to cover his eyes. 'Forgive me,' he said. 'I'm a sentimental old fool. I'll be getting off now. If you need anything, any of you, then just say the word. Your dad was a true gentleman and I'll do everything I can to look after his family now he's not here to do it himself.'

Max stood up and Pete shook his hand.

'I'll see you out, Peter,' said Caroline and she led him out of the room.

Max was grateful to her. He just needed a moment on his own to take it in. All that heartache and discord and the money was legitimate after all. The worst that his dad had done was to not declare it. And maybe he had been intending to do that eventually. They would never know. Max would hold on to that idea though. He was tired of his memories being tarnished by whisperings and hearsay.

He heard the front door open, Caroline saying thank you and goodbye to Pete and then the door closing again, but he didn't move. He just stood there until Caroline came back in.

'Bloody hell,' she said.

Max raised an eyebrow.

'Good job my fire-lighting skills are so bad,' she tried to joke, although her expression didn't match her words. 'We might have lost the lot and now it turns out that it's not dirty money after all. God, I'm so sorry, Max. I feel such an idiot. Maybe we can take what I burnt out of our savings and then we need never tell Ellie and Nathan.'

Max heard that she was talking but the words didn't really register. Now they knew the truth, they could tell the others the story of Tony and Pete and the returned investment, and just distribute the money as Nathan had wanted to do from the outset. But Max couldn't help feeling it wasn't going to be as easy as that. Things had been said that couldn't be unsaid. Lines had been crossed. There was a rift between them all now that hadn't been there before, and Max wasn't sure how they could go about fixing it, or even if it could be fixed at all.

EPILOGUE

They were going back to the Italian on the high street, the one where they had almost got their wine for free that time. It was the first occasion the four of them had been out for dinner since the funeral. Caroline didn't like to dwell on why that might be, the obvious reason not being something that she wanted to think about. In truth, they were all busy with their own lives and sometimes it could take longer than you might like to get a date in the diary. In her heart, though, she knew that wasn't the real reason. They had all been avoiding meeting up, letting the dust settle, perhaps, or maybe even re-evaluating their friendship. Caroline wasn't sure which.

Her forthcoming birthday had given her the perfect excuse to set something up. Her forty-first was nothing to write home about. In fact, she had decided that she was going to stop counting birthdays from this point on, but it felt important to get everyone together at least once before Christmas. The idea of the first Christmas without Tony was bad enough. That they might go into it with this awkwardness hanging over them was unthinkable – to Caroline at least.

And awkward was the perfect word to describe the atmosphere there still was between the Frosts and the Fishers. It didn't matter how many times Max told her she was imagining it, she knew she wasn't.

A distance had grown between them that hadn't been there before. It felt as if a sheet of glass had been slid in between the two families. They could still see what they could before, but they were prevented from getting close to one another, this invisible barrier preventing them from touching.

Rather than speaking every day as they always had done, she and Ellie had drifted to a conversation once a week, and that was more of an exchange of news than the intimate sharing of thoughts that had been there before.

At least the arguments had stopped after Pete's visit to their house. She and Max had quietly replaced the money she'd burnt, then they had taken the suitcase round to Ellie and James's. There had been no celebration that the money was rightfully theirs to distribute, though, no joyous popping of champagne corks or toasts to Tony and his canny nose for a deal. It had simply been a straightforward split three ways without ceremony, Max counting and James and Nathan watching over him like hawks. Caroline had found the whole exercise distasteful and upsetting; the others had been virtually salivating as they piled up their share of the cash, unable to keep the joy – or was it greed? – from their faces.

At least Nathan had had the good grace to even up what he had already had, which he'd done without any prompting from the others. That had been something at least, and Caroline had grasped on to this gesture as showing that the Frost children were basically honest, just as she had always believed them to be.

They had agreed to leave the five thousand stake money in the Perspex block for posterity's sake, although Nathan had taken some persuading. Then there had been a tricky moment as they discussed where the block should live, no one quite trusting anyone else to leave it intact.

In the end, Max had suggested they give it to Valerie to do with as she thought fit, and nobody had objected to that idea. Max and Caroline had paid their share straight into the bank, Max seeming to have no stomach for arguments over the tax implications. They intended to invest it for the boys in a trust fund. Caroline had never seen herself as the sort who might have a trust fund for her children, but it felt right that it should be Alex and Theo who benefited from Tony's wise investment. None of them had discussed the money at all since its distribution.

This evening they had arranged to meet at the restaurant rather than go for a drink beforehand, and when Max and Caroline arrived Ellie and James were already at the table, sitting down one side like an interview panel, or a rival team about to start a negotiation. Nathan wasn't there at all, having declined the invitation from the outset.

'Hi,' Caroline said as they approached the table. She could hear that her voice sounded over-bright, like she was making an effort, which she wouldn't have had to if everything had been fine between them.

Ellie gave her a wide smile. She was trying hard too, Caroline could see.

James stood up as they approached and Max offered his hand to shake as if nothing had changed. Caroline gave Ellie a hug, complimented her on her top, her hair. To the outside world, everything would have appeared perfectly normal, but Caroline knew different.

The conversation stumbled along. There were so many subjects they had to avoid. Ellie and James had put their house on the market but seemed reluctant to discuss where they were hoping to move to. There had been no holiday for them that summer either. Caroline, Max and the boys had had a lovely two weeks in a villa on Minorca, but it seemed tactless to bring it up, so she hadn't shared the details of that either. And Nathan seemed to be totally off the agenda, all of them certain that his share of the money would be gone already.

As they chatted, more like newish acquaintances than the oldest of friends, Caroline wondered about how they had got to this square. If she could have taken them all back to how they were with one another before she'd chased Monty into the box room and found the money, then she would have done in a heartbeat.

But would she have done anything differently, given that it had been her who had found the money? The answer to that was clear. Her integrity was still central to who she was. Her drive to do what was right, and, as importantly, to be seen doing it, ran through her body as the blood ran through her veins. It was who she was, who she would always be.

Yet maybe things weren't always quite as black and white as they first appeared. She could see now that there might be areas of grey. Caroline wasn't keen on grey but perhaps she could learn.

First, though, they had to get over the barriers that had grown up between them. Caroline didn't think she could bear it if this was how their friendships were going to look going forward. She missed Ellie so much. In many ways, it might have been better if she and James had just moved away. Then at least she would expect their friendship to change. As it was, it was limping along, a shadow of its former self, and that was what Caroline found so difficult.

She had to find a way to fix it.

And she thought she might be able to do it that night.

They were finishing their main courses and a couple of empty wine bottles stood on the table when she changed the subject.

'I don't think I ever told you,' Caroline began, her heart pounding in her chest, 'about what I did the night of your party, Ellie, when I went home early.'

She dampened down her feelings of apprehension and gave them the best grin she could muster, ignoring the warning looks Max was flashing at her.

'Went home to lie down, maybe?' laughed James. 'Given the amount of champagne you put away early on.' Had he forgotten what had been said, she wondered, or ever thought about how that might have contributed to her early departure? But she had to let that go.

'Well, yes. That,' said Caroline. 'But before then. I was really upset, having heard the row that you, Max and Nathan were having . . .'

She saw Ellie shifting in her chair as if she didn't want to be reminded of that at all.

'. . . and I knew it was me that had caused all the upset by wanting to get the money checked out before we spent it. So' – Caroline looked up and tried to smile as naturally as she could – 'to my champagne-befuddled brain, the most obvious thing to do was get rid of the lot. No money, no arguments. It seemed like a no-brainer.'

Ellie's brow creased, then her eyes narrowed and her mouth curled into a familiar smile. 'How do you mean?' she asked. 'What did you do, Caro?'

Caroline took a deep breath. This was a high-risk strategy, as Max could clearly tell given the faces he was pulling at her. But she was determined to continue. 'I put a match to it, tried to burn it,' she said. 'All of it.'

Caroline tried to keep her voice calm and matter-of-fact, even though her scalp was prickling with tension. Would her confession make things worse between them? Of course, she had failed in her mission to destroy the money, but what if she had been successful? She would have obliterated the windfall for all of them, not just her and Max.

She pressed on. 'I took the case out into the garden and set it on fire.'

Ellie's mouth fell open. James's too. There was a pause, a moment in time when everything around them seemed to slip into silence, the sounds of the busy restaurant falling away, the people moving around them in slow motion.

And then Ellie began to snigger. 'Oh, my God. You silly cow, Caro!' she said through her laughter. 'What an idiot! Only you could do something as ludicrous as that and think it was reasonable.'

'I blame the champagne,' replied Caroline sheepishly. She could feel her cheeks burning and hoped that the soft lighting would save her blushes. 'But to be honest, burning money is not as easy as it looks.'

'So what happened?' asked James. 'I assume you came to your senses in time, given that the money wasn't burnt to a crisp.'

'She trashed about a thousand of it,' said Max, relief surging across his face in light of the response her revelation seemed to be getting. 'I came home to find her surrounded by ash and spent matches! Don't worry, though. We replaced what she burnt before we divided it up.'

James leant back in his chair and shook his head, a grin creeping across his face, but Ellie was just staring at her, her eyes brimming with tears.

'I'm so sorry that you thought you had to do that, Caro,' she said quietly. 'It must have been really hard for you, to have reached the point where you believed that was the only solution. I don't think any of us really appreciated that. We just got so wrapped up in our own views. But I am really sorry.'

Caroline bit her lip. She wouldn't cry, not now.

'I'm sorry too,' she said. 'I didn't mean to cause all that bad feeling. I just . . .'

Caroline wanted to say that she just wanted to do what she knew was right, but she stopped herself. What was right was far more complicated, she understood now, than she could ever have believed. She dropped her gaze to the table.

'I know,' said Ellie. 'I know.'

ACKNOWLEDGEMENTS

I started writing this book towards the end of the UK's first period of coronavirus lockdown. The initial fear of the virus had worn off and we were becoming anxious to get back to something approaching normality. As a result, I started to notice that people across the country were interpreting the rules very differently. What seemed to be within the rules for one person appeared to be forbidden to another. That's when I realised that the idea that had been floating around in my head about finding a cache of hidden money was actually a book about integrity and honesty. As the story developed, the issue of reputation also became important, and I found myself turning to Shakespeare's *Othello*, which I studied at school many decades ago. Fear of losing one's good name is an age-old concern, it seems.

As always, what goes on in my head is only part of the process. Bringing the book to publication is a team effort and I would like to thank everyone at Amazon Publishing who work tirelessly to support their authors. Special thanks go to my editors: Victoria Pepe, for never failing to understand what it is that I'm trying to say, and Celine Kelly, for helping me to say it.

Thanks also to my family who have had to put up with me moaning that the house is too noisy to work in. Now they have all gone back to work and school I kind of miss the noise – but don't tell them that. I'll never live it down.

Thank you so much for reading *An Unwanted Inheritance*. I hope you enjoyed it, and if you did, please consider leaving a review. You can find out more about me and my books on my website www.imogenclark.com where there are also links to my social media accounts.

With very best wishes,

Imogen

ABOUT THE AUTHOR

Photo © 2020 Karen Ross Photography

Million-copy bestselling author Imogen Clark writes contemporary book club fiction.

Her books have reached number 1 in Kindle stores around the world and Where the Story Starts was shortlisted for Contemporary Romantic Novel of the Year 2020.

Imogen initially qualified as a lawyer, but after leaving her legal career behind to care for her four children, she returned to her first love—books. She went back to university to study English Literature whilst the children were at school, and then tried her hand at writing novels herself.

Her great love is travel and she is always planning her next adventure. She lives in Yorkshire with her husband and children.

If you'd like to get in touch then please visit her website at www.imogenclark.com where you can sign up to her monthly newsletter. Imogen can also be found on Facebook, Twitter and Instagram as Imogen Clark at Home.